EVA NOE

Rose in Bloom

CHARLIE BENT HIS HEAD TO KISS THE HANDS THAT
PUT A LITTLE WHITE ROSE IN HIS BUTTON-HOLE.

Rose in Bloom.   *Frontispiece (Page 156)*

Rose in Bloom

A SEQUEL TO "EIGHT COUSINS"

BY

LOUISA M. ALCOTT

Author of "Little Women," etc.

Complete Authorized Edition

Published by arrangement with Little, Brown and Company

GROSSET & DUNLAP
Publishers   New York

Printed in United States of America

Preface

AS authors may be supposed to know better **than** any one else what they intended to do when writing a book, I beg leave to say that there is **no** moral to this story. Rose is not designed for a model girl: and the Sequel was simply written in fulfilment of a promise; hoping to afford some amusement, and perhaps here and there a helpful **hint**, to other roses getting ready to bloom.

L. M. ALCOTT.

SEPTEMBER, 1876.

Contents

Rose in Bloom

CHAPTER I

COMING HOME

THREE young men stood together on a wharf
one bright October day, awaiting the arrival
of an ocean steamer with an impatience
which found a vent in lively skirmishes with a small
lad, who pervaded the premises like a will-o'-the-wisp,
and afforded much amusement to the other groups
assembled there.

"They are the Campbells, waiting for their cousin,
who has been abroad several years with her uncle, the
Doctor," whispered one lady to another, as the hand-
somest of the young men touched his hat to her as
he passed, lugging the boy, whom he had just rescued from a little expedition down among the piles.

"Which is that?" asked the stranger.

"Prince Charlie, as he's called, — a fine fellow, the
most promising of the seven; but a little fast, people
say," answered the first speaker, with a shake of the
head.

"Are the others his brothers?"

"No, cousins. The elder is Archie, a most exem-
plary young man. He has just gone into business
with the merchant uncle, and bids fair to be an honor

to his family. The other, with the eye-glasses and no gloves, is Mac, the odd one, just out of college."

" And the boy? "

" Oh, he is Jamie, the youngest brother of Archibald, and the pet of the whole family. Mercy on us! he'll be in if they don't hold on to him."

The ladies' chat came to a sudden end just there; for, by the time Jamie had been fished out of a hogshead, the steamer hove in sight and every thing else was forgotten. As it swung slowly round to enter the dock, a boyish voice shouted, —

" There she is! I see her and uncle and Phebe! Hooray for Cousin Rose!" and three small cheers were given with a will by Jamie, as he stood on a post waving his arms like a windmill, while his brother held on to the tail of his jacket.

Yes, there they were, — Uncle Alec swinging his hat like a boy, with Phebe smiling and nodding on one side, and Rose kissing both hands delightedly on the other, as she recognized familiar faces and heard familiar voices welcoming her home.

" Bless her dear heart, she's bonnier than ever! Looks like a Madonna, — does n't she? — with that blue cloak round her, and her bright hair flying in the wind!" said Charlie excitedly, as they watched the group upon the deck with eager eyes.

" Madonnas don't wear hats like that. Rose has n't changed much, but Phebe has. Why, she's a regular beauty!" answered Archie, staring with all his might at the dark-eyed young woman, with the brilliant color and glossy, black braids shining in the sun.

" Dear old uncle! does n't it seem good to have him back?" was all Mac said; but he was not looking at

" dear old uncle," as he made the fervent remark, for he saw only the slender blonde girl near by, and stretched out his hands to meet hers, forgetful of the green water tumbling between them.

During the confusion that reigned for a moment as the steamer settled to her moorings, Rose looked down into the three faces upturned to hers, and seemed to read in them something that both pleased and pained her. It was only a glance, and her own eyes were full; but through the mist of happy tears she received the impression that Archie was about the same, that Mac had decidedly improved, and that something was amiss with Charlie. There was no time for observation, however; for in a moment the shoreward rush began, and, before she could grasp her travelling bag, Jamie was clinging to her like an ecstatic young bear. She was with difficulty released from his embrace, to fall into the gentler ones of the elder cousins, who took advantage of the general ex-citement to welcome both blooming girls with affectionate impartiality. Then the wanderers were borne ashore in a triumphal procession, while Jamie danced rapturous jigs before them even on the gangway.

Archie remained to help his uncle get the luggage through the Custom House, and the others escorted the damsels home. No sooner were they shut up in a carriage, however, than a new and curious constraint seemed to fall upon the young people; for they realized, all at once, that their former playmates were men and women now. Fortunately, Jamie was quite free from this feeling of restraint, and, sitting bodkin-wise between the ladies, took all sorts of liberties with them and their belongings.

"Well, my mannikin, what do you think of us?" asked Rose, to break an awkward pause.

"You've both grown so pretty, I can't decide which I like best. Phebe is the biggest and brightest looking, and I was always fond of Phebe; but, somehow you are so kind of sweet and precious, I really think I *must* hug you again," and the small youth did it tempestuously.

"If you love me best, I shall not mind a bit about your thinking Phebe the handsomest, because she *is*. Isn't she, boys?" asked Rose, with a mischievous look at the gentlemen opposite, whose faces expressed a respectful admiration which much amused her.

"I'm so dazzled by the brilliancy and beauty that has suddenly burst upon me, I have no words to express my emotions," answered Charlie, gallantly dodging the dangerous question.

"I can't say yet, for I have not had time to look at any one. I will now, if you don't mind;" and, to the great amusement of the rest, Mac gravely adjusted his eye-glasses and took an observation.

"Well?" said Phebe, smiling and blushing under his honest stare, yet seeming not to resent it as she did the lordly sort of approval which made her answer the glance of Charlie's audacious blue eyes with a flash of her black ones.

"I think if you were my sister, I should be very proud of you, because your face shows what I admire more than its beauty, — truth and courage, Phebe," answered Mac, with a little bow, full of such genuine respect that surprise and pleasure brought a sudden dew to quench the fire of the girl's eyes, and soothe the sensitive pride of the girl's heart.

Rose clapped her hands just as she used to do when any thing delighted her, and beamed at Mac approvingly, as she said, —

"Now that's a criticism worth having, and we are much obliged. I was sure *you'd* admire my Phebe when you knew her: but I didn't believe you would be wise enough to see it at once; and you have gone up many pegs in my estimation, I assure you."

"I was always fond of mineralogy you remember, and I've been tapping round a good deal lately, so I've learned to know precious metals when I see them," Mac said with his shrewd smile.

"That is the last hobby, then? Your letters have amused us immensely; for each one had a new theory or experiment, and the latest was always the best. I thought uncle would have died of laughing over the vegetarian mania: it was so funny to imagine you living on bread and milk, baked apples, and potatoes roasted in your own fire," continued Rose, changing the subject again.

"This old chap was the laughing-stock of his class. They called him Don Quixote; and the way he went at windmills of all sorts was a sight to see," put in Charlie, evidently feeling that Mac had been patted on the head quite as much as was good for him.

"But in spite of that the Don got through college with all the honors. Oh, wasn't I proud when Aunt Jane wrote us about it! and didn't she rejoice that her boy kept at the head of his class, and won the medal!" cried Rose, shaking Mac by both hands in a way that caused Charlie to wish "the old chap" had been left behind with Dr. Alec.

"Oh come, that's all mother's nonsense. I began

earlier than the other fellows and liked it better : so
I don't deserve any praise.   Prince is right, though : I
did make a regular jack of myself; but, on the whole,
I'm not sure that my wild oats were n't better than
some I've seen sowed.   Anyway, they did n't cost
much, and I'm none the worse for them," said Mac,
placidly.

"I know what 'wild oats' mean.   I heard Uncle
Mac say Charlie was sowing 'em too fast, and I asked
mamma, so she told me.   And I know that he was
suspelled or expended, I don't remember which, but
it was something bad, and Aunt Clara cried," added
Jamie, all in one breath; for he possessed a fatal gift
of making *malapropos* remarks, which caused him to
be a terror to his family.

" Do you want to go on the box again? " demanded
Prince, with a warning frown.

" No, I don't."

" Then hold your tongue."

" Well, Mac need n't kick me; for I was only " —
began the culprit, innocently trying to make a bad
matter worse.

" That will do," interrupted Charlie, sternly, and
James subsided a crushed boy, consoling himself with
Rose's new watch for the indignities he suffered at
the hands of the " old fellows," as he vengefully called
his elders.

Mac and Charlie immediately began to talk as hard
as their tongues could wag, bringing up all sorts of
pleasant subjects so successfully that peals of laughter
made passers-by look after the merry load with sympathetic smiles.

An avalanche of aunts fell upon Rose as soon as

she reached home, and for the rest of the day the old house buzzed like a beehive. Evening found the whole tribe collected in the drawing-rooms, with the exception of Aunt Peace, whose place was empty now.

Naturally enough, the elders settled into one group after a while, and the young fellows clustered about the girls, like butterflies round two attractive flowers. Dr. Alec was the central figure in one room and Rose in the other; for the little girl, whom they had all loved and petted, had bloomed into a woman; and two years of absence had wrought a curious change in the relative positions of the cousins, especially the three elder ones, who eyed her with a mixture of boyish affection and manly admiration that was both new and pleasant.

Something sweet yet spirited about her charmed them and piqued their curiosity; for she was not quite like other girls, and rather startled them now and then by some independent little speech or act, which made them look at one another with a sly smile, as if reminded that Rose was "uncle's girl."

Let us listen, as in duty bound, to what the elders are saying first; for they are already building castles in the air for the boys and girls to inhabit.

"Dear child! how nice it is to see her safely back, so well and happy and like her sweet little self!" said Aunt Plenty, folding her hands as if giving thanks for a great happiness.

"I should n't wonder if you found that you'd brought a firebrand into the family, Alec. Two, in fact; for Phebe is a fine girl, and the lads have found it out already, if I'm not mistaken," added Uncle Mac, with a nod toward the other room.

All eyes followed his, and a highly suggestive tableau presented itself to the paternal and maternal
audience in the back parlor.

Rose and Phebe, sitting side by side on the sofa,
had evidently assumed at once the places which they
were destined to fill by right of youth, sex, and beauty;
for Phebe had long since ceased to be the maid and
become the friend, and Rose meant to have that fact
established at once.

Jamie occupied the rug, on which Will and Geordie
stood at ease, showing their uniforms to the best advantage; for they were now in a great school, where
military drill was the delight of their souls. Steve
posed gracefully in an arm-chair, with Mac lounging
over the back of it; while Archie leaned on one
corner of the low chimney-piece, looking down at
Phebe as she listened to his chat with smiling lips,
and cheeks almost as rich in color as the carnations
in her belt.

But Charlie was particularly effective, although he
sat upon a music-stool, that most trying position for
any man not gifted with grace in the management
of his legs. Fortunately Prince was, and had fallen
into an easy attitude, with one arm over the back of
the sofa, his handsome head bent a little, as he monop-
olized Rose, with a devoted air and a very becoming
expression of contentment on his face.

Aunt Clara smiled as if well pleased; Aunt Jessie
looked thoughtful; Aunt Jane's keen eyes went from
dapper Steve to broad-shouldered Mac with an anxious glance; Mrs. Myra murmured something about
her "blessed Caroline"; and Aunt Plenty said
warmly, —

"Bless the dears! any one might be proud of such a bonny flock of bairns as that."

"I am all ready to play chaperon as soon as you please, Alec; for I suppose the dear girl will come out at once, as she did not before you went away. My services won't be wanted long, I fancy; for with her many advantages she will be carried off in her first season or I'm much mistaken," said Mrs. Clara, with significant nods and smiles.

"You must settle all those matters with Rose: I am no longer captain, only first mate now, you know," answered Dr. Alec, adding soberly, half to himself, half to his brother, — "I wonder people are in such haste to 'bring out' their daughters, as it's called. To me there is something almost pathetic in the sight of a young girl standing on the threshold of the world, so innocent and hopeful, so ignorant of all that lies before her, and usually so ill prepared to meet the ups and downs of life. We do our duty better by the boys; but the poor little women are seldom provided with any armor worth having; and, sooner or later, they are sure to need it, for every one must fight her own battle, and only the brave and strong can win."

"You can't reproach yourself with neglect of that sort, Alec, for you have done your duty faithfully by George's girl; and I envy you the pride and happiness of having such a daughter, for she is that to you," answered old Mac, unexpectedly betraying the paternal sort of tenderness men seldom feel for their sons.

"I've tried, Mac, and I *am* both proud and happy; but with every year my anxiety seems to increase. I've done my best to fit Rose for what may come, as far as I can foresee it; but now she must stand alone, and all my care is powerless to keep her heart from aching, her life from being saddened by mistakes, or thwarted by the acts of others. I can only stand by ready to share her joy and sorrow, and watch her shape her life."

"Why, Alec, what is the child going to do, that you need look so solemn?" exclaimed Mrs. Clara, who seemed to have assumed a sort of right to Rose already.

"Hark! and let her tell you herself," answered Dr. Alec, as Rose's voice was heard saying very earnestly, —

"Now you have all told your plans for the future, why don't you ask us ours?"

"Because we know that there is only one thing for a pretty girl to do, — break a dozen or so of hearts before she finds one to suit, then marry and settle," answered Charlie, as if no other reply was possible.

"That may be the case with many, but not with us; for Phebe and I believe that it is as much a right and a duty for women to do something with their lives as for men; and we are not going to be satisfied with such frivolous parts as you give us," cried Rose, with kindling eyes. "I mean what I say, and you cannot laugh me down. Would *you* be contented to be told to enjoy yourself for a little while, then marry and do nothing more till you die?" she added, turning to Archie.

"Of course not: that is only a part of a man's life," he answered decidedly.

"A very precious and lovely part, but not *all*," continued Rose; "neither should it be for a woman: for we 've got minds and souls as well as hearts; ambition and talents, as well as beauty and accomplishments; and we want to live and learn as well as love and be loved. I'm sick of being told that is all a woman is fit for! I won't have any thing to do with love till I prove that I am something beside a housekeeper and baby-tender!"

"Heaven preserve us! here's woman's rights with a vengeance!" cried Charlie, starting up with mock horror, while the others regarded Rose with mingled surprise and amusement, evidently fancying it all a girlish outbreak.

"Ah, you need n't pretend to be shocked: you will be in earnest presently; for this is only the beginning of my strong-mindedness," continued Rose, nothing daunted by the smiles of good-natured incredulity or derision on the faces of her cousins. "I have made up my mind not to be cheated out of the real things that make one good and happy; and, just because I'm a rich girl, fold my hands and drift as so many do. I have n't lived with Phebe all these years in vain: I know what courage and self-reliance can do for one; and I sometimes wish I had n't a penny in the world so that I could go and earn my bread with her, and be as brave and independent as she will be pretty soon."

It was evident that Rose was in earnest now; for, as she spoke, she turned to her friend with such respect as well as love in her face that the look told better than any words how heartily the rich girl appreciated the virtues hard experience had given the poor girl, and how eagerly she desired to earn what all her fortune could not buy for her.

Something in the glance exchanged between the

friends impressed the young men in spite of their
prejudices; and it was in a perfectly serious tone that
Archie said, —

"I fancy you'll find your hands full, cousin, if you
want work; for I've heard people say that wealth has
its troubles and trials as well as poverty."

"I know it, and I'm going to try and fill my place
well. I've got some capital little plans all made, and
have begun to study my profession already," answered
Rose, with an energetic nod.

"Could I ask what it is to be?" inquired Charlie,
in a tone of awe.

"Guess!" and Rose looked up at him with an ex
pression half-earnest, half-merry.

"Well, I should say that you were fitted for a beauty
and a belle; but, as that is evidently not to your taste,
I am afraid you are going to study medicine and be
a doctor. Won't your patients have a heavenly time
though? It will be easy dying with an angel to
poison them."

"Now, Charlie, that's base of you, when you know
how well women have succeeded in this profession,
and what a comfort Dr. Mary Kirk was to dear Aunt
Peace. I did want to study medicine; but uncle
thought it would n't do to have so many M.D.'s in one
family, since Mac thinks of trying it. Besides, I seem
to have other work put into my hands that I am better
fitted for."

"You are fitted for any thing that is generous
and good; and I'll stand by you, no matter what
you've chosen," cried Mac heartily; for this was a
new style of talk from a girl's lips, and he liked it
immensely.

"Philanthropy is a generous, good, and beautiful profession; and I've chosen it for mine because I have much to give. I'm only the steward of the fortune papa left me; and I think, if I use it wisely for the happiness of others, it will be more blest than if I keep it all for myself."

Very sweetly and simply was this said, but it was curious to see how differently the various hearers received it.

Charlie shot a quick look at his mother, who exclaimed, as if in spite of herself, —

"Now, Alec, *are* you going to let that girl squander a fine fortune on all sorts of charitable nonsense and wild schemes, for the prevention of pauperism and crime?"

"'They who give to the poor lend to the Lord,' and practical Christianity is the kind He loves the best," was all Dr. Alec answered; but it silenced the aunts, and caused even prudent Uncle Mac to think with sudden satisfaction of certain secret investments he had made, which paid him no interest but the thanks of the poor.

Archie and Mac looked well pleased, and promised their advice and assistance with the enthusiasm of generous young hearts. Steve shook his head, but said nothing; and the lads on the rug at once proposed founding a hospital for invalid dogs and horses, white mice and wounded heroes.

"Don't you think that will be a better way for a woman to spend her life, than in dancing, dressing, and husband-hunting, Charlie?" asked Rose, observing his silence and anxious for his approval.

"Very pretty for a little while, and very effective

too; for I don't know any thing more captivating than
a sweet girl in a meek little bonnet, going on charitable errands and glorifying poor people's houses
with a delightful mixture of beauty and benevolence.
Fortunately, the dear souls soon tire of it, but it's
heavenly while it lasts."

Charlie spoke in a tone of mingled admiration and
contempt, and smiled a superior sort of smile, as if
he understood all the innocent delusions as well as
the artful devices of the sex, and expected nothing
more from them. It both surprised and grieved
Rose, for it did not sound like the Charlie she had
left two years ago. But she only said, with a reproachful look and a proud little gesture of head and
hand, as if she put the subject aside since it was not
treated with respect, —

"I am sorry you have so low an opinion of women: there *was* a time when you believed in them
sincerely."

"I do still, upon my word I do! They have n't a
more devoted admirer and slave in the world than I
am. Just try me and see," cried Charlie, gallantly
kissing his hand to the sex in general.

But Rose was not appeased, and gave a disdainful
shrug, as she answered with a look in her eyes that
his lordship did not like, —

"Thank you: I don't want admirers or slaves, but
friends and helpers. I 've lived so long with a wise,
good man that I am rather hard to suit, perhaps; but
I don't intend to lower my standard, and any one
who cares for my regard must at least try to live up
to it."

"Whew! here 's a wrathful dove! Come and

smooth her ruffled plumage, Mac. I'll dodge before I do further mischief," and Charlie strolled away into the other room, privately lamenting that Uncle Alec had spoiled a fine girl by making her strong-minded.

He wished himself back again in five minutes; for Mac said something that produced a gale of laughter, and when he took a look over his shoulder the "wrathful dove" was cooing so peacefully and pleasantly he was sorely tempted to return and share the fun. But Charlie had been spoiled by too much indulgence, and it was hard for him to own himself in the wrong even when he knew it. He always got what he wanted sooner or later; and, having long ago made up his mind that Rose and her fortune were to be his, he was secretly displeased at the new plans and beliefs of the young lady, but flattered himself that they would soon be changed when she saw how unfashionable and inconvenient they were.

Musing over the delightful future he had laid out, ne made himself comfortable in the sofa corner near his mother, till the appearance of a slight refection caused both groups to melt into one. Aunt Plenty believed in eating and drinking; so the slightest excuse for festivity delighted her hospitable soul, and on this joyful occasion she surpassed herself.

It was during this informal banquet that Rose, roaming about from one admiring relative to another, came upon the three younger lads, who were having a quiet little scuffle in a secluded corner.

"Come out here and let me have a look at you," she said enticingly; for she predicted an explosion and public disgrace if peace was not speedily restored.

Hastily smoothing themselves down, the young gentlemen presented three flushed and merry countenances for inspection, feeling highly honored by the command.

"Dear me, how you two have grown! You big things! how dare you get ahead of me in this way?" she said, standing on tiptoe to pat the curly pates before her; for Will and Geordie had shot up like weeds, and now grinned cheerfully down upon her as she surveyed them in comic amazement.

"The Campbells are all fine, tall fellows; and we mean to be the best of the lot. Should n't wonder if we were six-footers, like Grandpa," observed Will proudly, looking so like a young Shanghae rooster, all legs and an insignificant head, that Rose kept her countenance with difficulty.

"We shall broaden out when we get our growth. We are taller than Steve now, a half a head, both of us," added Geordie, with his nose in the air.

Rose turned to look at Steve, and, with a sudden smile, beckoned to him. He dropped his napkin, and flew to obey the summons; for she was queen of the hour, and he had openly announced his deathless loyalty.

"Tell the other boys to come here. I 've a fancy to stand you all in a row and look you over, as you did me that dreadful day when you nearly frightened me out of my wits," she said, laughing at the memory of it as she spoke.

They came in a body, and, standing shoulder to shoulder, made such an imposing array that the young commander was rather daunted for a moment. But she had seen too much of the world lately to be

abashed by a trifle; and the desire to try a girlish test
gave her courage to face the line of smiling cousins
with dignity and spirit.

"Now I'm going to stare at you as you stared at
me. It is my revenge on you seven bad boys for en-
trapping one poor little girl, and enjoying her alarm.
I'm not a bit afraid of you now; so tremble and
beware!"

As she spoke, Rose looked up into Archie's face
and nodded approvingly; for the steady gray eyes
met hers fairly, and softened as they did so, — a
becoming change, for naturally they were rather keen
than kind.

"A true Campbell, bless you!" she said, and shook
his hand heartily as she passed on.

Charlie came next, and here she felt less satisfied,
though scarcely conscious why; for, as she looked,
there came a defiant sort of flash, changing suddenly
to something warmer than anger, stronger than pride,
making her shrink a little and say, hastily, —

"I don't find the Charlie I left; but the Prince is
there still, I see."

Turning to Mac with a sense of relief, she gently
took off his "winkers," as Jamie called them, and
looked straight into the honest blue eyes that looked
straight back at her, full of a frank and friendly affection that warmed her heart, and made her own eyes
brighten as she gave back the glasses, saying, with a
look and tone of cordial satisfaction, —

"*You* are not changed, my dear old Mac; and I'm
so glad of that!"

"Now say something extra sweet to me, because
I'm the flower of the family," said Steve, twirling the

blonde moustache, which was evidently the pride of his life.

Rose saw at a glance that Dandy deserved his name more than ever, and promptly quenched his vanities by answering, with a provoking laugh, —

"Then the name of the flower of the family is Cock's-comb."

"Ah, ha! who's got it now?" jeered Will.

"Let us off easy, please," whispered Geordie, mindful that their turn came next.

"You blessed beanstalks! I'm proud of you: only don't grow quite out of sight, or ever be ashamed to look a woman in the face," answered Rose, with a gentle pat on the cheek of either bashful young giant; for both were as red as peonies, though their boyish eyes were as clear and calm as summer lakes.

"Now me!" And Jamie assumed his manliest air, feeling that he did not appear to advantage among his tall kinsmen. But he went to the head of the class in every one's opinion when Rose put her arms round him, saying, with a kiss, —

"You must be my boy now; for all the others are too old, and I want a faithful little page to do my errands for me."

"I will, I will! and I'll marry you too, if you'll just hold on till I grow up!" cried Jamie, rather losing his head at this sudden promotion.

"Bless the baby, what is he talking about?" laughed Rose, looking down at her little knight, as he clung about her with grateful ardor.

"Oh, I heard the aunts say that you'd better marry one of us, and keep the property in the family; so I speak first, because you are very fond of me, and I *do* love curls."

Alas for Jamie! this awful speech had hardly left his innocent lips when Will and Geordie swept him out of the room like a whirlwind; and the howls of that hapless boy were heard from the torture-hall, where being shut into the skeleton-case was one of the mildest punishments inflicted upon him.

Dismay fell upon the unfortunates who remained: but their confusion was soon ended; for Rose, with a look which they had never seen upon her face before, dismissed them with the brief command, "Break ranks, — the review is over," and walked away to Phebe.

"Confound that boy! You ought to shut him up, or gag him!" fumed Charlie, irritably.

"He shall be attended to," answered poor Archie, who was trying to bring up the little marplot with the success of most parents and guardians.

"The whole thing was deuced disagreeable," growled Steve, who felt that he had not distinguished himself in the late engagement.

"Truth generally is," observed Mac dryly, as he strolled away with his odd smile.

As if he suspected discord somewhere, Dr. Alec proposed music at this crisis; and the young people felt that it was a happy thought.

"I want you to hear both my birds; for they have improved immensely, and I am very proud of them," said the Doctor, twirling up the stool and pulling out the old music-books.

"I had better come first, for after you have heard the nightingale you won't care for the canary," added Rose, wishing to put Phebe at her ease; for she sat

among them looking like a picture, but rather shy
and silent, remembering the days when her place was
in the kitchen.

"I'll give you some of the dear old songs you used
to like so much. This was a favorite, I think;" and
sitting down she sang the first familiar air that came,
and sang it well in a pleasant, but by no means
finished, manner.

It chanced to be "The Birks of Aberfeldie," and
vividly recalled the time when Mac was ill, and she
took care of him. The memory was sweet to her, and
involuntarily her eye wandered in search of him. He
was not far away, sitting just as he used to sit when
she soothed his most despondent moods, — astride of
a chair with his head down on his arms, as if the song
suggested the attitude. Her heart quite softened to
him as she looked, and she decided to forgive *him* if
no one else; for she was sure that he had no merce-
nary plans about her tiresome money.

Charlie had assumed a pensive air, and fixed his
fine eyes upon her with an expression of tender admiration, which made her laugh in spite of all her efforts
to seem unconscious of it. She was both amused and
annoyed at his very evident desire to remind her of
certain sentimental passages in the last year of their
girl and boyhood, and to change what she had considered a childish joke into romantic earnest. This
did not suit her; for, young as she was, Rose had
very serious ideas of love, and had no intention of
being beguiled into even a flirtation with her handsome cousin.

So Charlie attitudinized unnoticed, and was getting
rather out of temper when Phebe began to sing; and

he forgot all about himself in admiration of her. It took every one by surprise: for two years of foreign training added to several at home had worked wonders; and the beautiful voice that used to warble cheerily over pots and kettles, now rang out melodiously or melted to a mellow music that woke a sympathetic thrill in those who listened. Rose glowed with pride as she accompanied her friend; for Phebe was in her own world now, — a lovely world where no depressing memory of poor-house or kitchen, ignorance or loneliness, came to trouble her; a happy world where she could be herself, and rule others by the magic of her sweet gift.

Yes, Phebe was herself now, and showed it in the change that came over her at the first note of music. No longer shy and silent, no longer the image of a handsome girl, but a blooming woman, alive and full of the eloquence her art gave her, as she laid her hands softly together, fixed her eye on the light, and just poured out her song as simply and joyfully as the lark does soaring toward the sun.

"My faith, Alec! that's the sort of voice that wins a man's heart out of his breast!" exclaimed Uncle Mac, wiping his eyes after one of the plaintive ballads that never grow old.

"So it would!" answered Dr. Alec, delightedly.

"So it has," added Archie to himself; and he was right: for, just at that moment, he fell in love with Phebe. He actually did, and could fix the time almost to a second: for, at a quarter past nine, he merely thought her a very charming young person; at twenty minutes past, he considered her the loveliest woman he ever beheld; at five and twenty minutes past, she

was an angel singing his soul away; and at half after
nine he was a lost man, floating over a delicious sea
to that temporary heaven on earth where lovers usually land after the first rapturous plunge.

If any one had mentioned this astonishing fact,
nobody would have believed it; nevertheless, it was
quite true : and sober, business-like Archie suddenly
discovered a fund of romance at the bottom of his
hitherto well-conducted heart that amazed him. He
was not quite clear what had happened to him at first,
and sat about in a dazed sort of way; seeing, hearing,
knowing nothing but Phebe : while the unconscious
idol found something wanting in the cordial praise
so modestly received, because Mr. Archie never said
a word.

This was one of the remarkable things which occurred that evening; another was that Mac paid Rose
a compliment, which was such an unprecedented fact,
it produced a great sensation, though only one person
heard it.

Everybody had gone but Mac and his father, who
was busy with the Doctor. Aunt Plenty was counting
the teaspoons in the dining-room, and Phebe was
helping her as of old. Mac and Rose were alone, — he
apparently in a brown study, leaning his elbows on
the chimney-piece ; and she lying back in a low chair,
looking thoughtfully at the fire. She was tired; and
the quiet was grateful to her : so she kept silence and
Mac respectfully held his tongue. Presently, however,
she became conscious that he was looking at her as
intently as eyes and glasses could do it; and, without
stirring from her comfortable attitude, she said, smiling up at him, —

" He looks as wise as an owl: I wonder what he 's thinking about? "

" You, cousin."

" Something good, I hope? "

" I was thinking Leigh Hunt was about right when he said, ' A girl is the sweetest thing God ever made.' "

" Why, Mac!" and Rose sat bolt upright with an astonished face: this was such an entirely unexpected sort of remark for the philosopher to make.

Evidently interested in the new discovery, Mac placidly continued, " Do you know, it seems as if I never really saw a girl before, or had any idea what agreeable creatures they could be. I fancy you are a remarkably good specimen, Rose."

" No, indeed! I 'm only hearty and happy; and being safe at home again may make me look better than usual perhaps: but I 'm no beauty except to uncle."

" ' Hearty and happy,' — that must be it," echoed Mac, soberly investigating the problem. " Most girls are sickly or silly, I think I have observed; and that is probably why I am so struck with you."

" Of all queer boys you are the queerest! Do you really mean that you don't like or notice girls? " asked Rose, much amused at this new peculiarity of her studious cousin.

" Well, no: I am only conscious of two sorts, — noisy and quiet ones. I prefer the latter: but, as a general thing, I don't notice any of them much more than I do flies, unless they bother me; then I 'd like to flap them away; but, as that won't do, I hide."

Rose leaned back and laughed till her eyes were full: it was so comical to hear Mac sink his voice to a confidential whisper at the last words, and see him smile with sinful satisfaction at the memory of the tormentors he had eluded.

"You need n't laugh: it's a fact, I assure you. Charlie likes the creatures, and they spoil him; Steve follows suit, of course. Archie is a respectful slave when he can't help himself. As for me, I don't often give them a chance; and, when I get caught, I talk science and dead languages till they run for their lives. Now and then I find a sensible one, and then we get on excellently."

"A sad prospect for Phebe and me," sighed Rose, trying to keep sober.

"Phebe is evidently a quiet one. I know she is sensible, or you would n't care for her. I can see that she is pleasant to look at, so I fancy I shall like her. As for you, I helped bring you up; therefore I am a little anxious to see how you turn out. I was afraid your foreign polish might spoil you, but I think it has not. In fact, I find you quite satisfactory so far, if you don't mind my saying it. I don't quite know what the charm is, though. Must be the power of inward graces, since you insist that you have no outward ones."

Mac was peering at her with a shrewd smile on his lips, but such a kindly look behind the glasses, that she found both words and glance very pleasant, and answered merrily, —

"I am glad you approve of me, and much obliged for your care of my early youth. I hope to be a credit to you, and depend on your keeping me straight; for I'm afraid I shall be spoilt among you all."

"I'll keep my eye on you upon one condition," replied the youthful Mentor.

"Name it."

"If you are going to have a lot of lovers round, I wash my hands of you. If not, I'm your man."

"You must be sheep-dog, and help keep them away; for I don't want any yet awhile; and, between ourselves, I don't believe I shall have any if it is known that I am strong-minded. That fact will scare most men away like a yellow flag," said Rose: for, thanks to Dr. Alec's guardianship, she had wasted neither heart nor time in the foolish flirtations so many girls fritter away their youth upon.

"Hum! I rather doubt that," muttered Mac, as he surveyed the damsel before him.

She certainly did not look unpleasantly strong-minded, for she *was* beautiful in spite of her modest denials. Beautiful with the truest sort of beauty; for nobility of character lent its subtle charm to the bloom of youth, the freshness of health, the innocence of a nature whose sweet maidenliness Mac felt but could not describe. Gentle yet full of spirit, and all aglow with the earnestness that suggests lovely possibilities, and makes one hope that such human flowers may have heaven's purest air and warmest sunshine to blossom in.

"Wait and see," answered Rose; then, as her uncle's voice was heard in the hall, she held out her hand, adding pleasantly, "The old times are to begin again, so come soon and tell me all your doings, and help me with mine just as you used to do."

"You really mean it?" and Mac looked much pleased.

"I really do. You are so little altered, except to grow big, that I don't feel at all strange with you, and want to begin where we left off."

"That will be capital. Good-night, cousin," and to her great amazement he gave her a hearty kiss.

"Oh, but that is not the old way at all!" cried Rose, stepping back in merry confusion; while the audacious youth assumed an air of mild surprise, as he innocently asked, —

"Did n't we always say good-night in that way? I had an impression that we did, and were to begin just as we left off."

"Of course not; no power on earth would have bribed you to do it, as you know well enough. I don't mind the first night, but we are too old for that sort of thing now."

"I'll remember. It was the force of habit, I suppose; for I'm sure I must have done it in former times, it seemed so natural. Coming, father!" and Mac retired, evidently convinced that he was right.

"Dear old thing! he is as much a boy as ever, and that is such a comfort; for some of the others have grown up very fast," said Rose to herself, recalling Charlie's sentimental airs, and Archie's beatified expression while Phebe sang.

CHAPTER II

OLD FRIENDS WITH NEW FACES

"IT is *so* good to be at home again! I wonder how we ever made up our minds to go away!" exclaimed Rose, as she went roaming about the old house next morning, full of the satisfaction one feels at revisiting familiar nooks and corners, and finding them unchanged.

"That we might have the pleasure of coming back again," answered Phebe, walking down the hall beside her little mistress, as happy as she.

"Every thing seems just as we left it, even to the 'ose-leaves we used to tuck in here," continued the younger girl, peeping into one of the tall India jars that stood about the hall.

"Don't you remember how Jamie and Pokey used to play Forty Thieves with them, and how you tried to get into that blue one and got stuck, and the other boys found us before I could pull you out?" asked Phebe, laughing.

"Yes, indeed; and speaking of angels one is apt to hear the rustling of their wings," added Rose, as a shrill whistle came up the avenue, accompanied by the clatter of hoofs.

"It is the circus!" cried Phebe, gayly, as they both recalled the red cart and the charge of the clan.

There was only one boy now, alas! but he made
noise enough for half a dozen; and, before Rose could
run to the door, Jamie came bouncing in with a "shining morning face," a bat over his shoulder, a red and
white jockey cap on his head, one pocket bulging with
a big ball, the other overflowing with cookies, and his
mouth full of the apple he was just finishing off in
hot haste.

"Morning! I just looked in to make sure you'd
really come, and see that you were all right," he
observed, saluting with the bat and doffing the gay
cap with one effective twitch.

"Good-morning, dear. Yes, we are really here, and
getting to rights as fast as possible. But it seems to
me you are rather gorgeous, Jamie. What do you
belong to, — a fire company or a jockey club?" asked
Rose, turning up the once chubby face, which now
was getting brown, and square about the chin.

"No, *ma'am!* Why, don't you know? I'm captain of the Base Ball Star Club. Look at that, will
you?" and, as if the fact was one of national importance, Jamie flung open his jacket to display upon
his proudly swelling chest a heart-shaped red-flannel
shield, decorated with a white cotton star the size of
a tea-plate.

"Superb! I've been away so long I forgot there
was such a game. And *you* are the captain?" cried
Rose, deeply impressed by the high honor to which
her kinsman had arrived.

"I just am, and it's no joke you'd better believe;
for we knock our teeth out, black our eyes, and split
our fingers almost as well as the big fellows. You
come down to the Common between one and two

and see us play a match; then you'll understand what hard work it is. I'll teach you to bat now if you'll come out on the lawn," added Jamie, fired with a wish to exhibit his prowess.

"No, thank you, captain. The grass is wet, and you'll be late at school if you stay for us."

"I'm not afraid. Girls are not good for much generally; but you never used to mind a little wet, and played cricket like a good one. Can't you ever do that sort of thing now?" asked the boy, with a pitying look at these hapless creatures, debarred from the joys and perils of manly sports.

"I can run still: and I'll get to the gate before you; see if I don't;" and, yielding to the impulse of the moment, Rose darted down the steps before astonished Jamie could mount and follow.

He was off in a moment: but Rose had the start; and, though old Sheltie did his best, she reached the goal just ahead, and stood there laughing and panting, all rosy with the fresh October air, a pretty picture for several gentlemen who were driving by.

"Good for you, Rose!" said Archie, jumping out to shake hands, while Will and Geordie saluted, and Uncle Mac laughed at Jamie, who looked as if girls had risen slightly in his opinion.

"I'm glad it is you, because you won't be shocked. But I'm so happy to be back I forgot I was not little Rose still," said Atalanta, smoothing down her flying hair.

"You look very like her, with the curls on your shoulders in the old way. I missed them last night, and wondered what it was. How is uncle and Phebe?" asked Archie. whose eyes had been looking over Rose's head while he spoke toward the piazza, where a female figure was visible among the reddening woodbines.

"All well, thanks. Won't you come up and see for yourselves?"

"Can't, my dear, can't possibly. Business, you know, business. This fellow is my right-hand man, and I can't spare him a minute. Come, Arch, we must be off, or these boys will miss their train," answered Uncle Mac, pulling out his watch.

With a last look from the light-haired figure at the gate to the dark-haired one among the vines, Archie drove away, and Jamie cantered after, consoling himself for his defeat with apple number two.

Rose lingered a moment, feeling much inclined to continue her run, and pop in upon all the aunts in succession; but, remembering her uncovered head, was about to turn back, when a cheerful "Ahoy! ahoy!" made her look up, to see Mac approaching at a great pace, waving his hat as he came.

"The Campbells are coming thick and fast this morning, and the more the merrier," she said, running to meet him. "You look like a good boy going to school, and virtuously conning your lesson by the way," she added, smiling to see him take his finger out of the book he had evidently been reading, and tuck it under his arm, just as he used to do years ago.

"I *am* a school-boy going to the school I like best," he answered, waving a plumy spray of asters, as if pointing out the lovely autumn world about them, full of gay hues, fresh airs, and mellow sunshine.

"That reminds me that I didn't get a chance to
hear much about your plans last night: the other
boys all talked at once, and you only got in a word
now and then. What have you decided to be, Mac?"
asked Rose, as they went up the avenue side by side.

"A man first, and a good one if possible; after that,
what God pleases."

Something in the tone, as well as the words, made
Rose look up quickly into Mac's face, to see a new
expression there. It was indescribable; but she felt
as she had often done when watching the mists part
suddenly, giving glimpses of some mountain-top,
shining serene and high against the blue.

"I think you *will* be something splendid; for you
really look quite glorified, walking under this arch of
yellow leaves with the sunshine on your face," she
exclaimed, conscious of a sudden admiration never
felt before; for Mac was the plainest of all the
cousins.

"I don't know about that; but I have my dreams
and aspirations, and some of them are pretty high
ones. Aim at the best, you know, and keep climbing
if you want to get on," he said, looking at the asters
with an inward sort of smile, as if he and they had
some sweet secret between them.

"You are queerer than ever. But I like your ambition, and hope you will get on. Only mustn't you
begin at something soon? I fancied you would study
medicine with uncle: that used to be our plan, you
know."

"I shall, for the present at least, because I quite
agree with you that it is necessary to have an anchor
somewhere, and not go floating off into the world of

imagination without ballast of the right sort. Uncle and I had some talk about it last night, and I 'm going up to begin as soon as possible; for I 've mooned long enough," and giving himself a shake, Mac threw down the pretty spray, adding half aloud, —

> "Chide me not, laborious band,
>   For the idle flowers I brought:
> Every aster in my hand
>   Goes home laden with a thought."

Rose caught the words and smiled, thinking to herself, "Oh, that 's it: he is getting into the sentimental age, and Aunt Jane has been lecturing him. Dear me, how we *are* growing up!"

"You look as if you did n't like the prospect very well," she said aloud; for Mac had rammed the volume of Shelley into his pocket, and the glorified expression was so entirely gone Rose fancied that she had been mistaken about the mountain-top behind the mists.

"Yes, well enough: I always thought the profession a grand one; and where could I find a better teacher than uncle? I 've got into lazy ways lately, and it is high time I went at something useful; so here I go," and Mac abruptly vanished into the study, while Rose joined Phebe in Aunt Plenty's room.

The dear old lady had just decided, after long and earnest discussion, which of six favorite puddings should be served for dinner, and thus had a few moments to devote to sentiment; so, when Rose came in, she held out her arms, saying fondly, —

"I shall not feel as if I 'd got my child back again, until I have her in my lap a minute. No, you 're not a bit too heavy; my rheumatism does n't begin much

before November: so sit here, darling, and put your
two arms round my neck."

Rose obeyed, and neither spoke for a moment, as
the old woman held the young one close, and appeased
the two years' longing of a motherly heart by the
caresses women give the creatures dearest to them.
Right in the middle of a kiss, however, she stopped
suddenly; and, holding out one arm, caught Phebe,
who was trying to steal away unobserved.

"Don't go: there's room for both in my love,
though there is n't in my lap. I'm so grateful to get
my dear girls safely home again, that I hardly know
what I'm about," said Aunt Plenty, embracing Phebe
so heartily that she could not feel left out in the cold,
and stood there with her black eyes shining through
the happiest tears.

"There, now I've had a good hug, and feel as if I
was all right again. I wish you'd set that cap in
order, Rose: I went to bed in such a hurry I pulled
the strings off and left it all in a heap. Phebe, dear,
you shall dust round a mite, just as you used to; for
I have n't had any one to do it as I like since you've
been gone, and it will do me good to see all my knick-
knacks straightened out in your tidy way," said the
elder lady, getting up with a refreshed expression on
her rosy old face.

"Shall I dust in here too?" asked Phebe, glancing toward an inner room which used to be her care.

"No, dear, I'd rather do that myself. Go in if you
like; nothing is changed. I *must* go and see to my
pudding;" and Aunt Plenty trotted abruptly away,
with a quiver of emotion in her voice which made
even her last words pathetic.

3

Pausing on the threshold as if it was a sacred place, the girls looked in with eyes soon dimmed by tender tears; for it seemed as if the gentle occupant was still there. Sunshine shone on the old geraniums by the window; the cushioned chair stood in its accustomed place, with the white wrapper hung across it, and the faded slippers lying ready. Books and basket, knitting and spectacles, were all just as she had left them; and the beautiful tranquillity that always filled the room seemed so natural both lookers turned involuntarily toward the bed where Aunt Peace used to greet them with a smile. There was no sweet old face upon the pillow now, yet the tears that wet the blooming cheeks were not for her who had gone, but for her who was left; because they saw something which spoke eloquently of the love which outlives death and makes the humblest thing beautiful and sacred.

A well-worn footstool stood beside the bed, and in the high-piled whiteness of the empty couch there was a little hollow where a gray head nightly rested, while Aunt Plenty said the prayers her mother taught her seventy years ago.

Without a word, the girls softly shut the door: and, while Phebe put the room in the most exquisite order, Rose retrimmed the plain white cap, where pink and yellow ribbons never rustled now; both feeling honored by their tasks, and better for their knowledge of the faithful love and piety which sanctified a good old woman's life.

"You darling creature, I'm *so* glad to get you back! I know it's shamefully early; but I really could n't keep away another minute. Let me help you: I'm dying to see all your splendid things; for I saw the trunks pass, and I know you've quantities of treasures," cried Annabel Bliss, all in one breath as she embraced Rose an hour later, and glanced about the room bestrewn with a variety of agreeable objects.

"How well you are looking! Sit down and I'll show you my lovely photographs. Uncle chose all the best for me, and it's a treat to see them," answered Rose, putting a roll on the table and looking about for more.

"Oh, thanks! I have n't time now: one needs hours to study such things. Show me your Paris dresses, there's a dear: I'm perfectly aching to see the last styles," and Annabel cast a hungry eye toward certain large boxes delightfully suggestive of French finery.

"I have n't got any," said Rose, fondly surveying the fine photographs as she laid them away.

Rose Campbell! you don't mean to say that you did n't get one Paris dress at least?" cried Annabel, scandalized at the bare idea of such neglect.

"Not one for myself: Aunt Clara ordered several, and will be charmed to show them when her box comes."

"Such a chance! right there and plenty of money! How *could* you love your uncle after such cruelty?" sighed Annabel, with a face full of sympathy.

Rose looked puzzled for a minute, then seemed to understand, and assumed a superior air which became her very well, as she said, good-naturedly opening a box of laces, "Uncle did not forbid my doing it, and I had money enough; but I chose not to spend it on things of that sort."

"Could and did n't! I can't believe it!" And Annabel sunk into a chair, as if the thought was too much for her.

"I did rather want to at first, just for the fun of the thing; in fact, I went and looked at some amazing gowns. But they were very expensive, very much trimmed, and not my style at all; so I gave them up, and kept what I valued more than all the gowns Worth ever made."

"What in the world was it?" cried Annabel, hoping she would say diamonds.

"Uncle's good opinion," answered Rose, looking thoughtfully into the depths of a packing case, where lay the lovely picture that would always remind her of the little triumph over girlish vanity, which not only kept but increased "Uncle's good opinion."

"Oh, indeed!" said Annabel, blankly, and fell to examining Aunt Plenty's lace; while Rose went on with a happy smile in her eyes as she dived into another trunk.

"Uncle thinks one has no right to waste money on such things; but he is very generous, and loves to give useful, beautiful, or curious gifts. See, all these pretty ornaments are for presents; and you shall choose first whatever you like."

"He 's a perfect dear!" cried Annabel, revelling in the crystal, filigree, coral, and mosaic trinkets spread before her; while Rose completed her rapture by adding sundry tasteful trifles fresh from Paris.

"Now tell me, when do you mean to have your coming-out party? I ask because I've nothing ready, and want plenty of time; for, I suppose, it will be *the*

event of the season," asked Annabel, a few minutes
later, as she wavered between a pink coral and a blue
lava set.

"I came out when I went to Europe; but I suppose
Aunty Plen will want to have some sort of merry-
making to celebrate our return. I shall begin as I
mean to go on, and have a simple, sociable sort of
party, and invite every one whom I like, no matter
in what 'set' they happen to belong. No one
shall ever say *I* am aristocratic and exclusive: so
prepare yourself to be shocked; for old friends
and young, rich and poor, will be asked to all my
parties."

"Oh, my heart! you *are* going to be odd just as
mamma predicted!" sighed Annabel, clasping her
hands in despair, and studying the effect of three
bracelets on her chubby arm in the midst of her
woe.

"In my own house I'm going to do as I think best;
and, if people call me odd, I can't help it. I shall
endeavor not to do any thing very dreadful; but I
seem to inherit uncle's love for experiments, and mean
to try some. I dare say they will fail and I shall get
laughed at; I intend to do it nevertheless, so you had
better drop me now before I begin," said Rose, with
an air of resolution that was rather alarming.

"What shall you wear at this new sort of party of
yours?" asked Annabel, wisely turning a deaf ear to
all delicate or dangerous topics and keeping to matters
she understood.

"That white thing over there. It is fresh and
pretty, and Phebe has one like it. I never want to
dress more than she does; and gowns of that sort are

always most appropriate and becoming to girls of
our age."

"Phebe! you don't mean to say you are going to
make a lady of *her!*" gasped Annabel, upsetting her
treasures, as she fell back with a gesture that made
the little chair creak again; for Miss Bliss was as
plump as a partridge.

"She *is* one already, and anybody who slights her
slights me; for she is the best girl I know and the
dearest," cried Rose, warmly.

"Yes, of course, — I was only surprised, — you are
quite right; for she *may* turn out to be somebody,
and then how glad you'll feel that you were so good
to her!" said Annabel, veering round at once, seeing
which way the wind blew.

Before Rose could speak again, a cheery voice
called from the hall, —

"Little mistress, where are you?"

"In my room, Phebe, dear," and up came the girl
Rose was going to "make a lady of," looking so like
one that Annabel opened her china-blue eyes, and
smiled involuntarily as Phebe dropped a little courtesy
in playful imitation of her old manner, and said
quietly, —

"How do you do, Miss Bliss?"

"Glad to see you back, Miss Moore," answered
Annabel, shaking hands in a way that settled the question of Phebe's place in *her* mind for ever; for the
stout damsel had a kind heart in spite of a weak head,
and was really fond of Rose. It was evidently, "Love
me, love my Phebe"; so she made up her mind on
the spot that Phebe *was* somebody, and that gave an
air of romance even to the poor-house.

She could not help staring a little, as she watched the two friends work together, and listened to their happy talk over each new treasure as it came to light; for every look and word plainly showed that years of close companionship had made them very dear to one another. It was pretty to see Rose try to do the hardest part of any little job herself: still prettier to see Phebe circumvent her, and untie the hard knots, fold the stiff papers, or lift the heavy trays with her own strong hands; and prettiest of all to hear her say in a motherly tone, as she put Rose into an easy chair, —

"Now, my deary, sit and rest; for you will have to see company all day, and I can't let you get tired out so early."

"That is no reason why I should let you either. Call Jane to help or I 'll bob up again directly," answered Rose, with a very bad assumption of authority.

"Jane may take my place downstairs; but no one shall wait on you here except me, as long as I 'm with you," said stately Phebe, stooping to put a hassock under the feet of her little mistress.

"It is very nice and pretty to see ; but I don't know what people *will* say when she goes into society with the rest of us. I do hope Rose won't be *very* odd," said Annabel to herself as she went away to circulate the depressing news that there was to be no grand ball; and, saddest disappointment of all, that Rose had not a single Paris costume with which to refresh the eyes and rouse the envy of her amiable friends.

"Now I 've seen or heard from all the boys but Charlie, and I suppose he is too busy. I wonder what he is about," thought Rose, turning from the hall door, whither she had courteously accompanied her guest.

The wish was granted a moment after; for, going into the parlor to decide where some of her pictures should hang, she saw a pair of boots at one end of the sofa, a tawny-brown head at the other, and discovered that Charlie was busily occupied in doing nothing.

"The voice of the Bliss was heard in the land, so I dodged till she went upstairs, and then took a brief *siesta* while waiting to pay my respects to the distin guished traveller, Lady Hester Stanhope," he said, leaping up to make his best bow.

"The voice of the sluggard would be a more appropriate quotation, I think. Does Annabel still pine for you?" asked Rose, recalling certain youthful jokes upon the subject of unrequited affections.

"Not a bit of it. Fun has cut me out, and the fair Annabella will be Mrs. Tokio before the winter is over, if I'm not much mistaken."

"What, little Fun See? How droll it seems to think of him grown up and married to Annabel of all people! She never said a word about him; but this accounts for her admiring my pretty Chinese things, and being so interested in Canton."

"Little Fun is a great swell now, and much enamoured of our fat friend, who will take to chopsticks whenever he says the word. I need n't ask how you do, cousin; for you beat that Aurora all hollow in the way of color. I should have been up before, but I thought you'd like a good rest after your voyage."

"I was running a race with Jamie before nine o'clock. What were you doing, young man?"

"'Sleeping I dreamed, love, dreamed, love, of thee,'"

began Charlie; but Rose cut him short by saying as reproachfully as she could, while the culprit stood regarding her with placid satisfaction, —

"You ought to have been up and at work like the rest of the boys. I felt like a drone in a hive of very busy bees, when I saw them all hurrying off to their business."

"But, my dear girl, I've got no business. I'm making up my mind, you see, and do the ornamental while I'm deciding. There always ought to be one gentleman in a family, and that seems to be rather my line," answered Charlie, posing for the character, with an assumption of languid elegance which would have been very effective if his twinkling eyes had not spoilt it.

"There are none *but* gentlemen in our family, I hope," answered Rose, with the proud air she always wore when any thing was said derogatory to the name of Campbell.

"Of course, of course. I should have said gentleman of leisure. You see it is against my principles to slave as Archie does. What's the use? Don't need the money, got plenty; so why not enjoy it, and keep jolly as long as possible? I'm sure cheerful people are public benefactors in this world of woe."

It was not easy to object to this proposition, especially when made by a comely young man, who looked the picture of health and happiness as he sat on the arm of the sofa, smiling at his cousin in the most engaging manner. Rose knew very well that the Epicurean philosophy was not the true one to begin life upon; but it was difficult to reason with Charlie, because he always dodged sober subjects, and was so full of cheery spirits, one hated to lessen the sort of sunshine which certainly is a public benefactor.

"You have such a clever way of putting things that I don't know how to contradict you, though I still think I'm right," she said gravely. "Mac likes to idle as well as you; but he is not going to do it, because he knows it's bad for him to fritter away his time. He is going to study a profession like a wise boy; though he would much prefer to live among his beloved books, or ride his hobbies in peace."

"That's all very well for *him*, because *he* does n't care for society, and may as well be studying medicine as philandering about the woods with his pockets full of musty philosophers and old-fashioned poets," answered Charlie, with a shrug which plainly expressed his opinion of Mac.

"I wonder if musty philosophers, like Socrates and Aristotle, and old-fashioned poets, like Shakspeare and Milton, are not safer company for him to keep than some of the more modern friends you have?" said Rose, remembering Jamie's hints about wild oats; for she could be a little sharp sometimes, and had not lectured "the boys" for so long it seemed unusually pleasant.

But Charlie changed the subject skilfully by exclaiming with an anxious expression, —

"I do believe you are going to be like Aunt Jane; for that's just the way she comes down on me when-

ever she gets a chance! Don't take her for a model, I beg: she is a good woman, but a mighty disagreeable one, in my humble opinion."

The fear of being disagreeable is a great bugbear to a girl, as this artful young man well knew, and Rose fell into the trap at once; for Aunt Jane was far from being her model, though she could not help respecting her worth.

"Have you given up your painting?" she asked rather abruptly, turning to a gilded Fra Angelico angel which leaned in the sofa corner.

"Sweetest face I ever saw, and very like you about the eyes, is n't it?" said Charlie, who seemed to have a Yankee trick of replying to one question with another.

"I want an answer, not a compliment," and Rose tried to look severe, as she put away the picture more quickly than she took it up.

"Have I given up painting? Oh, no! I daub a little in oils, slop a little in water-colors, sketch now and then, and poke about the studios when the artistic fit comes on."

"How is the music?"

"More flourishing. I don't practise much, but sing a good deal in company. Set up a guitar last summer, and went troubadouring round in great style. The girls like it, and it 's jolly among the fellows."

"Are you studying any thing?"

"Well, I have some law books on my table, — good, big, wise-looking chaps, — and I take a turn at them semi-occasionally, when pleasure palls or parents chide. But I doubt if I do more than learn what ' a allybi' is this year," and a sly laugh in Charlie's eye sug-

gested that he sometimes availed himself of this **bit**
of legal knowledge.

"What *do* you do then?"

"Fair catechist, I enjoy myself. Private theatricals have been the rage of late, and I have won such
laurels that I seriously think of adopting the stage
as my profession."

"Really!" cried Rose, alarmed.

"Why not? if I *must* go to work, is n't that as good
as any thing?"

"Not without more talent than I think you possess.
With genius one can do any thing: without it one had
better let the stage alone."

"There's a quencher for the 'star of the goodlie
companie' to which I belong. Mac has n't a ray of
genius for any thing, yet you admire him for trying to
be an M.D.," cried Charlie, rather nettled by her words.

"It is respectable, at all events; and I 'd rather be
a second-rate doctor than a second-rate actor. But
I know you don't mean it, and only say so to frighten
me."

"Exactly. I always bring it up when any one
begins to lecture, and it works wonders. Uncle Mac
turns pale, the aunts hold up their hands in holy
horror, and a general panic ensues. Then I magnani-
mously promise not to disgrace the family; and in
the first burst of gratitude the dear souls agree to
every thing I ask; so peace is restored, and I go on
my way rejoicing."

"Just the way you used to threaten to run off to
sea, if your mother objected to any of your whims.
You are not changed in that respect, though you are
in others. You had great plans and projects once,

Charlie; and now you seem to be contented with being a 'jack of all trades and master of none.'"

"Boyish nonsense! Time has brought wisdom, and I don't see the sense of tying myself down to one particular thing, and grinding away at it year after year. People of one idea get so deucedly narrow and tame, I've no patience with them. Culture is the thing; and the sort one gets by ranging over a wide field is the easiest to acquire, the handiest to have, and the most successful in the end. At any rate, it is the kind I like, and the only kind I intend to bother myself about."

With this declaration, Charlie smoothed his brow, clasped his hands over his head, and, leaning back, gently warbled the chorus of a college song, as if it expressed his views of life better than he could : —

> "While our rosy fillets shed
> Blushes o'er each fervid head,
> With many a cup and many a smile
> The festal moments we beguile."

"Some of my saints here were people of one idea; and, though they were not very successful in a worldly point of view while alive, they were loved and canonized when dead," said Rose, who had been turning over a pile of photographs upon the table, and, just then, found her favorite, St. Francis, among them.

"This is more to my taste. Those worn-out, cadaverous fellows give me the blues; but here's a gentlemanly saint, who takes things easy, and does good as he goes along, without howling over his own sins, or making other people miserable by telling them of theirs." And Charlie laid a handsome St. Martin beside the brown-frocked monk.

Rose looked at both, and understood why her cousin preferred the soldierly figure with the sword to the ascetic with his crucifix. One was riding bravely through the world in purple and fine linen, with horse and hound, and squires at his back; the other was in a lazar-house, praying over the dead and dying. The contrast was a strong one; and the girl's eyes lingered longest on the knight, though she said thoughtfully, —

"Yours is certainly the pleasantest: and yet I never heard of any good deed he did, except divide his cloak with a beggar; while my St. Francis gave himself to charity just when life was most tempting, and spent years working for God without reward. He's old and poor, and in a dreadful place, but I won't give him up; and you may have your gay St. Martin, if you want him."

"No, thank you; saints are not in my line: but I'd like the golden-haired angel in the blue gown, if you'll let me have her. She shall be my little Madonna, and I'll pray to her like a good Catholic," answered Charlie, turning to the delicate, deep-eyed figure, with the lilies in its hand.

"With all my heart, and any others that you like. Choose some for your mother, and give them to her with my love."

So Charlie sat down beside Rose to turn and talk over the pictures for a long and pleasant hour. But when they went away to lunch, if there had been any one to observe so small but significant a trifle, good St. Francis lay face downward behind the sofa, while gallant St. Martin stood erect upon the chimney-piece.

CHAPTER III

MISS CAMPBELL

WHILE the travellers unpack their trunks, we will pick up, as briefly as possible, the dropped stitches in the little romance we are weaving.

Rose's life had been a very busy and quiet one for the four years following the May-day when she made her choice. Study, exercise, house-work, and many wholesome pleasures, kept her a happy, hearty creature, yearly growing in womanly graces, yet always preserving the innocent freshness girls lose so soon when too early sent upon the world's stage, and given a part to play.

Not a remarkably gifted girl in any way, and far from perfect; full of all manner of youthful whims and fancies ; a little spoiled by much love ; rather apt to think all lives as safe and sweet as her own ; and, when want or pain appealed to her, the tender heart overflowed with a remorseful charity, which gave of its abundance recklessly. Yet, with all her human imperfections, the upright nature of the child kept her desires climbing toward the just and pure and true, as flowers struggle to the light; and the woman's soul was budding beautifully under the green leaves behind the little thorns.

At seventeen, Dr. Alec pronounced her ready for the voyage round the world, which he considered a better finishing off than any school could give her. But just then Aunt Peace began to fail, and soon slipped quietly away to rejoin the lover she had waited for so long. Youth seemed to come back in a mysterious way to touch the dead face with lost loveliness, and all the romance of her past to gather round her memory. Unlike most aged women, her friends were among the young; and, at her funeral, the gray heads gave place to the band of loving girls who made the sweet old maiden ready for her rest, bore her pall, and covered her grave with the white flowers she had never worn.

When this was over, poor Aunt Plenty seemed so lost without her life-long charge that Dr. Alec would not leave her; and Rose gladly paid the debt she owed by the tender service which comforts without words. But Aunt Plenty, having lived for others all her days, soon rebelled against this willing sacrifice, soon found strength in her own sincere piety, solace in cheerful occupation, and amusement in nursing Aunt Myra, who was a capital patient, as she never died and never got well.

So, at last, the moment came when, with free minds, the travellers could set out; and on Rose's eighteenth birthday, with Uncle Alec and the faithful Phebe, she sailed away to see and study the big, beautiful world, which lies ready for us all, if we only know how to use and to enjoy it.

Phebe was set to studying music in the best schools; and, while she trained her lovely voice with happy industry, Rose and her uncle roamed about in the most delightful way, till two years were gone like a dream, and those at home clamored for their return.

Back they came, and now the heiress must make ready to take her place; for at twenty-one she came into possession of the fortune she had been trying to learn how to use well. Great plans fermented in her brain; for, though the heart was as generous as ever, time had taught her prudence, and observation shown her that the wisest charity is that which helps the poor to help themselves.

Dr. Alec found it a little difficult to restrain the ardor of this young philanthropist, who wanted to begin at once to endow hospitals, build homes, adopt children, and befriend all mankind.

"Take a little time to look about you and get your bearings, child; for the world you have been living in is a much simpler, honester one than that you are now to enter. Test yourself a bit, and see if the old ways seem best after all; for you are old enough to decide, and wise enough to discover, what is for your truest good, I hope," he said, trying to feel ready to let the bird escape from under his wing, and make little flights alone.

"Now, uncle, I'm very much afraid you are going to be disappointed in me," answered Rose, with unusual hesitation, yet a very strong desire visible in her eyes. "You like to have me quite honest, and I've learned to tell you all my foolish thoughts: so I'll speak out, and if you find my wish very wrong and silly, please say so; for I don't want you to cast me off entirely, though I am grown up. You say, wait a little, test myself, and try if the old ways are best. I should like to do that; and can I in a better way

than by leading the life other girls lead, just for a
little while," she added, as her uncle's face grew grave.

He *was* disappointed; yet acknowledged that the
desire was natural, and in a moment saw that a trial
of this sort might have its advantages.   Nevertheless,
he dreaded it; for he had intended to choose her society carefully, and try to keep her unspoiled by the
world as long as possible, like many another fond
parent and guardian.   But the spirit of Eve is strong
in all her daughters: forbidden fruit will look rosier
to them than any in their own orchards, and the
temptation to take just one little bite proves irresistible to the wisest.   So Rose, looking out from the safe
seclusion of her girlhood into the woman's kingdom
which she was about to take possession of, felt a
sudden wish to try its pleasures before assuming its
responsibilities, and was too sincere to hide the
longing.

"Very well, my dear, try it if you like, only take
care of your health: be temperate in your gayety,
and don't lose more than you gain; if that is possible," he added under his breath, endeavoring to speak
cheerfully and not look anxious.

"I know it is foolish; but I do want to be a regular
butterfly for a little while and see what it is like.
You know I couldn't help seeing a good deal of
fashionable life abroad, though we were not in it; and
here at home the girls tell me about all sorts of
pleasant things that are to happen this winter; so, if
you won't despise me *very* much, I should like to
try it."

"For how long?"

"Would three months be too long?   New Year is

a good time to take a fresh start. Every one is going to welcome me; so I must be gay in spite of myself, unless I'm willing to seem very ungrateful and morose," said Rose, glad to have so good a reason to offer for her new experiment.

"You may like it so well that the three months may become years. Pleasure is very sweet when we are young."

"Do you think it will intoxicate me?"

"We shall see, my dear."

"We shall!" and Rose marched away; looking as if she had taken a pledge of some sort, and meant to keep it.

It was a great relief to the public mind when it became known that Miss Campbell was really coming out at last; and invitations to Aunt Plenty's party were promptly accepted. Aunt Clara was much disappointed about the grand ball she had planned; but Rose stood firm, and the dear old lady had her way about every thing.

The consequence was a delightfully informal gathering of friends to welcome the travellers home. Just a good, old-fashioned, hospitable house-warming; so simple, cordial, and genuine that those who came to criticise remained to enjoy, and many owned the charm they could neither describe nor imitate.

Much curiosity was felt about Phebe, and much gossip went on behind fans that evening; for those who had known her years ago found it hard to recognize the little house-maid in the handsome young woman who bore herself with such quiet dignity, and charmed them all with her fine voice. "Cinderella has turned out a princess," was the general verdict;

and Rose enjoyed the little sensation immensely; for she had had many battles to fight for her Phebe since she came among them, and now her faith was vindicated.

Miss Campbell herself was in great demand, and did the honors so prettily that even Miss Bliss forgave her for her sad neglect of Worth; though she shook her head over the white gowns, just alike except that Phebe wore crimson and Rose blue trimmings.

The girls swarmed eagerly round their recovered friend; for Rose had been a favorite before she went away, and found her throne waiting for her now. The young men privately pronounced Phebe the hand-somest, — "But then you know there's neither family nor money; so it's no use." Phebe, therefore, was admired as one of the ornamental properties belonging to the house, and let respectfully alone.

But bonny Rose was "all right," as these amiable youths expressed it; and many a wistful eye followed the bright head as it flitted about the rooms, as if it were a second Golden Fleece to be won with diffi-culty; for stalwart kinsmen hedged it round, and watchful aunts kept guard.

Little wonder that the girl found her new world an enchanting one, and that her first sip of pleasure rather went to her head; for everybody welcomed and smiled on her, flattered and praised, whispered agree-able prophecies in her ear, and looked the compliments and congratulations they dared not utter, till she felt as if she must have left her old self somewhere abroad, and suddenly become a new and wonderfully gifted being.

"It is very nice, uncle; and I'm not sure that I

may n't want another three months of it when the first
are gone," she whispered to Dr. Alec, as he stood
watching the dance she was leading with Charlie in
the long hall after supper.

" Steady, my lass, steady; and remember that you
are not really a butterfly, but a mortal girl with a
head that will ache to-morrow," he answered, watching the flushed and smiling face before him.

" I almost wish there was n't any to-morrow, but
that to-night would last for ever: it is so pleasant,
and every one so kind," she said with a little sigh of
happiness, as she gathered up her fleecy skirts like a
white bird pluming itself for flight.

" I 'll ask your opinion about that at two A.M.,"
began her uncle, with a warning nod.

" I 'll give it honestly," was all Rose had time to
say before Charlie swept her away into the parti-
colored cloud before them.

" It 's no use, Alec: train a girl as wisely as you
choose, she will break loose when the time comes, and
go in for pleasure as eagerly as the most frivolous;
for ' 't is their nature to,' " said Uncle Mac, keeping
time to the music as if he would not mind " going in "
for a bit of pleasure himself.

" My girl shall taste and try; but, unless I 'm much
mistaken, a little of it will satisfy her. I want to see
if she will stand the test; for, if not, all my work is a
failure, and I 'd like to know it," answered the doctor,
with a hopeful smile on his lips, but an anxious look
in his eyes.

" She will come out all right, — bless her heart! so
let her sow her innocent wild oats and enjoy herself
till she is ready to settle down. I wish all our young

folks were likely to have as small a crop, and get through as safely as she will," added Uncle Mac, with a shake of the head, as he glanced at some of the young men revolving before him.

"Nothing amiss with your lads, I hope?"

"No, thank heaven! So far I 've had little trouble with either; though Mac is an odd stick, and Steve a puppy. I don't complain; for both will outgrow that sort of thing, and are good fellows at heart, thanks to their mother. But Clara's boy is in a bad way; and she will spoil him as a man as she has as a boy, if his father does n't interfere."

"I told brother Stephen all about him when I was in Calcutta last year, and he wrote to the boy; but Clara has got no end of plans in her head, and so she insisted on keeping Charlie a year longer when his father ordered him off to India," replied the doctor, as they walked away.

"It is too late to 'order': Charlie is a man now, and Stephen will find that he has been too easy with him all these years. Poor fellow, it has been hard lines for him, and is likely to be harder, I fancy, unless he comes home and straightens things out."

"He won't do that if he can help it; for he has lost all his energy living in that climate, and hates worry more than ever: so you can imagine what an effort it would be to manage a foolish woman and a headstrong boy. We must lend a hand, Mac, and do our best for poor old Steve."

"The best we can do for the lad is to marry and settle him as soon as possible."

"My dear fellow, he is only three and twenty," began the doctor, as if the idea was preposterous:

then a sudden change came over him, as he added with a melancholy smile, " I forget how much one can hope and suffer, even at twenty-three."

" And be all the better for, if bravely outlived," said Uncle Mac, with his hand on his brother's shoulder, and the sincerest approval in his voice. Then, kindly returning to the younger people, he went on inquiringly, " You don't incline to Clara's view of a certain matter, I fancy?"

" Decidedly not. My girl must have the best, and Clara's training would spoil an angel," answered Dr. Alec, quickly.

" But we shall find it hard to let our little Rose go out of the family. How would Archie do? He has been well brought up, and is a thoroughly excellent lad."

The brothers had retired to the study by this time, and were alone; yet Dr. Alec lowered his voice as he said with a tender sort of anxiety pleasant to see, —

" You know I do not approve of cousins marrying, so I'm in a quandary, Mac; for I love the child as if she were my own, and feel as if I could not give her up to any man whom I did not know and trust entirely. It is of no use for us to plan; for she must choose for herself: yet I do wish we could keep her among us, and give one of our boys a wife worth having."

" We must; so never mind your theories, but devote yourself to testing our elder lads, and making one of them a happy fellow. All are heart-whole, I believe, and, though young still for this sort of thing, we can be gently shaping matters for them, since no one knows how soon the moment may come. My

faith! it is like living in a powder-mill to be among
a lot of young folks now-a-days. All looks as calm
as possible, till a sudden spark produces an explosion, and heaven only knows where we find ourselves
after it is over."

And Uncle Mac sat himself comfortably down to
settle Rose's fate; while the doctor paced the room,
plucking at his beard and knitting his brows, as if he
found it hard to see his way.

"Yes, Archie is a good fellow," he said, answering
the question he had ignored before. "An upright,
steady, intelligent lad, who will make an excellent
husband, if he ever finds out that he has a heart. I
suppose I'm an old fool, but I do like a little more
romance in a young man than he seems to have;
more warmth and enthusiasm, you know. Bless the
boy! he might be forty instead of three or four and
twenty: he's so sober, calm, and cool. I'm younger
now than he is, and could go a-wooing like a Romeo
if I had any heart to offer a woman."

The doctor looked rather shamefaced as he spoke,
and his brother burst out laughing, —

"See here, Alec, it's a pity so much romance and
excellence as yours should be lost; so why don't you
set these young fellows an example, and go a-wooing
yourself? Jessie has been wondering how you have
managed to keep from falling in love with Phebe
all this time; and Clara is quite sure that you only
waited till she was safe under Aunt Plenty's wing to
offer yourself in the good old-fashioned style."

"I!" and the doctor stood aghast at the mere
idea; then he gave a resigned sort of sigh and
added like a martyr, "If those dear women would

let me alone, I'd thank them for ever. Put the idea
out of their minds for heaven's sake, Mac, or I shall
be having that poor girl flung at my head, and her
comfort destroyed. She is a fine creature, and I'm
proud of her; but she deserves a better lot than to
be tied to an old fellow like me, whose only merit
is his fidelity."

"As you please, I was only joking," and Uncle
Mac dropped the subject with secret relief; for the
excellent man thought a good deal of family, and
had been rather worried at the hints of the ladies.
After a moment's silence, he returned to a former
topic, which was rather a pet plan of his. " I don't
think you do Archie justice, Alec. You don't know
him as well as I do; but you'll find that he has
heart enough under his cool, quiet manner. I've
grown very fond of him, think highly of him, and
don't see how you could do better for Rose than
to give her to him."

"If she will go," said the doctor, smiling at his
brother's business-like way of disposing of the young
people.

"She'll do any thing to please you," began Uncle
Mac, in perfect good faith; for twenty-five years in
the society of a very prosaic wife had taken nearly
all the romance out of him.

"It is of no use for us to plan, and I shall never
interfere except to advise; but, if I *were* to choose
one of the boys, I should incline to my godson,"
answered the doctor, gravely.

"What, my Ugly Duckling!" exclaimed Uncle
Mac, in great surprise.

"The Ugly Duckling turned out a swan, you re-

member. I've always been fond of the boy, because
he's so genuine and original. Crude as a green
apple now, but sound at the core, and only needs
time to ripen. I'm sure he'll turn out a capital
specimen of the Campbell variety."

"Much obliged, Alec; but it will never do at all.
He's a good fellow, and may do something to be
proud of by and by; but he's not the mate for our
Rose. She needs some one who can manage her
property when we are gone; and Archie is the man
for that, depend upon it."

"Confound the property!" cried Dr. Alec, impetuously. "I want her to be *happy ;* and I don't care
how soon she gets rid of her money if it is going to
be a millstone round her neck. I declare to you, I
dreaded the thought of this time so much that I've
kept her away as long as I could, and trembled whenever a young fellow joined us while we were abroad.
Had one or two narrow escapes, and now I'm in for
it, as you can see by to-night's 'success,' as Clara
calls it. Thank heaven, I haven't *many* daughters
to look after!"

"Come, come, don't be anxious: take Archie, and
settle it right up safely and happily. That's my
advice, and you'll find it sound," replied the elder
conspirator, like one having experience.

"I'll think of it; but mind you, Mac, not a word
of this to the sisters. We are a couple of old fools to
be match-making so soon; but I see what is before
me, and it's a comfort to free my mind to some one."

"So it is. Depend on me; not a breath even to
Jane," answered Uncle Mac, with a hearty shake and
a sympathetic slap on the shoulder.

"Why, what dark and awful secrets are going on here? Is it a Freemasons' Lodge, and those the mystic signs?" asked a gay voice at the door; and there stood Rose, full of smiling wonder at the sight of her two uncles hand in hand, whispering and nodding to one another mysteriously.

They started, like school-boys caught plotting mischief, and looked so guilty that she took pity on them, innocently imagining that the brothers were indulging in a little sentiment on this joyful occasion; so she added quickly, as she beckoned, without crossing the threshold, —

"Women not allowed, of course: but both of you dear Odd Fellows are wanted; for Aunt Plenty begs we will have an old-fashioned contra dance, and I'm to lead off with Uncle Mac. I chose you, sir, because you do it in style, pigeon-wings and all. So, please come; and Phebe is waiting for you, Uncle Alec. She is rather shy you know, but will enjoy it with you to take care of her."

"Thank you, thank you!" cried both gentlemen, following with great alacrity.

Unconscious Rose enjoyed that Virginia reel immensely; for the pigeon-wings were superb, and her partner conducted her through the convolutions of the dance without a fault, going down the middle in his most gallant style. Landing safely at the bottom, she stood aside to let him get his breath; for stout Uncle Mac was bound to do or die on that occasion, and would have danced his pumps through without a murmur if she had desired it.

Leaning against the wall with his hair in his eyes, and a decidedly bored expression of countenance, was

Mac, Jr., who had been surveying the gymnastics of his parent with respectful astonishment.

"Come and take a turn, my lad. Rose is as fresh as a daisy; but we old fellows soon get enough of it, so you shall have my place," said his father, wiping his face, which glowed like a cheerful peony.

"No, thank you, sir: I can't stand that sort of thing. I'll race you round the piazza with pleasure, cousin; but this oven is too much for me," was Mac's uncivil reply, as he backed toward the open window, as if glad of an excuse to escape.

"Fragile creature, don't stay on my account, I beg. *I* can't leave my guests for a moonlight run, even if I dared to take it on a frosty night in a thin dress," said Rose, fanning herself, and not a bit ruffled by Mac's refusal; for she knew his ways, and they amused her.

"Not half so bad as all this dust, gas, heat, and noise. What do you suppose lungs are made of?" demanded Mac, ready for a discussion then and there.

"I used to know, but I've forgotten now. Been so busy with other things that I've neglected the hobbies I used to ride five or six years ago," she said, laughing.

"Ah, those were times worth having! Are you going in for much of this sort of thing, Rose?" he asked, with a disapproving glance at the dancers.

"About three months of it, I think."

"Then good-by till New Year," and Mac vanished behind the curtains.

"Rose, my dear, you really must take that fellow in hand before he gets to be quite a bear. Since you have been gone, he has lived in his books, and got on so finely that we have let him alone, though his

mother groans over his manners. Polish him up a
bit, I beg of you; for it is high time he mended his
odd ways, and did justice to the fine gifts he hides
behind them," said Uncle Mac, scandalized at the
bluntness of his son.

"I know my chestnut-burr too well to mind his
prickles. But others do not; so I *will* take him in
hand and make him a credit to the family," answered
Rose, readily.

"Take Archie for your model: he's one of a thousand; and the girl who gets him gets a prize I do
assure you," added Uncle Mac, who found match-
making to his taste, and thought that closing remark
a deep one.

"Oh me, how tired I am!" cried Rose, dropping
into a chair as the last carriage rolled away, somewhere
between one and two.

"What is your opinion now, Miss Campbell?"
asked the doctor, addressing her for the first time by
the name which had been uttered so often that night.

"My opinion is that Miss Campbell is likely to have
a gay life if she goes on as she has begun; and that
she finds it very delightful so far," answered the girl,
with lips still smiling from their first taste of what the
world calls pleasure.

CHAPTER IV

THORNS AMONG THE ROSES

FOR a time every thing went smoothly, and Rose was a happy girl; for the world seemed a beautiful and friendly place, and the fulfilment of her brightest dreams appeared to be a possibility. Of course, this could not last, and disappointment was inevitable; because young eyes look for a Paradise, and weep when they find a work-a-day world, which seems full of care and trouble, till one learns to gladden and glorify it with high thoughts and holy living.

Those who loved her waited anxiously for the disillusion which must come in spite of all their cherishing; for, till now, Rose had been so busy with her studies, travels, and home duties, that she knew very little of the triumphs, trials, and temptations of fashionable life. Birth and fortune placed her where she could not well escape some of them; and Dr. Alec, knowing that experience is the best teacher, wisely left her to learn this lesson as she must many another, devoutly hoping that it would not be a hard one.

October and November passed rapidly; and Christmas was at hand, with all its merry mysteries, home-gatherings, and good wishes.

Rose sat in her own little sanctum, opening from the parlor busily preparing gifts for the dear five hundred friends who seemed to grow fonder and fonder as the holidays drew near. The drawers of her commode stood open, giving glimpses of dainty trifles, which she was tying up with bright ribbons.

A young girl's face at such moments is apt to be a happy one; but Rose's was very grave as she worked, and now and then she threw a parcel into the drawer with a careless toss, as if no love made the gift precious. So unusual was this expression that it struck Dr. Alec as he came in, and brought an anxious look to his eyes; for any cloud on that other countenance dropped its shadow over his.

"Can you spare a minute from your pretty work to take a stitch in my old glove?" he asked, coming up to the table strewn with ribbon, lace, and colored papers.

"Yes, uncle, as many as you please."

The face brightened with sudden sunshine; both hands were put out to receive the shabby driving-glove; and the voice was full of that affectionate alacrity which makes the smallest service sweet.

"My Lady Bountiful is hard at work, I see. Can I help in any way?" he asked, glancing at the display before him.

"No, thank you; unless you can make me as full of interest and pleasure in these things as I used to be. Don't you think preparing presents a great bore, except for those you love, and who love you?" she added, in a tone which had a slight tremor in it as she uttered the last words.

"I don't give to people whom I care nothing for.

Can't do it; especially at Christmas, when good-will should go into every thing one does. If all these ' pretties' are for dear friends, you must have a great many."

" I thought they were friends; but I find many of them are not, and that's the trouble, sir."

" Tell me all about it, dear, and let the old glove go," he said, sitting down beside her with his most sympathetic air.

But she held the glove fast, saying eagerly, " No, no, I love to do this! I don't feel as if I could look at you while I tell what a bad, suspicious girl I am," she added, keeping her eyes upon her work.

" Very well, I 'm ready for confessions of any iniquity, and glad to get them; for sometimes lately I 've seen a cloud in my girl's eyes, and caught a worried tone in her voice. Is there a bitter drop in the cup that promised to be so sweet, Rose? "

" Yes, uncle. I 've tried to think there was not; but it *is* there, and I don't like it. I 'm ashamed to tell; and yet I want to, because you will show me how to make it sweet, or assure me that I shall be the better for it, as you used to do when I took medicine."

She paused a minute, sewing swiftly; then out came the trouble all in one burst of girlish grief and chagrin.

" Uncle, half the people who are so kind to me don't care a bit for me, but for what I can give them; and that makes me unhappy, because I was so glad and proud to be liked. I do wish I had n't a penny in the world, then I should know who my true friends were."

"Poor little lass! she has found out that all that glitters is not gold, and the dis-illusion has begun," said the doctor to himself, adding aloud, smiling yet pitiful, "And so all the pleasure is gone out of the pretty gifts, and Christmas is a failure?"

"Oh, no! not for those whom nothing can make me doubt. It is sweeter than ever to make *these* things, because my heart is in every stitch; and I know that, poor as they are, they will be dear to you, Aunty Plen, Aunt Jessie, Phebe, and the boys."

She opened a drawer where lay a pile of pretty gifts, wrought with loving care by her own hands; touching them tenderly as she spoke, and patting the sailor's knot of blue ribbon on one fat parcel with a smile that told how unshakable her faith in some one was. "But *these*," she said, pulling open another drawer, and tossing over its gay contents with an air half sad, half scornful, "these I *bought* and give because they are expected. *These* people only care for a rich gift, not one bit for the giver, whom they will secretly abuse if she is not as generous as they expect. How *can* I enjoy that sort of thing, uncle?"

"You cannot; but perhaps you do some of them injustice, my dear. Don't let the envy or selfishness of a few poison your faith in all. Are you sure that none of these girls care for you?" he asked, reading a name here and there on the parcels scattered about.

"I'm afraid I am. You see I heard several talking together the other evening at Annabel's, only a few words, but it hurt me very much; for nearly every one was speculating on what I would give them, and hoping it would be something fine. 'She's so rich

5

she ought to be generous,' said one. 'I've been perfectly devoted to her for weeks, and hope she won't forget it,' said another. 'If she does n't give me some of her gloves, I shall think she's very mean; for she has heaps, and I tried on a pair in fun so she could see they fitted and take a hint,' added a third. I did take the hint, you see;" and Rose opened a handsome box in which lay several pairs of her best gloves, with buttons enough to satisfy the heart of the most covetous.

"Plenty of silver paper and perfume, but not much love went into *that* bundle, I fancy?" and Dr. Alec could not help smiling at the disdainful little gesture with which Rose pushed away the box.

"Not a particle, nor in most of these. I have given them what they wanted, and taken back the confidence and respect they did n't care for. It is wrong, I know; but I can't bear to think all the seeming good-will and friendliness I 've been enjoying was insincere and for a purpose. That 's not the way *I* treat people."

"I am sure of it. Take things for what they are worth, dear, and try to find the wheat among the tares; for there is plenty if one knows how to look. Is that all the trouble?"

"No, sir, that is the lightest part of it. I shall soon get over my disappointment in those girls, and take them for what they are worth as you advise; but being deceived in them makes me suspicious of others, and that is hateful. If I cannot trust people, I 'd rather keep by myself and be happy. I do detest manœuvring and underhand plots and plans!"

Rose spoke petulantly, and twitched her silk till it

broke; while regret seemed to give place to anger as she spoke.

"There is evidently another thorn pricking. Let us have it out, and then ' I 'll kiss the place to make it well,' as I used to do when I took the splinters from the fingers you are pricking so unmercifully," said the doctor, anxious to relieve his pet patient as soon as possible.

Rose laughed, but the color deepened in her cheeks, as she answered with a pretty mixture of maidenly shyness and natural candor.

"Aunt Clara worries me by warning me against half the young men I meet, and insisting that they only want my money. Now that is dreadful, and I won't listen: but I can't help thinking of it sometimes; for they *are* very kind to me, and I 'm not vain enough to think it is my beauty. I suppose I am foolish, but I do like to feel that I am something beside an heiress."

The little quiver was in Rose's voice again as she ended; and Dr. Alec gave a quick sigh as he looked at the downcast face so full of the perplexity ingenuous spirits feel when doubt first mars their faith, and dims the innocent beliefs still left from childhood. He had been expecting this, and knew that what the girl just began to perceive and try modestly to tell, had long ago been plain to worldlier eyes. The heiress *was* the attraction to most of the young men whom she met. Good fellows enough, but educated, as nearly all are now-a-days, to believe that girls with beauty or money are brought to market to sell or buy as the case may be.

Rose could purchase any thing she liked, as she

combined both advantages; and was soon surrounded by many admirers, each striving to secure the prize. Not being trained to believe that the only end and aim of a woman's life was a good match, she was a little disturbed, when the first pleasing excitement was over, to discover that her fortune was her chief attraction.

It was impossible for her to help seeing, hearing, guessing this from a significant glance, a stray word, a slight hint here and there; and the quick instinct of a woman felt even before it understood the self-interest which chilled for her so many opening friendships. In her eyes love was a very sacred thing, hardly to be thought of till it came, reverently received, and cherished faithfully to the end. Therefore, it is not strange that she shrunk from hearing it flippantly discussed, and marriage treated as a bargain to be haggled over, with little thought of its high duties, great responsibilities, and tender joys. Many things perplexed her, and sometimes a doubt of all that till now she had believed and trusted made her feel as if at sea without a compass; for the new world was so unlike the one she had been living in that it bewildered while it charmed the novice.

Dr. Alec understood the mood in which he found her, and did his best to warn without saddening by too much worldly wisdom.

"You are something besides an heiress to those who know and love you; so take heart, my girl, and hold fast to the faith that is in you. There is a touch-stone for all these things, and whatever does not ring true doubt and avoid. Test and try men and women as they come along; and I am sure conscience, instinct, and experience will keep you from any dire mistake," he said, with a protecting arm about her, and a trustful look that was very comforting.

After a moment's pause she answered, while a sudden smile dimpled round her mouth, and the big glove went up to half hide her tell-tale cheeks, —

"Uncle, if I must have lovers, I do wish they 'd be more interesting. How can I like or respect men who go on as some of them do, and then imagine women *can* feel honored by the offer of their hands? hearts are out of fashion, so they don't say much about them."

"Ah, ha! that is the trouble is it? and we begin to have delicate distresses do we?" said Dr. Alec, glad to see her brightening, and full of interest in the new topic; for he *was* a romantic old fellow, as he confessed to his brother.

Rose put down the glove, and looked up with a droll mixture of amusement and disgust in her face. "Uncle, it is perfectly disgraceful! I 've wanted to tell you, but I was ashamed, because I never could boast of such things as some girls do; and they were so absurd I could n't feel as if they were worth repeating even to you. Perhaps I ought, though; for you may think proper to command me to make a good match, and of course I should have to obey," she added, trying to look meek.

"Tell, by all means. Don't I always keep your secrets, and give you the best advice, like a model guardian? You must have a confidant, and where find a better one than here?" he asked, tapping his waistcoat with an inviting gesture.

"Nowhere: so I 'll tell all but the names. I 'd

best be prudent; for I'm afraid you may get a little fierce: you do sometimes when people vex me," began Rose, rather liking the prospect of a confidential chat with uncle; for he had kept himself a good deal in the background lately.

"You know our ideas are old-fashioned; so I was not prepared to have men propose at all times and places, with no warning but a few smiles and soft speeches. I expected things of that sort would be very interesting and proper, not to say thrilling, on my part: but they are not; and I find myself laughing instead of crying, feeling angry instead of glad, and forgetting all about it very soon. Why, uncle, one absurd boy proposed when we'd only met half a dozen times. But he was dreadfully in debt, so that accounted for it perhaps," and Rose dusted her fingers, as if she had soiled them.

"I know him, and I thought he'd do it," observed the doctor with a shrug.

"You see and know every thing; so there's no need of going on, is there?"

"Do, do! who else? I won't even guess."

"Well, another went down upon his knees in Mrs. Van's greenhouse and poured forth his passion manfully, with a great cactus pricking his poor legs all the while. Kitty found him there, and it was impossible to keep sober; so he has hated me ever since."

The doctor's "Ha! ha!" was good to hear, and Rose joined him; for it was impossible to regard these episodes seriously, since no true sentiment redeemed them from absurdity.

"Another one sent me reams of poetry, and went

on so Byronically, that I began to wish I had red hair and my name was Betsey Ann. I burnt all the verses: so don't expect to see them; and he, poor fellow, is consoling himself with Emma. But the worst of all was the one who would make love in public, and insisted on proposing in the middle of a dance. I seldom dance round dances except with our boys; but that night I did, because the girls laughed at me for being so 'prudish,' as they called it. I don't mind them now; for I found I *was* right, and felt that I deserved my fate."

" Is that all?" asked her uncle, looking " fierce," as she predicted, at the idea of his beloved girl obliged to listen to a declaration, twirling about on the arm of a lover.

" One more: but him I shall not tell about; for I know *he* was in earnest and really suffered, though I was as kind as I knew how to be. I 'm young in these things yet, so I grieved for him, and treat his love with the tenderest respect."

Rose's voice sunk almost to a whisper as she ended; and Dr. Alec bent his head, as if involuntarily saluting a comrade in misfortune. Then he got up, saying with a keen look into the face he lifted by a finger under the chin, —

" Do you want another three months of this?"

" I 'll tell you on New Year's day, uncle."

" Very well: try to keep a straight course, my little captain; and, if you see dirty weather ahead, call on your first mate."

" Ay, ay, sir; I 'll remember."

CHAPTER V

PRINCE CHARMING

THE old glove lay upon the floor forgotten, while Rose sat musing, till a quick step sounded in the hall, and a voice drew near tunefully humming.

> " As he was walkin' doun the street
> The city for to view,
> Oh, there he spied a bonny lass,
> The window lookin' through."

> " Sae licht he jumpèd up the stair,
> And tirled at the pin;
> Oh, wha sae ready as hersel'
> To let the laddie in ? "

sung Rose, as the voice paused and a tap came at the door.

" Good morning, Rosamunda ; here are your letters, and your most devoted ready to execute any commissions you may have for him," was Charlie's greeting, as he came in looking comely, gay, and debonair as usual.

" Thanks: I've no errands unless you mail my replies, if these need answering; so by your leave, Prince," and Rose began to open the handful of notes he threw into her lap.

" Ha ! what sight is this to blast mine eyes ? " ejaculated Charlie, as he pointed to the glove with a melo-
dramatic start; for, like most accomplished amateur
actors, he was fond of introducing private theatricals
into his " daily walk and conversation."

" Uncle left it."

" 'Tis well; methought perchance a rival had been
here," and, picking it up, Charlie amused himself with
putting it on the head of a little Psyche, which or-
namented the mantle-piece, humming, as he did so,
another verse of the old song, —

> " He set his Jenny on his knee,
> All in his Highland dress ;
> For brawly well he kenned the way
> To please a bonny lass."

Rose went on reading her letters, but all the while
was thinking of her conversation with her uncle, and
something else, suggested by the newcomer and his
ditty.

During the three months since her return, she had
seen more of this cousin than any of the others; for
he seemed to be the only one who had leisure to " play
with Rose," as they used to say years ago. The other
boys were all at work, even little Jamie, many of whose
play hours were devoted to manful struggles with
Latin grammar, the evil genius of his boyish life.
Dr. Alec had many affairs to arrange after his long
absence; Phebe was busy with her music; and Aunt
Plenty still actively superintended her housekeeping.
Thus it fell out, quite naturally, that Charlie should
form the habit of lounging in at all hours with letters,
messages, bits of news, and agreeable plans for Rose.

He helped her with her sketching, rode with her, sung with her, and took her to parties, as a matter of course; for Aunt Clara, being the gayest of the sisters, played chaperon on all occasions.

For a time it was very pleasant; but, by and by, Rose began to wish Charlie would find something to do like the rest, and not make dawdling after her the business of his life. The family were used to his self-indulgent ways: and there was an amiable delusion in the minds of the boys that he had a right to the best of every thing; for to them he was still the Prince, the flower of the flock, and in time to be an honor to the name. No one exactly knew how: for, though full of talent, he seemed to have no especial gift or bias; and the elders began to shake their heads, because, in spite of many grand promises and projects, the moment for decisive action never came.

Rose saw all this, and longed to inspire her brilliant cousin with some manful purpose, which should win for him respect as well as admiration. But she found it very hard: for, though he listened with imperturbable good humor, and owned his shortcomings with delightful frankness, he always had some argument, reason, or excuse to offer, and out-talked her in five minutes; leaving her silenced, but unconvinced.

Of late she had observed that he seemed to feel as if her time and thoughts belonged exclusively to him, and rather resented the approach of any other claimant. This annoyed her, and suggested the idea that her affectionate interest and efforts were misunderstood by him, misrepresented and taken advantage of by Aunt Clara, who had been most urgent that she should "use her influence with the dear boy," though the fond mother resented all other interference. This troubled Rose, and made her feel as if caught in a snare; for, while she owned to herself that Charlie was the most attractive of her cousins, she was not ready to be taken possession of in this masterful way, especially since other and sometimes better men sought her favor more humbly.

These thoughts were floating vaguely in her mind as she read her letters, and unconsciously influenced her in the chat that followed.

"Only invitations, and I can't stop to answer them now, or I shall never get through this job," she said, returning to her work.

"Let me help. You do up, and I'll direct. Have a secretary; do now, and see what a comfort it will be," proposed Charlie, who could turn his hand to any thing, and had made himself quite at home in the sanctum.

"I'd rather finish this myself, but you may answer the notes if you will. Just regrets to all but two or three. Read the names as you go along, and I'll tell you which."

"To hear is to obey. Who says I'm a 'frivolous idler' now?" and Charlie sat down at the writing table with alacrity; for these hours in the little room were his best and happiest.

"Order is heaven's first law, and the view a lovely one, but I *don't* see any note-paper," he added, opening the desk and surveying its contents with interest.

"Right-hand drawer: violet monogram for the notes; plain paper for the business letter. I'll see to that, though," answered Rose, trying to decide whether Annabel or Emma should have the laced handkerchief.

"Confiding creature! Suppose I open the wrong drawer, and come upon the tender secrets of your soul?" continued the new secretary, rummaging out the delicate note-paper with masculine disregard of order.

"I have n't got any," answered Rose, demurely.

"What, not one despairing scrawl, one cherished miniature, one faded floweret, etc., etc.? I can't believe it, cousin," and he shook his head incredulously.

"If I had, I certainly should not show them to you, impertinent person! There *are* a few little souvenirs in that desk, but nothing very sentimental or interesting."

"How I'd like to see 'em! But I should never dare to ask," observed Charlie, peering over the top of the half-open lid with a most persuasive pair of eyes.

"You may if you want to, but you 'll be disappointed, Paul Pry. Lower left-hand drawer with the key in it."

"'Angel of goodness, how shall I requite thee? Interesting moment, with what palpitating emotions art thou fraught!'" and, quoting from the "Mysteries of Udolpho," he unlocked and opened the drawer with a tragic gesture.

"Seven locks of hair in a box, all light; for 'here's your straw color, your orange tawny, your French crown color, and your perfect yellow' Shakspeare. They look very familiar, and I fancy I know the heads they thatched."

"Yes, you all gave me one when I went away, you know; and I carried them round the world with me in that very box."

"I wish the heads had gone too. Here's a jolly little amber god, with a gold ring in his back and a most balmy breath," continued Charlie, taking a long sniff at the scent-bottle.

"Uncle brought me that long ago, and I'm very fond of it."

"This now looks suspicious, — a man's ring with a lotus cut on the stone and a note attached. I tremble as I ask, Who, when, and where?"

"A gentleman, on my birthday, in Calcutta."

"I breathe again: it was my sire?"

"Don't be absurd. Of course it was, and he did every thing to make my visit pleasant. I wish you'd go and see him like a dutiful son, instead of idling here."

"That's what Uncle Mac is eternally telling me, but I don't intend to be lectured into the tread-mill till I've had my fling first," muttered Charlie, rebelliously.

"If you fling yourself in the wrong direction, you may find it hard to get back again," began Rose, gravely.

"No fear, if you look after me as you seem to have promised to do, judging by the thanks you get in this note. Poor old governor! I *should* like to see him; for it's almost four years since he came home last, and he must be getting on."

Charlie was the only one of the boys who ever called his father "governor": perhaps because the others knew and loved their fathers, while he had

seen so little of his that the less respectful name
came more readily to his lips; since the elder man
seemed in truth a governor issuing requests or com-
mands, which the younger too often neglected or
resented.

Long ago Rose had discovered that Uncle Stephen
found home made so distasteful by his wife's devotion
to society, that he preferred to exile himself, taking
business as an excuse for his protracted absences.

The girl was thinking of this, as she watched her
cousin turn the ring about with a sudden sobriety
which became him well; and, believing that the moment was propitious, she said earnestly, —

"He *is* getting on.   Dear Charlie, do think of duty
more than pleasure in this case, and I 'm sure you
never will regret it."

"Do *you* want me to go?" he asked quickly.

"I think you ought."

"And I think you 'd be much more charming if
you would n't always be worrying about right and
wrong!   Uncle Alec taught you that along with the
rest of his queer notions."

"I 'm glad he did!" cried Rose, warmly; then
checked herself, and said with a patient sort of sigh,
"You know women always want the men they
care for to be good, and can't help trying to make
them so."

"So they do; and we ought to be a set of angels:
but I 've a strong conviction that, if we were, the dear
souls would n't like us half as well.   Would they
now?" asked Charlie, with an insinuating smile.

"Perhaps not; but that is dodging the point.   Will
you go?" persisted Rose, unwisely.

"No, I will not."

That was sufficiently decided; and an uncomfortable pause followed, during which Rose tied a knot unnecessarily tight, and Charlie went on exploring the drawer with more energy than interest.

"Why, here's an old thing I gave you ages ago!" he suddenly exclaimed in a pleased tone, holding up a little agate heart on a faded blue ribbon. "Will you let me take away the heart of stone and give you a heart of flesh?" he asked, half in earnest, half in jest, touched by the little trinket and the recollections it awakened.

"No, I will not," answered Rose, bluntly, much displeased by the irreverent and audacious question.

Charlie looked rather abashed for a moment; but his natural light-heartedness made it easy for him to get the better of his own brief fits of waywardness, and put others in good humor with him and themselves.

"Now we are even: let's drop the subject and start afresh," he said with irresistible affability, as he coolly put the little heart in his pocket, and prepared to shut the drawer. But something caught his eye, and exclaiming, "What's this? what's this?" he snatched up a photograph which lay half under a pile of letters with foreign post-marks.

"Oh! I forgot that was there," said Rose, hastily.

"Who is the man?" demanded Charlie, eying the good-looking countenance before him with a frown.

"That is the Honorable Gilbert Murry, who went up the Nile with us, and shot crocodiles and other small deer, being a mighty hunter, as I told you in my letters," answered Rose gayly, though ill-pleased at the little discovery just then; for this

had been one of the narrow escapes her uncle
spoke of.

"And they have n't eaten him yet, I infer from that
pile of letters?" said Charlie, jealously.

"I hope not. His sister did not mention it when
she wrote last."

"Ah! then she is your correspondent? Sisters are
dangerous things sometimes." And Charlie eyed the
packet suspiciously.

"In this case, a very convenient thing; for she
tells me all about her brother's wedding as no one
else would take the trouble to do."

"Oh! well, if he's married, I don't care a straw
about him. I fancied I'd found out why you are
such a hard-hearted charmer. But, if there is no
secret idol, I'm all at sea again." And Charlie tossed
the photograph into the drawer, as if it no longer
interested him.

"I'm hard-hearted because I'm particular, and, as
yet, do not find any one at all to my taste."

"No one?" with a tender glance.

"No one," with a rebellious blush, and the truth-
ful addition, "I see much to admire and like in many
persons, but none quite strong and good enough to
suit me. My heroes are old-fashioned, you know."

"Prigs, like Guy Carleton, Count Altenberg, and
John Halifax: I know the pattern you goody girls
like," sneered Charlie, who preferred the Guy Living-
ston, Beaucierc, and Rochester style.

"Then I'm not a 'goody girl,' for I don't like
prigs. I want a gentleman in the best sense of the
word, and I can wait; for I've seen one, and know
there are more in the world."

"The deuce you have! Do I know him?" asked Charlie, much alarmed.

"You think you do," answered Rose, with a mischievous sparkle in her eye.

"If it is n't Pem, I give it up. He is the best-bred fellow I know."

"Oh, dear, no! far superior to Mr. Pemberton, and many years older," said Rose, with so much respect that Charlie looked perplexed as well as anxious.

"Some apostolic minister, I fancy. You pious creatures always like to adore a parson. But all we know are married."

"He is n't."

"Give a name, for pity's sake: I 'm suffering tortures of suspense," begged Charlie.

"Alexander Campbell."

"Uncle? Well, upon my word, that 's a relief, but mighty absurd all the same. So, when you find a young saint of that sort, you intend to marry him, do you?" demanded Charlie, much amused and rather disappointed.

"When I find any man half as honest, good, and noble as uncle, I shall be proud to marry him, if he asks me," answered Rose, decidedly.

"What odd tastes women have!" And Charlie leaned his chin on his hand, to muse pensively for a moment over the blindness of one woman who could admire an excellent old uncle more than a dashing young cousin.

Rose, meanwhile, tied up her parcels industriously, hoping she had not been too severe; for it was very hard to lecture Charlie, though he seemed to like it sometimes, and came to confession voluntarily, know-

ing that women love to forgive when the sinners are
of his sort.

"It will be mail-time before you are done," she said
presently; for silence was less pleasant than his rattle.

Charlie took the hint, and dashed off several notes
in his best manner. Coming to the business-letter, he
glanced at it, and asked, with a puzzled expression, —

"What is all this? Cost of repairs, &c., from a
man named Buffum?"

"Never mind that: I'll see to it by and by."

"But I do mind, for I'm interested in all your affairs; and, though you think I've no head for business, you'll find I have, if you'll try me."

"This is only about my two old houses in the city,
which are being repaired and altered so that the rooms
can be let singly."

"Going to make tenement-houses of them? Well,
that's not a bad idea: such places pay well, I've
heard."

"That is just what I'm *not* going to do. I would n't
have a tenement-house on my conscience for a mil-
lion of dollars, — not as they are now," said Rose,
decidedly.

"Why, what do *you* know about it, except that
poor people live in them, and the owners turn a
penny on the rents?"

"I know a good deal about them; for I've seen
many such, both here and abroad. It was not all
pleasure with us, I assure you. Uncle was interested
in hospitals and prisons, and I sometimes went with
him: but they made me sad; so he suggested other
charities, that I could help about when we came home.
I visited Infant Schools, Working-women's Homes,

Orphan Asylums, and places of that sort.   You don't
know how much good it did me, and how glad I am
that I have the means of lightening a little some of
the misery in the world."

"But, my dear girl, you need n't make ducks and
drakes of your fortune trying to feed and cure and
clothe all the poor wretches you see.   Give, of course:
every one should do something in that line, and no
one likes it better than I.   But don't, for mercy's sake,
go at it as some women do, and get so desperately
earnest, practical, and charity-mad that there is no
living in peace with you," protested Charlie, looking
alarmed at the prospect.

"You can do as you please.   *I* intend to do all the
good I can by asking the advice and following the example of the most 'earnest,' 'practical,' and 'charitable' people I know: so, if you don't approve, you can
drop my acquaintance," answered Rose, emphasizing
the obnoxious words, and assuming the resolute air
she always wore when defending her hobbies.

"You 'll be laughed at."

"I 'm used to that."

"And criticised and shunned."

"Not by people whose opinion I value."

"Women should n't go poking into such places."

"I 've been taught that they should."

"Well, you 'll get some dreadful disease and lose
your beauty, and then where are you?" added Charlie,
thinking that might daunt the young philanthropist.

But it did not; for Rose answered, with a sudden
kindling of the eyes as she remembered her talk with
Uncle Alec, —

"I should n't like it: but there would be one satisfaction in it; for, when I'd lost my beauty and given away my money, I should know who really cared for me."

Charlie nibbled his pen in silence for a moment, then asked, meekly, —

"Could I respectfully inquire what great reform is to be carried on in the old houses which their amiable owner is repairing?"

"I am merely going to make them comfortable homes for poor but respectable women to live in. There is a class who cannot afford to pay much, yet suffer a great deal from being obliged to stay in noisy, dirty, crowded places like tenement-houses and cheap lodgings. I can help a few of them, and I'm going to try."

"May I humbly ask if these decayed gentlewomen are to inhabit their palatial retreat rent-free?"

"That was my first plan; but uncle showed me that it was wiser not to make genteel paupers of them, but let them pay a small rent and feel independent. I don't want the money of course, and shall use it in keeping the houses tidy, or helping other women in like case," said Rose, entirely ignoring her cousin's covert ridicule.

"Don't expect any gratitude, for you won't get it; nor much comfort with a lot of forlornities on your hands; and be sure that when it is too late you will tire of it all, and wish you had done as other people do."

"Thanks for your cheerful prophecies; but I think I'll venture."

She looked so undaunted that Charlie was a little nettled, and fired his last shot rather recklessly, —

"Well, one thing I do know: you'll never get a husband if you go on in this absurd way; and, by Jove! you need one to take care of you and keep the property together!"

Rose had a temper, but seldom let it get the better of her; now, however, it flashed up for a moment. Those last words were peculiarly unfortunate, because Aunt Clara had used them more than once, when warning her against impecunious suitors and generous projects. She was disappointed in her cousin, annoyed at having her little plans laughed at, and indignant with him for his final suggestion.

"I'll never have one, if I must give up the liberty of doing what I know is right; and I'd rather go into the poor-house to-morrow than 'keep the property together' in the selfish way you mean!"

That was all: but Charlie saw that he had gone too far, and hastened to make his peace with the skill of a lover; for, turning to the little cabinet piano behind him, he sung in his best style the sweet old song, —

"Oh were thou in the cauld blast,"

dwelling with great effect, not only upon the tender assurance that

"My plaid should shelter thee,"

but also that, even if a king,

"The brightest jewel in my crown
Wad be my queen, wad be my queen."

It was very evident that Prince Charming had not gone troubadouring in vain; for Orpheus himself could not have restored harmony more successfully.

The tuneful apology was accepted with a forgiving smile, and a frank, —

"I'm sorry I was cross; but you have n't forgotten how to tease, and I'm rather out of sorts to-day. Late hours don't agree with me."

"Then you won't feel like going to Mrs. Hope's to-morrow night, I'm afraid," and Charlie took up the last note with an expression of regret which was very flattering.

"I must go, because it is made for me; but I can come away early, and make up lost sleep. I do hate to be so fractious," and Rose rubbed the forehead that ached with too much racketing.

"But the German does not begin till late: I'm to lead, and depend upon you. Just stay this once to oblige me," pleaded Charlie; for he had set his heart on distinguishing himself.

"No: I promised uncle to be temperate in my pleasures, and I must keep my word. I'm so well now, it would be very foolish to get ill and make him anxious: not to mention losing my beauty, as you are good enough to call it; for that depends on health, you know."

"But the fun does n't begin till after supper. Every thing will be delightful, I assure you; and we'll have a gay old time as we did last week at Emma's."

"Then I certainly will not; for I'm ashamed of myself when I remember what a romp that was, and how sober uncle looked, as he let me in at three in the morning, all fagged out; my dress in rags, my head aching, my feet so tired I could hardly stand, and nothing to show for five hours' hard work but a pocketful of bonbons, artificial flowers, and tissue-

paper fool's-caps. Uncle said I'd better put one on
and go to bed; for I looked as if I'd been to a
French Bal Masqué. I never want to hear him say
so again, and I'll never let dawn catch me out in such
a plight any more."

"You were all right enough; for mother didn't
object, and I got you both home before daylight.
Uncle is notional about such things, so I should n't
mind; for we had a jolly time, and we were none the
worse for it."

"Indeed we were, every one of us! Aunt Clara
has n't got over her cold yet; I slept all the next day,
and you looked like a ghost, for you 'd been out every
night for weeks, I think."

"Oh, nonsense! every one does it during the
season, and you 'll get used to the pace very soon,"
began Charlie, bent on making her go; for he was
in his element in a ballroom, and never happier than
when he had his pretty cousin on his arm.

"Ah! but I don't want to get used to it; for it
costs too much in the end. I don't wish to get used
to being whisked about a hot room by men who have
taken too much wine; to turn day into night, wasting
time that might be better spent; and grow into a
fashionable fast girl who can't get on without excitement. I don't deny that much of it is pleasant, but
don't try to make me too fond of gayety. Help me
to resist what I know is hurtful, and please don't
laugh me out of the good habits uncle has tried so
hard to give me."

Rose was quite sincere in her appeal, and Charlie
knew she was right: but he always found it hard to
give up any thing he had set his heart upon, no matter

how trivial; for the maternal indulgence which had
harmed the boy had fostered the habit of self-indul-
gence which was ruining the man. So when Rose
looked up at him, with a very honest desire to save
him as well as herself from being swept into the giddy
vortex which keeps so many young people revolving
aimlessly, till they go down or are cast upon the
shore wrecks of what they might have been, he gave
a shrug and answered briefly, —

"As you please. I'll bring you home as early as
you like, and Effie Waring can take your place in the
German. What flowers shall I send you?"

Now, that was an artful speech of Charlie's; for
Miss Waring was a fast and fashionable damsel, who
openly admired Prince Charming, and had given him
the name. Rose disliked her, and was sure her influence was bad; for youth made frivolity forgivable,
wit hid want of refinement, and beauty always covers
a multitude of sins in a man's eyes. At the sound of
Effie's name, Rose wavered, and would have yielded
but for the memory of the " first mate's " last words.
She did desire to " keep a straight course "; so, though
the current of impulse set strongly in a southerly
direction, principle, the only compass worth having,
pointed due north, and she tried to obey it like a wise
young navigator, saying steadily, while she directed
to Annabel the parcel containing a capacious pair of
slippers intended for Uncle Mac, —

"Don't trouble yourself about me. I can go with
uncle, and slip away without disturbing anybody."

"I don't believe you'll have the heart to do it,"
said Charlie, incredulously, as he sealed the last note
"Wait and see."

" I will, but shall hope to the last," and, kissing his
hand to her, he departed to post her letters, quite
sure that Miss Waring would not lead the German.

It certainly looked for a moment as if Miss Campbell *would*, because she ran to the door with the
words " I 'll go " upon her lips.   But she did not open
it till she had stood a minute staring hard at the old
glove on Psyche's head; then, like one who had suddenly got a bright idea, she gave a decided nod and
walked slowly out of the room.

CHAPTER VI

POLISHING MAC

"PLEASE could I say one word?" was the question three times repeated before a rough head bobbed out from the grotto of books in which Mac usually sat when he studied.

"Did any one speak?" he asked, blinking in the flood of sunshine that entered with Rose.

"Only three times, thank you. Don't disturb yourself, I beg; for I merely want to say a word," answered Rose, as she prevented him from offering the easy-chair in which he sat.

"I was rather deep in a compound fracture, and didn't hear. What can I do for you, cousin?" and Mac shoved a stack of pamphlets off the chair near him, with a hospitable wave of the hand that sent his papers flying in all directions.

Rose sat down, but did not seem to find her "word" an easy one to utter; for she twisted her handkerchief about her fingers in embarrassed silence, till Mac put on his glasses, and, after a keen look, asked soberly, —

"Is it a splinter, a cut, or a whitlow, ma'am?"

"It is neither; do forget your tiresome surgery for a minute, and be the kindest cousin that ever was," answered Rose, beginning rather sharply and ending with her most engaging smile.

"Can't promise in the dark," said the wary youth.

"It is a favor, a great favor, and one I don't choose to ask any of the other boys," answered the artful damsel.

Mac looked pleased, and leaned forward, saying more affably, —

"Name it, and be sure I'll grant it if I can."

"Go with me to Mrs. Hope's party to-morrow night."

"What!" and Mac recoiled as if she had put a pistol to his head.

"I've left you in peace a long time: but it is your turn now; so do your duty like a man and a cousin."

"But I never go to parties!" cried the unhappy victim in great dismay.

"High time you began, sir."

"But I don't dance fit to be seen."

"I'll teach you."

"My dress-coat is n't decent, I know."

"Archie will lend you one: he is n't going."

"I'm afraid there's a lecture that I ought not to cut."

"No, there is n't: I asked uncle."

"I'm always so tired and dull in the evening."

"This sort of thing is just what you want to rest and freshen up your spirits."

Mac gave a groan and fell back vanquished; for it was evident that escape was impossible.

"What put such a perfectly wild idea into your head?" he demanded, rather roughly; for hitherto he *had* been "left in peace," and this sudden attack decidedly amazed him.

"Sheer necessity; but don't do it if it is so very

dreadful to you. I must go to several more parties, because they are made for me; but after that I'll refuse, and then no one need be troubled with me."

Something in Rose's voice made Mac answer penitently, even while he knit his brows in perplexity, —

"I didn't mean to be rude; and of course I'll go anywhere if I'm really needed. But I don't understand where the sudden necessity is, with three other fellows at command, all better dancers and beaux than I am."

"I don't want them, and I do want you; for I haven't the heart to drag uncle out any more, and you know I never go with any gentleman but those of my own family."

"Now look here, Rose: if Steve has been doing any thing to tease you just mention it, and I'll attend to him," cried Mac, plainly seeing that something was amiss, and fancying that Dandy was at the bottom of it, as he had done escort duty several times lately.

"No, Steve has been very good: but I know he had rather be with Kitty Van; so of course I feel like a marplot, though he is too polite to hint it."

"What a noodle that boy is! But there's Archie; he's as steady as a church, and has no sweetheart to interfere," continued Mac, bound to get at the truth, and half suspecting what it was.

"He is on his feet all day, and Aunt Jessie wants him in the evening. He does not care for dancing as he used, and I suppose he really does prefer to rest and read." Rose might have added, " and hear Phebe sing;" for Phebe did not go out as much as Rose did, and Aunt Jessie often came in to sit with the old lady when the young folks were away; and,

of course, dutiful Archie came with her; so willingly of late!

"What's amiss with Charlie? I thought *he* was the prince of cavaliers. Annabel says he dances 'like an angel,' and I know a dozen mothers couldn't keep him at home of an evening. Have you had a tiff with Adonis, and so fall back on poor me?" asked Mac, coming last to the person of whom he thought first, but did not mention, feeling shy about alluding to a subject often discussed behind her back.

"Yes, we have; and I don't intend to go with him any more for some time. His ways do not suit me, and mine do not suit him; so I want to be quite independent, and you can help me if you will," said Rose, rather nervously spinning the big globe close by.

Mac gave a low whistle, looking wide awake all in a minute, as he said with a gesture, as if he brushed a cobweb off his face, —

"Now, see here, cousin: I'm not good at mysteries, and shall only blunder if you put me blindfold into any nice manœuvre. Just tell me straight out what you want, and I'll do it if I can. Play I'm uncle, and free your mind; come now."

He spoke so kindly, and the honest eyes were so full of merry good-will, that Rose felt she might confide in him, and answered as frankly as he could desire, —

"You are right, Mac; and I don't mind talking to you almost as freely as to uncle, because you are such a reliable fellow, and won't think me silly for trying to do what I believe to be right. Charlie does, and so makes it hard for me to hold to my resolutions. I want to keep early hours, dress simply, and behave properly; no matter what fashionable people do. You will agree to that, I'm sure; and stand by me through thick and thin for principle's sake."

"I will; and begin by showing you that I understand the case. I don't wonder you are not pleased; for Charlie is too presuming, and you do need some one to help you head him off a bit. Hey, cousin?"

"What a way to put it!" and Rose laughed in spite of herself, adding with an air of relief, "That *is* it; and I do want some one to help me make him understand that I don't choose to be taken possession of in that lordly way, as if I belonged to him more than to the rest of the family. I don't like it; for people begin to talk, and Charlie won't see how disagreeable it is to me."

"Tell him so," was Mac's blunt advice.

"I have; but he only laughs and promises to behave, and then he does it again, when I am so placed that I can't say any thing. You will never understand, and I cannot explain; for it is only a look, or a word, or some little thing: but I won't have it, and the best way to cure him is to put it out of his power to annoy me so."

"He is a great flirt, and wants to teach you how, I suppose. I'll speak to him if you like, and tell him you don't want to learn. Shall I?" asked Mac, finding the case rather an interesting one.

"No, thank you: that would only make trouble. If you will kindly play escort a few times, it will show Charlie that I am in earnest without more words, and put a stop to the gossip," said Rose, coloring like a poppy at the recollection of what she heard one young man whisper to another, as Charlie led her through

a crowded supper-room with his most devoted air,
"Lucky dog! he is sure to get the heiress, and we
are nowhere."

"There's no danger of people's gossiping about us,
is there?" and Mac looked up, with the oddest of
all his odd expressions.

"Of course not: you're only a boy."

"I'm twenty-one, thank you; and Prince is but a
couple of years older," said Mac, promptly resenting
the slight put upon his manhood.

"Yes; but he is like other young men, while you
are a dear old bookworm. No one would ever mind
what *you* did; so you may go to parties with me
every night, and not a word would be said; or, if
there was, I shouldn't mind since it is 'only Mac,'"
answered Rose, smiling as she quoted a household
word often used to excuse his vagaries.

"Then *I* am nobody?" lifting his brows, as if the
discovery surprised and rather nettled him.

"Nobody in society as yet; but my very best
cousin in private, and I've just proved my regard
by making you my confidant, and choosing you for
my knight," said Rose, hastening to soothe the
feelings her careless words seemed to have ruffled
slightly.

"Much good *that* is likely to do me," grumbled
Mac.

"You ungrateful boy, not to appreciate the honor
I've conferred upon you! I know a dozen who would
be proud of the place: but you only care for compound fractures; so I won't detain you any longer,
except to ask if I may consider myself provided with
an escort for to-morrow night?" said Rose, a trifle

hurt at his indifference; for she was not used to refusals.

"If I may hope for the honor," and, rising, he made her a bow which was such a capital imitation of Charlie's grand manner that she forgave him at once, exclaiming with amused surprise, —

"Why, Mac! I didn't know you *could* be so elegant!"

"A fellow can be almost any thing he likes, if he tries hard enough," he answered, standing very straight, and looking so tall and dignified that Rose was quite impressed, and with a stately courtesy she retired, saying graciously, —

"I accept with thanks. Good-morning, Doctor Alexander Mackenzie Campbell."

When Friday evening came, and word was sent up that her escort had arrived, Rose ran down, devoutly hoping that he had not come in a velveteen jacket, top-boots, black gloves, or made any trifling mistake of that sort. A young gentleman was standing before the long mirror, apparently intent on the arrangement of his hair; and Rose paused suddenly as her eye went from the glossy broadcloth to the white-gloved hands, busy with an unruly lock that would not stay in place.

"Why, Charlie, I thought—" she began with an accent of surprise in her voice, but got no further; for the gentleman turned and she beheld Mac in immaculate evening costume, with his hair parted sweetly on his brow, a superior posy at his button-hole, and the expression of a martyr upon his face.

"Ah, don't you wish it was? No one but yourself to thank that it isn't he. Am I right? Dandy got

me up, and he ought to know what is what," demanded Mac, folding his hands and standing as stiff
as a ramrod.

"You are so regularly splendid that I don't know
you."

"Neither do I."

"I really had no idea you could look so like a gentleman," added Rose, surveying him with great approval.

"Nor I that I could feel so like a fool."

"Poor boy! he does look rather miserable. What
can I do to cheer him up, in return for the sacrifice
he is making?"

"Stop calling me a boy. It will soothe my agony
immensely, and give me courage to appear in a low-
necked coat and a curl on my forehead; for I'm not
used to such elegancies, and find them no end of a
trial."

Mac spoke in such a pathetic tone, and gave such
a gloomy glare at the aforesaid curl, that Rose laughed
in his face, and added to his woe by handing him her
cloak. He surveyed it gravely for a minute, then
carefully put it on wrong side out, and gave the
swan's-down hood a good pull over her head, to the
utter destruction of all smoothness to the curls
inside.

Rose uttered a cry and cast off the cloak, bidding
him learn to do it properly, which he meekly did,
and then led her down the hall without walking on
her skirts more than three times by the way. But
at the door she discovered that she had forgotten
her furred overshoes, and bade Mac get them.

"Never mind: it's not wet," he said, pulling his

cap over his eyes and plunging into his coat, regardless of the "elegancies" that afflicted him.

"But I can't walk on cold stones with thin slippers,
can I?" began Rose, showing a little white foot.

"You need n't, for — there you are, my lady;"
and, unceremoniously picking her up, Mac landed
her in the carriage before she could say a word.

"What an escort!" she exclaimed in comic dismay, as she rescued her delicate dress from the rug
in which he was about to tuck her up like a mummy.

"It 's 'only Mac,' so don't mind," and he cast himself into an opposite corner, with the air of a man who
had nerved himself to the accomplishment of many
painful duties, and was bound to do them or die.

"But gentlemen don't catch up ladies like bags of
meal, and poke them into carriages in this way. It
is evident that you need looking after, and it is high
time I undertook your society manners. Now, do
mind what you are about, and don't get yourself or
me into a scrape if you can help it," besought Rose,
feeling that on many accounts she had gone farther
and fared worse.

"I 'll behave like a Turveydrop: see if I don't."

Mac's idea of the immortal Turveydrop's behavior
seemed to be a peculiar one; for, after dancing once
with his cousin, he left her to her own devices, and
soon forgot all about her in a long conversation with
Professor Stumph, the learned geologist. Rose did
not care; for one dance proved to her that that
branch of Mac's education *had* been sadly neglected,
and she was glad to glide smoothly about with Steve,
though he was only an inch or two taller than herself.
She had plenty of partners, however, and plenty of

chaperons; for all the young men were her most devoted, and all the matrons beamed upon her with maternal benignity.

Charlie was not there; for when he found that Rose stood firm, and had moreover engaged Mac as a permanency, he would not go at all, and retired in high dudgeon to console himself with more dangerous pastimes. Rose feared it would be so; and, even in the midst of the gayety about her, an anxious mood came over her now and then, and made her thoughtful for a moment. She felt her power, and wanted to use it wisely; but did not know how to be kind to Charlie without being untrue to herself and giving him false hopes.

"I wish we were all children again, with no hearts to perplex us and no great temptations to try us," she said to herself, as she rested a moment in a quiet nook while her partner went to get a glass of water. Right in the midst of this half-sad, half-sentimental reverie, she heard a familiar voice behind her say earnestly, —

"And allophite is the new hydrous silicate of alumina and magnesia, much resembling pseudophite, which Websky found in Silesia."

"What *is* Mac talking about!" she thought: and, peeping behind a great azalea in full bloom, she saw her cousin in deep converse with the professor, evidently having a capital time; for his face had lost its melancholy expression and was all alive with interest, while the elder man was listening as if his remarks were both intelligent and agreeable.

"What is it?" asked Steve, coming up with the water, and seeing a smile on Rose's face.

She pointed out the scientific *tête-à-tête* going on behind the azalea, and Steve grinned as he peeped, then grew sober and said in a tone of despair, —

"If you had seen the pains I took with that fellow, the patience with which I brushed his wig, the time I spent trying to convince him that he must wear thin boots, and the fight I had to get him into that coat; you 'd understand my feelings when I see him now."

"Why, what is the matter with him?" asked Rose.

"Will you take a look, and see what a spectacle he has made of himself. He 'd better be sent home at once, or he will disgrace the family by looking as if he 'd been in a row."

Steve spoke in such a tragic tone that Rose took another peep and did sympathize with Dandy; for Mac's elegance was quite gone. His tie was under one ear, his posy hung upside down, his gloves were rolled into a ball, which he absently squeezed and pounded as he talked, and his hair looked as if a whirlwind had passed over it; for his ten fingers set it on end now and then, as they had a habit of doing when he studied or talked earnestly. But he looked so happy and wide awake, in spite of his dishevelment, that Rose gave an approving nod, and said behind her fan, —

"It *is* a trying spectacle, Steve: yet, on the whole, I think his own odd ways suit him best; and I fancy we shall yet be proud of him, for he knows more than all the rest of us put together. Hear that now," and Rose paused, that they might listen to the following burst of eloquence from Mac's lips: —

"You know Frenzel has shown that the globular forms of silicate of bismuth at Schneeburg and Johanngeorgenstadt are not isometric, but monoclinic in crystalline form; and consequently he separates them from the old eulytite, and gives them the new name Agricolite."

"Is n't it awful? Let us get out of this before there 's another avalanche, or we shall be globular silicates and isometric crystals in spite of ourselves," whispered Steve with a panic-stricken air; and they fled from the hail-storm of hard words that rattled about their ears, leaving Mac to enjoy himself in his own way.

But when Rose was ready to go home, and looked about for her escort, he was nowhere to be seen; for the professor had departed, and Mac with him, so absorbed in some new topic that he entirely forgot his cousin, and went placidly home, still pondering on the charms of geology. When this pleasing fact dawned upon Rose, her feelings may be imagined. She was both angry and amused: it was so like Mac to go mooning off and leave her to her fate. Not a hard one, however; for, though Steve was gone with Kitty before her plight was discovered, Mrs. Bliss was only too glad to take the deserted damsel under her wing, and bear her safely home.

Rose was warming her feet, and sipping the chocolate which Phebe always had ready for her, as she never ate suppers; when a hurried tap came at the long window whence the light streamed, and Mac's voice was heard softly asking to be let in "just for one minute."

Curious to know what had befallen him, Rose bade Phebe obey his call; and the delinquent cavalier ap peared, breathless, anxious, and more dilapidated than ever: for he had forgotten his overcoat; his tie **was** at the back of his neck now; and his hair as rampantly erect as if all the winds of heaven had been blowing freely through it, as they had; for he had been tearing to and fro the last half-hour trying to undo the dreadful deed he had so innocently committed.

"Don't take any notice of me ; for I don't deserve it. I only came to see that you were safe, cousin, and then go hang myself, as Steve advised," he began, in a remorseful tone, that would have been very effective, if he had not been obliged to catch his breath with a comical gasp now and then.

"I never thought *you* would be the one to desert me," said Rose, with a reproachful look; thinking it best not to relent too soon, though she was quite ready to do it when she saw how sincerely distressed he was.

"It was that confounded man! He was a regular walking encyclopædia; and, finding I could get a good deal out of him, I went in for general information, as the time was short. You know I always forget every thing else when I get hold of such a fellow."

"That is evident. I wonder how you came to remember me at all," answered Rose, on the brink of a laugh: it was so absurd.

"I did n't till Steve said something that reminded me: then it burst upon me, in one awful shock, that I 'd gone and left you; and you might have knocked me down with a feather," said honest Mac, hiding none of his iniquity.

"What did you do then?"

"Do! I went off like a shot, and never stopped till I reached the Hopes" —

"You did n't walk all that way?" cried Rose.

"Bless you, no: I ran. But you were gone with Mrs. Bliss: so I pelted back again to see with my own eyes that you were safe at home," answered Mac, wiping his hot forehead, with a sigh of relief.

"But it is three miles at least each way; and twelve o'clock, and dark and cold. O Mac! how could you!" exclaimed Rose, suddenly realizing what he had done, as she heard his labored breathing, saw the state of the thin boots, and detected the absence of an overcoat.

"Could n't do less, could I?" asked Mac, leaning up against the door and trying not to pant.

"There was no need of half-killing yourself for such a trifle. You might have known I could take care of myself for once, at least, with so many friends about. Sit down this minute. Bring another cup, please, Phebe: this boy is n't going home till he is rested and refreshed after such a run as that," commanded Rose.

"Don't be good to me: I'd rather take a scolding than a chair, and drink hemlock instead of chocolate if you happen to have any ready," answered Mac, with a pathetic puff, as he subsided on to the sofa, and meekly took the draught Phebe brought him.

"If you had any thing the matter with your heart, sir, a race of this sort might be the death of you: so never do it again," said Rose, offering her fan to cool his heated countenance.

"Have n't got any heart."

"Yes, you have, for I hear it beating like a trip-hammer, and it is my fault: I ought to have stopped as we went by, and told you I was all right."

"It's the mortification, not the miles, that upsets me. I often take that run for exercise, and think nothing of it; but to-night I was so mad I made extra good time, I fancy. Now don't you worry, but compose your mind, and 'sip your dish of tea,' as Evelina says," answered Mac, artfully turning the conversation from himself.

"What do you know about Evelina?" asked Rose, in great surprise.

"All about her. Do you suppose I never read a novel?"

"I thought you read nothing but Greek and Latin, with an occasional glance at Websky's pseudophites and the monoclinics of Johanngeorgenstadt."

Mac opened his eyes wide at this reply, then seemed to see the joke, and joined in the laugh with such heartiness that Aunt Plenty's voice was heard demanding from above, with sleepy anxiety, —

"*Is* the house afire?"

"No, ma'am, every thing is safe, and I'm only saying good-night," answered Mac, diving for his cap.

"Then go at once, and let that child have her sleep," added the old lady, retiring to her bed.

Rose ran into the hall, and, catching up her uncle's fur coat, met Mac as he came out of the study, absently looking about for his own.

"You haven't got any, you benighted boy! so take this, and have your wits about you next time, or I won't let you off so easily," she said, holding up the heavy garment, and peeping over it, with no sign of displeasure in her laughing eyes.

"Next time! Then you do forgive me? You will try me again, and give me a chance to prove that

I'm not a fool?" cried Mac, embracing the big coat with emotion.

"Of course I will; and, so far from thinking you a fool, I was much impressed with your learning to-night, and told Steve that we ought to be proud of our philosopher."

"Learning be hanged! I'll show you that I'm *not* a bookworm, but as much a man as any of them; and then you may be proud or not, as you like!" cried Mac, with a defiant nod, that caused the glasses to leap wildly off his nose, as he caught up his hat and departed as he came.

A day or two later, Rose went to call upon Aunt Jane, as she dutifully did once or twice a week. On her way upstairs, she heard a singular sound in the drawing-room, and involuntarily stopped to listen.

"One, two, three, slide! One, two, three, turn! Now then, come on!" said one voice, impatiently.

"It's very easy to say 'come on'; but what the dickens do I do with my left leg while I'm turning and sliding with my right?" demanded another voice, in a breathless and mournful tone.

Then the whistling and thumping went on more vigorously than before; and Rose, recognizing the voices, peeped through the half-open door to behold a sight which made her shake with suppressed laughter. Steve, with a red table-cloth tied round his waist, languished upon Mac's shoulder, dancing in perfect time to the air he whistled; for Dandy was a proficient in the graceful art, and plumed himself upon his skill. Mac, with a flushed face and dizzy eye, clutched his brother by the small of his back, vainly endeavoring to steer him down the long room without entangling his own legs in the table-cloth, treading on his partner's toes, or colliding with the furniture. It was very droll; and Rose enjoyed the spectacle, till Mac, in a frantic attempt to swing round, dashed himself against the wall, and landed Steve upon the floor. Then it was impossible to restrain her laughter any longer; and she walked in upon them, saying merrily, —

"It was splendid! Do it again, and I'll play for you."

Steve sprung up, and tore off the table-cloth in great confusion; while Mac, still rubbing his head, dropped into a chair, trying to look quite calm and cheerful as he gasped out, —

"How are you, cousin? When did you come? John should have told us."

"I'm glad he did n't, for then I should have missed this touching tableau of cousinly devotion and brotherly love. Getting ready for our next party, I see."

"Trying to; but there are so many things to remember all at once, — keep time, steer straight, dodge the petticoats, and manage my confounded legs, — that it is n't easy to get on at first," answered Mac, wiping his hot forehead, with a sigh of exhaustion.

"Hardest job *I* ever undertook; and, as I'm not a battering-ram, I decline to be knocked round any longer," growled Steve, dusting his knees, and ruefully surveying the feet that had been trampled on till they tingled; for his boots and broadcloth were dear to the heart of the dapper youth.

"Very good of you, and I'm much obliged. I've got the pace, I think, and can practise with a chair to keep my hand in," said Mac, with such a comic mix-

ture of gratitude and resignation that Rose went off
again so irresistibly that her cousins joined her with a
hearty roar.

" As you are making a martyr of yourself in my
service, the least I can do is to lend a hand. Play
for us, Steve, and I 'll give Mac a lesson, unless he
prefers the chair." And, throwing off hat and cloak,
Rose beckoned so invitingly that the gravest philosopher would have yielded.

" A thousand thanks, but I 'm afraid I shall hurt
you," began Mac, much gratified, but mindful of past
mishaps.

" I 'm not. Steve did n't manage his train well, for
good dancers always loop theirs up. I have none at
all : so that trouble is gone ; and the music will make
it much easier to keep step. Just do as I tell you,
and you 'll go beautifully after a few turns."

" I will, I will ! Pipe up, Steve ! Now, Rose ! "
And, brushing his hair out of his eyes with an air
of stern determination, Mac grasped Rose, and returned to the charge, bent on distinguishing himself
if he died in the attempt.

The second lesson prospered : for Steve marked
the time by a series of emphatic bangs ; Mac obeyed
orders as promptly as if his life depended on it ; and,
after several narrow escapes at exciting moments,
Rose had the satisfaction of being steered safely
down the room, and landed with a grand pirouette
at the bottom. Steve applauded, and Mac, much
elated, exclaimed with artless candor, —

" There really is a sort of inspiration about you,
Rose. I always detested dancing before ; but now,
do you know, I rather like it."

"I knew you would; only you must n't stand with your arm round your partner in this way when you are done. You must seat and fan her, if she likes it," said Rose, anxious to perfect a pupil who seemed so lamentably in need of a teacher.

"Yes, of course, I know how they do it;" and, releasing his cousin, Mac raised a small whirlwind round her with a folded newspaper, so full of grateful zeal that she had not the heart to chide him again.

"Well done, old fellow. I begin to have hopes of you, and will order you a new dress-coat at once, since you are really going in for the proprieties of life," said Steve from the music-stool, with the approving nod of one who was a judge of said proprieties. "Now, Rose, if you will just coach him a little in his small-talk, he won't make a laughing-stock of himself as he did the other night," added Steve. "I don't mean his geological gabble: that was bad enough, but his chat with Emma Curtis was much worse. Tell her, Mac, and see if she does n't think poor Emma had a right to think you a first-class bore."

"I don't see why, when I merely tried to have a little sensible conversation," began Mac, with reluctance; for he had been unmercifully chaffed by his cousins, to whom his brother had betrayed him.

"What did you say? I won't laugh if I can help it," said Rose, curious to hear; for Steve's eyes were twinkling with fun.

"Well, I knew she was fond of theatres; so I tried that first, and got on pretty well till I began to tell her how they managed those things in Greece. Most interesting subject, you know?"

"Very. Did you give her one of the choruses or a bit of Agamemnon, as you did when you described it to me?" asked Rose, keeping sober with difficulty as she recalled that serio-comic scene.

"Of course not; but I was advising her to read Prometheus, when she gaped behind her fan, and began to talk about Phebe. What a 'nice creature' she was, 'kept her place,' dressed according to her station, and that sort of twaddle. I suppose it *was* rather rude, but being pulled up so short confused me a bit, and I said the first thing that came into my head, which was that I thought Phebe the best-dressed woman in the room, because she was n't all fuss and feathers like most of the girls."

"O Mac! that to Emma, who makes it the labor of her life to be always in the height of the fashion, and was particularly splendid that night. What *did* she say?" cried Rose, full of sympathy for both parties.

"She bridled and looked daggers at me."

"And what did you do?"

"I bit my tongue, and tumbled out of one scrape into another. Following her example, I changed the subject by talking about the Charity Concert for the orphans; and, when she gushed about the 'little darlings,' I advised her to adopt one, and wondered why young ladies did n't do that sort of thing, instead of cuddling cats and lapdogs."

"Unhappy boy! her pug is the idol of her life, and she hates babies," said Rose.

"More fool she! Well, she got my opinion on the subject, anyway, and she 's very welcome; for I went on to say that I thought it would not only be a lovely charity, but excellent training for the time when they had little darlings of their own. No end of poor things die through the ignorance of mothers, you know," added Mac, so seriously that Rose dared not smile at what went before.

" Imagine Emma trotting round with a pauper baby under her arm instead of her cherished Toto," said Steve, with an ecstatic twirl on the stool.

"Did she seem to like your advice, Monsieur Malapropos?" asked Rose, wishing she had been there.

" No, she gave a little shriek, and said, ' Good gracious, Mr. Campbell, how droll you are! Take me to mamma, please,' which I did with a thankful heart. Catch me setting her pug's leg again," ended Mac, with a grim shake of the head.

" Never mind. You were unfortunate in your listener that time. Don't think all girls are so foolish. I can show you a dozen sensible ones, who would discuss dress reform and charity with you, and enjoy Greek tragedy if you did the chorus for them as you did for me," said Rose, consolingly; for Steve would only jeer.

" Give me a list of them, please; and I 'll cultivate their acquaintance. A fellow must have some reward for making a teetotum of himself."

" I will with pleasure; and if you dance well they will make it very pleasant for you, and you 'll enjoy parties in spite of yourself."

" I cannot be a ' glass of fashion and a mould of form ' like Dandy here, but I 'll do my best : only, if I had my choice, I 'd much rather go round the streets with an organ and a monkey," answered Mac, despondently.

"Thank you kindly for the compliment," and Rose made him a low courtesy, while Steve cried, —

"Now you *have* done it!" in a tone of reproach which reminded the culprit, all too late, that he was Rose's chosen escort.

"By the gods, so I have!" and, casting away the newspaper with a gesture of comic despair, Mac strode from the room, chanting tragically the words of Cassandra, —

"'Woe! woe! O Earth! O Apollo! I will dare to die; I will accost the gates of Hades, and make my prayer that I may receive a mortal blow!'"

CHAPTER VII

PHEBE

WHILE Rose was making discoveries and having experiences, Phebe was doing the same in a quieter way: but, though they usually compared notes during the bedtime *tête-à-tête* which always ended their day, certain topics were never mentioned; so each had a little world of her own into which even the eye of friendship did not peep.

Rose's life just now was the gayest, but Phebe's the happiest. Both went out a good deal; for the beautiful voice was welcomed everywhere, and many were ready to patronize the singer who would have been slow to recognize the woman. Phebe knew this, and made no attempt to assert herself; content to know that those whose regard she valued felt her worth, and hopeful of a time when she could gracefully take the place she was meant to fill.

Proud as a princess was Phebe about some things, though in most as humble as a child; therefore, when each year lessened the service she loved to give, and increased the obligations she would have refused from any other source, dependence became a burden which even the most fervent gratitude could not lighten. Hitherto the children had gone on together, finding no obstacles to their companionship in the secluded

world in which they lived : now that they were women
their paths inevitably diverged, and both reluctantly
felt that they must part before long.

It had been settled, when they went abroad, that
on their return Phebe should take her one gift in her
hand, and try her fortunes. On no other terms would
she accept the teaching which was to fit her for the
independence she desired. Faithfully had she used
the facilities so generously afforded both at home and
abroad, and now was ready to prove that they had
not been in vain. Much encouraged by the small
successes she won in drawing-rooms, and the praise
bestowed by interested friends, she began to feel that
she might venture on a larger field, and begin her
career as a concert singer; for she aimed no higher.

Just at this time, much interest was felt in a new
asylum for orphan girls, which could not be completed
for want of funds. The Campbells "well had borne
their part," and still labored to accomplish the much-
needed charity. Several fairs had been given for this
purpose, followed by a series of concerts. Rose had
thrown herself into the work with all her heart, and
now proposed that Phebe should make her *début* at
the last concert which was to be a peculiarly interesting one, as all the orphans were to be present, and
were expected to plead their own cause by the sight
of their innocent helplessness, as well as touch hearts
by the simple airs they were to sing.

Some of the family thought Phebe would object to
so humble a beginning : but Rose knew her better,
and was not disappointed; for, when she made her
proposal, Phebe answered readily, —

"Where could I find a fitter time and place to

come before the public than here among my little
sisters in misfortune? I'll sing for them with all my
heart: only I must be one of them, and have no
flourish made about me."

"You shall arrange it as you like; and, as there
is to be little vocal music but yours and the children's,
I'll see that you have every thing as you please,"
promised Rose.

It was well she did; for the family got much excited over the prospect of "our Phebe's *début*," and
would have made a flourish if the girls had not resisted. Aunt Clara was in despair about the dress;
because Phebe decided to wear a plain claret-colored
merino with frills at neck and wrists, so that she
might look as much as possible, like the other orphans
in their stuff gowns and white aprons. Aunt Plenty
wanted to have a little supper afterward in honor of
the occasion; but Phebe begged her to change it to
a Christmas dinner for the poor children. The boys
planned to throw bushels of flowers, and Charlie
claimed the honor of leading the singer in. But
Phebe, with tears in her eyes, declined their kindly
offers, saying earnestly, —

"I had better begin as I am to go on, and depend
upon myself entirely. Indeed, Mr. Charlie, I'd rather
walk in alone; for you'd be out of place among us,
and spoil the pathetic effect we wish to produce," and
a smile sparkled through the tears, as Phebe looked
at the piece of elegance before her, and thought of
the brown gowns and pinafores.

So, after much discussion, it was decided that she
should have her way in all things, and the family
content themselves with applauding from the front.

"We'll blister our hands every man of us, and carry you home in a chariot and four : see if we don't, you perverse prima donna ! " threatened Steve, not at all satisfied with the simplicity of the affair.

" A chariot and two will be very acceptable as soon as I'm done. I shall be quite steady till my part is all over, and then I may feel a little upset; so I'd like to get away before the confusion begins. Indeed I don't mean to be perverse : but you are all so kind to me, my heart is full whenever I think of it; and that would n't do if I'm to sing," said Phebe, dropping one of the tears on the little frill she was making.

No diamond could have adorned it better Archie thought, as he watched it shine there for a moment; and felt like shaking Steve for daring to pat the dark head with an encouraging, —

" All right. I'll be on hand, and whisk you away while the rest are splitting their gloves. No fear of your breaking down. If you feel the least bit like it, though, just look at me; and I'll glare at you and shake my fist, since kindness upsets you."

" I wish you would, because one of my ballads is rather touching, and I always want to cry when I sing it. The sight of you trying to glare will make me want to laugh, and that will steady me nicely : so sit in front, please, ready to slip out when I come off the last time."

" Depend upon me ! " And the little man departed, taking great credit to himself for his influence over tall, handsome Phebe.

If he had known what was going on in the mind of the silent young gentleman behind the newspaper, Steve would have been much astonished; for Archie,

though apparently engrossed by business, was fathoms
deep in love by this time. No one suspected this but
Rose; for he did his wooing with his eyes, and only
Phebe knew how eloquent they could be. He had
discovered what the matter was long ago, — had made
many attempts to reason himself out of it; but, finding
it a hopeless task, had given up trying, and let himself drift deliciously. The knowledge that the family
would not approve only seemed to add ardor to his
love and strength to his purpose: for the same energy
and persistence which he brought to business went
into every thing he did; and, having once made up
his mind to marry Phebe, nothing could change his
plan except a word from her.

He watched and waited for three months, so that
he might not be accused of precipitation, though it
did not take him one to decide that this was the
woman to make him happy. Her steadfast nature;
quiet, busy ways; and the reserved power and passion
betrayed sometimes by a flash of the black eyes, a
quiver of the firm lips, — suited Archie, who possessed many of the same attributes himself: while
the obscurity of her birth and isolation of her lot,
which would have deterred some lovers, not only
appealed to his kindly heart, but touched the hidden
romance which ran like a vein of gold through his
strong common-sense, and made practical, steady-
going Archie a poet when he fell in love. If Uncle
Mac had guessed what dreams and fancies went on in
the head bent over his ledgers, and what emotions
were fermenting in the bosom of his staid " right-hand
man," he would have tapped his forehead, and suggested a lunatic asylum. The boys thought Archie

had sobered down too soon. His mother began to
fear that the air of the counting-room did not suit
him: and Dr. Alec was deluded into the belief that
the fellow really began to "think of Rose;" he came
so often in the evening, seeming quite contented to
sit beside her work-table, and snip tape, or draw
patterns, while they chatted.

No one observed that, though he talked to Rose on
these occasions, he looked at Phebe, in her low chair
close by, busy but silent; for she always tried to
efface herself when Rose was near, and often mourned
that she was too big to keep out of sight. No matter
what he talked about, Archie always saw the glossy
black braids on the other side of the table, the damask
cheek curving down into the firm white throat, and
the dark lashes, lifted now and then, showing eyes so
deep and soft he dared not look into them long.
Even the swift needle charmed him, the little brooch
which rose and fell with her quiet breath, the plain
work she did, and the tidy way she gathered her bits
of thread into a tiny bag. He seldom spoke to her;
never touched her basket, though he ravaged Rose's
if he wanted string or scissors; very rarely ventured
to bring her some curious or pretty thing when ships
came in from China: only sat and thought of her;
imagined that this was *his* parlor, this *her* work-table,
and they two sitting there alone a happy man and
wife.

At this stage of the little evening drama, he would
be conscious of such a strong desire to do something
rash that he took refuge in a new form of intoxication,
and proposed music, sometimes so abruptly that Rose
would pause in the middle of a sentence and look at

him, surprised to meet a curiously excited look in the usually cool, gray eyes.

Then Phebe, folding up her work, would go to the piano, as if glad to find a vent for the inner life which she seemed to have no power of expressing except in song. Rose would follow to accompany her; and Archie, moving to a certain shady corner whence he could see Phebe's face as she sang, would give himself up to unmitigated rapture for half an hour. Phebe never sang so well as at such times: for the kindly atmosphere was like sunshine to a bird, criticisms were few and gentle, praises hearty and abundant; and she poured out her soul as freely as a spring gushes up when its hidden source is full.

Always comely, with a large and wholesome growth, in moments such as these Phebe was beautiful with the beauty that makes a man's eye brighten with honest admiration, and thrills his heart with a sense of womanly nobility and sweetness. Little wonder, then, that the chief spectator of this agreeable tableau grew nightly more enamoured; and, while the elders were deep in whist, the young people were playing that still more absorbing game in which hearts are always trumps.

Rose, having Dummy for a partner, soon discovered the fact, and lately had begun to feel as she fancied Wall must have done when Pyramus wooed Thisbe through its chinks. She was a little startled at first, then amused, then anxious, then heartily interested, as every woman is in such affairs, and willingly continued to be a medium, though sometimes she quite tingled with the electricity which seemed to pervade the air. She said nothing, waiting for Phebe to speak; but

Phebe was silent, seeming to doubt the truth, till
doubt became impossible, then to shrink as if suddenly conscious of wrong-doing, and seize every possible pretext for absenting herself from the " girls'
corner," as the pretty recess was called.

The concert plan afforded excellent opportunities
for doing this; and evening after evening she slipped
away to practise her songs upstairs, while Archie sat
staring disconsolately at the neglected work-basket
and mute piano. Rose pitied him, and longed to
say a word of comfort, but felt shy, — he was such a
reserved fellow, — so left him to conduct his quiet
wooing in his own way, feeling that the crisis would
soon arrive.

She was sure of this, as she sat beside him on the
evening of the concert; for while the rest of the
family nodded and smiled, chatted and laughed in
great spirits, Archie was as mute as a fish, and sat
with his arms tightly folded, as if to keep in any unruly emotions which might attempt to escape. He
never looked at the programme ; but Rose knew
when Phebe's turn came by the quick breath he drew,
and the intent look that came into his eyes so absent
before.

But her own excitement prevented much notice of
his; for Rose was in a flutter of hope and fear, sympathy and delight, about Phebe and her success.
The house was crowded; the audience sufficiently
mixed to make the general opinion impartial; and
the stage full of little orphans with shining faces, a
most effective reminder of the object in view.

" Little dears, how nice they look ! " " Poor
things, so young to be fatherless and motherless."

"It will be a disgrace to the city, if those girls are not taken proper care of." "Subscriptions are always in order, you know; and pretty Miss Campbell will give you her sweetest smile if you hand her a handsome check." "I 've heard this Phebe Moore, and she really has a delicious voice: such a pity she won't fit herself for opera!" "Only sings three times tonight; that 's modest I 'm sure, when she is the chief attraction; so we must give her an encore after the Italian piece." "The orphans lead off, I see: stop your ears if you like; but don't fail to applaud, or the ladies will never forgive you."

Chat of this sort went on briskly, while fans waved, programmes rustled, and ushers flew about distractedly; till an important gentleman appeared, made his bow, skipped upon the leader's stand, and with a wave of his bâton caused a general uprising of white pinafores, as the orphans led off with that much-enduring melody, "America," in shrill small voices, but with creditable attention to time and tune. Pity and patriotism produced a generous round of applause; and the little girls sat down, beaming with innocent satisfaction.

An instrumental piece followed, and then a youthful gentleman, with his hair in picturesque confusion, and what his friends called a "musical brow," bounded up the steps, and, clutching a roll of music with a pair of tightly gloved hands, proceeded to inform the audience, in a husky tenor voice, that

"It was a lovely violet."

What else the song contained in the way of sense or sentiment it was impossible to discover; as the three

pages of music appeared to consist of variations upon
that one line, ending with a prolonged quaver, which
flushed the musical brow, and left the youth quite
breathless when he made his bow.

"Now she's coming! O uncle, my heart beats as
if it was myself!" whispered Rose, clutching Dr.
Alec's arm with a little gasp, as the piano was rolled
forward, the leader's stand pushed back, and all eyes
turned toward tne anteroom door.

She forgot to glance at Archie, and it was as well
perhaps; for his heart was thumping almost audibly,
as he waited for his Phebe. Not from the anteroom,
but out from among the children, where she had sat
unseen in the shadow of the organ, came stately Phebe
in her wine-colored dress, with no ornament but her
fine hair and a white flower at her throat. Very pale,
but quite composed, apparently; for she stepped
slowly through the narrow lane of upturned faces,
holding back her skirts, lest they should rudely brush
against some little head. Straight to the front she
went, bowed hastily, and, with a gesture to the
accompanist, stood waiting to begin, her eyes fixed
on the great gilt clock at the opposite end of the
hall.

They never wandered from that point while she
sung; but, as she ended, they dropped for an instant
on an eager, girlish countenance, bending from a
front seat; then, with her hasty little bow, she went
quickly back among the children, who clapped and
nodded as she passed, well pleased with the ballad
she had sung.

Every one courteously followed their example; but
there was no enthusiasm, and it was evident that

Phebe had not produced a particularly favorable impression.

"Never sang so badly in her life," muttered Charlie, irefully.

"She was frightened, poor thing. Give her time, give her time," said Uncle Mac, kindly.

"I saw she was, and I glared like a gorgon, but she never looked at me," added Steve, smoothing his gloves and his brows at the same time.

"That first song was the hardest, and she got through much better than I expected," put in Dr. Alec, bound not to show the disappointment he felt.

"Don't be troubled. Phebe has courage enough for any thing, and she'll astonish you before the evening's over," prophesied Mac, with unabated confidence; for he knew something that the rest did not.

Rose said nothing, but, under cover of her burnous gave Archie's hand a sympathetic squeeze; for his arms were unfolded now, as if the strain was over, and one lay on his knee, while with the other he wiped his hot forehead with an air of relief.

Friends about them murmured complimentary fibs, and affected great delight and surprise at Miss Moore's "charming style," "exquisite simplicity," and "undoubted talent." But strangers freely criticised, and Rose was so indignant at some of their remarks, she could not listen to any thing upon the stage, though a fine overture was played, a man with a remarkable bass voice growled and roared melodiously, and the orphans sang a lively air with a chorus of "Tra, la, la," which was a great relief to little tongues unused to long silence.

"I've often heard that women's tongues were hung in the middle and went at both ends: now I'm sure of it," whispered Charlie, trying to cheer her up by pointing out the comical effect of some seventy-five open mouths, in each of which the unruly member was wagging briskly.

Rose laughed and let him fan her, leaning from his seat behind with the devoted air he always assumed in public; but her wounded feelings were not soothed, and she continued to frown at the stout man on the left, who had dared to say with a shrug and a glance at Phebe's next piece, "That young woman can no more sing this Italian thing than she can fly, and they ought not to let her attempt it."

Phebe did, however; and suddenly changed the stout man's opinion by singing it grandly; for the consciousness of her first failure pricked her pride and spurred her to do her best with the calm sort of determination which conquers fear, fires ambition, and changes defeat to success. She looked steadily at Rose now, or the flushed, intent face beside her; and throwing all her soul into the task let her voice ring out like a silver clarion, filling the great hall and setting the hearers' blood a-tingle with the exulting strain.

That settled Phebe's fate as cantatrice; for the applause was genuine and spontaneous this time, and broke out again and again with the generous desire to atone for former coldness. But she would not return, and the shadow of the great organ seemed to have swallowed her up; for no eye could find her, no pleasant clamor win her back.

"Now I can die content," said Rose, beaming with heart-felt satisfaction; while Archie looked steadfastly at his programme, trying to keep his face in order, and the rest of the family assumed a triumphant air, as if *they* had never doubted from the first.

"Very well, indeed," said the stout man, with an approving nod. "Quite promising for a beginner. Should n't wonder if in time they made a second Cary or Kellogg of her."

"Now you 'll forgive him, won't you?" murmured Charlie, in his cousin's ear.

"Yes; and I 'd like to pat him on the head. But take warning and never judge by first appearances again," whispered Rose, at peace now with all mankind.

Phebe's last song was another ballad; for she meant to devote her talent to that much neglected but always attractive branch of her art. It was a great surprise, therefore, to all but one person in the hall, when, instead of singing "Auld Robin Grey," she placed herself at the piano, and, with a smiling glance over her shoulder at the children, broke out in the old bird-song which first won Rose. But the chirping, twittering, and cooing were now the burden to three verses of a charming little song, full of spring-time and the awakening life that makes it lovely. A rippling accompaniment flowed through it all, and a burst of delighted laughter from the children filled up the first pause with a fitting answer to the voices that seemed calling to them from the vernal woods.

It was very beautiful, and novelty lent its charm to the surprise; for art and nature worked a pretty miracle, and the clever imitation, first heard from a kitchen hearth, now became the favorite in a crowded concert room. Phebe was quite herself again; color in the cheeks now; eyes that wandered smiling to and fro; and lips that sang as gayly and far more sweetly than when she kept time to her blithe music with a scrubbing brush.

This song was evidently intended for the children, and they appreciated the kindly thought; for, as Phebe went back among them, they clapped ecstatically, flapped their pinafores, and some caught her by the skirts with audible requests to " do it again, please; do it again."

But Phebe shook her head and vanished; for it was getting late for such small people, several of whom " lay sweetly slumbering there," till roused by the clamor round them. The elders, however, were not to be denied, and applauded persistently, especially Aunt Plenty, who seized Uncle Mac's cane and pounded with it as vigorously as " Mrs. Nubbles " at the play.

" Never mind your gloves, Steve; keep it up till she comes," cried Charlie, enjoying the fun like a boy; while Jamie lost his head with excitement, and standing up called " Phebe! Phebe!" in spite of his mother's attempts to silence him.

Even the stout man clapped, and Rose could only laugh delightedly as she turned to look at Archie, who seemed to have let himself loose at last, and was stamping with a dogged energy funny to see.

So Phebe had to come, and stood there meekly bowing, with a moved look on her face, that showed how glad and grateful she was, till a sudden hush came; then, as if inspired by the memory of the cause that brought her there, she looked down into the sea of friendly faces before her, with no trace of fear in her own, and sung the song that never will grow old.

That went straight to the hearts of those who heard her: for there was something inexpressibly touching in the sight of this sweet-voiced woman singing of home for the little creatures who were homeless; and Phebe made her tuneful plea irresistible by an almost involuntary gesture of the hands which had hung loosely clasped before her; till, with the last echo of the beloved word, they fell apart and were half-out-stretched as if pleading to be filled.

It was the touch of nature that works wonders; for it made full purses suddenly weigh heavily in pockets slow to open, brought tears to eyes unused to weep, and caused that group of red-gowned girls to grow very pathetic in the sight of fathers and mothers who had left little daughters safe asleep at home. This was evident from the stillness that remained un-broken for an instant after Phebe ended; and before people could get rid of their handkerchiefs she would have been gone, if the sudden appearance of a mite in a pinafore, climbing up the stairs from the anteroom, with a great bouquet grasped in both hands, had not arrested her.

Up came the little creature, intent on performing the mission for which rich bribes of sugar-plums had been promised, and trotting bravely across the stage, she held up the lovely nosegay, saying in her baby voice, " Dis for you, ma'am; " then, startled by the sudden outburst of applause, she hid her face in Phebe's gown, and' began to sob with fright.

An awkward minute for poor Phebe; but she showed unexpected presence of mind, and left behind her a pretty picture of the oldest and the youngest orphan, as she went quickly down the step, smiling over the great bouquet with the baby on her arm.

Nobody minded the closing piece; for people began to go, sleepy children to be carried off, and whispers grew into a buzz of conversation. In the general confusion, Rose looked to see if Steve had remembered his promise to help Phebe slip away before the rush began. No, there he was putting on Kitty's cloak, quite oblivious of any other duty; and, turning to ask Archie to hurry out, Rose found that he had already vanished, leaving his gloves behind him.

"Have you lost any thing?" asked Dr. Alec, catching a glimpse of her face.

"No, sir, I've found something," she whispered back, giving him the gloves to pocket along with her fan and glass, adding hastily as the concert ended, "Please, uncle, tell them all not to come with us. Phebe has had enough excitement, and ought to rest."

Rose's word was law to the family in all things concerning Phebe. So word was passed that there were to be no congratulations till to-morrow, and Dr. Alec got his party off as soon as possible. But all the way home, while he and Aunt Plenty were prophesying a brilliant future for the singer, Rose sat rejoicing over the happy present of the woman. She was sure that Archie had spoken, and imagined the whole scene with feminine delight, — how tenderly he had asked the momentous question, how gratefully Phebe had given the desired reply, and now how both were enjoying that delicious hour which Rose had been given to understand never came but once. Such a

pity to shorten it, she thought; and begged her uncle
to go home the longest way: the night was so mild,
the moonlight so clear, and herself so in need of fresh
air after the excitement of the evening.

"I thought you would want to rush into Phebe's
arms the instant she got done," said Aunt Plenty,
innocently wondering at the whims girls took into
their heads.

"So I should if I consulted my own wishes; but
as Phebe asked to be let alone I want to gratify her,"
answered Rose, making the best excuse she could.

"A little piqued," thought the doctor, fancying he
understood the case.

As the old lady's rheumatism forbade their driving
about till midnight, home was reached much too soon,
Rose thought, and tripped away to warn the lovers
the instant she entered the house. But study, parlor,
and boudoir were empty; and, when Jane appeared
with cake and wine, she reported that "Miss Phebe
went right upstairs, and wished to be excused, please,
being very tired."

"That is n't at all like Phebe: I hope she is n't ill,"
began Aunt Plenty, sitting down to toast her feet.

"She may be a little hysterical; for she is a proud
thing, and represses her emotions as long as she can.
I 'll step up and see if she does n't need a soothing
draught of some sort," and Dr. Alec threw off his
coat as he spoke.

"No, no, she 's only tired. I 'll run up to her: she
won't mind me; and I 'll report if any thing is amiss."

Away went Rose, quite trembling with suspense;
but Phebe's door was shut, no light shone underneath,
and no sound came from the room within. She

tapped, and, receiving no answer, went on to her own chamber, thinking to herself, —

"Love always makes people queer, I've heard; so I suppose they settled it all in the carriage, and the dear thing ran away to think about her happiness alone. I'll not disturb her. Why, Phebe!" added Rose, surprised; for, entering her room, there was the cantatrice, busy about the nightly services she always rendered her little mistress.

"I'm waiting for you, dear. Where have you been so long?" asked Phebe, poking the fire as if anxious to get some color into cheeks that were unnaturally pale.

The instant she spoke, Rose knew that something was wrong, and a glance at her face confirmed the fear. It was like a dash of cold water, and quenched her happy fancies in a moment; but being a delicate minded girl she respected Phebe's mood, and asked no questions, made no comments, and left her friend to speak or be silent as she chose.

"I was so excited I would take a turn in the moonlight to calm my nerves. O dearest Phebe, I am *so* glad, so proud, so full of wonder at your courage and skill and sweet ways altogether, that I cannot half tell you how I love and honor you!" she cried, kissing the white cheeks with such tender warmth they could not help glowing faintly, as Phebe held her little mistress close, sure that nothing could disturb this innocent affection.

"It is all your work, dear; because but for you I might still be scrubbing floors, and hardly dare to dream of any thing like this," she said, in her old grateful way; but in her voice there was a thrill of something deeper than gratitude, and at the last two words her head went up with a gesture of soft pride as if it had been newly crowned.

Rose heard and saw and guessed the meaning of both tone and gesture; feeling that her Phebe deserved both the singer's laurel and the bride's myrtle wreath. But she only looked up, saying very wistfully, —

"Then it *has* been a happy night for you as well as for us."

"The happiest of my life, and the hardest," answered Phebe briefly, as she looked away from the questioning eyes.

"You should have let us come nearer and help you through. I'm afraid you are very proud, my Jenny Lind."

"I have to be; for sometimes I feel as if I had nothing else to keep me up." She stopped short there, fearing that her voice would prove traitorous if she went on. In a moment, she asked in a tone that was almost hard, —

"You think I did well to-night?"

"They all think so, and were so delighted they wanted to come in a body and tell you so; but I sent them home, because I knew you'd be tired out. Perhaps I ought not to have done it, and you'd rather have had a crowd about you than just me?"

"It was the kindest thing you ever did, and what could I like better than 'just you,' my darling?"

Phebe seldom called her that, and when she did her heart was in the little word, making it so tender that Rose thought it the sweetest in the world, next to Uncle Alec's "my little girl." Now it was almost passionate, and Phebe's face grew rather tragical as she looked down at Rose. It was impossible to seem unconscious any longer, and Rose said, caressing Phebe's cheek, which burned with a feverish color now, —

"Then don't shut me out if you have a trouble; but let me share it as I let you share all mine."

"I will! Little mistress, I've got to go away, sooner even than we planned."

"Why, Phebe?"

"Because — Archie loves me."

"That's the very reason you should stay and make him happy."

"Not if it caused dissension in the family, and you know it would."

Rose opened her lips to deny this impetuously, but checked herself and answered honestly, —

"Uncle and I would be heartily glad; and I'm sure Aunt Jessie never could object, if you loved Archie as he does you."

"She has other hopes, I think; and kind as she is it *would* be a disappointment if he brought me home. She is right; they all are, and I alone am to blame. I should have gone long ago: I knew I should; but it was so pleasant I couldn't bear to go away alone."

"I kept you, and I am to blame if any one; but indeed, dear Phebe, I cannot see why you should care even if Aunt Myra croaks, and Aunt Clara exclaims, or Aunt Jane makes disagreeable remarks. Be happy, and never mind them," cried Rose; so much excited by all this that she felt the spirit of revolt rise up within her, and was ready to defy even that awe-inspiring institution "the family" for her friend's sake.

But Phebe shook her head with a sad smile; and answered, still with the hard tone in her voice as if forcing back all emotion that she might see her duty clearly, —

"*You* could do that, but *I* never can. Answer me this, Rose, and answer truly as you love me. If you had been taken into a house, a friendless, penniless, forlorn girl, and for years been heaped with benefits, trusted, taught, loved, and made, oh, so happy! could you think it right to steal away something that these good people valued very much? To have them feel that you had been ungrateful, had deceived them, and meant to thrust yourself into a high place not fit for you; when they had been generously helping you in other ways, far more than you deserved. Could you then say as you do now, 'Be happy and never mind them'?"

Phebe held Rose by the shoulders now, and searched her face so keenly that the other shrunk a little; for the black eyes were full of fire, and there was something almost grand about this girl who seemed suddenly to have become a woman. There was no need of words to answer the questions so swiftly asked; for Rose put herself in Phebe's place in the drawing of a breath, and her own pride made her truthfully reply, —

"No: I could not!"

"I knew you'd say that, and help me do my duty;" and all the coldness melted out of Phebe's manner, as she hugged her little mistress close, feeling the comfort of sympathy even through the blunt sincerity of Rose's words.

"I will if I know how. Now come and tell me all

about it;" and, seating herself in the great chair which had often held them both, Rose stretched out her hands as if glad and ready to give help of any sort.

But Phebe would not take her accustomed place; for, as if coming to confession, she knelt down upon the rug, and, leaning on the arm of the chair, told her love-story in the simplest words.

"I never thought he cared for me until a little while ago. I fancied it was you, and even when I knew he liked to hear me sing I supposed it was because you helped; and so I did my best, and was glad you were to be a happy girl. But his eyes told the truth; then I saw what I had been doing, and was frightened. He did not speak, so I believed, what is quite true, that he felt I was not a fit wife for him, and would never ask me. It was right: I was glad of it, yet I *was* proud; and, though I did not ask or hope for any thing, I did want him to see that I respected myself, remembered my duty, and could do right as well as he. I kept away; I planned to go as soon as possible, and resolved that at this concert I would do so well he should not be ashamed of poor Phebe and her one gift."

"It was this that made you so strange, then; preferring to go alone, and refusing every little favor at our hands!" asked Rose, feeling very sure now about the state of Phebe's heart.

"Yes; I wanted to do every thing myself, and not owe one jot of my success, if I had any, to even the dearest friend I've got. It was bad and foolish of me, and I was punished by that first dreadful failure. I was so frightened, Rose! My breath was all gone my eyes so dizzy I could hardly see, and that great crowd of faces seemed so near I dared not look. If it had not been for the clock, I never should have got through; and when I did, not knowing in the least how I 'd sung, one look at your distressed face told me that I 'd failed."

"But I smiled, Phebe, — indeed I did, — as sweetly as I could; for I was sure it was only fright," protested Rose, eagerly.

"So you did: but the smile was full of pity, not of pride, as I wanted it to be; and I rushed into a dark place behind the organ, feeling ready to kill myself. How angry and miserable I was! I set my teeth, clenched my hands, and vowed that I would do well next time, or never sing another note. I was quite desperate when my turn came, and felt as if I could do almost any thing; for I remembered that *he* was there. I 'm not sure how it was, but it seemed as if I was all voice; for I let myself go, trying to forget every thing except that two people must *not* be disappointed, though I died when the song was done."

"O Phebe, it was splendid! I nearly cried, I was so proud and glad to see you do yourself justice at last."

"And he?" whispered Phebe, with her face half hidden on the arm of the chair.

"Said not a word: but I saw his lips tremble and his eyes shine; and I knew he was the happiest creature there, because *I* was sure he did think you fit to be his wife, and did mean to speak very soon."

Phebe made no answer for a moment, seeming to forget the small success in the greater one which followed, and to comfort her sore heart with the knowledge that Rose was right.

"*He* sent the flowers; *he* came for me, and, on the way home, showed me how wrong I had been to doubt him for an hour. Don't ask me to tell that part, but be sure *I* was the happiest creature in the world then." And Phebe hid her face again, all wet with tender tears, that fell soft and sudden as a summer shower.

Rose let them flow undisturbed, while she silently caressed the bent head; wondering, with a wistful look in her own wet eyes, what this mysterious passion was, which could so move, ennoble, and beautify the beings whom it blessed.

An impertinent little clock upon the chimney-piece striking eleven broke the silence, and reminded Phebe that she could not indulge in love-dreams there. She started up, brushed off her tears, and said resolutely, —

"That is enough for to-night. Go happily to bed, and leave the troubles for to-morrow."

"But, Phebe, I must know what you said," cried Rose, like a child defrauded of half its bedtime story.

"I said 'No.'"

"Ah! but it will change to 'Yes' by and by; I'm sure of that: so I'll let you go to dream of 'him.' The Campbells *are* rather proud of being descendants of Robert Bruce; but they have common-sense and love you dearly, as you 'll see to-morrow."

"Perhaps." And, with a good-night kiss, poor Phebe went away, to lie awake till dawn.

CHAPTER VIII

BREAKERS AHEAD

ANXIOUS to smooth the way for Phebe, Rose was up betimes, and slipped into Aunt Plenty's room before the old lady had got her cap on.

"Aunty, I've something pleasant to tell you; and, while you listen, I'll brush your hair, as you like to have me," she began, well aware that the proposed process was a very soothing one.

"Yes, dear: only don't be too particular, because I'm late and must hurry down, or Jane won't get things straight; and it does fidget me to have the salt-cellars uneven, the tea-strainer forgotten, and your uncle's paper not aired," returned Miss Plenty, briskly unrolling the two gray curls she wore at her temples.

Then Rose, brushing away at the scanty back-hair led skilfully up to the crisis of her tale by describing Phebe's panic and brave efforts to conquer it; all about the flowers Archie sent her; and how Steve forgot, and dear, thoughtful Archie took his place. So far it went well, and Aunt Plenty was full of interest, sympathy, and approbation; but when Rose added, as if it was quite a matter of course, "So, on the way home, he told her he loved her," a great start twitched the gray locks out of her hands as the old lady turned round, with the little curls standing erect, exclaiming, in undisguised dismay, —

"Not seriously, Rose?"

"Yes, Aunty, very seriously. He never jokes about such things."

"Mercy on us! what *shall* we do about it?"

"Nothing, ma'am, but be as glad as we ought, and congratulate him as soon as she says 'Yes.'"

"Do you mean to say she did n't accept at once?"

"She never will if we don't welcome her as kindly as if she belonged to one of our best families, and I don't blame her."

"I'm glad the girl has so much sense. Of course we can't do any thing of the sort; and I'm surprised at Archie's forgetting what he owes to the family in this rash manner. Give me my cap, child: I must speak to Alec at once." And Aunt Plenty twisted her hair into a button at the back of her head with one energetic twirl.

"Do speak kindly, Aunty, and remember that it was not Phebe's fault. She never thought of this till very lately, and began at once to prepare for going away," said Rose, pleadingly.

"She ought to have gone long ago. I told Myra we should have trouble somewhere as soon as I saw what a good-looking creature she was; and here it is as bad as can be. Dear, dear! why can't young people have a little prudence?"

"I don't see that any one need object if Uncle Jem and Aunt Jessie approve; and I do think it will be very, very unkind to scold poor Phebe for being well-bred, pretty, and good, after doing all we could to make her so."

"Child, you don't understand these things yet; but you ought to feel your duty toward your family, and do all you can to keep the name as honorable as it always has been. What do you suppose our blessed ancestress Lady Marget, would say to our oldest boy taking a wife from the poor-house?"

As she spoke, Miss Plenty looked up, almost apprehensively, at one of the wooden-faced old portraits with which her room was hung, as if asking pardon of the severe-nosed matron, who stared back at her from under the sort of blue dish-cover which formed her head-gear.

"As Lady Marget died about two hundred years ago, I don't care a pin what she would say; especially as she looks like a very narrow-minded, haughty woman. But I do care very much what Miss Plenty Campbell says; for *she* is a very sensible, generous, discreet, and dear old lady, who would n't hurt a fly, much less a good and faithful girl who has been a sister to me. Would she?" entreated Rose, knowing well that the elder aunt led all the rest more or less.

But Miss Plenty had her cap on now, and consequently felt herself twice the woman she was without it; so she not only gave it a somewhat belligerent air by setting it well up, but she shook her head decidedly, smoothed down her stiff white apron, and stood up as if ready for battle.

" I shall do my duty, Rose, and expect the same of others. Don't say any more now: I must turn the matter over in my mind; for it has come upon me suddenly, and needs serious consideration."

With which unusually solemn address, she took up her keys and trotted away, leaving her niece to follow with an anxious countenance, uncertain whether her championship had done good or ill to the cause she had at heart.

She was much cheered by the sound of Phebe's voice in the study; for Rose was sure that if Uncle Alec was on their side all would be well. But the clouds lowered again when they came in to breakfast: for Phebe's heavy eyes and pale cheeks did not look encouraging; while Dr. Alec was as sober as a judge, and sent an inquiring glance toward Rose now and then as if curious to discover how she bore the news.

An uncomfortable meal, though all tried to seem as usual, and talked over last night's events with all the interest they could. But the old peace was disturbed by a word, as a pebble thrown into a quiet pool sends tell-tale circles rippling its surface far and wide. Aunt Plenty, while "turning the subject over in her mind," also seemed intent on upsetting every thing she touched, and made sad havoc in her tea-tray; Dr. Alec unsociably read his paper; Rose, having salted instead of sugared her oatmeal, absently ate it feeling that the sweetness had gone out of every thing; and Phebe, after choking down a cup of tea and crumbling a roll, excused herself, and went away, sternly resolving not to be a bone of contention to this beloved family.

As soon as the door was shut, Rose pushed away her plate, and going to Dr. Alec peeped over the paper with such an anxious face that he put it down at once.

"Uncle, this is a serious matter, and *we* must take our stand at once; for you are Phebe's guardian and I am her sister," began Rose, with pretty solemnity. "You have often been disappointed in me," she continued, "but I know I never shall be in you; because you are too wise and good to let any worldly pride or prudence spoil your sympathy with Archie and our Phebe. You won't desert them, will you?"

"Never!" answered Dr. Alec, with gratifying energy.

"Thank you! thank you!" cried Rose. "Now, if I have you and aunty on my side, I'm not afraid of anybody."

"Gently, gently, child. I don't intend to desert the lovers; but I certainly shall advise them to consider well what they are about. I'll own I *am* rather disappointed; because Archie is young to decide his life in this way, and Phebe's career seemed settled in another fashion. Old people don't like to have their plans upset, you know," he added, more lightly; for Rose's face fell as he went on.

"Old people shouldn't plan too much for the young ones then. We are very grateful, I'm sure; but we cannot always be disposed of in the most prudent and sensible way; so don't set your hearts on little arrangements of that sort, I beg," and Rose looked wondrous wise; for she could not help suspecting even her best uncle of "plans" in her behalf.

"You are quite right: we shouldn't; yet it is very hard to help it," confessed Dr. Alec, with a conscious air; and, returning hastily to the lovers, he added kindly, —

"I was much pleased with the straightforward way in which Phebe came to me this morning, and told me all about it, as if I really was her guardian. She did not own it in words: but it was perfectly evident that she loves Archie with all her heart; yet, knowing the objections which will be made, very sensibly and bravely proposes to go away at once, and end the matter, — as if that were possible, poor child," and the tender-hearted man gave a sigh of sympathy that did Rose good to hear, and mollified her rising indignation at the bare idea of ending Phebe's love affairs in such a summary way.

"You don't think she ought to go, I hope?"

"I think she will go."

"We must not let her."

"We have no right to keep her."

"O uncle! surely we have! Our Phebe, whom we all love so much."

"You forget that she is a woman now, and we have no claim upon her. Because we've befriended her for years is the very reason we should not make our benefits a burden, but leave her free; and, if she chooses to do this in spite of Archie, we must let her with a God-speed."

Before Rose could answer, Aunt Plenty spoke out like one having authority; for old-fashioned ways were dear to her soul, and she thought even love affairs should be conducted with a proper regard to the powers that be.

"The family must talk the matter over and decide what is best for the children, who of course will listen to reason and do nothing ill-advised. For my part, I am quite upset by the news, but shall not commit myself till I've seen Jessie and the boy. Jane, clear away, and bring me the hot water."

That ended the morning conference; and, leaving the old lady to soothe her mind by polishing spoons and washing cups, Rose went away to find Phebe, while the doctor retired to laugh over the downfall of brother Mac's match-making schemes.

The Campbells did not gossip about their concerns in public; but, being a very united family, it had long been the custom to " talk over " any interesting event which occurred to any member thereof, and every one gave his or her opinion, advice, or censure with the utmost candor. Therefore the first engagement, if such it could be called, created a great sensation, among the aunts especially; and they were in as much of a flutter as a flock of maternal birds when their young begin to hop out of the nest. So at all hours the excellent ladies were seen excitedly nodding their caps together, as they discussed the affair in all its bearings, without ever arriving at any unanimous decision.

The boys took it much more calmly. Mac was the only one who came out strongly in Archie's favor. Charlie thought the Chief ought to do better, and called Phebe " a siren, who had bewitched the sage youth." Steve was scandalized, and delivered long orations upon one's duty to society, keeping the old name up, and the danger of *mésalliances ;* while all the time he secretly sympathized with Archie, being much smitten with Kitty Van himself. Will and Geordie, unfortunately home for the holidays, considered it " a jolly lark "; and little Jamie nearly drove his elder brother distracted by curious inquiries as to " how folks felt when they were in love."

Uncle Mac's dismay was so comical that it kept

Dr. Alec in good spirits; for he alone knew how deep was the deluded man's chagrin at the failure of the little plot which he fancied was prospering finely.

" I 'll never set my heart on any thing of the sort again; and the young rascals may marry whom they like. I 'm prepared for any thing now: so if Steve brings home the washerwoman's daughter, and Mac runs away with our pretty chamber-maid, I shall say, ' Bless you my children,' with mournful resignation; for, upon my soul, that is all that 's left for a modern parent to do."

With which tragic burst, poor Uncle Mac washed his hands of the whole affair, and buried himself in the counting-house while the storm raged.

About this time, Archie might have echoed Rose's childish wish, that she had not *quite* so many aunts; for the tongues of those interested relatives made sad havoc with his little romance, and caused him to long fervently for a desert island, where he could woo and win his love in delicious peace. That nothing of the sort was possible soon became evident; since every word uttered only confirmed Phebe's resolution to go away, and proved to Rose how mistaken she had been in believing that she could bring every one to her way of thinking.

Prejudices are unmanageable things; and the good aunts, like most women, possessed a plentiful supply: so Rose found it like beating her head against a wall to try and convince them that Archie was wise in loving poor Phebe. His mother, who had hoped to have Rose for her daughter, — not because of her fortune, but the tender affection she felt for her, — put away her disappointment without a word, and welcomed Phebe as kindly as she could for her boy's sake. But the girl felt the truth with the quickness of a nature made sensitive by love, and clung to her resolve all the more tenaciously, though grateful for the motherly words that would have been so sweet if genuine happiness had prompted them.

Aunt Jane called it romantic nonsense, and advised strong measures, — "kind, but firm, Jessie." Aunt Clara was sadly distressed about "what people would say," if one of "our boys" married a nobody's daughter. And Aunt Myra not only seconded her views by painting portraits of Phebe's unknown relations in the darkest colors, but uttered direful prophecies regarding the disreputable beings who would start up in swarms the moment the girl made a good match.

These suggestions so wrought upon Aunt Plenty that she turned a deaf ear to the benevolent emotions native to her breast, and taking refuge behind "our blessed ancestress, Lady Marget," refused to sanction any engagement which could bring discredit upon the stainless name which was her pride.

So it all ended where it began; for Archie steadily refused to listen to any one but Phebe, and she as steadily reiterated her bitter "No;" fortifying herself half unconsciously with the hope that, by and by, when she had won a name, fate might be kinder.

While the rest talked, she had been working; for every hour showed her that her instinct had been a true one, and pride would not let her stay, though love pleaded eloquently. So, after a Christmas any thing but merry, Phebe packed her trunks, rich in gifts from those who generously gave her all but the one thing she desired; and, with a pocketful of letters to people who could further her plans, she went away to seek her fortune, with a brave face and a very heavy heart.

"Write often, and let me know all you do, my Phebe; and remember I shall never be contented till you come back again," whispered Rose, clinging to her till the last.

"She *will* come back; for in a year I'm going to bring her home, please God," said Archie, pale with the pain of parting, but as resolute as she.

"I'll earn my welcome: then perhaps it will be easier for them to give and me to receive it," answered Phebe, with a backward glance at the group of caps in the hall, as she went down the steps on Dr. Alec's arm.

"You earned it long ago, and it is always waiting for you while I am here. Remember that, and God bless you, my good girl," he said, with a paternal kiss that warmed her heart.

"I never shall forget it!" and Phebe never did.

CHAPTER IX

NEW-YEAR'S CALLS

"NOW I'm going to turn over a new leaf, as I promised. I wonder what I shall find on the next page?" said Rose, coming down on New-Year's morning, with a serious face, and a thick letter in her hand.

"Tired of frivolity, my dear?" asked her uncle, pausing, in his walk up and down the hall, to glance at her with the quick, bright look she liked to bring into his eyes.

"No, sir, and that's the sad part of it; but I've made up my mind to stop while I can, because I'm sure it is not good for me. I've had some very sober thoughts lately; for, since my Phebe went away, I've had no heart for gayety: so it is a good place to stop and make a fresh start," answered Rose, taking his arm, and walking on with him.

"An excellent time! Now, how are you going to fill the aching void?" he asked, well pleased.

"By trying to be as unselfish, brave, and good as she is." And Rose held the letter against her bosom with a tender touch, for Phebe's strength had inspired her with a desire to be as self-reliant. "I'm going to set about living in earnest, as she has; though I think it will be harder for me than for her, because she stands alone, and has a career marked out for her.

I'm nothing but a common-place sort of girl, with no end of relations to be consulted every time I wink, and a dreadful fortune hanging like a millstone round my neck, to weigh me down if I try to fly. It is a hard case, uncle, and I get low in my mind when I think about it," sighed Rose, oppressed with her blessings.

"Afflicted child! how can I relieve you?" And there was amusement as well as sympathy in Dr. Alec's face, as he patted the hand upon his arm.

"Please don't laugh, for I really *am* trying to be good. In the first place, help me to wean myself from foolish pleasures, and show me how to occupy my thoughts and time so that I may not idle about and dream, instead of doing great things."

"Good! we'll begin at once. Come to town with me this morning, and see your houses. They are all ready, and Mrs. Gardner has half a dozen poor souls waiting to go in as soon as you give the word," answered the doctor, promptly, glad to get his girl back again, though not surprised that she still looked with regretful eyes at the Vanity Fair, always so enticing when we are young.

"I'll give it to-day, and make the new year a happy one to those poor souls at least. I'm so sorry that it's impossible for me to go with you, but you know I must help Aunty Plen receive. We haven't been here for so long that she has set her heart on having a grand time to-day; and I particularly want to please her, because I have not been as amiable as I ought lately. I really couldn't forgive her for siding against Phebe."

"She did what she thought was right: so we must

not blame her. I am going to make my New-Year's calls to-day; and, as my friends live down that way, I 'll get the list of names from Mrs. G., and tell the poor ladies, with Miss Campbell's compliments, that their new home is ready. Shall I?"

"Yes, uncle, but take all the credit to yourself; for I never should have thought of it if you had not proposed the plan."

"Bless your heart! I 'm only your agent, and suggest now and then. I 've nothing to offer but advice: so I lavish that on all occasions."

"You have nothing because you 've given your substance all away as generously as you do your advice. Never mind: you shall never come to want while I live. I 'll save enough for us two, though I do make 'ducks and drakes of my fortune.'"

Dr. Alec laughed at the toss of the head with which she quoted Charlie's offensive words, then offered to take the letter, saying, as he looked at his watch, —

"I 'll post that for you in time for the early mail. I like a run before breakfast."

But Rose held her letter fast, dimpling with sudden smiles, half merry and half shy.

"No, thank you, sir: Archie likes to do that, and never fails to call for all I write. He gets a peep at Phebe's in return, and I cheer him up a bit; for, though he says nothing, he has a hard time of it, poor fellow."

"How many letters in five days?"

"Four, sir, to me: she does n't write to him, uncle."

"As yet. Well, you show hers: so it 's all right; and you are a set of sentimental youngsters." And the doctor walked away, looking as if he enjoyed the sentiment as much as any of them.

Old Miss Campbell was nearly as great a favorite as young Miss Campbell; so a succession of black coats and white gloves flowed in and out of the hospitable mansion pretty steadily all day. The clan were out in great force, and came by instalments to pay their duty to Aunt Plenty, and wish the compliments of the season to "our cousin." Archie appeared first, looking sad but steadfast, and went away with Phebe's letter in his left breast-pocket; feeling that life was still endurable, though his love was torn from him: for Rose had many comfortable things to say, and read him delicious bits from the voluminous correspondence lately begun.

Hardly was he gone, when Will and Geordie came marching in, looking as fine as gray uniforms with much scarlet piping could make them, and feeling peculiarly important, as this was their first essay in New-Year's call-making. Brief was their stay, for they planned to visit every friend they had; and Rose could not help laughing at the droll mixture of manly dignity and boyish delight with which they drove off in their own carriage, both as erect as ramrods, arms folded, and caps stuck at exactly the same angle on each blonde head.

"Here comes the other couple,—Steve, in full feather, with a big bouquet for Kitty; and poor Mac, looking like a gentleman and feeling like a martyr, I'm sure," said Rose, watching one carriage turn in as the other turned out of the great gate, with its arch of holly, ivy, and evergreen.

"Here he is: I've got him in tow for the day, and want you to cheer him up with a word of praise; for he came without a struggle, though planning to bolt somewhere with uncle," cried Steve, falling back to display his brother, who came in, looking remarkably well in his state and festival array; for polishing began to tell.

"A happy New Year, aunty; same to you, cousin, and best wishes for as many more as you deserve," said Mac, heeding Steve no more than if he had been a fly, as he gave the old lady a hearty kiss, and offered Rose a quaint little nosegay of pansies.

"Heart's-ease: do you think I need it?" she asked, looking up with sudden sobriety.

"We all do.   Could I give you any thing better on a day like this?"

"No: thank you very much," and a sudden dew came to Rose's eyes; for, though often blunt in speech, when Mac did do a tender thing, it always touched her; because he seemed to understand her moods so well.

"Has Archie been here?   He said he shouldn't go anywhere else; but I hope you talked that nonsense out of his head," said Steve, settling his tie before the mirror.

"Yes, dear, he came; but looked so out of spirits, I really felt reproached.   Rose cheered him up a little: but I don't believe he will feel equal to making calls, and I hope he won't; for his face tells the whole story much too plainly," answered Aunt Plenty, rustling about her bountiful table in her richest black silk, with all her old lace on.

"Oh, he'll get over it in a month or two, and
Phebe will soon find another lover; so don't be
worried about him, aunty," said Steve, with the air
of a man who knew all about that sort of thing.

"If Archie does forget, I shall despise him; and
I know Phebe won't try to find another lover,
though she'll probably have them: she is so sweet
and good!" cried Rose, indignantly; for, having
taken the pair under her protection, she defended
them valiantly.

"Then you'd have Arch hope against hope, and
never give up, would you?" asked Mac, putting on
his glasses to survey the thin boots which were his
especial abomination.

"Yes, I would! for a lover is not worth having if
he's not in earnest."

"Exactly: so you'd like them to wait and work
and keep on loving till they made you relent, or
plainly proved that it was no use."

"If they were good as well as constant, I think I
should relent in time."

"I'll mention that to Pemberton; for he seemed
to be hit the hardest, and a ray of hope will do him
good, whether he is equal to the ten years' wait or
not," put in Steve, who liked to rally Rose about her
lovers.

"I'll never forgive you if you say a word to any
one. It is only Mac's odd way of asking questions,
and I ought not to answer them. You *will* talk
about such things, and I can't stop you; but I don't
like it," said Rose, much annoyed.

"Poor little Penelope! she shall not be teased
about her suitors, but left in peace till her Ulysses

comes home," said Mac, sitting down to read the mottoes sticking out of certain fanciful bonbons on the table.

"It is this fuss about Archie which has demoralized us all. Even the owl waked up, and has n't got over the excitement yet, you see. He 's had no experience, poor fellow; so he does n't know how to behave," observed Steve, regarding his bouquet with tender interest.

"That 's true; and I asked for information, because I may be in love myself some day, and all this will be useful, don't you see?"

"You in love!" and Steve could not restrain a laugh at the idea of the bookworm a slave to the tender passion.

Quite unruffled, Mac leaned his chin in both hands, regarding them with a meditative eye, as he answered in his whimsical way, —

"Why not? I intend to study love as well as medicine; for it is one of the most mysterious and remarkable diseases that afflict mankind, and the best way to understand it is to have it. I may catch it some day, and then I should like to know how to treat and cure it."

"If you take it as badly as you did measles and whooping-cough, it will go hard with you, old fellow," said Steve, much amused with the fancy.

"I want it to: no great experience comes or goes easily; and this is the greatest we can know, I believe, except death."

Something in Mac's quiet tone and thoughtful eyes made Rose look at him in surprise; for she had never beard him speak in that way before. Steve also

stared for an instant, equally amazed; then said below
his breath, with an air of mock anxiety, —

"He's been catching something at the hospital,
typhoid probably, and is beginning to wander. I'll
take him quietly away before he gets any wilder.
Come, old lunatic, we must be off."

"Don't be alarmed: I'm all right and much
obliged for your advice; for I fancy I shall be a desperate lover when my time comes, if it ever does.
You don't think it impossible, do you?" and Mac
put the question so soberly that there was a general
smile.

"Certainly not: you'll be a regular Douglas,
tender and true," answered Rose, wondering what
queer question would come next.

"Thank you. The fact is, I've been with Archie
so much in his trouble lately that I've got interested
in this matter, and very naturally want to investigate
the subject as every rational man must, sooner or
later: that's all. Now, Steve, I'm ready," and Mac
got up as if the lesson was over.

"My dear, that boy is either a fool or a genius, and
I'm sure I should be glad to know which," said Aunt
Plenty, putting her bonbons to rights with a puzzled
shake of her best cap.

"Time will show; but I incline to think that he is
not a fool by any means," answered the girl, pulling
a cluster of white roses out of her bosom to make
room for the pansies, though they did not suit the
blue gown half so well.

Just then Aunt Jessie came in to help them receive,
with Jamie to make himself generally useful; which
he proceeded to do by hovering round the table like

a fly about a honey-pot, when not flattening his nose against the window-panes, to announce excitedly, " Here 's another man coming up the drive ! "

Charlie arrived next, in his most sunshiny humor; for any thing social and festive was his delight, and when in this mood the Prince was quite irresistible. He brought a pretty bracelet for Rose, and was graciously allowed to put it on, while she chid him gently for his extravagance.

" I am only following your example; for, you know, ' nothing is too good for those we love, and giving way is the best thing one can do,'" he retorted, quoting words of her own.

" I wish you would follow my example in some other things as well as you do in this," said Rose, soberly, as Aunt Plenty called him to come and see if the punch was right.

" Must conform to the customs of society. Aunty's heart would be broken, if we did not drink her health in the good old fashion. But don't be alarmed: I 've a strong head of my own, and that 's lucky; for I shall need it before I get through," laughed Charlie, showing a long list, as he turned away to gratify the old lady with all sorts of merry and affectionate compliments as the glasses touched.

Rose did feel rather alarmed; for, if he drank the health of all the owners of those names, she felt sure that Charlie would need a very strong head indeed. It was hard to say any thing, then and there, without seeming disrespect to Aunt Plenty: yet she longed to remind her cousin of the example she tried to set him in this respect; for Rose never touched wine, and the boys knew it. She was thoughtfully turning the

bracelet with its pretty device of turquoise forget-me-
nots, when the giver came back to her, still bubbling
over with good spirits.

"Dear little saint, you look as if you'd like to
smash all the punch-bowls in the city, and save us
jolly young fellows from to-morrow's headache."

"I should; for such headaches sometimes end in
heartaches, I'm afraid. Dear Charlie, don't be angry;
but you know better than I that this is a dangerous
day for such as you: so do be careful for my sake,"
she added, with an unwonted touch of tenderness in
her voice; for, looking at the gallant figure before
her, it was impossible to repress the womanly longing
to keep it always as brave and blithe as now.

Charlie saw that new softness in the eyes that never
looked unkindly on him, fancied that it meant more
than it did, and, with a sudden fervor in his own
voice, answered quickly, —

"My darling, I will!"

The glow which had risen to his face was reflected
in hers; for at that moment it seemed as if it would
be possible to love this cousin, who was so willing to
be led by her, and so much needed some helpful
influence to make a noble man of him. The thought
came and went like a flash; but gave her a quick
heart-throb, as if the old affection was trembling on
the verge of some warmer sentiment, and left her with
a sense of responsibility never felt before. Obeying
the impulse, she said, with a pretty blending of
earnestness and playfulness, —

"If I wear the bracelet to remember you by, you
must wear this to remind you of your promise."

"And you," whispered Charlie, bending his head

to kiss the hands that put a little white rose in his button-hole.

Just at that most interesting moment, they became aware of an arrival in the front drawing-room, whither Aunt Plenty had discreetly retired. Rose felt grateful for the interruption; because, not being at all sure of the state of her heart as yet, she was afraid of letting a sudden impulse lead her too far. But Charlie, conscious that a very propitious instant had been spoilt, regarded the newcomer with any thing but a benignant expression of countenance; and whispering, " Good-by, my Rose, I shall look in this evening to see how you are after the fatigues of the day," he went away, with such a cool nod to poor Fun See that the amiable Asiatic thought he must have mortally offended him.

Rose had little leisure to analyze the new emotions of which she was conscious: for Mr. Tokio came up at once to make his compliments with a comical mingling of Chinese courtesy and American awkwardness; and before he had got his hat on Jamie shouted with admiring energy, —

" Here 's another!   Oh, such a swell!"

They now came thick and fast for many hours; and the ladies stood bravely at their posts till late into the evening. Then Aunt Jessie went home, escorted by a very sleepy little son, and Aunt Plenty retired to bed used up. Dr. Alec had returned in good season; for *his* friends were not fashionable ones: but Aunt Myra had sent up for him in hot haste, and he had good-naturedly obeyed the summons. In fact, he was quite used to them now; for Mrs. Myra, having tried a variety of dangerous diseases, had finally deɩided upon heart-complaint as the ·one most likely to keep her friends in a chronic state of anxiety, and was continually sending word that she was dying. One gets used to palpitations as well as every thing else; so the doctor felt no alarm, but always went, and prescribed some harmless remedy with the most amiable sobriety and patience.

Rose was tired, but not sleepy, and wanted to think over several things; so instead of going to bed she sat down before the open fire in the study to wait for her uncle, and perhaps Charlie, though she did not expect him so late.

Aunt Myra's palpitations must have been unusually severe; for the clock struck twelve before Dr. Alec came, and Rose was preparing to end her reverie, when the sound of some one fumbling at the hall-door made her jump up, saying to herself, —

"Poor man! his hands are so cold he can't get his latch-key in. Is that you, uncle?" she added, running to admit him; for Jane was slow, and the night as bitter as it was brilliant.

A voice answered "Yes," and as the door swung open in walked, — not Dr. Alec, but Charlie, who immediately took one of the hall chairs, and sat there with his hat on, rubbing his gloveless hands, and blinking as if the light dazzled him, as he said in a rapid, abrupt sort of tone, —

"I told you I'd come — left the fellows keeping it up gloriously — going to see the old year out, you know. But I promised — never break my word — and here I am. Angel in blue, did you slay your thousands?"

"Hush! the waiters are still about: come to the

study fire and warm yourself; you must be frozen," said Rose, going before to roll up the easy-chair.

"Not at all — never warmer — looks very comfortable, though. Where's uncle?" asked Charlie, following with his hat still on, his hands in his pockets, and his eye fixed steadily on the bright head in front of him.

"Aunt Myra sent for him, and I was waiting up to see how she was," answered Rose, busily mending the fire.

Charlie laughed, and sat down upon a corner of the library table. "Poor old soul! what a pity she does n't die before he is quite worn out. A little too much ether some of these times would send her off quite comfortably, you know."

"Don't speak in that way. Uncle says imaginary troubles are often as hard to bear as real ones," said Rose, turning round displeased.

Till now she had not fairly looked at him; for recollections of the morning made her a little shy. His attitude and appearance surprised her as much as his words, and the quick change in her face seemed to remind him of his manners. Getting up, he hastily took off his hat, and stood looking at her with a curiously fixed yet absent look, as he said in the same rapid, abrupt way, as if, when once started, he found it hard to stop, —

"I beg pardon — only joking — very bad taste I know, and won't do it again. The heat of the room makes me a little dizzy, and I think I got a chill coming out. It *is* cold — I *am* frozen, I dare say — though I drove like the devil."

"Not that bad horse of yours, I hope? I know it is dangerous, so late and alone," said Rose, shrinking behind the big chair, as Charlie approached the fire, carefully avoiding a footstool in his way.

"Danger is exciting — that's why I like it. No man ever called me a coward — let him try it once. I never give in — and that horse shall *not* conquer me. I'll break his neck, if he breaks my spirit doing it. No — I don't mean that — never mind — it's all right," and Charlie laughed in a way that troubled her. beccause there was no mirth in it.

"Have you had a pleasant day?" asked Rose, looking at him intently, as he stood pondering over the cigar and match which he held, as if doubtful which to strike and which to smoke.

"Day? oh, yes, capital. About two thousand calls, and a nice little supper at the Club. Randal can't sing any more than a crow; but I left him with a glass of champagne upside-down trying to give them my old favorite,—

"'Tis better to laugh than be sighing;'"

and Charlie burst forth in that bacchanalian melody at the top of his voice, waving an allumette-holder over his head to represent Randal's inverted wine-glass.

"Hush! you'll wake aunty," cried Rose, in a tone so commanding that he broke off in the middle of a *roulade* to stare at her with a blank look, as he said apologetically,—

"I was merely showing how it should be done. Don't be angry, dearest — look at me as you did this morning, and I'll swear never to sing another note if you say so. I'm only a little gay — we drank your health handsomely, and they all congratulated

me. Told 'em it was n't out yet. Stop, though — I
did n't mean to mention that. No matter — I 'm
always in a scrape; but you always forgive me in the
sweetest way. Do it now, and don't be angry, little
darling; " and, dropping the vase, he went toward
her with a sudden excitement that made her shrink
behind the chair.

She was not angry, but shocked and frightened;
for she knew now what the matter was, and grew so
pale he saw it, and asked pardon before she could
utter a rebuke.

" We 'll talk of that to-morrow: it is very late; go
home, now, please, before uncle comes," she said, trying to speak naturally; yet betraying her distress by
the tremor of her voice, and the sad anxiety in her
eyes.

" Yes, yes, I will go — you are tired — I 'll make it
all right to-morrow; " and, as if the sound of his
uncle's name steadied him for an instant, Charlie
made for the door with an unevenness of gait which
would have told the shameful truth, if his words had
not already done so. Before he reached it, however,
the sound of wheels arrested him; and, leaning
against the wall, he listened with a look of dismay
mingled with amusement creeping over his face.
" Brutus has bolted — now I *am* in a fix. Can't walk
home with this horrid dizziness in my head. It 's the
cold, Rose, nothing else, I do assure you; and a chill
— yes, a chill. See here! let one of those fellows
there lend me an arm — no use to go after that brute.
Won't mother be frightened though, when he gets
home? " and with that empty laugh again, he fumbled
for the door-handle.

"No, no: don't let them see you! don't let any one know! Stay here till uncle comes, and he'll take care of you. O Charlie! how could you do it! how could you when you promised?" and, forgetting fear in the sudden sense of shame and anguish that came over her, Rose ran to him, caught his hand from the lock, and turned the key; then, as if she could not bear to see him standing there with that vacant smile upon his lips, she dropped into a chair and covered up her face.

The cry, the act, and more than all, the sight of the bowed head would have sobered poor Charlie, if it had not been too late. He looked about the room, with a vague, despairing look, as if to find the reason fast slipping from his control: but heat and cold, excitement and reckless pledging of many healths, had done their work too well to make instant sobriety possible, and owning his defeat with a groan, he turned away and threw himself face-downward on the sofa; one of the saddest sights the new year looked upon as it came in.

As she sat there with hidden eyes, Rose felt that something dear to her was dead for ever. The ideal, which all women cherish, look for, and too often think they have found when love glorifies a mortal man, is hard to give up, especially when it comes in the likeness of the first lover who touches a young girl's heart. Rose had just begun to feel that perhaps this cousin, despite his faults, might yet become the hero that he sometimes looked; and the thought that she might be his inspiration was growing sweet to her, although she had not entertained it until very lately. Alas, how short the tender dream had been, how rude

the awakening! how impossible it would be ever again
to surround that fallen figure with all the romance of
an innocent fancy, or gift it with the high attributes
beloved by a noble nature!

Breathing heavily in the sudden sleep that kindly
brought a brief oblivion of himself, he lay with flushed
cheeks, disordered hair, and at his feet the little rose,
that never would be fresh and fair again, — a pitiful
contrast now to the brave, blithe young man who
went so gayly out that morning to be so ignominiously
overthrown at night.

Many girls would have made light of a trespass so
readily forgiven by the world; but Rose had not yet
learned to offer temptation with a smile, and shut her
eyes to the weakness that makes a man a brute.   It
always grieved or disgusted her to see it in others, and
now it was very terrible to have it brought so near, —
not in its worst form, by any means, but bad enough
to wring her heart with shame and sorrow, and fill
her mind with dark forebodings for the future.   So
she could only sit mourning for the Charlie that
might have been, while watching the Charlie that was,
with an ache at her heart which found no relief till,
putting her hands there as if to ease the pain, they
touched the pansies, faded, but still showing gold
among the sombre purple; and then two great tears
dropped on them as she sighed, —

"Ah me!   I do need heart's-ease sooner than I
thought!"

Her uncle's step made her spring up and unlock
the door, showing him such an altered face that he
stopped short, ejaculating in dismay, —

"Good heavens, child! what's the matter?" adding,

as she pointed to the sofa in pathetic silence, "Is he hurt? — ill? — dead?"

"No, uncle: he is — " She could not utter the ugly word, but whispered, with a sob in her throat, "Be kind to him," and fled away to her own room, feeling as if a great disgrace had fallen on the house.

CHAPTER X

THE SAD AND SOBER PART

"HOW will he look? what will he say? can any thing make us forget and be happy again?" were the first questions Rose asked herself as soon as she woke from the brief sleep which followed a long, sad vigil. It seemed as if the whole world must be changed, because a trouble darkened it for her. She was too young yet to know how possible it is to forgive much greater sins than this forget far heavier disappointments, outlive higher hopes, and bury loves compared to which hers was but a girlish fancy. She wished it had not been so bright a day, wondered how her birds could sing with such shrill gayety, put no ribbon in her hair, and said, as she looked at the reflection of her own tired face in the glass, —

"Poor thing! you thought the new leaf would have something pleasant on it. The story has been very sweet and easy to read so far, but the sad and sober part is coming now."

A tap at the door reminded her that, in spite of her afflictions, breakfast must be eaten; and the sudden thought that Charlie might still be in the house made her hurry to the door, to find Dr. Alec waiting for her with his morning smile. She drew him in, and

whispered anxiously, as if some one lay dangerously
ill near by, —

"Is he better, uncle? Tell me all about it: I can
bear it now."

Some men would have smiled at her innocent distress, and told her this was only what was to be
expected and endured; but Dr. Alec believed in the
pure instincts that make youth beautiful, desired to
keep them true, and hoped his girl would never learn
to look unmoved by pain and pity upon any human
being vanquished by a vice, no matter how trivial it
seemed, how venial it was held. So his face grew
grave, though his voice was cheerful as he answered, —

"All right, I dare say, by this time; for sleep is
the best medicine in such cases. I took him home
last night, and no one knows he came but you
and I."

"No one ever shall. How did you do it, uncle?"

"Just slipped out of the long study-window, and
got him cannily off; for the air and motion, after a
dash of cold water, brought him round, and he was
glad to be safely landed at home. His rooms are
below, you know: so no one was disturbed, and I
left him sleeping nicely."

"Thank you so much," sighed Rose. "And
Brutus? were n't they frightened when he got back
alone?"

"Not at all: the sagacious beast went quietly to
the stable, and the sleepy groom asked no questions;
for Charlie often sends the horse round by himself
when it is late or stormy. Rest easy, dear: no eye
but ours saw the poor lad come and go, and we'll
forgive it for love's sake."

"Yes, but not forget it. *I* never can; and he will never be again to me the Charlie I've been so proud and fond of all these years. O uncle, such a pity! such a pity!"

"Don't break your tender heart about it, child; for it is not incurable, thank God! I don't make light of it; but I am sure that under better influences Charlie will redeem himself, because his impulses are good, and this his only vice. I can hardly blame him for what he is, because his mother did the harm. I declare to you, Rose, I sometimes feel as if I must break out against that woman, and thunder in her ears that she is ruining the immortal soul for which she is responsible to heaven."

Dr. Alec seldom spoke in this way, and when he did it was rather awful; for his indignation was of the righteous sort, and such thunder often rouses up a drowsy soul when sunshine has no effect. Rose liked it, and sincerely wished Aunt Clara had been there to get the benefit of the outbreak; for she needed just such an awakening from the self-indulgent dream in which she lived.

"Do it, and save Charlie before it is too late!" she cried, kindling herself as she watched him; for he looked like a roused lion, as he walked about the room, with his hand clenched and a spark in his eye, evidently in desperate earnest, and ready to do most any thing.

"Will you help?" he asked, stopping suddenly, with a look that made her stand up straight and strong as she answered with an eager voice, —

"I will."

"Then don't love him — yet."

That startled her; but she asked steadily, though her heart began to beat and her color to come, —

"Why not ? "

"Firstly, because no woman should give her happiness into the keeping of a man without fixed principles; secondly, because the hope of being worthy of you will help him more than any prayers or preaching of mine. Thirdly, because it will need all our wit and patience to undo the work of nearly four and twenty years. You understand what I mean ? "

"Yes, sir."

" Can you say ' No ' when he asks you to say ' Yes,' and wait a little for your happiness ? "

"I can."

" And will **you?** "

" I will."

" Then I 'm satisfied, and a great weight taken off my heart. I can't help seeing what goes on, or trembling when I think of you setting sail with no better pilot than poor Charlie. Now you answer as I hoped you would, and I am proud of my girl ! "

They had been standing with the width of the room between them, Dr. Alec looking very much like a commander issuing orders, Rose like a well-drilled private obediently receiving them; and both wore the air of soldiers getting ready for a battle, with the bracing of nerves and quickening of the blood brave souls feel as they put on their armor. At the last words he went to her, brushed back the hair, and kissed her on the forehead with a tender sort of gravity, and a look that made her feel as if he had endowed her with the Victoria cross for courage on the field.

No more was said then; for Aunt Plenty called
them down, and the day's duties began. But that
brief talk showed Rose what to do, and fitted her to
do it; for it set her to thinking of the duty one owes
one's self in loving as in all the other great passions
or experiences which make or mar a life.

She had plenty of time for quiet meditation that
day, because every one was resting after yesterday's
festivity; and she sat in her little room planning out
a new year, so full of good works, grand successes,
and beautiful romances, that if it could have been
realized the Millennium would have begun. It was a
great comfort to her, however, and lightened the long
hours haunted by a secret desire to know when
Charlie would come, and a secret fear of the first
meeting. She was sure he would be bowed down
with humiliation and repentance, and a struggle took
place in her mind between the pity she could not help
feeling, and the disapprobation she ought to show.
She decided to be gentle, but very frank; to reprove,
but also to console, and try to improve the softened
moment by inspiring the culprit with a wish for all the
virtues which make a perfect man.

This fond delusion grew quite absorbing, and her
mind was full of it as she sat watching the sun set
from her western window, and admiring with dreamy
eyes the fine effect of the distant hills clear and dark
against a daffodil sky, when the bang of a door made
her sit suddenly erect in her low chair, and say with
a catch in her breath, —

" He is coming! I must remember what I promised
uncle, and be very firm."

Usually Charlie announced his approach with music

of some sort: now he neither whistled, hummed, nor sung, but came so quietly Rose was sure that he dreaded the meeting as much as she did, and, compassionating his natural confusion, did not look round as the steps drew near. She thought perhaps he would go down upon his knees, as he used to after a boyish offence, but hoped not; for too much humility distressed her: so she waited for the first demonstration anxiously.

It was rather a shock when it came, however; for a great nosegay dropped into her lap, and a voice, bold and gay as usual, said lightly, —

" Here she is, as pretty and pensive as you please. Is the world hollow, our doll stuffed with sawdust, and do we want to go into a nunnery to-day, cousin?"

Rose was so taken aback by this unexpected coolness that the flowers lay unnoticed, as she looked up with a face so full of surprise, reproach, and something like shame, that it was impossible to mistake its meaning. Charlie did not; and had the grace to redden deeply, and his eyes fell, as he said quickly, though in the same light tone, —

"I humbly apologize for — coming so late last night. Don't be hard upon me, cousin: you know America expects every man to do his duty on New-Year's day."

"I am tired of forgiving! You make and break promises as easily as you did years ago, and I shall never ask you for another," answered Rose, putting the bouquet away; for the apology did not satisfy her, and she would not be bribed to silence.

" But, my dear girl, you are so very exacting, so peculiar in your notions, and so angry about trifles.

that a poor fellow can't please you, try as he will,"
began Charlie, ill at ease, but too proud to show half
the penitence he felt, not so much for the fault as for
her discovery of it.

"I am not angry: I am grieved and disappointed;
for *I* expect every man to do his duty in another way,
and keep his word to the uttermost, as I try to do.
If that is exacting, I'm sorry, and won't trouble you
with my old-fashioned notions any more."

"Bless my soul! what a rout about nothing! I
own that I forgot: I know I acted like a fool, and
I beg pardon; what more *can* I do?"

"Act like a man, and never let me be so terribly
ashamed of you again as I was last night," and Rose
gave a little shiver as she thought of it.

That involuntary act hurt Charlie more than her
words, and it was his turn now to feel "terribly
ashamed;" for the events of the previous evening
were very hazy in his mind, and fear magnified them
greatly. Turning sharply away, he went and stood
by the fire, quite at a loss how to make his peace this
time, because Rose was so unlike herself. Usually a
word of excuse sufficed, and she seemed glad to pardon and forget; now, though very quiet, there was
something almost stern about her that surprised and
daunted him; for how could he know that all the
while her pitiful heart was pleading for him, and the
very effort to control it made her seem a little hard
and cold? As he stood there, restlessly fingering the
ornaments upon the chimney-piece, his eye brightened
suddenly; and, taking up the pretty bracelet lying
there, he went slowly back to her, saying in a tone
that was humble and serious enough now, —

"I *will* act like a man, and you shall never be ashamed again. Only be kind to me : let me put this on, and promise afresh; this time I swear I'll keep it. Won't you trust me, Rose?"

It was very hard to resist the pleading voice and eyes: for this humility was dangerous; and, but for Uncle Alec, Rose would have answered "Yes." The blue forget-me-nots reminded her of her own promise; and she kept it with difficulty now, to be glad always afterward. Putting back the offered trinket with a gentle touch, she said firmly, though she dared not look up into the anxious face bending toward her, —

"No, Charlie: I can't wear it yet. My hands must be free if I'm to help you as I ought. I will be kind; I will trust you: but don't swear any thing, only try to resist temptation, and we'll all stand by you."

Charlie did not like that, and lost the ground he had gained by saying impetuously, —

"I don't want any one but you to stand by me, and I must be sure you won't desert me, else, while I'm mortifying soul and body to please you, some stranger will come and steal your heart away from me. I could n't bear that; so I give you fair warning, in such a case I'll break the bargain, and go straight to the devil."

The last sentence spoilt it all; for it was both masterful and defiant. Rose had the Campbell spirit in her, though it seldom showed; as yet she valued her liberty more than any love offered her, and she resented the authority he assumed too soon, — resented it all the more warmly, because of the effort she was making to reinstate her hero, who would insist on being a very faulty and ungrateful man. She rose straight out of her chair, saying with a look and tone which rather startled her hearer, and convinced him that she was no longer a tender-hearted child, but a woman with a will of her own, and a spirit as proud and fiery as any of her race, —

"My heart is my own, to dispose of as I please. Don't shut yourself out of it by presuming too much; for you have no claim on me but that of cousinship, and you never will have unless you earn it. Remember that, and neither threaten nor defy me any more."

For a minute it was doubtful whether Charlie would answer this flash with another, and a general explosion ensue; or wisely quench the flame with the mild answer which turneth away wrath. He chose the latter course, and made it very effective by throwing himself down before his offended goddess, as he had often done in jest; this time it was not acting, but serious earnest, and there was real passion in his voice, as he caught Rose's dress in both hands, saying eagerly, —

"No, no! don't shut your heart against me, or I shall turn desperate. I'm not half good enough for such a saint as you, but you can do what you will with me. I only need a motive to make a man of me, and where can I find a stronger one than in trying to keep your love?"

"It is not yours yet," began Rose, much moved, though all the while she felt as if she was on a stage, and had a part to play; for Charlie had made life so like a melodrama that it was hard for him to be quite simple even when most sincere.

"Let me earn it, then. Show me how, and I'll do any thing: for you are my good angel, Rose;

and, if you cast me off, I feel as if I should n't care
how soon there was an end of me," cried Charlie,
getting tragic in his earnestness, and putting both
arms round her, as if his only safety lay in clinging
to this beloved fellow-creature.

Behind footlights it would have been irresistible;
but somehow it did not touch the one spectator,
though she had neither time nor skill to discover
why. For all their ardor the words did not ring
quite true: despite the grace of the attitude, she
would have liked him better manfully erect upon his
feet; and, though the gesture was full of tenderness,
a subtle instinct made her shrink away, as she said
with a composure that surprised herself, even more
than it did him, —

"Please don't. No, I will promise nothing yet;
for I must respect the man I love."

That brought Charlie to his feet, pale with something deeper than anger; for the recoil told him more
plainly than the words how much he had fallen in her
regard since yesterday. The memory of the happy
moment when she gave the rose with that new softness in her eyes, the shy color, the sweet "for my
sake," came back with sudden vividness, contrasting
sharply with the now averted face, the hand out-
stretched to put him back, the shrinking figure: and
in that instant's silence poor Charlie realized what
he had lost; for a girl's first thought of love is as
delicate a thing as the rosy morning-glory, that a
breath of air can shatter. Only a hint of evil, only
an hour's debasement for him, a moment's glimpse
for her of the coarser pleasures men know, and the
innocent heart, just opening to bless and to be blessed,

closed again like a sensitive plant, and shut him out perhaps for ever.

The consciousness of this turned him pale with fear: for his love was deeper than she knew; and he proved this when he said in a tone so full of mingled pain and patience that it touched her to the heart, —

"You *shall* respect me if I can make you; and when I've earned it may I hope for something more?"

She looked up then, saw in his face the noble shame, the humble sort of courage, that shows repentance to be genuine, and gives promise of success, and, with a hopeful smile that was a cordial to him, answered heartily, —

"You may."

"Bless you for that! I'll make no promises, I'll ask for none: only trust me, Rose; and, while you treat me like a cousin, remember that no matter how many lovers you may have, you'll never be to any of them as dear as you are to me."

A traitorous break in his voice warned Charlie to stop there: and, with no other good-by, he very wisely went away, leaving Rose to put the neglected flowers into water with remorseful care, and lay away the bracelet, saying to herself, —

"I'll never wear it till I feel as I did before; then he shall put it on, and I'll say 'Yes.'"

CHAPTER XI

"O ROSE, I've got something *so* exciting to tell you!" cried Kitty Van Tassel, skipping into the carriage next morning when her friend called for her to go shopping.

Kitty always did have some "perfectly thrilling" communication to make, and Rose had learned to take them quietly: but the next demonstration was a new one; for, regardless alike of curious observers outside and disordered hats within, Kitty caught Rose round the neck, exclaiming in a rapturous whisper, —

"My dearest creature, I'm engaged!"

"I'm so glad!   Of course it is Steve?"

"Dear fellow, he did it last night in the nicest way, and mamma is *so* delighted.   Now what *shall* I be married in?" and Kitty composed herself with a face full of the deepest anxiety.

"How can you talk of that so soon?   Why, Kit, you unromantic girl, you ought to be thinking of your lover and not your clothes," said Rose, amused, yet rather scandalized at such want of sentiment.

"I *am* thinking of my lover; for he says he will *not* have a long engagement, so I *must* begin to think about the most important things at once, must n't I?"

"Ah, he wants to be sure of you; for you are such a slippery creature he is afraid you'll treat him as you did poor Jackson and the rest," interrupted Rose, shaking her finger at her prospective cousin, who had tried this pastime twice before, and was rather proud than otherwise of her brief engagements.

"You need n't scold, for I know I 'm right; and, when you 've been in society as long as I have, you 'll find that the only way to really know a man is to be engaged to him. While they want you, they are all devotion; but when they think they 've got you, then you find out what wretches they are," answered Kitty, with an air of worldly wisdom which contrasted oddly with her youthful face and giddy manners.

"A sad prospect for poor Steve, unless I give him a hint to look well to his ways."

"O my dear child, I 'm sure of him; for my experience has made me very sharp, and I 'm convinced I can manage him without a bit of trouble. We 've known each other for ages" (Steve was twenty and Kitty eighteen), "and always been the best of friends. Besides he is quite my ideal man: I never *could* bear big hands and feet, and his are simply adorable. Then he 's the best dancer I know, and dresses in perfect taste. I really do believe I fell in love with his pocket-handkerchiefs first; they were so enchanting I could n't resist," laughed Kitty, pulling a large one out of her pocket, and burying her little nose in the folds, which shed a delicious fragrance upon the air.

"Now that looks promising, and I begin to think you *have* got a little sentiment after all," said Rose, well pleased; for the merry brown eyes had softened suddenly, and a quick color came up in Kitty's cheek, as she answered, still half hiding her face in the beloved handkerchief, —

"Of course I have, lots of it; only I 'm ashamed

to show it to most people, because it 's the style to take every thing in the most nonchalant way. My gracious, Rose, you 'd have thought me a romantic goose last night while Steve proposed in the back parlor : for I actually cried ; he was so dreadfully in earnest when I pretended that I did n't care for him, and so very dear and nice when I told the truth. I did n't know he had it in him ; but he came out delightfully, and never cared a particle, though I dropped tears all over his lovely shirt-front. Was n't that good of him? for you know he hates his things to be mussed."

"He 's a true Campbell, and has got a good warm heart of his own under those fine fronts of his. Aunt Jane does n't believe in sentiment, so he has been trained never to show any : but it is there, and you must encourage him to let it out ; not foolishly, but in a way to make him more manly and serious."

"I will if I can ; for, though I would n't own this to everybody, I like it in him very much, and feel as if Steve and I should get on beautifully. Here we are : now be sure not to breathe a word if we meet any one ; I want it to be a profound secret for a week at least," added Kitty, whisking the handkerchief out of sight, as the carriage stopped before the fashionable store they were about to visit.

Rose promised with a smile ; for Kitty's face betrayed her without words, so full was it of the happiness which few eyes fail to understand wherever they see it.

"Just a glance at the silks. You ask my opinion about white ones, and I 'll look at the colors. Mamma says satin ; but that is out now, and I 've set my heart on the heaviest corded thing I can find," whispered Kitty, as they went rustling by the long counters strewn with all that could delight the feminine eye, and tempt the feminine pocket.

"Isn't that opal the loveliest thing you ever saw? I'm afraid I'm too dark to wear it, but it would just suit you. You'll need a variety you know," added Kitty in a significant aside, as Rose stood among the white silks, while her companion affected great interest in the delicate hues laid before her.

"But I have a variety now, and don't need a new dress of any sort."

"No matter, get it; else it will be gone: you've worn all yours several times already, and *must* have a new one whether you need it or not. Dear me! if I had as much pocket-money as you have, I'd come out in a fresh toilet at every party I went to," answered Kitty, casting an envious eye upon the rainbow piles before her.

The quick-witted shopman saw that a wedding was afoot; for when two pretty girls whisper, smile, and blush over their shopping, clerks scent bridal finery, and a transient gleam of interest brightens their imperturbable countenances, and lends a brief energy to languid voices weary with crying "Cash!" Gathering both silks with a practised turn of the hand, he held them up for inspection, detecting at a glance which was the bride-elect and which the friend; for Kitty fell back to study the effect of the silvery white folds with an absorbing interest impossible to mistake, while Rose sat looking at the opal as if she scarcely heard a bland voice saying, with the rustle of silk so dear to girlish ears, —

"A superb thing; just opened; all the rage in Paris; very rare shade; trying to most, as the lady says, but quite perfect for a blonde."

Rose was not listening to those words, but to others which Aunt Clara had lately uttered; laughed at then, but thought over more than once since.

"I 'm tired of hearing people wonder why Miss Campbell does not dress more. Simplicity is all very well for school-girls and women who can't afford any thing better, but *you* can, and you really ought. Your things are pretty enough in their way, and I rather like you to have a style of your own; but it looks odd and people will think you are mean if you don't make more show. Besides, you don't do justice to your beauty, which would be both peculiar and striking, if you 'd devote your mind to getting up ravishing costumes."

Much more to the same effect did her aunt say, discussing the subject quite artistically, and unconsciously appealing to several of Rose's ruling passions. One was a love for the delicate fabrics, colors, and ornaments which refined tastes enjoy, and whose costliness keeps them from ever growing common; another, her strong desire to please the eyes of those she cared for, and gratify their wishes in the smallest matter if she could. And last, but not least, the natural desire of a young and pretty woman to enhance the beauty which she so soon discovers to be her most potent charm for the other sex, her passport to a high place among her maiden peers.

She had thought seriously of surprising and delighting every one, by appearing in a costume which should do justice to the loveliness which was so modest that

it was apt to forget itself in admiring others, — what
girls call a " ravishing" dress, such as she could
imagine and easily procure by the magic of the
Fortunatus' purse in her pocket. She had planned
it all, the shimmer of pale silk through lace like woven
frostwork, ornaments of some classic pattern, and all
the dainty accessaries as perfect as time, taste, and
money could make them.

She knew that Uncle Alec's healthful training had
given her a figure that could venture on any fashion,
and Nature blessed her with a complexion that defied
all hues. So it was little wonder that she felt a
strong desire to use these gifts, not for the pleasure
of display, but to seem fair in the eyes that seldom
looked at her without a tender sort of admiration, all
the more winning when no words marred the involuntary homage women love.

These thoughts were busy in Rose's mind, as she
sat looking at the lovely silk, and wondering what
Charlie would say if she should some night burst
upon him in a pale, rosy cloud, like the Aurora to
whom he often likened her. She knew it would
please him very much, and she longed to do all she
honestly could to gratify the poor fellow; for her
tender heart already felt some remorseful pangs,
remembering how severe she had been the night
before. She could not revoke her words, because
she meant them every one; but she might be kind,
and show that she did not wholly shut him out from
her regard, by asking him to go with her to Kitty's
ball, and gratify his artistic taste by a lovely costume.
A very girlish but kindly plan; for that ball was to
be the last of her frivolities, so she wanted it to be a

pleasant one, and felt that "being friends" with
Charlie would add much to her enjoyment. This
idea made her fingers tighten on the gleaming fabric
so temptingly upheld, and she was about to take it
when, "If ye please, sir, would ye kindly tell me
where I'd be finding the flannel place?" said a voice
behind her; and, glancing up, she saw a meek little
Irishwoman looking quite lost and out of place among
the luxuries around her.

"Downstairs, turn to the left," was the clerk's hasty
reply, with a vague wave of the hand which left the
inquirer more in the dark than ever.

Rose saw the woman's perplexity, and said kindly.
"I'll show you: this way."

"I'm ashamed to be throublin' ye, miss; but it's
strange I am in it, and would n't be comin' here at all,
at all, barrin' they tould me I'd get the bit I'm
wantin' chaper in this big shop than the little ones
more becomin' the like o' me," explained the little
woman humbly.

Rose looked again, as she led the way through a
well-dressed crowd of busy shoppers: and something
in the anxious, tired face under the old woollen hood;
the bare, purple hands, holding fast a meagre wallet
and a faded scrap of the dotted flannel little children's
frocks are so often made of, — touched the generous
heart, that never could see want without an impulse
to relieve it.   She had meant only to point the way;
but, following a new impulse, she went on, listening
to the poor soul's motherly prattle about "me baby,'
and the "throuble" it was to "find clothes for the
growin' childer, when me man is out av work, and
the bit and sup inconvaynient these hard times." as

they descended to that darksome lower world, where necessities take refuge when luxuries crowd them out from the gayer place above.

The presence of a lady made Mrs. Sullivan's shopping very easy now; and her one poor "bit" of flannel grew miraculously into yards of several colors, since the shabby purse was no lighter when she went away, wiping her eyes on the corner of a big, brown bundle. A very little thing, and no one saw it but a wooden-faced clerk, who never told; yet it did Rose good, and sent her up into the light again with a sober face, thinking self-reproachfully, —

"What right have I to more gay gowns, when some poor babies have none; or to spend time making myself fine, while there is so much bitter want in the world?"

Nevertheless the pretty things were just as tempting as ever, and she yearned for the opal silk with a renewed yearning when she got back. I am not sure that it would not have been bought in spite of her better self, if a good angel in the likeness of a stout lady with silvery curls about the benevolent face, enshrined in a plain bonnet, had not accosted her as she joined Kitty, still brooding over the wedding gowns.

"I waited a moment for you, my dear, because I'm in haste, and very glad to save myself a journey or a note," began the newcomer in a low tone, as Rose shook hands with the most affectionate respect. "You know the great box factory was burned a day or two ago, and over a hundred girls thrown out of work. Some were hurt and are in the hospital, many have no homes to go to, and nearly all need temporary help

of some sort. We've had so many calls this winter
I hardly know which way to turn; for the want is
pressing, and I've had my finger in so many purses
I'm almost ashamed to ask again. Any little con-
tribution — ah, thank you; I was sure you would n't
fail me, my good child," and Mrs. Gardener warmly
pressed the hand that went so quickly into the little
portemonnaie, and came out so generously filled.

" Let me know how else I can help, and thank you
very much for allowing me to have a share in your
good works," said Rose, forgetting all about gay
gowns, as she watched the black bonnet go briskly
away, with an approving smile on the fine old face
inside it.

" You extravagant thing! how could you give so
much?" whispered Kitty, whose curious eye had seen
three figures on the single bill which had so rapidly
changed hands.

" I believe if Mrs. Gardener asked me for my head
I should give it to her," answered Rose lightly; then
turning to the silks she asked, " Which have you decided upon; the yellow white or the blue, the corded
or the striped?"

" I've decided nothing, except that *you* are to have
the pink, and wear it at my — ahem! ball," said
Kitty, who *had* made up her mind, but could not
give her orders till mamma had been consulted.

"No, I can't afford it just yet. I never overstep
my allowance, and I shall have to if I get any more
finery. Come, we ought not to waste time here, if
you have all the patterns you want," and Rose
walked quickly away, glad that it was out of her
power to break through two resolutions which hith-

erto had been faithfully kept, — one to dress simply for example's sake, the other not to be extravagant for charity's sake.

As Rosamond had her day of misfortunes, so this seemed to be one of small temptations to Rose. After she had set Kitty down at home and been to see her new houses, she drove about doing various errands for the aunts; and, while waiting in the carriage for the execution of an order, young Pemberton came by.

As Steve said, this gentleman had been " hard hit," and still hovered moth-like about the forbidden light. Being the most eligible *parti* of the season, his regard was considered a distinction to be proud of; and Rose had been well scolded by Aunt Clara for refusing so honorable a mate. The girl liked him; and he was the suitor of whom she had spoken so respectfully to Dr. Alec, because he had no need of the heiress, and had sincerely loved the woman. He had been away, and she hoped had got over his disappointment as happily as the rest; but now when he saw her, and came hurrying up so hungry for a word, she felt that he had not forgotten, and was too kind to chill him with the bow which plainly says, " Don't stop."

A personable youth was Pemberton, and had brought with him from the wilds of Canada a sable-lined overcoat, which was the envy of every masculine and the admiration of every feminine friend he had; and, as he stood at her carriage window, Rose knew that this luxurious garment and its stalwart wearer were objects of interest to the passers-by. It chanced that the tide of shoppers flowed in that direction; and, as she chatted, familiar faces often passed with glances, smiles, and nods of varying curiosity, significance, and wonder.

She could not help feeling a certain satisfaction in giving him a moment's pleasure, since she could do no more; but it was not that amiable desire alone which made her ignore the neat white parcels which the druggist's boy deposited on the front seat, and kept her lingering a little longer to enjoy one of the small triumphs which girls often risk more than a cold in the head to display. The sight of several snow-flakes on the broad shoulders which partially obstructed her view, as well as the rapidly increasing animation of Pemberton's chat, reminded her that it was high time to go.

" I mustn't keep you: it is beginning to storm," she said, taking up her muff, much to old Jacob's satisfaction; for small talk is not exciting to a hungry man whose nose feels like an icicle.

" Is it? I thought the sun was shining." And the absorbed gentleman turned to the outer world with visible reluctance, for it looked very warm and cosey in the red-lined carriage.

" Wise people say we must carry our sunshine with us," answered Rose, taking refuge in commonplaces, for the face at the window grew pensive suddenly, as he answered, with a longing look, —

" I wish I could: " then, smiling gratefully, he added, " Thank you for giving me a little of yours."

" You are very welcome." And Rose offered him her hand, while her eyes mutely asked pardon for withholding her leave to keep it.

He pressed it silently, and, shouldering the umbrella which he forgot to open, turned away, with an " up-again-and-take-another" expression, which caused the soft eyes to follow him admiringly.

" I ought not to have kept him a minute longer than I could help: for it was n't all pity; it was my foolish wish to show off and do as I liked for a minute, to pay for being good about the gown. Oh me! how weak and silly I am in spite of all my trying!" And Miss Campbell fell into a remorseful reverie, which lasted till she got home.

" Now, young man, what brought you out in this driving storm?" asked Rose, as Jamie came stamping in that same afternoon.

" Mamma sent you a new book,— thought you 'd like it: *I* don't mind your old storms!" replied the boy, wrestling his way out of his coat, and presenting a face as round and red and shiny as a well-polished Baldwin apple.

" Much obliged: it is just the day to enjoy it, and I was longing for something nice to read," said Rose, as Jamie sat down upon the lower stair for a protracted struggle with his rubber boots.

" Here you are, then — no — yes — I do believe I 've forgotten it, after all! " cried Jamie, slapping his pockets one after the other, with a dismayed expression of countenance.

" Never mind: I 'll hunt up something else. Let me help with those: your hands are so cold." And Rose good-naturedly gave a tug at the boots, while Jamie clutched the banisters; murmuring somewhat incoherently, as his legs flew up and down, —

" I 'll go back if you want me to. I 'm so sorry! It 's very good of you, I 'm sure. Getting these horrid things on made me forget. Mother would make me wear 'em, though I told her they'd stick like — like gumdrops," he added, inspired by recollections of certain dire disappointments when the above-mentioned sweetmeat melted in his pockets, and refused to come out.

"Now what shall we do?" asked Rose, when he was finally extricated. "Since I've nothing to read, I may as well play."

"I'll teach you to pitch and toss. You catch very well for a girl, but you can't throw worth a cent," replied Jamie, gambading down the hall in his slippers, and producing a ball from some of the mysterious receptacles in which boys have the art of storing rubbish enough to fill a peck measure.

Of course Rose agreed, and cheerfully risked getting her eyes blackened and her fingers bruised, till her young preceptor gratefully observed that "it was no fun playing where you had to look out for windows and jars and things; so I'd like that jolly book about Captain Nemo and the 'Nautilus,' please."

Being gratified, he spread himself upon the couch, crossed his legs in the air, and without another word dived "Twenty Thousand Leagues Under the Sea," where he remained for two mortal hours, to the general satisfaction of his relatives.

Bereft both of her unexpected playfellow and the much-desired book, Rose went into the parlor, there to discover a French novel, which Kitty had taken from a library and left in the carriage among the bundles. Settling herself in her favorite lounging-chair, she read as diligently as Jamie, while the wind howled and snow fell fast without.

For an hour, nothing disturbed the cosey quiet of

the house; for Aunt Plenty was napping upstairs, and Dr. Alec writing in his own sanctum; at least, Rose thought so, till his step made her hastily drop the book, and look up with very much the expression she used to wear when caught in mischief years ago.

"Did I startle you? Have a screen: you are burning your face before this hot fire." And Dr. Alec pulled one forward.

"Thank you, uncle; I did n't feel it." And the color seemed to deepen in spite of the screen, while the uneasy eyes fell upon the book in her lap.

"Have you got the 'Quarterly' there? I want to glance at an article in it, if you can spare it for a moment," he said, leaning toward her with an inquiring glance.

"No, sir: I am reading —" And, without mentioning the name, Rose put the book into his hand.

The instant his eye fell on the title, he understood the look she wore, and knew what "mischief" she had been in. He knit his brows: then smiled, because it was impossible to help it; Rose looked so conscience-stricken in spite of her twenty years.

"How do you find it? — interesting?"

"Oh, very! I felt as if I was in another world, and forgot all about this."

"Not a very good world, I fancy, if you were afraid or ashamed to be found in it. Where did this come from?" asked Dr. Alec, surveying the book with great disfavor.

Rose told him, and added slowly, —

"I particularly wanted to read it, and fancied I might, because you did when it was so much talked about the winter we were in Rome."

" I did read it to see if it was fit for you."

" And decided that it was not, I suppose; since you never gave it to me?"

" Yes."

" Then I won't finish it. But, uncle, I don't see why I should not," added Rose, wistfully; for she had reached the heart of the romance and found it wonderfully fascinating.

"You may not *see*, but don't you *feel* why not?" asked Dr. Alec, gravely.

Rose leaned her flushed cheek on her hand and thought a minute; then looked up, and answered honestly, —

" Yes, I do: but can't explain it; except that I know something *must* be wrong, because I blushed and started when you came in."

" Exactly," and the doctor gave an emphatic nod, as if the symptoms pleased him.

" But I really don't see any harm in the book so far. It is by a famous author, wonderfully well written as you know, and the characters so life-like that I feel as if I should really meet them somewhere."

" I hope not!" ejaculated the doctor, shutting the book quickly, as if to keep the objectionable beings from escaping.

Rose laughed, but persisted in her defence; for she did want to finish the absorbing story, yet would not without leave.

" I have read French novels before, and you gave them to me. Not many to be sure, but the best; so I think I know what is good, and should n't like this if it was harmful."

Her uncle's answer was to reopen the volume and

turn the leaves an instant as if to find a particular place; then he put it into her hand, saying quietly,—

"Read a page or two aloud, translating as you go. You used to like that: try it again."

Rose obeyed, and went glibly down a page, doing her best to give the sense in her purest English. Presently she went more slowly, then skipped a sentence here and there, and finally stopped short, looking as if she needed a screen again.

"What's the matter?" asked her uncle, who had been watching her with a serious eye.

"Some phrases are untranslatable, and it only spoils them to try. They are not amiss in French, but sound coarse and bad in our blunt English," she said a little pettishly; for she felt annoyed by her failure to prove the contested point.

"Ah, my dear! if the fine phrases won't bear putting into honest English, the thoughts they express won't bear putting into your innocent mind. That chapter is the key to the whole book; and if you had been led up, or rather down, to it artfully and artistically, you might have read it to yourself without seeing how bad it is. All the worse for the undeniable talent which hides the evil so subtly and makes the danger so delightful."

He paused a moment, then added with an anxious glance at the book, over which she was still bending, —

"Finish it if you choose: only remember, my girl, that one may read at forty what is unsafe at twenty, and that we never can be too careful what food we give that precious yet perilous thing called imagination."

And taking his "Review" he went away to look over a learned article which interested him much less than the workings of a young mind near by.

Another long silence, broken only by an occasional excited bounce from Jamie, when the sociable cuttle-fish looked in at the windows, or the "Nautilus" scuttled a ship or two in its terrific course. A bell rang, and the doctor popped his head out to see if he was wanted. It was only a message for Aunt Plenty, and he was about to pop in again when his eye was caught by a square parcel on the slab.

"What's this?" he asked, taking it up.

"Rose wants me to leave it at Kitty Van's when I go. I forgot to bring her book from mamma; so I shall go and get it as soon as ever I've done this," replied Jamie, from his nest.

As the volume in his hands was a corpulent one, and Jamie only a third of the way through, Dr. Alec thought Rose's prospect rather doubtful; and, slipping the parcel into his pocket, he walked away, saying with a satisfied air, —

"Virtue does n't always get rewarded; but it shall be this time, if I can do it."

More than half an hour afterward, Rose woke from a little nap, and found the various old favorites with which she had tried to solace herself, replaced by the simple, wholesome story promised by Aunt Jessie.

"Good boy! I'll go and thank him," she said, half-aloud; jumping up, wide awake and much pleased.

But she did not go; for, just then, she espied her

uncle standing on the rug warming his hands with
a generally fresh and breezy look about him, which
suggested a recent struggle with the elements.

" How did this come? " she asked suspiciously.

" A man brought it."

" This man? O uncle! why did you take so much
trouble just to gratify a wish of mine?" she cried,
taking both the cold hands in hers, with a tenderly
reproachful glance from the storm without to the
ruddy face above her.

" Because, having taken away your French bonbons
with the poisonous color on them, I wanted to get
you something better. Here it is, all pure sugar; the
sort that sweetens the heart as well as the tongue,
and leaves no bad taste behind."

" How good you are to me! I don't deserve it;
for I did n't resist temptation, though I tried. Uncle,
after I 'd put the book away, I thought I *must* just
see how it ended, and I 'm afraid I should have read
it all if it had not been gone," said Rose, laying her
face down on the hands she held, as humbly as a
repentant child.

But Uncle Alec lifted up the bent head, and looking into the eyes that met his frankly, though either
held a tear, he said, with the energy that always made
his words remembered, —

" My little girl, I would face a dozen storms far
worse than this to keep your soul as stainless as
snow; for it is the small temptations which under-
mine integrity, unless we watch and pray, and never
think them too trivial to be resisted."

Some people would consider Dr. Alec an over-
careful man: but Rose felt that he was right; and.

when she said her prayers that night, added a meek petition to be kept from yielding to three of the small temptations which beset a rich, pretty, and romantic girl, — extravagance, coquetry, and novel-reading.

CHAPTER XII

ROSE had no new gown to wear on this festive occasion, and gave one little sigh of regret as she put on the pale blue silk, refreshed with clouds of *gaze de Chambéry*. But a smile followed, very bright and sweet, as she added the clusters of forget-me-not which Charlie had conjured up through the agency of an old German florist: for one part of her plan *had* been carried out, and Prince was invited to be her escort, much to his delight; though he wisely made no protestations of any sort, and showed his gratitude by being a model gentleman. This pleased Rose; for the late humiliation and a very sincere desire to atone for it, gave him an air of pensive dignity which was very effective.

Aunt Clara could not go; for a certain new cosmetic, privately used to improve the once fine complexion, which had been her pride till late hours impaired it, had brought out an unsightly eruption, reducing her to the depths of woe, and leaving her no solace for her disappointment but the sight of the elegant velvet dress spread forth upon her bed in melancholy state.

So Aunt Jessie was chaperon, to Rose's great satisfaction, and looked as "pretty as a pink," Archie thought, in her matronly pearl-colored gown, with a dainty trifle of rich lace on her still abundant hair. He was very proud of his little mamma, and as devoted as a lover, " to keep his hand in against Phebe's return," she said laughingly, when he brought her a nosegay of blush-roses to light up her quiet costume.

A happier mother did not live than Mrs. Jessie, as she sat contentedly beside Sister Jane (who graced the frivolous scene in a serious black gown with a diadem of purple asters nodding above her severe brow), both watching their boys with the maternal conviction that no other parent could show such remarkable specimens as these.   Each had done her best according to her light; and years of faithful care were now beginning to bear fruit in the promise of goodly men, so dear to the hearts of true mothers.

Mrs. Jessie watched her three tall sons with something like wonder; for Archie was a fine fellow, grave and rather stately, but full of the cordial courtesy and respect we see so little of now-a-days, and which is the sure sign of good home-training.   " The cadets," as Will and Geordie called themselves, were there as gorgeous as you please; and the agonies they suffered that night with tight boots and stiff collars no pen can fitly tell.   But only to one another did they confide these sufferings, in the rare moments of repose when they could stand on one aching foot with heads comfortably sunken inside the excruciating collars, which rasped their ears and made the lobes thereof a pleasing scarlet.   Brief were these moments, however; and the Spartan boys danced on with smiling faces, undaunted by the hidden anguish which preyed upon them " fore and aft," as Will expressed it.

Mrs. Jane's pair were an odd contrast, and even the stern disciplinarian herself could not help smiling as she watched them. Steve was superb, and might have been married on the spot, so superfine was his broadcloth, glossy his linen, and perfect the fit of his gloves; while pride and happiness so fermented in his youthful bosom, that there would have been danger of spontaneous combustion if dancing had not proved a safety-valve; for his strong sense of the proprieties would not permit him to vent his emotions in any other way.

Kitty felt no such restraint, and looked like a blissful little gypsy, with her brunette prettiness set off by a dashing costume of cardinal and cream color, and every hair on her head curled in a Merry Pecksniffian crop; for youth was her strong point, and she much enjoyed the fact that she had been engaged three times before she was nineteen.

To see her and Steve spin round the room was a sight to bring a smile to the lips of the crustiest bachelor or saddest spinster; for happy lovers are always a pleasing spectacle, and two such merry little grigs as these are seldom seen.

Mac, meantime, with glasses astride of his nose, surveyed his brother's performances " on the light fantastic " very much as a benevolent Newfoundland would the gambols of a toy terrier, receiving with thanks the hasty hints for his guidance which Steve breathed into his ear as he passed, and forgetting all about them the next minute. When not thus engaged, Mac stood about with his thumbs in his vest pockets, regarding the lively crowd like a meditative philosopher of a cheerful aspect, often smiling to himself at some whimsical fancy of his own, knitting his brows as some bit of ill-natured gossip met his ear, or staring with undisguised admiration as a beautiful face or figure caught his eye.

"I hope that girl knows what a treasure she has got. But I doubt if she ever fully appreciates it," said Mrs. Jane, bringing her spectacles to bear upon Kitty, as she whisked by, causing quite a gale with her flying skirts.

"I think she will: for Steve has been so well brought up, she cannot but see and feel the worth of what she has never had; and being so young she will profit by it," answered Mrs. Jessie, softly; thinking of the days when she and her Jem danced together, just betrothed.

"I've done my duty by both the boys, and done it *thoroughly:* or their father would have spoilt them; for he's no more idea of discipline than a child," and Aunt Jane gave her own palm a smart rap with her closed fan, emphasizing the word "thoroughly" in a most suggestive manner.

"I've often wished I had your firmness, Jane: but after all, I'm not sure that I don't like my own way best, at least with my boys; for plenty of love, and plenty of patience, seem to have succeeded pretty well;" and Aunt Jessie lifted the nosegay from her lap, feeling as if that unfailing love and patience were already blooming into her life, as beautifully as the sweet-breathed roses given by her boy refreshed and brightened these long hours of patient waiting in a corner.

"I don't deny that you've done well, Jessie; but you've been let alone, and had no one to hold your

hand or interfere. If my Mac had gone to sea as
your Jem did, I never should have been as severe as
I am. Men are so perverse and short-sighted, they
don't trouble about the future as long as things are
quiet and comfortable in the present," continued Mrs.
Jane, quite forgetting that the short-sighted partner
of the firm, physically speaking at least, was herself.

"Ah, yes! we mothers love to foresee and foretell
our children's lives even before they are born, and
are very apt to be disappointed if they do not turn
out as we planned. I know I am: yet I really have
no cause to complain, and am learning to see that
all we can do is to give the dear boys good principles,
and the best training we may, then leave them to
finish what we have begun;" and Mrs. Jessie's eye
wandered away to Archie, dancing with Rose, quite
unconscious what a pretty little castle in the air
tumbled down when he fell in love with Phebe.

"Right, quite right: on that point we agree exactly.
I have spared nothing to give my boys good principles and good habits, and I am willing to trust them
anywhere. Nine times did I whip my Steve to cure
him of fibbing, and over and over again did Mac go
without his dinner rather than wash his hands. But
I whipped and starved them both into obedience, and
now I have my reward," concluded the "stern parent,"
with a proud wave of the fan, which looked very like
a ferule, being as big, hard, and uncompromising as
such an article could be.

Mrs. Jessie gave a mild murmur of assent, but could
not help thinking, with a smile, that, in spite of their
early tribulations, the sins for which the boys suffered
had got a little mixed in their result; for fibbing

Steve was now the tidy one, and careless Mac the truth-teller. But such small contradictions will happen in the best-regulated families, and all perplexed parents can do is to keep up a steadfast preaching and practising, in the hope that it will bear fruit sometime; for according to the old proverb, —

> " ' Children pick up words as pigeons pease,
> To utter them again as God shall please.' "

" I hope they won't dance the child to death among them; for each one seems bound to have his turn, even your sober Mac," said Mrs. Jessie, a few minutes later, as she saw Archie hand Rose over to his cousin, who carried her off with an air of triumph from several other claimants.

" She 's very good to him, and her influence is excellent; for he is of an age now when a young woman's opinion has more weight than an old one's. Though he is always good to his mother, and I feel as if I should take great comfort in him. He 's one of the sort who will not marry till late, if ever, being fond of books and a quiet life," responded Mrs. Jane, remembering how often her son had expressed his belief that philosophers should not marry, and brought up Plato as an example of the serene wisdom only to be attained by a single man, while her husband sided with Socrates, for whom he felt a profound sympathy, though he did n't dare to own it.

" Well, I don't know about that. Since my Archie surprised me by losing his heart as he did, I 'm prepared for any thing, and advise you to do likewise. I really should n't wonder if Mac did something remarkable in that line, though he shows no signs of it yet, I confess," answered Mrs. Jessie, laughing.

"It won't be in that direction, you may be sure; for *her* fate is sealed. Dear me, how sad it is to see a superior girl, like that, about to throw herself away on a handsome scapegrace. I won't mention names, but you understand me; " and Mrs. Jane shook her head, as if she *could* mention the name of one superior girl who had thrown herself away, and now saw the folly of it.

"I 'm very anxious, of course, and so is Alec: but it may be the saving of one party, and the happiness of the other; for some women love to give more than they receive," said Mrs. Jessie, privately wondering, for the thousandth time, why brother Mac ever married the learned Miss Humphries.

"You 'll see that it won't prosper; and I shall always maintain that a wife cannot entirely undo a mother's work. Rose will have her hands full if she tries to set all Clara's mistakes right," answered Aunt Jane, grimly; then began to fan violently as their hostess approached to have a dish of chat about "our dear young people."

Rose was in a merry mood that night, and found Mac quite ready for fun, which was fortunate, since her first remark set them off on a droll subject.

"O Mac! Annabel has just confided to me that she is engaged to Fun See! Think of her going to housekeeping in Canton some day, and having to order rats, puppies, and birds'-nest soup for dinner," whispered Rose, too much amused to keep the news to herself.

"By Confucius! is n't that a sweet prospect?" and

Mac burst out laughing, to the great surprise of his neighbors, who wondered what there was amusing about the Chinese sage. "It is rather alarming, though, to have these infants going on at this rate. Seems to be catching; a new sort of scarlet-fever, to judge by Annabel's cheeks and Kitty's gown," he added, regarding the aforesaid ladies with eyes still twinkling with merriment.

"Don't be ungallant, but go and do likewise; for it is all the fashion. I heard Mrs. Van tell old Mrs. Joy that it was going to be a marrying year; so you'll be sure to catch it," answered Rose, reefing her skirts; for, with all his training, Mac still found it difficult to keep his long legs out of the man-traps.

"It does n't look like a painful disease; but I must be careful, for I 've no time to be ill now. What are the symptoms?" asked Mac, trying to combine business with pleasure, and improve his mind while doing his duty.

"If you ever come back I'll tell you," laughed Rose, as he danced away into the wrong corner, bumped smartly against another gentleman, and returned as soberly as if that was the proper figure.

"Well, tell me 'how not to do it,'" he said, subsiding for a moment's talk when Rose had floated to and fro in her turn.

"Oh! you see some young girl who strikes you as particularly charming, — whether she really is or not does n't matter a bit, — and you begin to think about her a great deal, to want to see her, and to get generally sentimental and absurd," began Rose, finding it difficult to give a diagnosis of the most mysterious disease under the sun.

"Don't think it sounds enticing. Can't I find an antidote somewhere; for if it is in the air this year I'm sure to get it, and it may be fatal," said Mac, who felt pretty lively and liked to make Rose merry; for he suspected that she had a little trouble from a hint Dr. Alec had given him.

"I hope you will catch it, because you'll be so funny."

"Will you take care of me as you did before, or have you got your hands full?"

"I'll help; but really with Archie and Steve and — Charlie, I shall have enough to do. You'd better take it lightly the first time, and so won't need much care."

"Very well, how shall I begin? Enlighten my ignorance and start me right, I beg."

"Go about and see people; make yourself agreeable, and not sit in corners observing other people as if they were puppets dancing for your amusement. I heard Mrs. Van once say that propinquity works wonders; and she ought to know, having married off two daughters, and just engaged a third to 'a most charming young man.'"

"Good lack! the cure sounds worse than the disease. Propinquity, hey? Why, I may be in danger this identical moment, and can't flee for my life," said Mac, gently catching her round the waist for a general waltz.

"Don't be alarmed, but mind your steps; for Charlie is looking at us, and I want you to do your best. That's perfect: take me quite round; for I love to waltz, and seldom get a good turn except with you boys," said Rose, smiling up at him approvingly, as his strong arm guided her among the revolving couples, and his feet kept time without a fault.

"This certainly is a great improvement on the chair business, to which I have devoted myself with such energy that I've broken the backs of two partners and dislocated the arm of the old rocker. I took an occasional turn with that heavy party, thinking it good practice in case I ever happen to dance with stout ladies," and Mac nodded toward Annabel, pounding gayly away with Mr. Tokio, whose yellow countenance beamed as his beady eyes rested on his plump *fiancée*.

Pausing in the midst of her merriment at the image of Mac and the old rocking-chair, Rose said reprovingly, —

"Though a heathen Chinee, Fun puts you to shame; for *he* did not ask foolish questions, but went a wooing like a sensible little man; and I've no doubt Annabel will be very happy."

"Choose me a suitable divinity, and I will try to adore. Can I do more than that to retrieve my character?" answered Mac, safely landing his partner, and plying the fan according to instructions.

"How would Emma do?" inquired Rose, whose sense of the ludicrous was strong, and who could not resist the temptation of horrifying Mac by the suggestion.

"Never! It sets my teeth on edge to look at her to-night. I suppose that dress is 'a sweet thing just out'; but, upon my word, she reminds me of nothing but a harlequin ice," and Mac turned his back on her with a shudder; for he was sensitive to discords of all kinds.

" She certainly does ; and that mixture of chocolate, pea green, and pink is simply detestable, though many people would consider it decidedly ' chic,' to use her favorite word.   I suppose you will dress your wife like a Spartan matron of the time of Lycurgus," added Rose, much tickled by his new conceit.

" I 'll wait till I get her before I decide.   But one thing I 'm sure of, — she shall *not* dress like a Greek dancer of the time of Pericles," answered Mac, regarding with great disfavor a young lady who, having a statuesque figure, affected drapery of the scanty and clinging description.

" Then it is of no use to suggest that classic creature ; so, as you reject my first attempts, I won't go on, but look about me quietly, and you had better do the same.   Seriously, Mac, more gayety and less study would do you good ; for you will grow old before your time, if you shut yourself up and pore over books so much."

" I don't believe there is a younger or a jollier feeling fellow in the room than I am, though I may not conduct myself like a dancing dervish.   But I own you may be right about the books ; for there are many sorts of intemperance, and a library is as irresistible to me as a bar-room to a toper.   I shall have to sign a pledge, and cork up the only bottle that tempts me, — my inkstand."

" I 'll tell you how to make it easier to abstain. Stop studying, and write a novel into which you can put all your wise things, and so clear your brains for a new start by and by.   Do : I should *so* like to read it," cried Rose, delighted with the project ; for she was sure Mac could do any thing he liked in that line.

"First live, then write. How can I go to romancing till I know what romance means?" he asked soberly, feeling that so far he had had very little in his life.

"Then you must find out, and nothing will help you more than to love some one very much. Do as I've advised, and be a modern Diogenes going about with spectacles, instead of a lantern, in search, not of an honest man, but a perfect woman. I do hope you will be successful," and Rose made her courtesy as the dance ended.

"I don't expect perfection, but I *should* like one as good as they ever make them now-a-days. If you are looking for the honest man, I wish you success in return," said Mac, relinquishing her fan with a glance of such sympathetic significance that a quick flush of feeling rose to the girl's face, as she answered very low, —

"If honesty was all I wanted, I certainly have found it in you."

Then she went away with Charlie, who was waiting for his turn, and Mac roamed about, wondering if anywhere in all that crowd his future wife was hidden, saying to himself, as he glanced from face to face, quite unresponsive to the various allurements displayed, —

"What care I how fair she be,
If she be not fair for me?"

Just before supper, several young ladies met in the dressing-room to repair damages; and, being friends, they fell into discourse, as they smoothed their locks, and had their tattered furbelows sewed or pinned up by the neat-handed Phillis in waiting.

When each had asked the other, "How do I look to-night, dear?" and been answered with reciprocal enthusiasm, "Perfectly lovely, darling!" Kitty said to Rose, who was helping her to restore order out of the chaos to which much exercise had reduced her curls, —

"By the way, young Randal is dying to be presented to you.   May I after supper?"

"No, thank you," answered Rose, very decidedly.

"Well, I'm sure I don't see why not," began Kitty, looking displeased, but not surprised.

"I think you do, else why didn't you present him when he asked?   You seldom stop to think of etiquette : why did you now?"

"I didn't like to do it till I had — you are so particular — I thought you'd say 'No'; but I couldn't tell him so," stammered Kitty, feeling that she had better have settled the matter herself; for Rose *was* very particular, and had especial reason to dislike this person, because he was not only a dissipated young reprobate himself, but seemed possessed of Satan to lead others astray likewise.

"I don't wish to be rude, dear : but I really must decline; for I cannot know such people, even though I meet them here," said Rose, remembering Charlie's revelations on New-Year's night, and hardening her heart against the man who had been his undoing on that as well as on other occasions, she had reason to believe.

"I couldn't help it!   Old Mr. Randal and papa are friends; and, though I spoke of it, brother Alf wouldn't hear of passing that bad boy over," explained Kitty, eagerly.

" Yet Alf forbade your driving or skating with him; for he knows better than we how unfit he is to come among us."

" I 'd drop him to-morrow if I could; but I must be civil in my own house. His mother brought him, and he won't dare to behave here as he does at their bachelor parties."

" She ought not to have brought him till he had shown some desire to mend his ways. It is none of my business, I know; but I do wish people would n't be so inconsistent, letting boys go to destruction, and then expecting us girls to receive them like decent people." Rose spoke in an energetic whisper, but Annabel heard her, and exclaimed, as she turned round with a powder-puff in her hand, —

" My goodness, Rose! what is all that about going to destruction?"

" She is being strong-minded; and I don't very much blame her in this case. But it leaves me in a dreadful scrape," said Kitty, supporting her spirits with a sniff of aromatic vinegar.

" I appeal to you, since you heard me, and there 's no one here but ourselves: do you consider young Randal a nice person to know?" and Rose turned to Annabel and Emma with an anxious eye; for she did not find it easy to abide by her principles when so doing annoyed friends.

" No, indeed: he 's perfectly horrid! Papa says he and Gorham are the wildest young men he knows, and enough to spoil the whole set. I 'm so glad I 've got no brothers," responded Annabel, placidly powdering her pink arms, quite undeterred by the memory of sundry white streaks left on sundry coat-sleeves.

"*I* think that sort of scrupulousness is very ill-bred, if you 'll excuse my saying so, Rose. *We* are not supposed to know any thing about fastness, and wildness, and so on; but to treat every man alike, and not be fussy and prudish," said Emma, settling her many-colored streamers with the superior air of a woman of the world, aged twenty.

"Ah! but we do know; and, if our silence and civility have no effect, we ought to try something else, and not encourage wickedness of any kind. We need n't scold and preach, but we *can* refuse to know such people; and that will do some good, for they don't like to be shunned and shut out from respectable society. Uncle Alec told me not to know that man, and I won't." Rose spoke with unusual warmth, forgetting that she could not tell the real reason for her strong prejudice against " that man."

"Well, *I* know him: *I* think him very jolly, and I 'm engaged to dance the German with him after supper. He leads quite as well as your cousin Charlie, and is quite as fascinating, some people think," returned Emma, tossing her head disdainfully; for Prince Charming did not worship at her shrine, and it piqued her vanity.

In spite of her quandary, Rose could not help smiling as she recalled Mac's comparison; for Emma turned so red with spiteful chagrin, she seemed to have added strawberry-ice to the other varieties composing the Harlequin.

"Each must judge for herself. I shall follow Aunt Jessie's advice, and try to keep my atmosphere as pure as I can; for she says every woman has her own little circle, and in it can use her influence for

good, if she will. I do will heartily; and I'll prove
that I'm neither proud nor fussy by receiving, here
or at home, any respectable man you like to present
to me, no matter how poor or plain or insignificant
he may be."

With which declaration Rose ended her protest,
and the four damsels streamed downstairs together
like a wandering rainbow. But Kitty laid to heart
what she had said; Annabel took credit to herself for
siding with her; and Emma owned that *she* was not
trying to keep her atmosphere pure when she came
to dance with the objectionable Randal. So Rose's
"little circle" was the better for the influence she
tried to exert, although she never knew it.

All supper-time, Charlie kept near her, and she
was quite content with him; for he drank only coffee,
and she saw him shake his head with a frown when
young Van beckoned him toward an anteroom, from
whence the sound of popping corks had issued with
increasing frequency as the evening wore on.

"Dear fellow, he does try," thought Rose, longing
to show how she admired his self-denial; but she
could only say, as they left the supper-room with the
aunts, who were going early, —

"If I had not promised uncle to get home as
soon after midnight as possible, I'd stay and dance
the German with you; for you deserve a reward
to-night."

"A thousand thanks! but I am going when you
do," answered Charlie, understanding both her look
and words, and very grateful for them.

"Really?" cried Rose, delighted.

"Really. I'll be in the hall when you come down."

14

And Charlie thought the Fra Angelico angel was not half so bright and beautiful as the one who looked back at him out of a pale-blue cloud, as Rose went upstairs as if on wings.

When she came down again, Charlie was not in the hall, however; and, after waiting a few minutes, Mac offered to go and find him, for Aunt Jane was still hunting a lost rubber above.

" Please say I 'm ready, but he need n't come if he does n't want to," said Rose, not wishing to demand too much of her promising penitent.

" If he has gone into that bar-room, I 'll have him out, no matter who is there ! " growled Mac to himself, as he made his way to the small apartment whither the gentlemen retired for a little private refreshment when the spirit moved, as it often did.

The door was ajar, and Charlie seemed to have just entered; for Mac heard a familiar voice call out, in a jovial tone, —

" Come, Prince ! you 're just in time to help us drink Steve's health with all the honors."

" Can't stop ; only ran in to say good-night, Van. Had a capital time; but I 'm on duty, and must go."

" That 's a new dodge. Take a stirrup-cup any-way, and come back in time for a merry-go-rounder when you 've disposed of the ladies," answered the young host, diving into the wine-cooler for another bottle.

" Charlie 's going in for sanctity, and it does n't seem to agree with him," laughed one of the two other young men, who occupied several chairs apiece, resting their soles in every sense of the word.

" Apron-strings are coming into fashion, — the

bluer the better: hey, Prince?" added the other,
trying to be witty, with the usual success.

"You'd better go home early yourself, Barrow, or
that tongue of yours will get you into trouble," retorted Charlie, conscious that he ought to take his
own advice, yet lingering, nervously putting on his
gloves while the glasses were being filled.

"Now, brother-in-law, fire away! Here you are,
Prince." And Steve handed a glass across the table
to his cousin, feeling too much elated with various
pleasurable emotions to think what he was doing; for
the boys all knew Charlie's weakness, and usually
tried to defend him from it.

Before the glass could be taken, however, Mac
entered in a great hurry, delivering his message in
an abbreviated and rather peremptory form, —

"Rose is waiting for you. Hurry up!"

"All right. Good-night, old fellows!" And Charlie
was off, as if the name had power to stop him in the
very act of breaking the promise made to himself.

"Come, Solon, take a social drop, and give us an
epithalamium in your best Greek. Here's to you!"
And Steve was lifting the wine to his own lips, when
Mac knocked the glass out of his hand, with a flash
of the eye that caused his brother to stare at him,
with his mouth open, in an imbecile sort of way, which
seemed to excite Mac still more; for, turning to
his young host, he said, in a low voice, and with a
look that made the gentlemen on the chairs sit up
suddenly, —

"I beg pardon, Van, for making a mess; but I
can't stand by and see my own brother tempt another
man beyond his strength, or make a brute of himself.

That's plain English: but I can't help speaking out;
for I know not one of you would willingly hurt Charlie,
and you will if you don't let him alone."

"What do you pitch into me for? I've done
nothing. A fellow must be civil in his own house,
must n't he?" asked Van, good-humoredly, as he
faced about, corkscrew in hand.

"Yes, but it is not civil to urge or joke a guest
into doing what you know and he knows is bad for
him. That's only a glass of wine to you, but it
is perdition to Charlie; and, if Steve knew what he
was about, he'd cut his right hand off before he'd
offer it."

"Do you mean to say I'm tipsy?" demanded Steve,
ruffling up like a little game-cock; for, though he
saw now what he had done and was ashamed of it,
he hated to have Mac air his peculiar notions before
other people.

"With excitement, not champagne, I hope; for I
would n't own you if you were," answered Mac, in
whom indignation was effervescing like the wine in
the forgotten bottle; for the men were all young,
friends of Steve's and admirers of Charlie's. "Look
here, boys," he went on more quietly: "I know I
ought not to explode in this violent sort of way, but
upon my life I could n't help it, when I heard what
you were saying and saw what Steve was doing.
Since I *have* begun I may as well finish, and tell you
straight out that Prince can't stand this sort of thing.
He is trying to flee temptation, and whoever leads
him into it does a cowardly and sinful act; for the
loss of one's own self-respect is bad enough, without
losing the more precious things that make life worth

having. Don't tell him I've said this, but lend a hand if you can, and never have to reproach yourselves with the knowledge that you helped to ruin a fellow-creature, soul and body."

It was well for the success of Mac's first crusade, that his hearers were gentlemen and sober: so his outburst was not received with jeers or laughter, but listened to in silence, while the expression of the faces changed from one of surprise to regret and respect; for earnestness is always effective, and championship of this sort seldom fails to touch hearts as yet unspoiled. As he paused with an eloquent little quiver in his eager voice, Van corked the bottle at a blow, threw down the corkscrew, and offered Mac his hand, saying heartily, in spite of his slang, —

"You are a first-class old brick! I'll lend a hand for one, and do my best to back up Charlie; for he's the finest fellow I know, and shan't go to the devil like poor Randal if *I* can help it."

Murmurs of applause from the others seemed to express a general assent to this vigorous statement; and, giving the hand a grateful shake, Mac retreated to the door, anxious to be off now that he had freed his mind with such unusual impetuosity.

"Count on me for any thing I can do in return for this, Van. I'm sorry to be such a marplot, but you can take it out in quizzing me after I'm gone. I'm fair game, and Steve can set you going."

With that, Mac departed as abruptly as he came, feeling that he *had* "made a mess" of it; but comforting himself with the thought that perhaps he had secured help for Charlie at his own expense, and

thinking with a droll smile as he went back to his
mother, —

"My romance begins by looking after other girls'
lovers instead of finding a sweetheart for myself; but
I can't tell Rose, so *she* won't laugh at me."

CHAPTER XIII

BOTH SIDES

STEVE'S engagement made a great stir in the
family: a pleasant one this time; for nobody
objected, every thing seemed felicitous, and
the course of true love ran very smoothly for the
young couple, who promised to remove the only
obstacle to their union by growing old and wise as
soon as possible. If he had not been so genuinely
happy, the little lover's airs would have been unbear-
able; for he patronized all mankind in general, his
brother and elder cousins in particular.

"Now that is the way to manage matters," he
declared, standing before the fire in Aunt Clara's
billiard room a day or two after the ball, with his
hands behind his back, — "no nonsense, no delay,
no domestic rows or tragic separations. Just choose
with taste and judgment, make yourself agreeable
through thick and thin; and, when it is perfectly
evident that the dear creature adores the ground
you walk on, say the word like a man, and there
you are."

"All very easy to do that with a girl like Kitty,
who has no confounded notions to spoil her and trip
you up every time you don't exactly toe the mark,"
muttered Charlie, knocking the balls about as if it
were a relief to hit something; for he was in a glo-

riously bad humor that evening, because time hung
heavy on his hands since he had forsworn the company he could not keep without danger to himself.

"You should humor those little notions; for all
women have them, and it needs tact to steer clear of
them. Kitty's got dozens; but I treat them with
respect, have my own way when I can, give in without growling when I can't, and we get on like a
couple of — "

"Spoons," put in Charlie, who felt that he had *not*
steered clear, and so suffered shipwreck in sight of
land.

Steve meant to have said "doves," but his cousin's
levity caused him to add with calm dignity, " reason-
able beings," and then revenged himself by making a
good shot which won him the game.

"You always were a lucky little dog, Steve. I
don't begrudge you a particle of your happiness, but
it does seem as if things were n't quite fair sometimes," said Archie, suppressing an envious sigh;
for, though he seldom complained, it was impossible
to contrast his own and his cousin's prospects with
perfect equanimity.

> "'His worth shines forth the brightest who in hope
> Always confides: the abject soul despairs,'"

observed Mac, quoting Euripides in a conversational
tone, as he lay upon a divan reposing after a hard
day's work.

"Thank you," said Archie, brightening a little; for
a hopeful word from any source was very comfortable.

"That's your favorite Rip, is n't it? He was a
wise old boy, but you could find advice as good as

that nearer home," put in Steve, who just then felt
equal to slapping Plato on the shoulder; so elated
was he at being engaged "first of all the lot," as he
gracefully expressed it.

"Don't halloo till you are out of the wood, Dandy:
Mrs. Kit has jilted two men, and may a third; so
you'd better not brag of your wisdom too soon; for
she may make a fool of you yet," said Charlie,
cynically, his views of life being very gloomy about
this time.

"No, she won't, Steve, if you do your part honestly.
There's the making of a good little woman in Kitty,
and she has proved it by taking you instead of those
other fellows. You are not a Solomon, but you're
not spoilt yet; and she had the sense to see it," said
Mac, encouragingly from his corner; for he and his
brother were better friends than ever since the little
scene at the Van Tassels.

"Hear! hear!" cried Steve, looking more than
ever like a cheerful young cockerel trying to crow, as
he stood upon the hearth-rug with his hands under
his coat-tails, rising and falling alternately upon the
toes and heels of his neat little boots.

"Come, you've given them each a pat on the head:
haven't you got one for me? I need it enough; for
if ever there was a poor devil born under an evil star,
it is C. C. Campbell," exclaimed Charlie, leaning his
chin on his cue with a discontented expression of
countenance; for trying to be good is often very
hard work till one gets used to it.

"Oh, yes! I can accommodate you;" and, as if
his words suggested the selection, Mac, still lying flat
upon his back, repeated one of his favorite bits from

Beaumont and Fletcher; for he had a wonderful memory, and could reel off poetry by the hour together.

> "'Man is his own star: and the soul that can
> Render an honest and a perfect man
> Commands all light, all influence, all fate.
> Nothing to him falls early or too late.
> Our acts our angels are; or good or ill,
> Our fatal shadows that walk by us still.'"

"Confoundedly bad angels they are too," muttered Charlie, ruefully; remembering the one that undid him.

His cousins never knew exactly what occurred on New-Year's night, but suspected that something was amiss; for Charlie had the blues, and Rose, though as kind as ever, expressed no surprise at his long absences. They had all observed and wondered at this state of things, yet discreetly made no remark, till Steve, who was as inquisitive as a magpie, seized this opportunity to say in a friendly tone, which showed that he bore no malice for the dark prophecy regarding his Kitty's faithfulness, —

"What's the trouble, Prince? You are so seldom in a bad humor that we don't know what to make of it, and all feel out of spirits when you have the blues. Had a tiff with Rose?"

"Never you mind, little boy; but this I will say, — the better women are, the more unreasonable they are. They don't require us to be saints like themselves, which is lucky; but they do expect us to render 'an honest and a perfect man' sometimes, and that is asking rather too much in a fallen world like this," said Charlie, glad to get a little sympathy, though he had no intention of confessing his transgressions.

"No, it is n't," said Mac, decidedly.

"Much you know about it," began Charlie, ill pleased to be so flatly contradicted.

"Well, I know this much," added Mac, suddenly sitting up with his hair in a highly dishevelled condition. "It is very unreasonable in us to ask women to be saints, and then expect them to feel honored when we offer them our damaged hearts, or, at best, one not half as good as theirs. If they were n't blinded by love, they 'd see what a mean advantage we take of them, and not make such bad bargains."

"Upon my word, the philosopher is coming out strong upon the subject! We shall have him preaching 'Women's Rights' directly," cried Steve, much amazed at this outburst.

"I 've begun, you see, and much good may it do you," answered Mac, laying himself placidly down again.

"Well, but look here, man: you are arguing on the wrong side," put in Archie, quite agreeing with him, but feeling that he must stand by his order at all costs.

"Never mind sides, uphold the right wherever you find it. You need n't stare, Steve: I told you I was going to look into this matter, and I am. You think I 'm wrapt up in books: but I see a great deal more of what is going on round me than you imagine; and I 'm getting on in this new branch, let me tell you; quite as fast as is good for me, I dare say."

"Going in for perfection, are you?" asked Charlie, both amused and interested: for he respected Mac more than he owned even to himself, and though he had never alluded to the timely warning, neither forgot.

"Yes, I think of it."

"How will you begin?"

"Do my best all round: keep good company, read good books, love good things, and cultivate soul and body as faithfully and wisely as I can."

"And you expect to succeed, do you?"

"Please God, I will."

The quiet energy of Mac's last words produced a momentary silence. Charlie thoughtfully studied the carpet; Archie, who had been absently poking the fire, looked over at Mac as if he thanked him again, and Steve, forgetting his self-conceit, began to wonder if it was not possible to improve himself a little for Kitty's sake. Only a minute; for young men do not give much time to thoughts of this kind, even when love stirs up the noblest impulses within them. To act rather than to talk is more natural to most of them, as Charlie's next question showed; for, having the matter much at heart, he ventured to ask in an off-hand way, as he laughed and twirled his cue,—

"Do you intend to reach the highest point of perfection before you address one of the fair saints, or shall you ask her to lend a hand somewhere short of that?"

"As it takes a long lifetime to do what I plan, I think I shall ask some good woman 'to lend a hand' when I 've got any thing worth offering her. Not a saint, for I never shall be one myself, but a gentle creature who will help me, as I shall try to help her; so that we can go on together, and finish our work hereafter, if we have n't time to do it here."

If Mac had been a lover, he would not have discussed the subject in this simple and sincere fashion, though he might have felt it far more deeply; but being quite heart-free he frankly showed his interest, and, curiously enough, out of his wise young head unconsciously gave the three lovers before him counsel which they valued, because he practised what he preached.

"Well, I hope you'll find her!" said Charlie, heartily, as he went back to his game.

"I think I shall," and, while the others played, Mac lay staring at the window-curtain, as contentedly as if, through it, he beheld "a dream of fair women," from which to choose his future mate.

A few days after this talk in the billiard-room, Kitty went to call upon Rose; for, as she was about to enter the family, she felt it her duty to become acquainted with all its branches. This branch, however, she cultivated more assiduously than any other, and was continually running in to confer with "Cousin Rose," whom she considered the wisest, dearest, kindest girl ever created. And Rose, finding that, in spite of her flighty head, Kitty had a good heart of her own, did her best to encourage all the new hopes and aspirations springing up in it under the warmth of the first genuine affection she had ever known.

"My dear, I want to have some serious conversation with you upon a subject in which I take an interest for the first time in my life," began Miss Kitty, seating herself and pulling off her gloves, as if the subject was one which needed a firm grasp.

"Tell away, and don't mind if I go on working, as I want to finish this job to-day," answered Rose, with a long-handled paint-brush in her hand, and a great pair of shears at her side.

"You are always so busy! What is it now? Let me help: I can talk faster when I'm doing something," which seemed hardly possible; for Kitty's tongue went like a mill-clapper at all hours.

"Making picture-books for my sick babies at the hospital. Pretty work, isn't it? You cut out, and I'll paste them ɔn these squares of gay cambric: then we just tie up a few pages with a ribbon; and there is a nice, light, durable book for the poor dears to look at as they lie in their little beds."

"A capital idea. Do you go there often? How ever do you find the time for such things?" asked Kitty, busily cutting from a big sheet the touching picture of a parent bird with a red head and a blue tail, offering what looked like a small boa-constrictor to one of its nestlings; a fat young squab with a green head, yellow body, and no tail at all.

"I have plenty of time now I don't go out so much; for a party uses up two days generally, — one to prepare for it, and one to get over it, you know."

"People think it is so odd of you to give up society all of a sudden. They say you have 'turned pious,' and it is owing to your peculiar bringing up. I always take your part, and say it is a pity other girls haven't as sensible an education; for I don't know one who is as satisfactory on the whole as you are."

"Much obliged. You may also tell people I gave up gayety because I valued health more. But I haven't forsworn every thing of the kind, Kit. I go to concerts and lectures, and all sorts of early things, and have nice times at home, as you know. I like fun as well as ever: but I'm getting on, you see, and must be preparing a little for the serious part of life; one never knows when it may come," said Rose, thoughtfully, as she pasted a squirrel upside-down on the pink cotton page before her.

"That reminds me of what I wanted to say. If you'll believe me, my dear, Steve has got that very idea into his head! Did you or Mac put it there?" asked Kitty, industriously clashing her shears.

"No, I've given up lecturing the boys lately: they are so big now they don't like it, and I fancy I'd got into a way that was rather tiresome."

"Well, then, *he* is 'turning pious' too. And what is very singular, I like it. Now don't smile: I really do; and I want to be getting ready for the 'serious part of life,' as you call it. That is, I want to grow better as fast as I can; for Steve says he isn't half good enough for me. Just think of that!"

Kitty looked so surprised and pleased and proud, that Rose felt no desire to laugh at her sudden fancy for sobriety, but said in her most sympathetic tone, —

"I'm very glad to hear it; for it shows that he loves you in the right way."

"Is there more than one way?"

"Yes, I fancy so; because some people improve so much after they fall in love, and others do not at all. Have you never observed that?"

"I never learned how to observe. Of course, I know that some matches turn out well and some don't; but I never thought much about it."

"Well, I have; for I was rather interested in the

subject lately, and had a talk with Aunt Jessie and uncle about it."

"Gracious! you don't talk to them about such things, do you?"

"Yes, indeed; I ask any question I like, and always get a good answer. It is such a nice way to learn, Kitty; for you don't have to poke over books, but as things come along you talk about them, and remember; and when they are spoken of afterward you understand and are interested, though you don't say a word," explained Rose.

"It must be nice; but I have n't any one to do so for me. Papa is too busy, and mamma always says when I ask questions, ' Don't trouble your head with such things, child ; ' so I don't. What did you learn about matches turning out well? I'm interested in that, because I want mine to be quite perfect in all respects."

"After thinking it over, I came to the conclusion that uncle *was* right, and it is *not* always safe to marry a person just because you love him," began Rose, trying to enlighten Kitty without betraying herself.

"Of course not : if they have n't money or are bad. But otherwise I don't see what more is needed," said Kitty, wonderingly.

"One should stop and see if it is a wise love, likely to help both parties, and wear well; for you know it ought to last all one's lifetime, and it is very sad if it does n't."

"I declare it quite scares me to think of it; for I don't usually go beyond my wedding-day in making plans. I remember, though, that when I was engaged the first time (you don't know the man: it was just after you went away, and I was only sixteen), some one very ill-naturedly said I should 'marry in haste and repent at leisure;' and that made me try to imagine how it would seem to go on year after year with Gustavus (who had a dreadful temper, by the way), and it worried me so to think of it that I broke the engagement, and was so glad ever afterward."

"You were a wise girl; and I hope you'll do it again, if you find, after a time, that you and Steve do not truly trust and respect as well as love one another. If you don't, you'll be miserable when it is too late, as so many people are who do marry in haste and have a lifetime to repent in. Aunt Jessie says so, and she knows."

"Don't be solemn, Rose. It fidgets me to think about lifetimes, and respecting, and all those responsible things. I'm not used to it, and I don't know how to do it."

"But you *must* think, and you must learn how before you take the responsibility upon yourself. That is what your life is for; and you must n't spoil it by doing a very solemn thing without seeing if you are ready for it."

"Do you think about all this?" asked Kitty, shrugging up her shoulders as if responsibility of any sort did not sit comfortably on them.

"One has to sometimes, you know. But is that all you wanted to tell me?" added Rose, anxious to turn the conversation from herself.

"Oh, dear, no! The most serious thing of all is this. Steve is putting himself in order generally, and so I want to do my part; and I must begin right away before my thoughts get distracted with clothes, and all sorts of dear, delightful, frivolous things that I can't help liking. Now I wish you'd tell me where to begin. Should n't I improve my mind by reading something solid?" and Kitty looked over at the well-filled book-case, as if to see if it contained any thing large and dry enough to be considered "solid."

"It would be an excellent plan, and we'll look up something. What do you feel as if you needed most?"

"A little of every thing I should say; for when I look into my mind there really does n't seem to be much there but odds and ends, and yet I'm sure I've read a great deal more than some girls do. I suppose novels don't count, though, and are of no use; for, goodness knows, the people and things they describe are n't a bit like the real ones."

"Some novels are very useful and do as much good as sermons, I've heard uncle say; because they not only describe truly, but teach so pleasantly that people like to learn in that way," said Rose, who knew the sort of books Kitty had read, and did not wonder that she felt rather astray when she tried to guide herself by their teaching.

"You pick me out some of the right kind, and I'll apply my mind to them. Then I ought to have some 'serious views' and 'methods' and 'principles;' Steve said 'principles,' good firm ones, you know," and Kitty gave a little pull at the bit of cambric she was cutting, as housewives pull cotton or calico when they want "a good firm article."

Rose could not help laughing now, though much pleased; for Kitty was so prettily in earnest, and yet so perfectly ignorant how to begin on the self-improvement she very much needed, that it was pathetic as well as comical to see and hear her.

"You certainly want some of those, and must begin at once to get them: but Aunt Jessie can help you there better than I can; or Aunt Jane, for she has very 'firm' ones, I assure you," said Rose, sobering down as quickly as possible.

"Mercy on us! I should never dare to say a word about it to Mrs. Mac: for I'm dreadfully afraid of her, she is so stern; and how I'm ever to get on when she is my mother-in-law I don't know!" cried Kitty, clasping her hands in dismay at the idea.

"She isn't half as stern as she looks; and if you go to her without fear, you've no idea how sensible and helpful she is. I used to be frightened out of my wits with her, but now I'm not a bit, and we get on nicely; indeed I'm fond of her, she is so reliable and upright in all things."

"She certainly is the straightest woman I ever saw, and the most precise. I never shall forget how scared I was when Steve took me up to see her that first time. I put on all my plainest things, did my hair in a meek knob, and tried to act like a sober, sedate young woman. Steve would laugh at me, and say I looked like a pretty nun, so I couldn't be as proper as I wished. Mrs. Mac was very kind, of course; but her eye was so sharp I felt as if she saw right through me, and knew that I'd pinned on my bonnet-strings, lost a button off my boot, and didn't brush my hair for ten minutes every night," said Kitty, in an awe-stricken tone.

"She likes you, though, and so does uncle, and he's set his heart on having you live with them by and by; so don't mind her eyes, but look straight up at her, and you'll see how kind they can grow."

"Mac likes me too, and that did please me; for he does n't like girls generally. Steve told me he said I had the 'making of a capital little woman in me.' Was n't it nice of him? Steve was *so* proud, though he does laugh at Mac sometimes."

"Don't disappoint them, dear. Encourage Steve in all the good things he likes or wants, make friends with Mac, love Aunt Jane, and be a daughter to uncle, and you'll find yourself a very happy girl."

"I truly will, and thank you very much for not making fun of me. I know I'm a little goose; but lately I've felt as if I might come to something if I had the right sort of help. I'll go up and see Aunt Jessie to-morrow; I'm not a bit afraid of her: and then if you'll just quietly find out from Uncle Doctor what I must read, I'll work as hard as I can. Don't tell any one, please; they'll think it odd and affected, and I can't bear to be laughed at, though I dare say it is good discipline."

Rose promised, and both worked in silence for a moment; then Kitty asked rather timidly, —

"Are you and Charlie trying this plan too? Since you've left off going out so much, he keeps away also; and we don't know what to make of it."

"He has had what he calls an 'artistic fit' lately, set up a studio, and is doing some crayon sketches of us all. If he'd only finish his things, they would be excellent; but he likes to try a great variety at once. I'll take you in sometime, and perhaps he will do a portrait of you for Steve. He likes girls' faces, and gets the likenesses wonderfully well."

"People say you are engaged: but I contradict it; because, of course, *I* should know if you were."

"We are not."

"I'm glad of it; for really, Rose, I'm afraid Charlie has n't got 'firm principles,' though he is a fascinating fellow and one can't scold him. You don't mind my saying so, do you, dear?" added Kitty; for Rose did not answer at once.

"Not in the least: for you are one of us now, and I can speak frankly, and I will; for I think in one way you *can* help Steve very much. You are right about Charlie, both as to the principles and the fascination: Steve admires him exceedingly, and always from a boy liked to imitate his pleasant ways. Some of them are very harmless and do Steve good, but some are not. I need n't talk about it, only you must show your boy that you depend on him to keep out of harm, and help him do it."

"I will, I will! and then perhaps, when he is a perfect model, Charlie will imitate him. I really begin to feel as if I had a great deal to do," and Kitty looked as if she was beginning to like it also.

"We all have; and the sooner we go to work the better for us and those we love. You would n't think now that Phebe was doing any thing for Archie, but she is; and writes such splendid letters, they stir him up wonderfully, and make us all love and admire her more than ever."

"How is she getting on?" asked Kitty, who, though she called herself a "little goose," had tact enough to see that Rose did not care to talk about Charlie.

"Nicely; for you know she used to sing in our choir, so that was a good recommendation for another. She got a fine place in the new church at L——; and that gives her a comfortable salary, though she has something put away. She was always a saving creature and kept her wages carefully; uncle invested them, and she begins to feel quite independent already. No fear but my Phebe will get on: she has such energy, and manages so well. I sometimes wish I could run away and work with her."

"Ah, my dear! we rich girls have our trials as well as poor ones, though we don't get as much pity as they do," sighed Kitty. "Nobody knows what I suffer sometimes from worries that I can't talk about, and I should n't get much sympathy if I did; just because I live in a big house, wear good gowns, and have lots of lovers. Annabel used to say she envied me above all created beings; but she does n't now, and is perfectly absorbed in her dear little Chinaman. Do you see how she ever could like him?"

So they began to gossip, and the sober talk was over for that time; but when Kitty departed, after criticising all her dear friends and their respective sweethearts, she had a helpful little book in her muff, a resolute expression on her bright face, and so many excellent plans for self-improvement in her busy brain, that she and Steve bid fair to turn out the model couple of the century.

CHAPTER XIV

AUNT CLARA'S PLAN

BEING seriously alarmed by the fear of losing the desire of his heart, Charlie had gone resolutely to work, and, like many another young reformer, he rather overdid the matter; for, in trying to keep out of the way of temptation, he denied himself much innocent enjoyment. The artistic fit was a good excuse for the seclusion which he fancied would be a proper penance; and he sat listlessly plying crayon or paint-brush, with daily wild rides on black Brutus, which seemed to do him good; for danger of that sort was his delight.

People were used to his whims, and made light of what they considered a new one; but, when it lasted week after week and all attempts to draw him out were vain, his jolly comrades gave him up, and the family began to say approvingly, — "Now he really *is* going to settle down and do something." Fortunately, his mother let him alone; for though Dr. Alec had not "thundered in her ear," as he threatened, he *had* talked with her in a way which first made her very angry, then anxious, and, lastly, quite submissive; for her heart was set on her boy's winning Rose, and she would have had him put on sackcloth and ashes if that would have secured the prize. She made light of the cause of Rose's displeasure, considering her extremely foolish and straitlaced; "for all young

men of any spirit had their little vices, and came out
well enough when the wild oats were sowed." So she
indulged Charlie in his new vagary, as she had in all
his others, and treated him like an ill-used being,
which was neither an inspiring nor helpful course on
her part. Poor soul! she saw her mistake by and by,
and when too late repented of it bitterly.

Rose wanted to be kind, and tried in various ways
to help her cousin, feeling very sure she should succeed as many another hopeful woman has done, quite
unconscious how much stronger an undisciplined will
is than the truest love; and what a difficult task the
wisest find it to undo the mistakes of a bad education.
But it was a hard thing to do: for, at the least
hint of commendation or encouragement, he looked
so hopeful that she was afraid of seeming to promise
too much, and, of all things, she desired to escape
the accusation of having trifled with him.

So life was not very comfortable to either just
then; and, while Charlie was "mortifying soul and
body" to please her, she was studying how to serve
him best. Aunt Jessie helped her very much, and no
one guessed, when they saw pretty Miss Campbell
going up and down the hill with such a serious face,
that she was intent on any thing except taking,
with praiseworthy regularity, the constitutionals which
gave her such a charming color.

Matters were in this state, when one day a note
came to Rose from Mrs. Clara.

" My sweet Child, — Do take pity on my poor boy, and
cheer him up with a sight of you ; for he is so *triste* it breaks
my heart to see him. He has a new plan in his head, which

strikes me as an excellent one, if you will only favor it. Let him come and take you for a drive this fine afternoon, and talk things over. It will do him a world of good and deeply oblige

" Your ever loving

" AUNT CLARA."

Rose read the note twice, and stood a moment pondering, with her eyes absently fixed on the little bay before her window. The sight of several black figures moving briskly to and fro across its frozen surface seemed to suggest a mode of escape from the drive she dreaded in more ways than one. "That will be safer and pleasanter," she said, and going to her desk wrote her answer.

" DEAR AUNTY, — I'm afraid of Brutus; but, if Charlie will go skating with me, I should enjoy it very much, and it would do us both good. I can listen to the new plan with an undivided mind there; so give him my love, please, and say I shall expect him at three.

"Affectionately,

" ROSE."

Punctually at three, Charlie appeared with his skates over his arm, and a very contented face, which brightened wonderfully as Rose came downstairs in a seal-skin suit and scarlet skirt, so like the one she wore years ago that he involuntarily exclaimed as he took her skates, —

"You look so like little Rose I hardly know you, and it seems so like old times I feel sixteen again."

"That is just the way one ought to feel such a day as this. Now let us be off and have a good spin before any one comes. There are only a few children there now; but it is Saturday, you know, and everybody will be out before long," answered Rose, carefully putting on her mittens as she talked : for her heart was not as light as the one little Rose carried under the brown jacket ; and the boy of sixteen never looked at her with the love and longing she read in the eyes of the young man before her.

Away they went, and were soon almost as merry and warm as the children round them; for the ice was in good condition, the February sunshine brilliant, and the keen wind set their blood a-tingle with a healthful glow.

" Now tell me the plan your mother spoke of," began Rose, as they went gliding across the wide expanse before them; for Charlie seemed to have forgotten every thing but the bliss of having her all to himself for a little while.

" Plan? Oh, yes! it is simply this. I 'm going out to father next month."

" Really? " and Rose looked both surprised and incredulous; for this plan was not a new one.

" Really. You don't believe it, but I am; and mother means to go with me. We 've had another letter from the governor, and he says if she can't part from her big baby to come along too, and all be happy together. What do you think of that? " he asked, eying her intently; for they were face to face, as she went backward and he held both her hands to steer and steady her.

" I like it immensely, and I do believe it now: only it rather takes my breath away to think of aunty's going, when she never would hear of it before."

" She does n't like the plan very well now, and consents to go only on one condition."

"What is that?" asked Rose, trying to free her hands; for a look at Charlie made her suspect what was coming.

"That you go with us;" and, holding the hands fast, he added rapidly, "Let me finish before you speak. I don't mean that any thing is to be changed till you are ready; but if *you* go I'm willing to give up every thing else, and live anywhere as long as you like. Why shouldn't you come to us for a year or two? We've never had our share. Father would be delighted, mother contented, and I the happiest man alive."

"Who made this plan?" asked Rose, as soon as she got the breath which certainly *had* been rather taken away by this entirely new and by no means agreeable scheme.

"Mother suggested it: I shouldn't have dared to even dream of such richness. I'd made up my mind to go alone; and when I told her she was in despair, till this superb idea came into her head. After that, of course it was easy enough for me to stick to the resolution I'd made."

"Why did *you* decide to go, Charlie?" and Rose looked up into the eyes that were fixed beseechingly on hers.

They wavered and glanced aside; then met hers honestly, yet full of a humility which made her own fall as he answered very low, —

"Because I don't *dare* to stay."

"Is it so hard?" she said pitifully.

"Very hard. I haven't the moral courage to own up and face ridicule, and it seems so mean to hide for fear of breaking my word. I *will* keep

it this time, Rose, if I go to the ends of the earth to
do it."

"It is not cowardly to flee temptation; and nobody whose opinion is worth having will ridicule any
brave attempt to conquer one's self. Don't mind it,
Charlie, but stand fast; and I am sure you will
succeed."

"You don't know what it is, and I can't tell you;
for till I tried to give it up I never guessed what a
grip it had on me. I thought it was only a habit,
easy to drop when I liked: but it is stronger than I;
and sometimes I feel as if possessed of a devil that
will get the better of me, try as I may."

He dropped her hands abruptly as he said that,
with the energy of despair; and, as if afraid of saying
too much, he left her for a minute, striking away at
full speed, as if in truth he would "go to the ends of
the earth" to escape the enemy within himself.

Rose stood still, appalled by this sudden knowledge
of how much greater the evil was than she had dreamed.
What ought she to do? Go with her cousin, and by
so doing tacitly pledge herself as his companion
on that longer journey for which he was as yet so
poorly equipped? Both heart and conscience protested against this so strongly that she put the thought
away. But compassion pleaded for him tenderly;
and the spirit of self-sacrifice, which makes women
love to give more than they receive, caused her to
feel as if in a measure this man's fate lay in her hands,
to be decided for good or ill through her. How
should she be true both to him and to herself?

Before this question could be answered, he was
back again, looking as if he had left his care behind

him; for his moods varied like the wind. Her attitude, as she stood motionless and alone with downcast face, was so unlike the cheerful creature who came to meet him an hour ago, it filled him with self-reproach; and, coming up, he drew one hand through his arm, saying, as she involuntarily followed him, —

"You must not stand still. Forget my heroics, and answer my question. Will you go with us, Rose?"

"Not now: that is asking too much, Charlie, and I will promise nothing, because I cannot do it honestly," she answered, so firmly that he knew appeal was useless.

"Am I to go alone, then, leaving all I care for behind me?"

"No, take your mother with you, and do your best to reunite your parents. You could not give yourself to a better task."

"She won't go without you."

"I think she will if you hold fast to your resolution. You won't give that up, I hope?"

"No: I must go somewhere, for I can't stay here; and it may as well be India, since that pleases father," answered Charlie, doggedly.

"It will more than you can imagine. Tell him all the truth, and see how glad he will be to help you, and how sincerely he will respect you for what you 've done."

"If you respect me, I don't care much about the opinion of any one else," answered Charlie, clinging with a lover's pertinacity to the hope that was dearest.

"I shall, if you go manfully away, and do the duty you owe your father and yourself."

"And, when I 've done it, may I come back to be rewarded, Rose?" he asked, taking possession of the hand on his arm, as if it was already his.

"I wish I could say what you want me to. But how can I promise when I am not sure of any thing? I don't love you as I ought, and perhaps I never shall: so why persist in making me bind myself in this way? Be generous, Charlie, and don't ask it," implored Rose, much afflicted by his persistence.

"I thought you did love me: it looked very like it a month ago, unless you have turned coquette, and I can't quite believe that," he answered bitterly.

"I *was* beginning to love you, but you made me afraid to go on," murmured Rose, trying to tell the truth kindly.

"That cursed custom! What *can* a man do when his hostess asks him to drink wine with her?" And Charlie looked as if he could have cursed himself even more heartily.

"He can say 'No.'"

"I can't."

"Ah, that 's the trouble! You never learned to say it even to yourself; and now it is so hard you want me to help you."

"And you won't."

"Yes, I will, by showing you that I *can* say it to myself, for your sake." And Rose looked up with a face so full of tender sorrow he could not doubt the words which both reproached and comforted him.

"My little saint! I don't deserve one half your goodness to me, but I will, and go away without one complaint to do my best, for your sake," he cried, touched by her grief, and stirred to emulation by the example of courage and integrity she tried to set him.

Here Steve and Kitty bore down upon them; and, obeying the impulse to put care behind them which makes it possible for young hearts to ache one minute and dance the next, Rose and Charlie banished their troubles, joined in the sport that soon turned the lonely little bay into a ballroom, and enjoyed the splendors of a winter sunset, forgetful of separation and Calcutta.

CHAPTER XV

ALAS FOR CHARLIE!

IN spite of much internal rebellion, Charlie held fast to his resolution; and Aunt Clara, finding all persuasions vain, gave in, and prepared to accompany him, in a state of chronic indignation against the world in general and Rose in particular. The poor girl had a hard time of it, and, but for her uncle, would have fared still worse. He was a sort of shield, upon which Mrs. Clara's lamentations, reproaches, and irate glances fell unavailingly, instead of wounding the heart against which they were aimed.

The days passed very quickly now; for every one seemed anxious to have the parting over, and preparations went on rapidly. The big house was made ready to shut up for a year at least, comforts for the long voyage laid in, and farewell visits paid. The general activity and excitement rendered it impossible for Charlie to lead the life of an artistic hermit any longer: and he fell into a restless condition, which caused Rose to long for the departure of the " Rajah," when she felt that he would be safe; for these farewell festivities were dangerous to one who was just learning to say "No."

" Half the month safely gone. If we can only get well over these last weeks, a great weight will be off my mind," thought Rose, as she went down one wild, wet morning toward the end of February.

Opening the study-door to greet her uncle, she exclaimed, "Why, Archie!" then paused upon the threshold, transfixed by fear; for in her cousin's white face she read the tidings of some great affliction.

"Hush! don't be frightened. Come in and I'll tell you," he whispered, putting down the bottle he had just taken from the doctor's medicine-closet.

Rose understood and obeyed; for Aunt Plenty was poorly with her rheumatism, and depended on her morning doze.

"What is it?" she said, looking about the room with a shiver, as if expecting to see again what she saw there New-Year's night. Archie was alone, however, and, drawing her toward the closet, answered, with an evident effort to be quite calm and steady, —

"Charlie is hurt! Uncle wants more ether, and the wide bandages in some drawer or other. He told me, but I forget. You keep this place in order : find them for me. Quick!"

Before he had done, Rose was at the drawer, turning over the bandages with hands that trembled as they searched.

"All narrow! I must make some. Can you wait?" And, catching up a piece of old linen, she tore it into wide strips, adding, in the same quick tone, as she began to roll them, —

"Now tell me."

"I can wait: those are not needed just yet. I didn't mean any one should know, you least of all," began Archie, smoothing out the strips as they lay across the table, and evidently surprised at the girl's nerve and skill.

" I can bear it: make haste! Is he much hurt?"

" I'm afraid he is. Uncle looks sober, and the poor boy suffers so I could n't stay," answered Archie, turning still whiter about the lips that never had so hard a tale to tell before.

" You see, he went to town last evening to meet the man who is going to buy Brutus —"

" And Brutus did it? I knew he would!" cried Rose, dropping her work to wring her hands, as if she guessed the ending of the story now.

" Yes, and if he was n't shot already I 'd do it myself with pleasure; for he 's done his best to kill Charlie," muttered Charlie's mate with a grim look; then gave a great sigh, and added with averted face, —

" I should n't blame the brute; it was n't his fault; he needed a firm hand, and —" he stopped there, but Rose said quickly, —

" Go on. I *must* know."

" Charlie met some of his old cronies, quite by accident; there was a dinner-party, and they made him go, just for a good-by they said. He could n't refuse, and it was too much for him. He would come home alone in the storm, though they tried to keep him as he was n't fit. Down by the new bridge, — that high embankment you know, — the wind had put the lantern out — he forgot — or something scared Brutus, and all went down together."

Archie had spoken fast and brokenly; but Rose understood, and at the last word hid her face with a little moan, as if she saw it all.

"Drink this and never mind the rest," he said, dashing into the next room and coming back with a glass of water, longing to be done and away; for this sort of pain seemed almost as bad as that he had left.

Rose drank, but held his arm tightly as he would have turned away, saying in a tone of command he could not disobey, —

"Don't keep any thing back: tell me the worst at once."

"We knew nothing of it," he went on obediently. "Aunt Clara thought he was with me, and no one found him till early this morning. A workman recognized him; and he was brought home, dead they thought. I came for uncle an hour ago. Charlie is conscious now, but awfully hurt; and I'm afraid from the way Mac and uncle look at one another that — Oh! think of it, Rose! crushed and helpless, alone in the rain all night, and I never knew, I never knew!"

With that poor Archie broke down entirely; and, flinging himself into a chair, laid his face on the table, sobbing like a girl. Rose had never seen a man cry before, and it was so unlike a woman's gentler grief that it moved her very much. Putting by her own anguish, she tried to comfort his, and going to him lifted up his head and made him lean on her; for in such hours as this women are the stronger. It was a very little to do, but it did comfort Archie; for the poor fellow felt as if fate was very hard upon him just then, and into this faithful bosom he could pour his brief but pathetic plaint.

"Phebe's gone, and now if Charlie's taken I don't see how I *can* bear it!"

"Phebe will come back, dear, and let us hope poor Charlie is n't going to be taken yet. Such things always seem worse at first, I 've heard people say; so cheer up and hope for the best," answered Rose, seeking for some comfortable words to say, and finding very few.

They took effect, however; for Archie did cheer up like a man. Wiping away the tears which he so seldom shed that they did not know where to go, he got up, gave himself a little shake, and said with a long breath, as if he had been under water, —

"Now I 'm all right, thank you. I could n't help it: the shock of being waked suddenly to find the dear old fellow in such a pitiful state upset me. I ought to go: are these ready?"

"In a minute. Tell uncle to send for me if I can be of any use. Oh, poor Aunt Clara! how does she bear it?"

"Almost distracted. I took mother to her, and she will do all that anybody can. Heaven only knows what aunt will do if — "

"And Heaven only can help her," added Rose, as Archie stopped at the words he could not utter. "Now take them, and let me know often."

"You brave little soul, I will," and Archie went away through the rain with his sad burden, wondering how Rose could be so calm, when the beloved Prince might be dying.

A long dark day followed, with nothing to break its melancholy monotony except the bulletins that came from hour to hour, reporting little change either for better or for worse. Rose broke the news gently to Aunt Plenty, and set herself to the task of keeping up

the old lady's spirits; for, being helpless, the good
soul felt as if every thing would go wrong without her.
At dusk she fell asleep, and Rose went down to order
lights and fire in the parlor, with tea ready to serve at
any moment; for she felt sure some of the men would
come, and that a cheerful greeting and creature comforts would suit them better than tears, darkness, and
desolation.

Presently Mac arrived, saying the instant he entered
the room, —

"More comfortable, cousin."

"Thank Heaven!" cried Rose, unclasping her
hands. Then seeing how worn out, wet, and weary
Mac looked as he came into the light, she added
in a tone that was a cordial in itself, "Poor boy, how
tired you are! Come here, and let me make you
comfortable."

"I was going home to freshen up a bit; for I
must be back in an hour. Mother took my place;
so I could be spared, and came off, as uncle refused
to stir."

"Don't go home; for if aunty is n't there it will be
very dismal. Step into uncle's room and refresh, then
come back and I'll give you your tea. Let me, let
me! I can't help in any other way; and I *must* do
something, this waiting is so dreadful."

Her last words betrayed how much suspense was
trying her; and Mac yielded at once, glad to comfort
and be comforted. When he came back, looking
much revived, a tempting little tea-table stood before
the fire; and Rose went to meet him, saying with a
faint smile, as she liberally bedewed him with the
contents of a cologne flask, —

"I can't bear the smell of ether: it suggests such dreadful things."

"What curious creatures women are! Archie told us you bore the news like a hero, and now you turn pale at a whiff of bad air. I can't explain it," mused Mac, as he meekly endured the fragrant shower-bath.

"Neither can I; but I 've been imagining horrors all day, and made myself nervous. Don't let us talk about it; but come and have some tea."

"That 's another queer thing. Tea is your panacea for all human ills; yet there is n't any nourishment in it. I 'd rather have a glass of milk, thank you," said Mac, taking an easy-chair and stretching his feet to the fire.

She brought it to him and made him eat something; then, as he shut his eyes wearily, she went away to the piano, and having no heart to sing, played softly till he seemed asleep. But, at the stroke of six, he was up and ready to be off again.

"He gave me that: take it with you and put some on his hair; he likes it, and I do so want to help a little," she said, slipping the pretty flagon into his pocket, with such a wistful look, Mac never thought of smiling at this very feminine request.

"I 'll tell him. Is there any thing else I can do for you, cousin?" he asked, holding the cold hand that had been serving him so helpfully.

"Only this: if there is any sudden change, promise to send for me, no matter at what hour it is: I *must* say ' Good-by.' "

"I will come for you. But, Rose, I am sure you may sleep in peace to-night; and I hope to have good news for you in the morning."

"Bless you for that! Come early, and let me see him soon. I will be very good, and I know it will not do him any harm."

"No fear of that: the first thing he said when he could speak was, 'Tell Rose carefully;' and, as I came away, he guessed where I was going, and tried to kiss his hand in the old way, you know."

Mac thought it would cheer her to hear that Charlie remembered her; but the sudden thought that she might never see that familiar little gesture any more was the last drop that made her full heart overflow, and Mac saw the " hero" of the morning sink down at his feet in a passion of tears that frightened him. He took her to the sofa, and tried to comfort her; but, as soon as the bitter sobbing quieted, she looked up and said quite steadily, great drops rolling down her cheeks the while, —

"Let me cry: it is what I need, and I shall be all the better for it by and by. Go to Charlie now, and tell him I said with all my heart, 'Good-night!'"

"I will!" and Mac trudged away, marvelling in his turn at the curiously blended strength and weakness of womankind.

That was the longest night Rose ever spent; but joy came in the morning with the early message, "He is better. You are to come by and by." Then Aunt Plenty forgot her lumbago and arose; Aunt Myra, who had come to have a social croak, took off her black bonnet as if it would not be needed at present, and the girl made ready to go and say "Welcome back," not the hard "Good-by."

It seemed very long to wait; for no summons came

till afternoon, then her uncle arrived, and at the first sight of his face Rose began to tremble.

"I came for my little girl myself, because we must go back at once," he said, as she hurried toward him hat in hand.

"I'm ready, sir;" but her hands shook as she tried to tie the ribbons, and her eyes never left the face that was so full of tender pity for her.

He took her quickly into the carriage, and, as they rolled away, said with the quiet directness which soothes such agitation better than any sympathetic demonstration, —

"Charlie is worse. I feared it when the pain went so suddenly this morning; but the chief injuries are internal, and one can never tell what the chances are. He insists that he is better, but will soon begin to fail, I fear; become unconscious, and slip away without more suffering. This is the time for you to see him; for he has set his heart on it, and nothing can hurt him now. My child, it is very hard; but we must help each other bear it."

Rose tried to say "Yes, uncle," bravely; but the words would not come; and she could only slip her hand into his with a look of mute submission. He laid her head on his shoulder, and went on talking so quietly that any one who did not see how worn and haggard his face had grown with two days and a night of sharp anxiety might have thought him cold.

"Jessie has gone home to rest, and Jane is with poor Clara, who has dropped asleep at last. I've sent for Steve and the other boys. There will be time for them later; but he so begged to see you

now, I thought it best to come while this temporary
strength keeps him up. I have told him how it is,
but he will not believe me. If he asks you, answer
honestly; and try to fit him a little for this sudden
ending of so many hopes."

"How soon, uncle?"

"A few hours, probably. This tranquil moment is
yours: make the most of it; and, when we can do no
more for him, we'll comfort one another."

Mac met them in the hall: but Rose hardly saw
him; she was conscious only of the task before her;
and, when her uncle led her to the door, she said
quietly, —

"Let me go in alone, please."

Archie, who had been hanging over the bed,
slipped away into the inner room as she appeared;
and Rose found Charlie waiting for her with such a
happy face, she could not believe what she had heard,
and found it easy to say almost cheerfully, as she
took his eager hand in both of hers, —

"Dear Charlie, I'm so glad you sent for me. I
longed to come, but waited till you were better. You
surely are?" she added, as a second glance showed
her the indescribable change which had come upon
the face which at first seemed to have both light and
color in it.

"Uncle says not: but I think he is mistaken, because the agony is all gone; and, except for this odd
sinking now and then, I don't feel so much amiss,"
he answered feebly, but with something of the old
lightness in his voice.

"You will hardly be able to sail in the 'Rajah,' I
fear; but you won't mind waiting a little, while we

nurse you," said poor Rose, trying to talk on quietly, with her heart growing heavier every minute.

"I shall go if I'm carried! I'll keep that promise, though it costs me my life. O Rose! you know? they've told you?" and, with a sudden memory of what brought him there, he hid his face in the pillow.

"You broke no promise; for I would not let you make one, you remember. Forget all that, and let us talk about the better time that may be coming for you."

"Always so generous, so kind!" he murmured, with her hand against his feverish cheek; then, looking up, he went on in a tone so humbly contrite it made her eyes fill with slow, hot tears.

"I tried to flee temptation: I tried to say 'No;' but I am so pitiably weak, I couldn't. You must despise me. But don't give me up entirely: for, if I live, I'll do better; I'll go away to father and begin again."

Rose tried to keep back the bitter drops; but they would fall, to hear him still speak hopefully when there was no hope. Something in the mute anguish of her face seemed to tell him what she could not speak; and a quick change came over him as he grasped her hand tighter, saying in a sharp whisper,—

"Have I really got to die, Rose?"

Her only answer was to kneel down and put her arms about him, as if she tried to keep death away a little longer. He believed it then, and lay so still, she looked up in a moment, fearing she knew not what.

But Charlie bore it manfully; for he had the courage

which can face a great danger bravely, though not the strength to fight a bosom-sin and conquer it. His eyes were fixed, as if trying to look into the unseen world whither he was going, and his lips firmly set that no word of complaint should spoil the proof he meant to give that, though he had not known how to live, he did know how to die. It seemed to Rose as if for one brief instant she saw the man that might have been, if early training had taught him how to rule himself; and the first words he uttered with a long sigh, as his eye came back to her, showed that he felt the failure and owned it with pathetic candor.

"Better so, perhaps; better go before I bring any more sorrow to you, and shame to myself. I'd like to stay a little longer, and try to redeem the past; it seems so wasted now: but, if I can't, don't grieve, Rose; I'm no loss to any one, and perhaps it *is* too late to mend."

"Oh, don't say that! no one will fill your place among us : we never can forget how much we loved you; and you must believe how freely we forgive as we would be forgiven," cried Rose, steadied by the pale despair that had fallen on Charlie's face with those bitter words.

"'Forgive us our trespasses!' Yes, I should say that. Rose, I'm not ready; it is so sudden: what can I do?" he whispered, clinging to her, as if he had no anchor except the creature whom he loved so much.

"Uncle will tell you: I am not good enough; I can only pray for you," and she moved as if to call in the help so sorely needed.

"No, no, not yet! stay by me, darling: read something; there, in grandfather's old book, some prayer for such as I. It will do me more good from you than any minister alive."

She got the venerable book, — given to Charlie because he bore the good man's name, — and, turning to the " Prayer for the Dying," read it brokenly; while the voice beside her echoed now and then some word that reproved or comforted.

" The testimony of a good conscience." " By the sadness of his countenance may his heart be made better." " Christian patience and fortitude." " Leave the world in peace." " Amen."

There was silence for a little; then Rose, seeing how wan he looked, said softly, " Shall I call uncle now? "

" If you will; but first — don't smile at my foolishness, dear — I want my little heart. They took it off: please give it back, and let me keep it always," he answered, with the old fondness strong as ever, even when he could only show it by holding fast the childish trinket which she found and gave him, — the old agate heart with the faded ribbon. " Put it on, and never let them take it off," he said; and, when she asked if there was any thing else she could do for him, he tried to stretch out his arms to her with a look which asked for more.

She kissed him very tenderly on lips and forehead; tried to say " Good-by," but could not speak, and groped her way to the door. Turning for a last look, Charlie's hopeful spirit rose for a moment, as if anxious to send her away more cheerful, and he said with a shadow of the old blithe smile, a feeble attempt at the familiar farewell gesture, —

" Till to-morrow, Rose."

Alas, for Charlie! his to-morrow never came : and, when she saw him next, he lay there looking so serene and noble, it seemed as if it must be well with him ; for all the pain was past ; temptation ended ; doubt and fear, hope and love, could no more stir his quiet heart, and in solemn truth he *had* gone to meet his Father, and begin again.

CHAPTER XVI

GOOD WORKS

THE "Rajah" was delayed awhile, and when it sailed poor Mrs. Clara was on board; for every thing was ready, all thought she had better go to comfort her husband, and since her boy died she seemed to care very little what became of her. So, with friends to cheer the long voyage, she sailed away, a heavy-hearted woman, yet not quite disconsolate; for she knew her mourning was excessively becoming, and felt sure that Stephen would not find her altered by her trials as much as might have been expected.

Then nothing was left of that gay household but the empty rooms, silence never broken by a blithe voice any more, and pictures full of promise, but all unfinished, like poor Charlie's life.

There was much mourning for the bonny Prince, but no need to tell of it except as it affected Rose; for it is with her we have most to do, the other characters being of secondary importance.

When time had soothed the first shock of sudden loss, she was surprised to find that the memory of his faults and failings, short life and piteous death, grew dim as if a kindly hand wiped out the record, and gave him back to her in the likeness of the brave, bright boy she had loved, not as the wayward, passionate young man who had loved her.

This comforted her very much; and, folding down the last blotted leaf where his name was written, she gladly turned back to reopen and reread the happier chapters which painted the youthful knight before he went out to fall in his first battle. None of the bitterness of love bereaved marred this memory for Rose, because she found that the warmer sentiment, just budding in her heart, had died with Charlie, and lay cold and quiet in his grave. She wondered, yet was glad; though sometimes a remorseful pang smote her when she discovered how possible it was to go on without him, feeling almost as if a burden had been lifted off, since his happiness was taken out of her hands. The time had not yet come when the knowledge that a man's heart was in her keeping would make the pride and joy of her life; and while she waited for that moment she enjoyed the liberty she seemed to have recovered.

Such being her inward state, it much annoyed her to be regarded as a broken-hearted girl, and pitied for the loss of her young lover. She could not explain to all the world, so let it pass, and occupied her mind with the good works which always lie ready to be taken up and carried on. Having chosen philanthropy as her profession, she felt that it was high time to begin the task too long neglected.

Her projects were excellent, but did not prosper as rapidly as she hoped; for, having to deal with people, not things, unexpected obstacles were constantly arising. The "Home for Decayed Gentlewomen," as the boys insisted on calling her two

newly repaired houses, started finely; and it was a
pleasant sight to see the comfortable rooms filled with
respectable women busy at their various tasks, surrounded by the decencies and many of the comforts
which make life endurable.   But, presently, Rose was
disturbed to find that the good people expected her
to take care of them in a way she had not bargained
for.   Buffum, her agent, was constantly reporting
complaints, new wants, and general discontent if they
were not attended to.   Things were neglected, water-
pipes froze and burst, drains got out of order, yards
were in a mess, and rents behindhand.   Worst of all,
outsiders, instead of sympathizing, only laughed and
said, " We told you so," which is a most discouraging
remark to older and wiser workers than Rose.

Uncle Alec, however, stood by her staunchly, and
helped her out of many of her woes by good advice,
and an occasional visit of inspection, which did much
to impress upon the dwellers there the fact that, if
they did not do their part, their leases would be short
ones.

" I did n't expect to make any thing out of it, but
I did think they would be grateful," said Rose, on
one occasion when several complaints had come in
at once, and Buffum had reported great difficulty in
collecting the low rents.

" If you do this thing for the sake of the gratitude,
then it *is* a failure: but if it is done for the love of
helping those who need help it is a success; for in
spite of their worry every one of those women feel
what privileges they enjoy and value them highly,"
said Dr. Alec, as they went home after one of these
unsatisfactory calls.

"Then the least they can do is to say 'Thank you.' I'm afraid I *have* thought more of the gratitude than the work; but if there is n't any I must make up my mind to go without," answered Rose, feeling defrauded of her due.

"Favors often separate instead of attracting people nearer to one another, and I've seen many a friendship spoilt by the obligation being all on one side. Can't explain it, but it is so; and I've come to the conclusion that it is as hard to give in the right spirit as it is to receive. Puzzle it out, my dear, while you are learning to do good for its own sake."

"I know one sort of people who *are* grateful, and I'm going to devote my mind to them. They thank me in many ways, and helping them is all pleasure and no worry. Come in to the hospital and see the dear babies, or the Asylum and carry oranges to Phebe's orphans: *they* don't complain and fidget one's life out, bless their hearts!" cried Rose, clearing up suddenly.

After that she left Buffum to manage the "Retreat," and devoted her energies to the little folks, always so ready to receive the smallest gift, and repay the giver with their artless thanks. Here she found plenty to do, and did it with such sweet good-will that she won her way like sunshine, making many a little heart dance over splendid dolls, gay picture-books, and pots of flowers, as well as food, fire, and clothes for the small bodies pinched with want and pain.

As spring came, new plans sprung up as naturally as dandelions. The poor children longed for the country; and, as the green fields could not come to them, Rose carried them to the green fields. **Down**

17

on the Point stood an old farmhouse, often used by the Campbell tribe for summer holidays. That spring it was set to rights unusually early, several women installed as housekeeper, cook, and nurses; and, when the May days grew bright and warm, squads of pale children came to toddle in the grass, run over the rocks, and play upon the smooth sands of the beach. A pretty sight, and one that well repaid those who brought it to pass.

Every one took an interest in the " Rose Garden," as Mac named it; and the women-folk were continually driving over to the Point with something for the "poor dears." Aunt Plenty sowed gingerbread broadcast; Aunt Jessie made pinafores by the dozen; while Aunt Jane "kept her eye" on the nurses, and Aunt Myra supplied medicines so liberally that the mortality would have been awful, if Dr. Alec had not taken them in charge. To him this was the most delightful spot in the world: and well it might be; for he suggested the idea, and gave Rose all the credit of it. He was often there, and his appearance was always greeted with shrieks of rapture, as the children gathered from all quarters: creeping, running, hopping on crutches, or carried in arms which they gladly left to sit on " Uncle Doctor's" knee; for that was the title by which he went among them.

He seemed as young as any of his comrades, though the curly head was getting gray; and the frolics that went on when he arrived were better than any medicine to children who had never learned to play. It was a standing joke among the friends that the bachelor brother had the largest family, and was the most domestic man of the remaining four; though Uncle Mac did his part manfully, and kept Aunt Jane in a constant fidget, by his rash propositions to adopt the heartiest boys and prettiest girls to amuse him and employ her.

On one occasion she had a very narrow escape; and the culprit being her son, not her husband, she felt free to repay herself for many scares of this sort by a good scolding; which, unlike many, produced excellent results.

One bright June day, as Rose came cantering home from the Point on her pretty bay pony, she saw a man sitting on a fallen tree beside the road, and something in his despondent attitude arrested her attention. As she drew nearer, he turned his head, and she stopped short, exclaiming in great surprise, —

"Why, Mac! what *are* you doing here?"

"Trying to solve a problem," he answered, looking up with a whimsical expression of perplexity and amusement in his face, which made Rose smile, till his next words turned her sober in a twinkling, —

"I've eloped with a young lady, and don't know what to do with her. I took her home, of course; but mother turned her out of the house, and I'm in a quandary."

"Is that her baggage?" asked Rose, pointing with her whip to the large bundle which he held; while the wild idea flashed through her head that perhaps he really *had* done some rash deed of this sort.

"No, this is the young lady herself;" and, opening a corner of the brown shawl, he displayed a child of three, — so pale, so thin, and tiny, that she looked like a small scared bird just fallen from the nest, as she shrunk away from the light with great frightened eyes, and a hand like a little claw tightly clutching a button of Mac's coat.

" Poor baby! where did it come from? " cried Rose, leaning down to look.

" I 'll tell you the story, and then you shall advise me what to do. At our hospital, we 've had a poor woman who got hurt, and died two days ago. I had nothing to do with her, only took her a bit of fruit once or twice; for she had big, wistful sort of eyes that haunted me. The day she died I stopped a minute, and the nurse said she 'd been wanting to speak to me, but did n't dare. So I asked if I could do any thing for her; and, though she could hardly breathe for pain, — being almost gone, — she implored me to take care of baby. I found out where the child was, and promised I 'd see after her; for the poor soul could n't seem to die till I 'd given her that comfort. I never can forget the look in her eyes, as I held her hand, and said, ' Baby shall be taken care of.' She tried to thank me, and died soon after quite peacefully. Well, I went to-day and hunted up the poor little wretch. Found her in a miserable place, left in the care of an old hag, who had shut her up alone to keep her out of the way, and there this mite was, huddled in a corner crying, ' Marmar, marmar ! ' fit to touch a heart of stone. I blew up the woman, and took baby straight away, for she had been abused; and it was high time. Look there, will you? "

Mac turned the little skinny arm, and showed a blue mark which made Rose drop her reins, and stretch out both hands, crying with a tender sort of indignation, —

"How dared they do it? Give her to me; poor, little, motherless thing!"

Mac laid the bundle in her arms, and Rose began to cuddle it in the fond, foolish way women have, — a most comfortable and effective way, nevertheless; and baby evidently felt that things were changing for the better, when warm lips touched her cheeks, a soft hand smoothed her tumbled hair, and a womanly face bent over her, with the inarticulate cooings and purrings mothers make. The frightened eyes went up to this gentle countenance, and rested there as if reassured; the little claw crept to the girl's neck, and poor baby nestled to her with a long sigh, and a plaintive murmur of "Marmar, marmar," that certainly would have touched a stony heart.

"Now, go on. No, Rosa, not you," said the new nurse, as the intelligent animal looked round to see if things were all right before she proceeded.

"I took the child home to mother, not knowing what else to do; but she would n't have it at any price, even for a night. She does n't like children, you know, and father has joked so much about the Pointers that she is quite rampant at the mere idea of a child in the house. She told me to take it to the Rose Garden. I said it was running over now, and no room even for a mite like this. 'Go to the Hospital,' says she. 'Baby is n't ill, ma'am,' says I. 'Orphan Asylum,' says she. 'Not an orphan: got a father who can't take care of her,' says I. 'Take her to the Foundling place, or Mrs. Gardener, or some one whose business it is. I will *not* have the creature here, sick and dirty and noisy. Carry it back, and ask Rose to tell you what to do with it.' So my cruel parent cast me forth; but relented as I shouldered baby, gave me a shawl to put her in, a jumble to feed her with, and money to pay her board in some good place. Mother's bark is always worse than her bite, you know."

"And you were trying to think of the ' good place ' as you sat here?" asked Rose, looking down at him with great approval, as he stood patting Rosa's glossy neck.

"Exactly. I did n't want to trouble you, for you have your house full already; and I really could n't lay my hand on any good soul who would be bothered with this little forlornity. She has nothing to recommend her, you see, — not pretty, feeble, and shy as a mouse; no end of care, I dare say: yet she needs every bit she can get to keep soul and body together, if I 'm any judge."

Rose opened her lips impulsively, but closed them without speaking, and sat a minute looking straight between Rosa's ears, as if forcing herself to think twice before she spoke. Mac watched her out of the corner of his eye, as he said, in a musing tone, tucking the shawl round a pair of shabby little feet the while, —

"This seems to be one of the charities that no one wants to undertake; yet I can't help feeling that my promise to the mother binds me to something more than merely handing baby over to some busy matron or careless nurse in any of our over-crowded institutions. She is such a frail creature she won't trouble any one long, perhaps; and I *should* like to give her just a taste of comfort, if not love, before she finds her ' Marmar ' again."

"Lead Rosa: I 'm going to take this child home:

and, if uncle is willing, I'll adopt her, and she *shall*
be happy!" cried Rose, with the sudden glow of feeling that always made her lovely. And, gathering poor
baby close, she went on her way like a modern Brito-
mart, ready to redress the wrongs of any who had
need of her.

As he led the slowly stepping horse along the quiet
road, Mac could not help thinking that they looked a
little like the Flight into Egypt: but he did not say
so, being a reverent youth, — only glanced back now
and then at the figure above him; for Rose had taken
off her hat to keep the light from baby's eyes, and sat
with the sunshine turning her uncovered hair to gold,
as she looked down at the little creature resting on
the saddle before her, with the sweet thoughtfulness
one sees in some of Correggio's young Madonnas.

No one else saw the picture, but Mac long remembered it; and ever after there was a touch of reverence added to the warm affection he had always borne
his cousin Rose.

"What is the child's name?" was the sudden question which disturbed a brief silence, broken only by
the sound of pacing hoofs, the rustle of green boughs
overhead, and the blithe carolling of birds.

"I'm sure I don't know," answered Mac, suddenly
aware that he had fallen out of one quandary into
another.

"Didn't you ask?"

"No: the mother called her 'Baby;' the old
woman, 'Brat.' And that is all I know of the first
name: the last is Kennedy. You can Christen her
what you like."

"Then I shall name her Dulcinea, as you are her

knight, and call her Dulce for short. That is a sweet diminutive, I'm sure," laughed Rose, much amused at the idea.

Don Quixote looked pleased, and vowed to defend his little lady stoutly, beginning his services on the spot by filling the small hands with buttercups, thereby winning for himself the first smile baby's face had known for weeks.

When they got home, Aunt Plenty received her new guest with her accustomed hospitality, and, on learning the story, was as warmly interested as even enthusiastic Rose could desire, bustling about to make the child comfortable with an energy pleasant to see; for the grandmotherly instincts were strong in the old lady, and of late had been beautifully developed.

In less than half an hour from the time baby went upstairs, she came down again on Rose's arm, freshly washed and brushed, in a pink gown much too large, and a white apron decidedly too small; an immaculate pair of socks, but no shoes; a neat bandage on the bruised arm, and a string of spools for a plaything hanging on the other. A resigned expression sat upon her little face; but the frightened eyes were only shy now, and the forlorn heart evidently much comforted.

"There! how do you like your Dulce now?" said Rose, proudly displaying the work of her hands, as she came in with her habit pinned up, and carrying a silver porringer of bread and milk.

Mac knelt down, took the small, reluctant hand, and kissed it as devoutly as ever good Alonzo Quixada did that of the Duchess; while he said, merrily quoting from the immortal story, —

"'High and Sovereign Lady, thine till death, the Knight of the Rueful Countenance.'"

But baby had no heart for play, and, withdrawing her hand, pointed to the porringer, with the suggestive remark, —

"Din-din, *now*."

So Rose sat down and fed the Duchess, while the Don stood by and watched the feast with much satisfaction.

"How nice she looks! Do you consider shoes unhealthy?" he asked, surveying the socks with respectful interest.

"No: her shoes are drying. You must have let her go in the mud."

"I only put her down for a minute when she howled; and she made for a puddle, like a duck. I'll buy her some new ones, — clothes too. Where do I go, what do I ask for, and how much do I get?" he said, diving for his pocket-book, amiably anxious, but pitiably ignorant.

"I'll see to that. We always have things on hand for the Pointers as they come along, and can soon fit Dulce out. You may make some inquiries about the father if you will; for I don't want to have her taken away just as I get fond of her. Do you know any thing about him?"

"Only that he is in State Prison for twenty-one years, and not likely to trouble you."

"How dreadful! I really think Phebe was better off to have none at all. I'll go to work at once, then, and try to bring up the convict's little daughter to be a good woman; so that she will have an honest name of her own, since he has nothing but disgrace to give her."

" Uncle can show you how to do that, if you need any help. He has been so successful in his first attempt I fancy you won't require much," said Mac, picking up the spools for the sixth time.

" Yes, I shall; for it is a great responsibility, and I do not undertake it lightly," answered Rose, soberly; though the double-barrelled compliment pleased her very much.

" I'm sure Phebe has turned out splendidly, and you began very early with her."

" So I did! that's encouraging. Dear thing, how bewildered she looked when I proposed adopting her. I remember all about it; for uncle had just come, and I was quite crazy over a box of presents, and rushed at Phebe as she was cleaning brasses. How little I thought my childish offer would end so well! " and Rose fell a musing with a happy smile on her face, while baby picked the last morsels out of the porringer with her own busy fingers.

It certainly had ended well; for Phebe at the end of six months not only had a good place as choir singer, but several young pupils, and excellent prospects for the next winter.

> " ' Accept the blessing of a poor young man,
> Whose lucky steps have led him to your door,'

and let me help as much as I can.   Good-by, my Dul-
cinea," and, with a farewell stroke of the smooth head, Mac went away to report his success to his mother, who, in spite of her seeming harshness, was already planning how she could best befriend this inconvenient baby.

CHAPTER XVII

AMONG THE HAY-COCKS

U NCLE ALEC did not object; and, finding
that no one had any claim upon the child,
permitted Rose to keep it for a time at least.
So little Dulce, newly equipped even to a name, took
her place among them and slowly began to thrive.
But she did not grow pretty, and never was a gay,
attractive child; for she seemed to have been born
in sorrow and brought up in misery. A pale, pensive
little creature, always creeping into corners and looking timidly out, as if asking leave to live, and, when
offered playthings, taking them with a meek surprise
that was very touching.

Rose soon won her heart, and then almost wished
she had not; for baby clung to her with inconvenient
fondness, changing her former wail of " Marmar "
into a lament for " Aunty Wose " if separated long.
Nevertheless, there was great satisfaction in cherishing the little waif; for she learned more than she
could teach, and felt a sense of responsibility which
was excellent ballast for her enthusiastic nature.

Kitty Van, who made Rose her model in all things,
was immediately inspired to go and do likewise, to
the great amusement as well as annoyance of her
family. Selecting the prettiest, liveliest child in the

Asylum, she took it home on trial for a week. "A
perfect cherub" she pronounced it the first day, but
an "*enfant terrible*" before the week was over; for the
young hero rioted by day, howled by night, ravaged
the house from top to bottom, and kept his guardians
in a series of panics by his hair-breadth escapes. So
early on Saturday, poor, exhausted Kitty restored
the "cherub" with many thanks, and decided to
wait till her views of education were rather more
advanced.

As the warm weather came on, Rose announced
that Dulce needed mountain air; for she dutifully
repeated as many of Dr. Alec's prescriptions as possible, and, remembering how much good Cosy Corner
did her long ago, resolved to try it on her baby.
Aunt Jessie and Jamie went with her, and Mother
Atkinson received them as cordially as ever. The
pretty daughters were all married and gone, but a
stout damsel took their place; and nothing seemed
changed except that the old heads were grayer and
the young ones a good deal taller than six years ago.

Jamie immediately fraternized with neighboring
boys, and devoted himself to fishing with an ardor
which deserved greater success. Aunt Jessie rev-
elled in the reading, for which she had no time at
home; and lay in her hammock a happy woman,
with no socks to darn, buttons to sew, or housekeeping cares to vex her soul.

Rose went about with Dulce like a very devoted
hen with one rather feeble chicken; for she was anxious to have this treatment work well, and tended her
little patient with daily increasing satisfaction. Dr.
Alec came up to pass a few days, and pronounced

the child in a most promising condition. But the grand event of the season was the unexpected arrival of Phebe.

Two of her pupils had invited her to join them in a trip to the mountains, and she ran away from the great hotel to surprise her little mistress with a sight of her, so well and happy that Rose had no anxiety left on her account.

Three delightful days they spent, roaming about together, talking as only girls can talk after a long separation, and enjoying one another like a pair of lovers. As if to make it quite perfect, by one of those remarkable coincidences which sometimes occur, Archie happened to run up for the Sunday; so Phebe had *her* surprise, and Aunt Jessie and the telegraph kept their secret so well, no one ever knew what maternal machinations brought the happy accident to pass.

Then Rose saw a very pretty, pastoral bit of love-making, and long after it was over, and Phebe gone one way, Archie another, the echo of sweet words seemed to linger in the air, tender ghosts to haunt the pine-grove, and even the big coffee-pot had a halo of romance about it; for its burnished sides reflected the soft glances the lovers interchanged, as one filled the other's cup at that last breakfast.

Rose found these reminiscences more interesting than any novel she had read, and often beguiled her long leisure by planning a splendid future for her Phebe, as she trotted about after her baby in the lovely July weather.

On one of the most perfect days, she sat under an old apple-tree on the slope behind the house where

they used to play.   Before her opened the wide inter-
vale, dotted with hay-makers at their picturesque work.
On the left, flowed the swift river fringed with graceful elms in their bravest greenery; on the right, rose
the purple hills serene and grand; and overhead
glowed the midsummer sky which glorified it all.

Little Dulce tired of play, lay fast asleep in the nest
she had made in one of the hay cocks close by; and
Rose leaned against the gnarled old tree, dreaming
day-dreams with her work at her feet.   Happy and
absorbing fancies they seemed to be; for her face was
beautifully tranquil, and she took no heed of the train
which suddenly went speeding down the valley, leaving
a white cloud behind.   Its rumble concealed the sound
of approaching steps, and her eyes never turned from
the distant hills, till the abrupt appearance of a very
sunburnt but smiling young man made her jump up,
exclaiming joyfully, —

"Why, Mac! where did you drop from?"

"The top of Mount Washington. How do you
do?"

"Never better. Won't you go in? You must be
tired after such a fall."

"No, thank you; I've seen the old lady.   She told
me Aunt Jessie and the boy had gone to town, and
that you were ' settin' round ' in the old place; so I
came on at once, and will take a lounge here, if you
don't mind," answered Mac, unstrapping his knapsack,
and taking a hay-cock as if it were a chair.

Rose subsided into her former seat, surveying her
cousin with much satisfaction, as she said, —

"This is the third surprise I've had since I came.
Uncle popped in upon us first, then Phebe, and now

you. Have you had a pleasant tramp? Uncle said you were off."

"Delightful! I feel as if I 'd been in heaven, or near it, for about three weeks; and thought I 'd break the shock of coming down to the earth by calling here on my way home."

"You look as if heaven suited you. Brown as a berry; but so fresh and happy, I should never guess you had been scrambling down a mountain," said Rose, trying to discover why he looked so well in spite of the blue-flannel suit and dusty shoes; for there was a certain sylvan freshness about him, as he sat there full of the reposeful strength the hills seemed to have given, the wholesome cheerfulness days of air and sunshine put into a man, and the clear, bright look of one who had caught glimpses of a new world from the mountain-top.

"Tramping agrees with me. I took a dip in the river as I came along, and made my toilet in a place where Milton's Sabrina might have lived," he said, shaking back his damp hair, and settling the knot of scarlet bunch-berries stuck in his button-hole.

"You look as if you found the nymph at home," said Rose, knowing how much he liked the Comus.

"I found her *here*," and he made a little bow.

"That 's very pretty; and I 'll give you one in return. You grow more like Uncle Alec every day, and I think I 'll call you Alec, Jr."

"Alexander the Great would n't thank you for that," and Mac did not look as grateful as she had expected.

"Very like, indeed, except the forehead. His is broad and benevolent; yours high and arched. Do you know if you had no beard, and wore your hair

long, I really think you 'd look like Milton," added
Rose, sure that would please him.

It certainly did amuse him; for he lay back on the
hay and laughed so heartily that his merriment scared
the squirrel on the wall and woke Dulce.

" You ungrateful boy! will nothing suit you?
When I say you look like the best man I know, you
give a shrug; and, when I liken you to a great poet,
you shout: I 'm afraid you are very conceited, Mac;"
and Rose laughed too, glad to see him so gay.

" If I am, it is your fault. Nothing I can do will
ever make a Milton of me, unless I go blind some
day," he said, sobering at the thought.

" You once said a man could be what he liked if he
tried hard enough; so why should n't you be a poet?"
asked Rose, liking to trip him up with his own words,
as he often did her.

" I thought I was to be an M.D."

" You might be both. There have been poetical
doctors, you know."

" Would you like me to be such an one?" asked
Mac, looking at her as seriously as if he really thought
of trying it.

" No: I 'd rather have you one or the other. I
don't care which, only you must be famous in either
you choose. I 'm very ambitious for you; because, I
insist upon it, you are a genius of some sort. I think
it is beginning to simmer already, and I 've a great
curiosity to know what it will turn out to be."

Mac's eyes shone as she said that, but before he
could speak a little voice said, " Aunty Wose!" and
he turned to find Dulce sitting up in her nest, staring
at the broad blue back before her with round eyes.

"Do you know your Don?" he asked, offering his hand with respectful gentleness; for she seemed a little doubtful whether he was friend or stranger.

"It is 'Mat,'" said Rose, and that familiar word seemed to reassure the child at once; for, leaning forward, she kissed him as if quite used to doing it.

"I picked up some toys for her by the way, and she shall have them at once to pay for that. I did n't expect to be so graciously received by this shy mouse," said Mac, much gratified; for Dulce was very chary of her favors.

"She knew you; for I always carry my home-album with me, and when she comes to your picture she always kisses it, because I never want her to forget her first friend," explained Rose, pleased with her pupil.

"First, but not best," answered Mac, rummaging in his knapsack for the promised toys, which he set forth upon the hay before delighted Dulce.

Neither picture-books nor sweeties; but berries strung on long stems of grass, acorns and pretty cones, bits of rock shining with mica, several blue-birds' feathers, and a nest of moss with white pebbles for eggs.

"Dearest Nature, strong and kind," knows what children love, and has plenty of such playthings ready for them all, if one only knows how to find them. These were received with rapture; and, leaving the little creature to enjoy them in her own quiet way, Mac began to tumble the things back into his knapsack again. Two or three books lay near Rose, and she took up one which opened at a place marked by a scribbled paper.

"Keats? I did n't know you condescended to read any thing so modern," she said, moving the paper to see the page beneath.

Mac looked up, snatched the book out of her hand, and shook down several more scraps; then returned it with a curiously shame-faced expression, saying, as he crammed the papers into his pocket, —

"I beg pardon, but it was full of rubbish. Oh, yes! I 'm fond of Keats; don't you know him?"

"I used to read him a good deal; but uncle found me crying over the 'Pot of Basil,' and advised me to read less poetry for a while or I should get too sentimental," answered Rose, turning the pages without seeing them; for a new idea had just popped into her head.

"'The Eve of St. Agnes' is the most perfect love-story in the world, I think," said Mac, enthusiastically.

"Read it to me. I feel just like hearing poetry, and you will do it justice if you are fond of it," said Rose, handing him the book with an innocent air.

"Nothing I 'd like better; but it is rather long."

"I 'll tell you to stop if I get tired. Baby won't interrupt; she will be contented for an hour with those pretty things."

As if well pleased with his task, Mac laid himself comfortably on the grass, and leaning his head on his hand read the lovely story as only one could who entered fully into the spirit of it. Rose watched him closely, and saw how his face brightened over some quaint fancy, delicate description, or delicious word; heard how smoothly the melodious measures fell from his lips, and read something more than admiration in his eyes, as he looked up now and then to mark if she enjoyed it as much as he.

She could not help enjoying it; for the poet's pen painted as well as wrote, and the little romance lived before her: but she was not thinking of John Keats as she listened; she was wondering if this cousin was a kindred spirit, born to make such music and leave as sweet an echo behind him. It seemed as if it might be; and, after going through the rough caterpillar and the pent-up chrysalis changes, the beautiful butterfly would appear to astonish and delight them all. So full of this fancy was she that she never thanked him when the story ended; but, leaning forward, asked in a tone that made him start and look as if he had fallen from the clouds, —

"Mac, do you ever write poetry?"

"Never."

"What do you call the song Phebe sang with her bird chorus?"

"That was nothing till she put the music to it. But she promised not to tell."

"She didn't; I suspected, and now I know," laughed Rose, delighted to have caught him.

Much discomfited, Mac gave poor Keats a fling, and leaning on both elbows tried to hide his face; for it had reddened like that of a modest girl when teased about her lover.

"You needn't look so guilty; it is no sin to write poetry," said Rose, amused at his confusion.

"It's a sin to call that rubbish poetry," muttered Mac, with great scorn.

"It is a greater sin to tell a fib, and say you never write it."

"Reading so much sets one thinking about such things, and every fellow scribbles a little jingle when he is lazy or in love, you know," explained Mac, looking very guilty.

Rose could not quite understand the change she saw in him, till his last words suggested a cause which she knew by experience was apt to inspire young men. Leaning forward again, she asked solemnly, though her eyes danced with fun, —

"Mac, are you in love?"

"Do I look like it?" and he sat up with such an injured and indignant face, that she apologized at once; for he certainly did not look lover-like with hay-seed in his hair, several lively crickets playing leap-frog over his back, and a pair of long legs stretching from tree to hay-cock.

"No, you don't; and I humbly beg your pardon for making such an unwarrantable insinuation. It merely occurred to me that the general upliftedness I observe in you might be owing to that, since it was n't poetry."

"It is the good company I 've been keeping, if any thing. A fellow can't spend 'A Week' with Thoreau and not be the better for it. I 'm glad I show it; because in the scramble life is to most of us, even an hour with such a sane, simple, and sagacious soul as his must help one," said Mac, taking a much worn book out of his pocket with the air of introducing a dear and honored friend.

"I 've read bits, and like them: they are so original and fresh and sometimes droll," said Rose, smiling to see what natural and appropriate marks of approbation the elements seemed to set upon the pages Mac

was turning eagerly; for one had evidently been rained on, a crushed berry stained another, some appreciative field-mouse or squirrel had nibbled one corner, and the cover was faded with the sunshine, which seemed to have filtered through to the thoughts within.

" Here's a characteristic bit for you : —

" ' I would rather sit on a pumpkin, and have it all to myself, than be crowded on a velvet cushion. I would rather ride on earth in an ox-cart, with free circulation, than go to heaven in the fancy car of an excursion train, and breathe malaria all the way.'

" I 've tried both and quite agree with him," laughed Mac; and, skimming down another page, gave her a paragraph here and there.

" ' Read the best books first, or you may not have a chance to read them at all.'

" ' We do not learn much from learned books, but from sincere human books: frank, honest biographies.'

" ' At least let us have healthy books. Let the poet be as vigorous as a sugar-maple, with sap enough to maintain his own verdure, besides what runs into the trough; and not like a vine which, being cut in the spring, bears no fruit, but bleeds to death in the endeavor to heal its wounds.' "

" That will do for you," said Rose, still thinking of the new suspicion which pleased her by its very improbability.

Mac flashed a quick look at her and shut the book, saying quietly, though his eyes shone, and a conscious smile lurked about his mouth, —

"We shall see, and no one need meddle; for, as my Thoreau says, —

> "'Whate'er we leave to God, God does
> And blesses us :
> The work we choose should be our own
> God lets alone.'"

Rose sat silent, as if conscious that she deserved his poetical reproof.

"Come, you have catechised me pretty well; now I'll take my turn and ask why *you* look 'uplifted,' as you call it. What have you been doing to make yourself more like your namesake than ever?" asked Mac, carrying war into the enemy's camp with the sudden question.

"Nothing but live, and enjoy doing it. I actually sit here, day after day, as happy and contented with little things as Dulce is, and feel as if I wasn't much older than she," answered the girl, feeling as if some change was going on in that pleasant sort of pause, but unable to describe it.

> "'As if a rose should shut and be a bud again,'"

murmured Mac, borrowing from his beloved Keats.

"Ah, but I can't do that! I must go on blooming whether I like it or not, and the only trouble I have is to know what leaf I ought to unfold next," said Rose, playfully smoothing out the white gown, in which she looked very like a daisy among the green.

"How far have you got?" asked Mac, continuing his catechism as if the fancy suited him.

"Let me see. Since I came home last year, I've been gay, then sad, then busy, and now I am simply happy. I don't know why; but seem to be waiting for what is to come next, and getting ready for it, perhaps unconsciously," she said, looking dreamily away to the hills again, as if the new experience was coming to her from afar.

Mac watched her thoughtfully for a minute, wondering how many more leaves must unfold, before the golden heart of this human flower would lie open to the sun. He felt a curious desire to help in some way, and could think of none better than to offer her what he had found most helpful to himself. Picking up another book, he opened it at a place where an oak leaf lay, and, handing it to her, said, as if presenting something very excellent and precious, —

"If you want to be ready to take whatever comes in a brave and noble way, read that, and the one where the page is turned down."

Rose took it, saw the words " Self-Reliance," and, turning the leaves, read here and there a passage which was marked : —

"'My life is for itself, and not for a spectacle.'

"'Insist on yourself: never imitate. That which each can do best, none but his Maker can teach him.'

"'Do that which is assigned to you, and you cannot hope or dare too much.'"

Then coming to the folded leaf, whose title was " Heroism," she read, and brightened as she read, —

"'Let the maiden, with erect soul, walk serenely on her way; accept the hint of each new experience; search in turn all the objects that solicit her eye, that she may learn the power and the charm of her new-born being.'

"'The fair girl who repels interference by a decided and proud choice of influences inspires every beholder with something of her own nobleness; and the silent heart encourages her. O friend, never strike sail to a fear! Come into port greatly, or sail with God the seas.'"

"You understand that, don't you?" asked Mac, as she glanced up with the look of one who had found something suited to her taste and need.

"Yes, but I never dared to read these Essays, because I thought they were too wise for me."

"The wisest things are sometimes the simplest, I think. Every one welcomes light and air, and cannot do without them; yet very few could explain them truly. I don't ask you to read or understand all of that, — don't myself, — but I do recommend the two essays I've marked, as well as 'Love and Friendship.' Try them, and let me know how they suit. I'll leave you the book."

"Thanks. I wanted something fine to read up here; and, judging by what I see, I fancy this *will* suit. Only Aunt Jessie may think I'm putting on airs, if I try Emerson."

"Why should she? He has done more to set young men and women thinking, than any man in this century at least. Don't you be afraid: if it is what you want, take it, and go ahead as he tells you, —

> "'Without halting, without rest,
> Lifting Better up to Best.'"

"I'll try," said Rose, meekly; feeling that Mac had been going ahead himself much faster than she had any suspicion.

Here a voice exclaimed "Hallo!" and, looking round, Jamie was discovered surveying them critically,

as he stood in an independent attitude, like a small
Colossus of Rhodes in brown linen, with a bundle of
molasses-candy in one hand, several new fish-hooks
cherished carefully in the other, and his hat well on
the back of his head, displaying as many freckles as
one somewhat limited nose could reasonably accommodate.

" How are you, young one? " said Mac, nodding.

" Tip-top. Glad it 's you: thought Archie might
have turned up again, and he 's no fun. Where did
you come from? What did you come for? How
long are you going to stay? Want a bit? It 's jolly
good."

With which varied remarks Jamie approached,
shook hands in a manly way, and, sitting down beside
his long cousin, hospitably offered sticks of candy all
round.

" Did you get any letters? " asked Rose, declining
the sticky treat.

" Lots: but mamma forgot to give 'em to me, and I
was rather in a hurry; for Mrs. Atkinson said somebody had come, and I could n't wait," explained Jamie,
reposing luxuriously with his head on Mac's legs, and
his mouth full.

" I 'll step and get them. Aunty must be tired,
and we should enjoy reading the news together."

" She is the most convenient girl that ever was,"
observed Jamie, as Rose departed, thinking Mac
might like some more substantial refreshment than
sweetmeats.

" I should think so, if you let her run your errands,
you lazy little scamp," answered Mac, looking after
her as she went up the green slope; for there was

something very attractive to him about the slender figure in a plain white gown, with a black sash about the waist, and all the wavy hair gathered to the top of the head with a little black bow.

"Sort of pre-Raphaelite, and quite refreshing after the furbelowed creatures at the hotels," he said to himself, as she vanished under the arch of scarlet-runners over the garden-gate.

"Oh, well! she likes it. Rose is fond of me, and I'm very good to her when I have time," continued Jamie, calmly explaining. "I let her cut out a fish-hook, when it caught in my leg, with a sharp pen-knife; and you'd better believe it hurt: but I never squirmed a bit, and she said I was a brave boy. And then, one day I got left on my desert island, — out in the pond, you know, — the boat floated off, and there I was for as much as an hour before I could make any one hear. But Rose thought I might be there; and down she came, and told me to swim ashore. It was n't far; but the water was horrid cold, and I did n't like it. I started though, just as she said, and got on all right, till about half way, then cramp or something made me shut up and howl, and she came after me slapdash, and pulled me ashore. Yes, sir, as wet as a turtle, and looked so funny, I laughed; and that cured the cramp. Was n't I good to mind when she said, 'Come on'?"

"She was, to dive after such a scapegrace. I guess you lead her a life of it, and I'd better take you home with me in the morning," suggested Mac, rolling the boy over, and giving him a good-natured pummelling on the hay-cock, while Dulce applauded from her nest.

When Rose returned with ice-cold milk, ginger-bread, and letters, she found the reader of Emerson up in the tree, pelting and being pelted with green apples, as Jamie vainly endeavored to get at him. The siege ended when Aunt Jessie appeared; and the rest of the afternoon was spent in chat about home affairs.

Early the next morning Mac was off, and Rose went as far as the old church with him.

"Shall you walk all the way?" she asked, as he strode along beside her, in the dewy freshness of the young day.

"Only about twenty miles, then take car and whisk back to my work," he answered, breaking a delicate fern for her.

"Are you never lonely?"

"Never: I take my best friends along, you know," and he gave a slap to the pocket from which peeped the volume of Thoreau.

"I 'm afraid you leave your very best behind you," said Rose, alluding to the book he had lent her yesterday.

"I 'm glad to share it with you. I have much of it here; and a little goes a great way, as you will soon discover," he answered, tapping his head.

"I hope the reading will do as much for me as it seems to have done for you. I 'm happy; but you are wise and good: I want to be, also."

"Read away, and digest it well; then write, and tell me what you think of it. Will you?" he asked, as they paused where the four roads met.

"If you will answer. Shall you have time with all your other work? Poetry -- I beg pardon -- medicine is very absorbing, you know," answered Rose, mischievously; for just then, as he stood bareheaded with the shadows of the leaves playing over his fine forehead, she remembered the chat among the haycocks, and he did not look at all like an M.D.

"I'll make time."

"Good-by, Milton."

"Good-by, Sabrina."

CHAPTER XVIII

WHICH WAS IT?

ROSE did read and digest, and found her days much richer for the good company she kept; for an introduction to so much that was wise, beautiful, and true, could not but make that month a memorable one. It is not strange that while the young man most admired " Heroism " and " Self-Reliance," the girl preferred " Love " and " Friendship," reading them over and over like prose poems, as they are, to the fitting accompaniment of sunshine, solitude, and sympathy; for letters went to and fro, with praiseworthy regularity.

Rose much enjoyed this correspondence, and found herself regretting that it was at an end when she went home in September; for Mac wrote better than he talked, though he could do that remarkably well when he chose. But she had no chance to express either pleasure or regret; for, the first time she saw him after her return, the great change in his appearance made her forget everything else. Some whim had seized him to be shaven and shorn, and when he presented himself to welcome Rose she hardly knew him; for the shaggy hair was nicely trimmed and brushed, the cherished brown beard entirely gone, showing a well cut mouth and handsome chin, and giving a new expression to the whole face.

"Are you trying to look like Keats?" she asked after a critical glance, which left her undecided whether the change was an improvement or not.

"I am trying not to look like uncle," answered Mac, coolly.

"And why, if you please?" demanded Rose, in great surprise.

"Because I prefer to look like myself, and not resemble any other man, no matter how good or great he may be."

"You have n't succeeded then; for you look now very much like the Young Augustus," returned Rose, rather pleased, on the whole, to see what a finely shaped head appeared after the rough thatch was off.

"Trust a woman to find a comparison for every thing under the sun!" laughed Mac, not at all flattered by the one just made. "What do you think of me, on the whole?" he asked a minute later, as he found Rose still scrutinizing him with a meditative air.

"Have n't made up my mind. It is such an entire change I don't know you, and feel as if I ought to be introduced. You certainly look much more tidy; and I fancy I *shall* like it, when I 'm used to seeing a somewhat distinguished-looking man about the house instead of my old friend Orson," answered Rose, with her head on one side to get a profile view.

"Don't tell uncle why I did it, please: he thinks it was for the sake of coolness, and likes it, so take no notice; they are all used to me now, and don't mind," said Mac, roving about the room as if rather ashamed of his whim after all.

"No, I won't; but you must n't mind if I 'm not as sociable as usual for a while. I never can be with

strangers, and you really do seem like one. That
will be a punishment for your want of taste and love
of originality," returned Rose, resolved to punish him
for the slight put upon her beloved uncle.

"As you like. I won't trouble you much anyway;
for I 'm going to be very busy. May go to L—— this
winter, if uncle thinks best; and then my 'originality'
can't annoy you."

"I hope you won't go. Why, Mac, I 'm just getting
to know and enjoy you, and thought we 'd have a nice
time this winter reading something together. Must
you go?" and Rose seemed to forget his strangeness,
as she held him still by one button while she talked.

"That *would* be nice. But I feel as if I must go:
my plans are all made, and I 've set my heart on it,"
answered Mac, looking so eager that Rose released
him, saying sadly, —

"I suppose it is natural for you all to get restless,
and push off; but it is hard for me to let you go one
after the other, and stay here alone. Charlie is gone,
Archie and Steve are wrapt up in their sweethearts,
the boys away, and only Jamie left to 'play with
Rose.'"

"But I 'll come back, and you 'll be glad I went if
I bring you my —" began Mac, with sudden animation; then stopped abruptly to bite his lips, as if he
had nearly said too much.

"Your what?" asked Rose, curiously; for he neither
looked nor acted like himself.

"I forgot how long it takes to get a diploma," he
said, walking away again.

"There will be one comfort if you go: you 'll see
Phebe, and can tell me all about her; for she is so

modest she does n't half do it. I shall want to know
how she gets on, if she is engaged to sing ballads in
the concerts they talk of for next winter. You will
write, won't you?"

"Oh, yes! no doubt of that," and Mac laughed
low to himself, as he stooped to look at the little
Psyche on the mantel-piece. "What a pretty thing
it is!" he added soberly, as he took it up.

"Be careful. Uncle gave it to me last New-Year,
and I'm very fond of it. She is just lifting her lamp
to see what Cupid is like; for she has n't seen him
yet," said Rose, busy putting her work-table in order.

"You ought to have a Cupid for her to look at.
She has been waiting patiently a whole year, with
nothing but a bronze lizard in sight," said Mac, with
the half-shy, half-daring look which was so new and
puzzling.

"Cupid flew away as soon as she woke him, you
know, and she had a bad time of it. She must wait
longer till she can find and keep him."

"Do you know she looks like you? Hair tied
up in a knot, and a spiritual sort of face. Don't you
see it?" asked Mac, turning the graceful little figure
toward her.

"Not a bit of it. I wonder whom I shall resemble
next! I 've been compared to a Fra Angelico angel,
Saint Agnes, and now 'Syke,' as Annabel once called
her."

"You 'd see what I mean, if you 'd ever watched
your own face when you were listening to music, talking earnestly, or much moved; then your soul gets
into your eyes and you are — like Psyche."

"Tell me the next time you see me in a 'soulful'

state, and I'll look in the glass; for I'd like to see if
it is becoming," said Rose, merrily, as she sorted her
gay worsteds.

> "'Your feet in the full-grown grasses,
>   Moved soft as a soft wind blows;
>   You passed me as April passes,
>   With a face made out of a rose,'"

murmured Mac, under his breath, thinking of the
white figure going up a green slope one summer day;
then, as if chiding himself for sentimentality, he set
Psyche down with great care, and began to talk about
a course of solid reading for the winter.

After that, Rose saw very little of him for several
weeks, as he seemed to be making up for lost time,
and was more odd and absent than ever when he did
appear. As she became accustomed to the change in
his external appearance, she discovered that he was
altering fast in other ways, and watched the "distinguished-looking gentleman" with much interest; saying to herself, when she saw a new sort of dignity
about him alternating with an unusual restlessness
of manner, and now and then a touch of sentiment,
"Genius is simmering, just as I predicted."

As the family were in mourning, there were no festivities on Rose's twenty-first birthday, though the
boys had planned all sorts of rejoicings. Every one
felt particularly tender toward their girl on that day,
remembering how "poor Charlie" had loved her;
and they tried to show it in the gifts and good wishes
they sent her. She found her sanctum all aglow with
autumn leaves, and on her table so many rare and
pretty things she quite forgot she was an heiress, and
only felt how rich she was in loving friends

One gift greatly pleased her, though she could not help smiling at the source from whence it came; for Mac sent her a Cupid, — not the chubby child with a face of naughty merriment, but a slender, winged youth, leaning on his unstrung bow, with a broken arrow at his feet. A poem, " To Psyche," came with it: and Rose was much surprised at the beauty of the lines; for, instead of being witty, complimentary, or gay, there was something nobler than mere sentiment in them, and the sweet old fable lived again in language which fitly painted the maiden Soul looking for a Love worthy to possess it.

Rose read them over and over, as she sat among the gold and scarlet leaves which glorified her little room, and each time found new depth and beauty in them; looking from the words that made music in her ear to the lovely shapes that spoke with their mute grace to her eye. The whole thing suited her exactly, it was so delicate and perfect in its way; for she was tired of costly gifts, and valued very much this proof of her cousin's taste and talent, seeing nothing in it but an affectionate desire to please her.

All the rest dropped in at intervals through the day to say a loving word, and last of all came Mac. Rose happened to be alone with Dulce, enjoying a splendid sunset from her western window; for October gave her child a beautiful good-night.

Rose turned round as he entered, and, putting down the little girl, went to him with the evening red shining on her happy face. as she said gratefully, —

"Dear Mac, it was *so* lovely! I don't know how to thank you for it in any way but this." And, drawing down his tall head, she gave him the birthday kiss she had given all the others.

But this time it produced a singular effect: for Mac turned scarlet, then grew pale; and when Rose added playfully, thinking to relieve the shyness of so young a poet, " Never say again you don't write poetry, or call your verses rubbish: I *knew* you were a genius, and now I'm sure of it," he broke out, as if against his will, —

" No. It is n't genius: it is — love!" Then, as she shrunk a little, startled at his energy, he added, with an effort at self-control which made his voice sound strange, —

" I did n't mean to speak, but I can't suffer you to deceive yourself so. I *must* tell the truth, and not let you kiss me like a cousin when I love you with all my heart and soul!"

" O Mac, don't joke!" cried Rose, bewildered by this sudden glimpse into a heart she thought she knew so well.

" I'm in solemn earnest," he answered, steadily, in such a quiet tone that, but for the pale excitement of his face, she might have doubted his words. " Be angry, if you will. I expect it, for I know it is too soon to speak. I ought to wait for years, perhaps; but you seemed so happy I dared to hope you had forgotten."

" Forgotten what?" asked Rose, sharply.

" Charlie."

" Ah! you all will insist on believing that I loved him better than I did!" she cried, with both pain and impatience in her voice; for the family delusion tried her very much at times.

" How could we help it, when he was every thing women most admire? " said Mac, not bitterly, but as if he sometimes wondered at their want of insight.

"*I* do not admire weakness of any sort: I could never love without either confidence or respect. Do me the justice to believe that, for I 'm tired of being pitied."

She spoke almost passionately, being more excited by Mac's repressed emotion than she had ever been by Charlie's most touching demonstration, though she did not know why.

" But he loved you so ! " began Mac; feeling as if a barrier had suddenly gone down, but not daring to venture in as yet.

" That was the hard part of it ! That was why I tried to love him, — why I hoped he would stand fast for my sake, if not for his own; and why I found it so sad sometimes not to be able to help despising him for his want of courage. I don't know how others feel, but, to me, love is n't all. I must look up, not down, trust and honor with my whole heart, and find strength and integrity to lean on. I have had it so far, and I know I could not live without it."

" Your ideal is a high one. Do you hope to find it, Rose? " Mac asked, feeling, with the humility of a genuine love, that *he* could not give her all she desired.

" Yes," she answered, with a face full of the beautiful confidence in virtue, the instinctive desire for the best which so many of us lose too soon, to find again after life's great lessons are well learned. " I do hope to find it, because I try not to be unreasonable and expect perfection. Smile if you will, but I won't give up my hero yet," and she tried to speak lightly, hoping to lead him away from a more dangerous topic.

"You'll have to look a long while, I'm afraid," and all the glow was gone out of Mac's face; for he understood her wish, and knew his answer had been given.

"I have uncle to help me; and I think my ideal grew out of my knowledge of him. How can I fail to believe in goodness, when he shows me what it can be and do?"

"It is no use for me to say any more; for I have very little to offer. I did not mean to say a word, till I'd earned a right to hope for something in return. I cannot take it back; but I can wish you success, and I do, because you deserve the very best," and Mac moved, as if he was going away without more words, accepting the inevitable as manfully as he could.

"Thank you: that makes me feel very ungrateful and unkind. I wish I could answer as you want me to; for, indeed, dear Mac, I'm very fond of you in my own way," and Rose looked up with such tender pity and frank affection in her face, it was no wonder the poor fellow caught at a ray of hope, and, brightening suddenly, said in his own odd way, —

"Couldn't you take me on trial, while you are waiting for the true hero? It may be years before you find him; meantime, you could be practising on me in ways that would be useful when you get him."

"O Mac! what *shall* I do with you?" exclaimed Rose, so curiously affected by this very characteristic wooing, that she did not know whether to laugh or cry; for he was looking at her with his heart in his eyes, though his proposition was the queerest ever made at such a time.

"Just go on being fond of me in your own way, and let me love you as much as I like in mine. I'll try to be satisfied with that," and he took both her hands so beseechingly that she felt more ungrateful than ever.

"No, it would not be fair: for you would love the most; and, if the hero did appear, what would become of you?"

"I should resemble Uncle Alec in one thing at least, — fidelity; for my first love would be my last."

That went straight to Rose's heart; and for a minute she stood silent, looking down at the two strong hands that held hers so firmly, yet so gently; and the thought went through her mind, "Must he too be solitary all his life? I have no dear lover as my mother had, why cannot I make him happy and forget myself?"

It did not seem very hard; and she owned that, even while she told herself to remember that compassion was no equivalent for love. She wanted to give all she could, and keep as much of Mac's affection as she honestly might; because it seemed to grow more sweet and precious when she thought of putting it away.

"You will be like uncle in happier ways than that, I hope; for you, too, must have a high ideal, and find her and be happy," she said, resolving to be true to the voice of conscience, not be swayed by the impulse of the moment.

"I *have* found her, but I don't see any prospect of happiness, do you?" he asked, wistfully.

"Dear Mac, I cannot give you the love you want, but I do trust and respect you from the bottom of my heart, if that is any comfort," began Rose, looking up with eyes full of contrition, for the pain her reply must give.

She got no further, however; for those last words wrought a marvellous change in Mac. Dropping her hands, he stood erect, as if inspired with sudden energy and hope, while over his face there came a brave, bright look, which for the moment made him a nobler and a comelier man than ever handsome Prince had been.

"It *is* a comfort!" he said, in a tone of gratitude, that touched her very much. "You said your love must be founded on respect, and that you have given me: why can I not earn the rest? I'm nothing now; but every thing is possible when one loves with all his heart and soul and strength. Rose, *I* will be your hero if a mortal man can, even though I have to work and wait for years. I'll *make* you love me, and be glad to do it. Don't be frightened. I've not lost my wits: I've just found them. I don't ask any thing: I'll never speak of my hope, but it is no use to stop me; I *must* try it, and I *will* succeed!"

With the last words, uttered in a ringing voice, while his face glowed, his eyes shone, and he looked as if carried out of himself by the passion that possessed him, Mac abruptly left the room, like one eager to change words to deeds and begin his task at once.

Rose was so amazed by all this, that she sat down trembling a little, not with fear or anger, but a feeling half pleasure, half pain; and a sense of some new power — subtle, strong, and sweet — that had come into her life. It seemed as if another Mac had taken the place of the one she had known so long, — an ardent, ambitious man, ready for any work, now that the magical moment had come, when every thing seems possible to love. If hope could work such a marvellous change for a moment, could not happiness do it for a lifetime? It would be an exciting experiment to try, she thought, remembering the sudden illumination which made that familiar face both beautiful and strange.

She could not help wondering how long this unsuspected sentiment had been growing in his heart, and felt perplexed by its peculiar demonstration; for she had never had a lover like this before. It touched and flattered her, nevertheless: and she could not but feel honored by a love so genuine and generous; for it seemed to make a man of Mac all at once, and a manly man too, who was not daunted by disappointment, but could "hope against hope," and resolve to *make* her love him if it took years to do it.

There was the charm of novelty about this sort of wooing, and she tried to guess how he would set about it, felt curious to see how he would behave when next they met, and was half angry with herself for not being able to decide how she ought to act. The more she thought the more bewildered she grew; for, having made up her mind that Mac was a genius, it disturbed all her plans to find him a lover, and such an ardent one. As it was impossible to predict what would come next, she gave up trying to prepare for it; and, tired with vain speculations, carried Dulce off to bed, wishing she could tuck away her love-troubles as quietly and comfortably as she did her sleepy little charge.

Simple and sincere in all things, Mac gave Rose a new surprise by keeping his promise to the letter, — asked nothing of her, said nothing of his hope, and went on as if nothing had happened, quite in the old friendly way. No, not quite; for now and then, when she least expected it, she saw again that indescribable expression in his face, a look that seemed to shed a sudden sunshine over her, making her eyes fall involuntarily, her color rise, and her heart beat quicker for a moment. Not a word did he say, but she felt that a new atmosphere surrounded her when he was by; and, although he used none of the little devices most lovers employ to keep the flame alight, it was impossible to forget that underneath his quietude there was a hidden world of fire and force, ready to appear at a touch, a word from her.

This was rather dangerous knowledge for Rose, and she soon began to feel that there were more subtle temptations than she had suspected; for it was impossible to be unconscious of her power, or always to resist the trials of it which daily came unsought. She had never felt this desire before: for Charlie was the only one who had touched her heart; and he was constantly asking as well as giving, and wearied her by demanding too much, or oppressed by offering more than she could accept.

Mac did neither: he only loved her, silently, patiently, hopefully; and this generous sort of fidelity was very eloquent to a nature like hers. She could not refuse or chide, since nothing was asked or urged : there was no need of coldness, for he never presumed ; no call for pity, since he never complained. All that could be done was to try and be as just and true as he was, and to wait as trustfully for the end, whatever it was to be.

For a time she liked the new interest it put into her life, yet did nothing to encourage it; and thought that if she gave this love no food it would soon starve to death. But it seemed to thrive on air; and presently she began to feel as if a very strong will was slowly but steadily influencing her in many ways. If Mac had never told her that he meant to " *make* her love him," she might have yielded unconsciously ; but now she mistook the impulse to obey this undercurrent for compassion, and resisted stoutly, not comprehending yet the reason of the unrest which took possession of her about this time.

She had as many moods as an April day; and would have much surprised Dr. Alec by her vagaries, had he known them all. He saw enough, however, to guess what was the matter, but took no notice; for he knew this fever must run its course, and much medicine only does harm. The others were busy about their own affairs, and Aunt Plenty was too much absorbed in her rheumatism to think of love; for the cold weather set in early, and the poor lady kept her room for days at a time, with Rose as nurse.

Mac had spoken of going away in November, and Rose began to hope he would; for she decided that this silent sort of adoration was bad for her, as it prevented her from steadily pursuing the employments she had marked out for that year. What was the use of trying to read useful books, when her thoughts continually wandered to those charming essays on " Love and Friendship "? to copy antique casts, when all the masculine heads looked like Cupid, and the feminine ones like the Psyche on her mantel-piece? to practise the best music, if it ended in singing over and over the pretty spring-song without Phebe's bird-chorus? Dulce's company was pleasantest now; for Dulce seldom talked, so much meditation was possible. Even Aunt Plenty's red flannel, camphor, and Pond's Extract were preferable to general society; and long solitary rides on Rosa seemed the only thing to put her in tune after one of her attempts to find out what she ought to do or leave undone.

She made up her mind at last; and arming herself with an unmade pen, like Fanny Squeers, she boldly went into the study to confer with Dr. Alec, at an hour when Mac was usually absent.

" I want a pen for marking: can you make me one, uncle?" she asked, popping in her head to be sure he was alone.

" Yes, my dear," answered a voice so like the doctor's that she entered without delay.

But before she had taken three steps she stopped, looking rather annoyed; for the head that rose from behind the tall desk was not rough and gray, but brown and smooth, and Mac, not Uncle Alec, sat there writing. Late experience had taught her that she had nothing to fear from a *tête-à-tête ;* and, having with difficulty taken a resolution, she did not like to fail of carrying it out.

" Don't get up: I won't trouble you if you are busy;

there is no hurry," she said, not quite sure whether **it**
were wiser to stay or run away.

Mac settled the point, by taking the pen out of her
hand and beginning to cut it, as quietly as Nicholas
did on that "thrilling" occasion. Perhaps he was
thinking of that; for he smiled as he asked, —

"Hard or soft?"

Rose evidently had forgotten that the family of
Squeers ever existed, for she answered,

"Hard, please," in a voice to match. "I'm glad to
see you doing that," she added, taking courage from
his composure, and going as straight to her point as
could be expected of a woman.

"And I am very glad to do it."

"I don't mean making pens, but the romance I
advised," and she touched the closely written page
before him, looking as if she would like to read it.

"That is my abstract of a lecture on the circulation
of the blood," he answered, kindly turning it so that
she could see. "I don't write romances: I'm living
one," and he glanced up with the happy, hopeful
expression which always made her feel as if he was
heaping coals of fire on her head.

"I wish you would n't look at me in that way: it
fidgets me," she said a little petulantly; for she had
been out riding, and knew that she did not present a
"spiritual" appearance, after the frosty air had reddened nose as well as cheeks.

"I'll try to remember.   It does itself before I know
it.   Perhaps this may mend matters," and, taking out
the blue glasses he sometimes wore in the wind, he
gravely put them on.

Rose could not help laughing: but his obedience

only aggravated her; for she knew he could observe her all the better behind his ugly screen.

"No, it won't: they are not becoming; and I don't want to look blue when I do not feel so," she said, finding it impossible to guess what he would do next, or to help enjoying his peculiarities.

"But you don't to me; for in spite of the goggles every thing is rose-colored now," and he pocketed the glasses, without a murmur at the charming inconsistency of his idol.

"Really, Mac, I'm tired of this nonsense; it worries me and wastes your time."

"Never worked harder. But does it *really* trouble you to know I love you?" he asked anxiously.

"Don't you see how cross it makes me?" and she walked away, feeling that things were not going as she intended to have them at all.

"I don't mind the thorns if I get the rose at last; and I still hope I may, some ten years hence," said this persistent suitor, quite undaunted by the prospect of a "long wait."

"I think it is rather hard to be loved whether I like it or not," objected Rose, at a loss how to make any headway against such indomitable hopefulness.

"But you can't help it, nor can I: so I must go on doing it with all my heart till you marry; and then — well, then I'm afraid I may hate somebody instead," and Mac spoilt the pen by an involuntary slash of his knife.

"Please don't, Mac!"

"Don't which, love or hate?"

"Don't do either: go and care for some one else; there are plenty of nice girls who will be glad to make

you happy," said Rose, intent upon ending her dis-
quiet in some way.

"That is too easy. I enjoy working for my blessings; and the harder I have to work the more I value
them when they come."

"Then if I suddenly grew very kind would you stop
caring about me?" asked Rose, wondering if that
treatment would free her from a passion which both
touched and tormented her.

"Try and see;" but there was a traitorous glimmer
in Mac's eyes which plainly showed what a failure it
would be.

"No, I'll get something to do, so absorbing I shall
forget all about you."

"Don't think about me if it troubles you," he said
tenderly.

"I can't help it." Rose tried to catch back the
words: but it was too late; and she added hastily,
"That is, I cannot help wishing you would forget *me*.
It is a great disappointment to find I was mistaken
when I hoped such fine things of you."

"Yes, you were very sure that it was love when it
was poetry; and now you want poetry when I've
nothing on hand but love. Will both together please
you?"

"Try and see."

"I'll do my best. Any thing else?" he asked,
forgetting the small task she had given him, in his
eagerness to attempt the greater.

"Tell me one thing. I've often wanted to know;
and now you speak of it I'll venture to ask. Did
you care about me when you read Keats to me last
summer?"

" No."

" When *did* you begin? " asked Rose, smiling in spite of herself at his unflattering honesty.

" How can I tell? Perhaps it did begin up there, though; for that talk set us writing, and the letters showed me what a beautiful soul you had. I loved that first: it was so quick to recognize good things, to use them when they came, and give them out again as unconsciously as a flower does its breath. I longed for you to come home, and wanted you to find me altered for the better in some way as I had found you. And when you came it was very easy to see why I needed you, — to love you entirely, and to tell you so. That 's all, Rose."

A short story, but it was enough: the voice that told it with such simple truth made the few words so eloquent Rose felt strongly tempted to add the sequel Mac desired. But her eyes had fallen as he spoke; for she knew his were fixed upon her, dark and dilated, with the same repressed emotion that put such fervor into his quiet tones, and, just as she was about to look up, they fell on a shabby little footstool. Trifles affect women curiously, and often most irresistibly when some agitation sways them: the sight of the old hassock vividly recalled Charlie; for he had kicked it on the night she never liked to remember; like a spark it fired a long train of recollections, and the thought went through her mind, —

" I fancied I loved him, and let him see it; but I deceived myself, and he reproached me for a single look that said too much. This feeling is very different, but too new and sudden to be trusted. I 'll neither look nor speak till I am quite sure; for Mac's love is far deeper than poor Charlie's, and I must be very true."

Not in words did the resolve shape itself, but in a quick impulse, which she obeyed, — certain that it was right, since it was hard to yield to it. Only an instant's silence followed Mac's answer, as she stood looking down with fingers intertwined, and color varying in her cheeks. A foolish attitude; but Mac thought it a sweet picture of maiden hesitation, and began to hope that a month's wooing was about to end in winning for a lifetime. He deceived himself, however; and cold water fell upon his flame, subduing but by no means quenching it, when Rose looked up with an air of determination, which could not escape eyes that were growing wonderfully far-sighted lately.

"I came in here to beg uncle to advise you to go away soon. You are very patient and forbearing, and I feel it more than I can tell. But it is not good for you to depend on any one so much for your happiness, I think; and I know it is bad for me to feel that I have so much power over a fellow-creature. Go away, Mac, and see if this isn't all a mistake. Don't let a fancy for me change or delay your work, because it may end as suddenly as it began, and then we should both reproach ourselves and each other. Please do! I respect and care for you so much, I can't be happy to take all and give nothing. I try to, but I'm not sure — I want to think — it is too soon to know yet —"

Rose began bravely, but ended in a fluttered sort of way, as she moved toward the door; for Mac's face, though it fell at first, brightened as she went on, and at the last word, uttered almost involuntarily, he actually laughed low to himself, as if this order into exile pleased him much.

"Don't say that you give nothing, when you 've just shown me that I 'm getting on. I 'll go; I 'll go at once; and see if absence won't help you ' to think, to know, and to be sure,' as it did me. I wish I could do something more for you; as I can't, good-by."

"Are you going *now?*" and Rose paused in her retreat, to look back with a startled face, as he offered her a badly made pen, and opened the door for her just as Dr. Alec always did; for, in spite of himself, Mac did resemble the best of uncles.

" Not yet; but you seem to be."

Rose turned as red as a poppy, snatched the pen, and flew upstairs, to call herself hard names, as she industriously spoiled all Aunt Plenty's new pocket-handkerchiefs by marking them "A. M. C."

Three days later Mac said "Good-by" in earnest; and no one was surprised that he left somewhat abruptly, such being his way, and a course of lectures by a famous physician the ostensible reason for a trip to L——.   Uncle Alec deserted most shamefully at the last moment by sending word that he would be at the station to see the traveller off: Aunt Plenty was still in her room; so, when Mac came down from his fare- well to her, Rose met him in the hall, as if anxious not to delay him.   She was a little afraid of another *tête-à-tête*, as she fared so badly at the last, and had assumed a calm and cousinly air, which she flattered herself would plainly show on what terms she wished to part.

Mac apparently understood, and not only took the

hint, but surpassed her in cheerful composure; **for,** merely saying, " Good-by, cousin; write when you feel like it," he shook hands, and walked out of the house as tranquilly as if only a day instead of three months were to pass before they met again. Rose felt as if a sudden shower-bath had chilled her, and was about to retire, saying to herself with disdainful decision, —

" There 's no love about it after all; only one of the eccentricities of genius," when a rush of cold air made her turn, to find herself in what appeared to be the embrace of an impetuous overcoat, which wrapt her close for an instant, then vanished as suddenly as it came, leaving her to hide in the sanctum, and confide to Psyche with a tender sort of triumph in her breathless voice, —

" No, no, it is n't genius: *that* must be love ! "

CHAPTER XIX

BEHIND THE FOUNTAIN

TWO days after Christmas, a young man of a serious aspect might have been seen entering one of the large churches at L——. Being shown to a seat, he joined in the services with praiseworthy devotion, especially the music, to which he listened with such evident pleasure that a gentleman who sat near by felt moved to address this appreciative stranger after church.

"Fine sermon to-day. Ever heard our minister before, sir?" he began, as they went down the aisle together among the last; for the young man had lingered as if admiring the ancient building.

"Very fine. No, sir, I have never had that pleasure. I've often wished to see this old place, and am not at all disappointed. Your choir, too, is unusually good," answered the stranger, glancing up at several bonnets bobbing about behind the half-drawn curtains above.

"Finest in the city, sir. We pride ourselves on our music, and always have the best. People often come for that alone," and the old gentleman looked as satisfied as if a choir of cherubim and seraphim "continually did cry" in his organ-loft.

"Who is the contralto? That solo was beautifully sung," observed the younger man, pausing to read a tablet in the wall.

"That is Miss Moore. Been here about a year, and is universally admired. Excellent young lady: could n't do without her. Sings superbly in oratorios. Ever heard her?"

"Never. She came from X——, I believe?"

"Yes; highly recommended. She was brought up by one of the first families there. Campbell is the name. If you come from X——, you doubtless know them."

"I have met them. Good morning." And with bows the gentlemen parted; for at that instant the young man caught sight of a tall lady going down the church-steps, with a devout expression in her fine eyes, and a prayer-book in her hand.

Hastening after her, the serious-minded young man accosted her just as she turned into a quiet street.

"Phebe!"

Only a word, but it wrought a marvellous change, for the devout expression vanished in the drawing of a breath, and the quiet face blossomed suddenly with color, warmth, and "the light that never was on sea or land," as she turned to meet her lover, with an answering word as eloquent as his, —

"Archie!"

"The year is out to-day. I told you I should come. Have you forgotten?"

"No: I knew you 'd come."

"And you are glad?"

"How can I help it?"

"You can't: don't try. Come into this little park, and let us talk." And, drawing her hand through his arm, Archie led her into what to other eyes was a very dismal square. with a boarded-up fountain in

the middle, sodden grass-plots, and dead leaves dancing in the wintry wind.

But to them it was a summery Paradise; and they
walked to and fro in the pale sunshine, quite unconscious that they were objects of interest to several
ladies and gentlemen waiting anxiously for their dinner, or yawning over the dull books kept for Sunday
reading.

"Are you ready to come home now, Phebe?"
asked Archie, tenderly, as he looked at the downcast
face beside him, and wondered why all women did
not wear delightful little black velvet bonnets, with
one deep-red flower against their hair.

"Not yet. I have n't done enough," began Phebe,
finding it very hard to keep the resolution made a
year ago.

"You have proved that you can support yourself,
make friends, and earn a name, if you choose. No
one can deny that; and we are all getting proud of
you. What more can you ask, my dearest?"

"I don't quite know, but I am very ambitious.
I want to be famous, to do something for you all, to
make some sacrifice for Rose, and, if I can, to have
something to give up for your sake. Let me wait
and work longer: I know I have n't earned my welcome yet," pleaded Phebe, so earnestly that her lover
knew it would be vain to try and turn her; so wisely
contented himself with half, since he could not have
the whole.

"Such a proud woman! Yet I love you all the
better for it, and understand your feeling. Rose
made me see how it seems to you; and I don't
wonder that you cannot forget the unkind things that

were looked, if not said, by some of my amiable aunts.
I'll try to be patient on one condition, Phebe."

"And what is that?"

"You are to let me come sometimes while I wait,
and wear this lest you should forget me," he said,
pulling a ring from his pocket, and gently drawing
a warm, bare hand out of the muff where it lay
hidden.

"Yes, Archie, but not here, — not now!" cried
Phebe, glancing about her, as if suddenly aware that
they were not alone.

"No one can see us here: I thought of that. Give
me one happy minute, after this long, long year of
waiting," answered Archie, pausing just where the
fountain hid them from all eyes, for there were houses
only on one side.

Phebe submitted; and never did a plain gold ring
slip more easily to its place than the one he put on in
such a hurry that cold December day. Then one
hand went back into the muff red with the grasp he
gave it, and the other to its old place on his arm, with
a confiding gesture, as if it had a right there.

"Now I feel sure of you," said Archie, as they went
on again, and no one the wiser for that tender trans-
action behind the ugly pyramid of boards. "Mac
wrote me that you were much admired by your
church people, and that certain wealthy bachelors
evidently had designs on the retiring Miss Moore. I
was horribly jealous, but now I defy every man of
them."

Phebe smiled with the air of proud humility that
was so becoming, and answered briefly, —

"There was no danger: kings could not change

me, whether you ever came or not.   But Mac should
not have told you."

"You shall be revenged on him, then; for, as he
told secrets about you, I'll tell you one about him.
Phebe, he loves Rose!"   And Archie looked as
if he expected to make a great sensation with his
news.

"I know it."   And Phebe laughed at his sudden
change of countenance, as he added inquiringly,—

"She told you, then?"

"Not a word. I guessed it from her letters: for
lately she says nothing about Mac, and before there
was a good deal; so I suspected what the silence
meant, and asked no questions."

"Wise girl! then you think she does care for the
dear old fellow?"

"Of course she does. Did n't he tell you so?"

"No, he only said when he went away, 'Take care
of my Rose, and I'll take care of your Phebe,' and not
another thing could I get out of him; for *I* did ask
questions. He stood by me like a hero, and kept
Aunt Jane from driving me stark mad with her 'advice.' I don't forget that, and burned to lend him a
hand somewhere; but he begged me to let him manage his wooing in his own way. And from what I see
I should say he knew how to do it," added Archie,
finding it very delightful to gossip about love affairs
with his sweetheart.

"Dear little mistress! how does she behave?" asked
Phebe, longing for news, but too grateful to ask at
headquarters; remembering how generously Rose had
tried to help her, even by silence, the greatest sacrifice
a woman can make at such interesting periods.

"Very sweet and shy and charming. I try not to watch: but upon my word I cannot help it sometimes; she is so 'cunning,' as you girls say. When I carry her a letter from Mac she tries so hard not to show how glad she is, that I want to laugh, and tell her I know all about it. But I look as sober as a judge, and as stupid as an owl by daylight; and she enjoys her letter in peace, and thinks I'm so absorbed by my own passion that I'm blind to hers."

"But why did Mac come away? He says lectures brought him, and he goes; but I am sure something else is in his mind, he looks so happy at times. I don't see him very often, but when I do I'm conscious that he isn't the Mac I left a year ago," said Phebe, leading Archie away: for inexorable propriety forbade a longer stay, even if prudence and duty had not given her a reminding nudge; as it was very cold, and afternoon church came in an hour.

"Well, you see Mac was always peculiar, and he cannot even grow up like other fellows. I don't understand him yet, and am sure he's got some plan in his head that no one suspects, unless it is Uncle Alec. Love makes us all cut queer capers; and I've an idea that the Don will distinguish himself in some uncommon way. So be prepared to applaud whatever it is. We owe him that, you know."

"Indeed we do! If Rose ever speaks of him to you, tell her I shall see that he comes to no harm, and she must do the same for my Archie."

That unusual demonstration of tenderness from reserved Phebe very naturally turned the conversation into a more personal channel; and Archie devoted himself to building castles in the air so successfully that they passed the material mansion without either being aware of it.

"Will you come in?" asked Phebe, when the mistake was rectified, and she stood on her own steps looking down at her escort, who had discreetly released her before a pull at the bell caused five heads to pop up at five different windows.

"No, thanks. I shall be at church this afternoon, and the oratorio this evening. I must be off early in the morning, so let me make the most of precious time, and come home with you to-night as I did before," answered Archie, making his best bow, and quite sure of consent.

"You may," and Phebe vanished, closing the door softly, as if she found it hard to shut out so much love and happiness as that in the heart of the sedate young gentleman, who went briskly down the street, humming a verse of old " Clyde " like a tuneful bass viol.

> "' Oh, let our mingling voices rise
> In grateful rapture to the skies,
>   Where love has had its birth.
> Let songs of joy this day declare
> That spirits come their bliss to share
>   With all the sons of earth.' "

That afternoon Miss Moore sang remarkably well, and that evening quite electrified even her best friends by the skill and power with which she rendered " Inflammatus " in the oratorio.

"If that is not genius, I should like to know what it is?" said one young man to another, as they went out just before the general crush at the end.

"Some genius and a great deal of love. They are a grand team, and, when well driven, astonish the world by the time they make in the great race," answered the second young man, with the look of one inclined to try his hand at driving that immortal span.

"Dare say you are right. Can't stop now: she's waiting for me. Don't sit up, Mac."

"The gods go with you, Archie."

And the cousins separated: one to write till midnight, the other to bid his Phebe good-by, little dreaming how unexpectedly and successfully she was to earn her welcome home.

CHAPTER XX

WHAT MAC DID

ROSE, meantime, was trying to find out what the sentiment was with which she regarded her cousin Mac. She could not seem to reconcile the character she had known so long with the new one lately shown her; and the idea of loving the droll, bookish, absent-minded Mac of former times appeared quite impossible and absurd: but the new Mac, wide awake, full of talent, ardent and high-minded, was such a surprise to her she felt as if her heart was being won by a stranger, and it became her to study him well before yielding to a charm which she could not deny.

Affection came naturally, and had always been strong for the boy; regard for the studious youth easily deepened to respect for the integrity of the young man: and now something warmer was growing up within her; but at first she could not decide whether it was admiration for the rapid unfolding of talent of some sort, or love answering to love.

As if to settle that point, Mac sent her on New Year's day a little book plainly bound and modestly entitled "Songs and Sonnets." After reading this with ever-growing surprise and delight, Rose never had another doubt about the writer's being a poet;

for, though she was no critic, she had read the best
authors and knew what was good. Unpretending as
it was, this had the true ring, and its very simplicity
showed conscious power; for, unlike so many first
attempts, the book was not full of " My Lady," neither
did it indulge in Swinburnian convulsions about

> " The lilies and languors of peace,
> The roses and raptures of love ; "

or contain any of the highly colored mediæval word
pictures so much in vogue. " My book should smell
of pines, and resound with the hum of insects," might
have been its motto : so sweet and wholesome was it
with a spring-like sort of freshness, which plainly betrayed that the author had learned some of Nature's
deepest secrets, and possessed the skill to tell them
in tuneful words. The songs went ringing through
one's memory long after they were read ; and the
sonnets were full of the subtle beauty, insight, and
half-unconscious wisdom, which seem to prove that
" genius is divine when young."

Many faults it had, but was so full of promise that
it was evident Mac had not " kept good company,
read good books, loved good things, and cultivated
soul and body as faithfully as he could," in vain. It
all told now ; for truth and virtue had blossomed into
character, and had a language of their own more
eloquent than the poetry to which they were what
the fragrance is to the flower. Wiser critics than
Rose felt and admired this ; less partial ones could
not deny their praise to a first effort, which seemed
as spontaneous and aspiring as a lark's song ; and,
when one or two of these Jupiters had given a nod

of approval, Mac found himself, not exactly famous, but much talked about. One set abused, the other set praised, and the little book was sadly mauled among them: for it was too original to be ignored, and too robust to be killed by hard usage; so it came out of the fray none the worse, but rather brighter, if any thing, for the friction which proved the gold genuine.

This took time, however, and Rose could only sit at home reading all the notices she could get, as well as the literary gossip Phebe sent her: for Mac seldom wrote, and never a word about himself; so Phebe skilfully extracted from him in their occasional meetings all the personal news her feminine wit could collect, and faithfully reported it.

It was a little singular that without a word of inquiry on either side, the letters of the girls were principally filled with tidings of their respective lovers. Phebe wrote about Mac; Rose answered with minute particulars about Archie; and both added hasty items concerning their own affairs, as if these were of little consequence.

Phebe got the most satisfaction out of the correspondence; for, soon after the book appeared, Rose began to want Mac home again, and to be rather jealous of the new duties and delights that kept him. She was immensely proud of her poet, and had little jubilees over the beautiful fulfilment of her prophecies; for even Aunt Plenty owned now with contrition that "the boy was not a fool." Every word of praise was read aloud on the house-tops, so to speak, by happy Rose; every adverse criticism was hotly disputed; and the whole family were in a great state of pleasant excitement over this unexpectedly successful first flight of the Ugly Duckling, now generally considered by his relatives as the most promising young swan of the flock.

Aunt Jane was particularly funny in her new position of mother to a callow poet, and conducted herself like a proud but bewildered hen when one of her brood takes to the water. She pored over the poems trying to appreciate them, but quite failing to do so; for life was all prose to her, and she vainly tried to discover where Mac got his talent from. It was pretty to see the new respect with which she treated his possessions now; the old books were dusted with a sort of reverence; scraps of paper laid carefully by lest some immortal verse be lost; and a certain shabby velvet jacket fondly smoothed, when no one was by to smile at the maternal pride which filled her heart, and caused her once severe countenance to shine with unwonted benignity.

Uncle Mac talked about "my son" with ill-concealed satisfaction, and evidently began to feel as if his boy was going to confer distinction upon the whole race of Campbell, which had already possessed one poet. Steve exulted with irrepressible delight, and went about quoting "Songs and Sonnets," till he bored his friends dreadfully by his fraternal raptures.

Archie took it more quietly, and even suggested that it was too soon to crow yet; for the dear old fellow's first burst might be his last, since it was impossible to predict what he would do next. Having proved that he *could* write poetry, he might drop it for some new world to conquer, quoting his favorite Thoreau, who, having made a perfect pencil, gave up the business, and took to writing books with the sort of indelible ink which grows clearer with time.

The aunts of course had their "views," and enjoyed much prophetic gossip, as they wagged their caps over many social cups of tea. The younger boys thought it "very jolly, and hoped the Don would go ahead and come to glory as soon as possible," which was all that could be expected of "Young America," with whom poetry is not usually a passion.

But Dr. Alec was a sight for "sair een:" so full of concentrated contentment was he. No one but Rose, perhaps, knew how proud and pleased the good man felt at this first small success of his godson; for he had always had high hopes of the boy, because in spite of his oddities he had such an upright nature, and promising little did much, with the quiet persistence which foretells a manly character. All the romance of the doctor's heart was stirred by this poetic bud of promise, and the love that made it bloom so early; for Mac had confided his hopes to uncle, finding great consolation and support in his sympathy and advice. Like a wise man, Dr. Alec left the young people to learn the great lesson in their own way, counselling Mac to work, and Rose to wait, till both were quite certain that their love was built on a surer foundation than admiration or youthful romance.

Meantime he went about with a well-worn little book in his pocket, humming bits from a new set of songs, and repeating with great fervor certain sonnets which seemed to him quite equal, if not superior, to any that Shakspeare ever wrote. As Rose was doing the same thing, they often met for a private

" read and warble," as they called it; and, while discussing the safe subject of Mac's poetry, both arrived at a pretty clear idea of what Mac's reward was to be when he came home.

He seemed in no hurry to do this, however, and continued to astonish his family by going into society, and coming out brilliantly in that line. It takes very little to make a lion, as every one knows who has seen what poor specimens are patted and petted every year, in spite of their bad manners, foolish vagaries, and very feeble roaring. Mac did not want to be lionized and took it rather scornfully, which only added to the charm that people suddenly discovered about the nineteenth cousin of Thomas Campbell, the poet. He desired to be distinguished in the best sense of the word, as well as to look so, and thought a little of the polish society gives would not be amiss, remembering Rose's efforts in that line. For her sake he came out of his shell, and went about seeing and testing all sorts of people with those observing eyes of his, which saw so much in spite of their nearsightedness. What use he meant to make of these new experiences no one knew; for he wrote short letters, and, when questioned, answered with imperturbable patience, —

" Wait till I get through; then I 'll come home and talk about it."

So every one waited for the poet, till something happened which produced a greater sensation in the family than if all the boys had simultaneously taken to rhyming.

Dr. Alec got very impatient, and suddenly announced that he was going to L—— to see after those young people; for Phebe was rapidly singing herself into public favor, with the sweet old ballads which she rendered so beautifully that hearts were touched as well as ears delighted, and her prospects brightening every month.

"Will you come with me, Rose, and surprise this ambitious pair, who are getting famous so fast they'll forget their home-keeping friends if we don't remind them of us now and then?" he said, when he proposed the trip one wild March morning.

"No, thank you, sir; I'll stay with auntie: that is all I'm fit for; and I should only be in the way among those fine people," answered Rose, snipping away at the plants blooming in the study window.

There was a slight bitterness in her voice and a cloud on her face, which her uncle heard and saw at once, half-guessed the meaning of, and could not rest till he had found out.

"Do you think Phebe and Mac would not care to see you?" he asked, putting down a letter in which Mac gave a glowing account of a concert at which Phebe surpassed herself.

"No, but they must be very busy," began Rose, wishing she had held her tongue.

"Then what is the matter?" persisted Dr. Alec.

Rose did not speak for a moment, and decapitated two fine geraniums with a reckless slash of her scissors, as if pent-up vexation of some kind must find a vent. It did in words also; for, as if quite against her will, she exclaimed impetuously, —

"The truth is, I'm jealous of them both!"

"Bless my soul! what now?" ejaculated the doctor, in great surprise.

Rose put down her watering-pot and shears, came and stood before him with her hands nervously twisted together, and said, just as she used to do when she was a little girl confessing some misdeed, —

"Uncle, I must tell you; for I've been getting very envious, discontented, and bad lately. No, don't be good to me yet; for you don't know how little I deserve it. Scold me well, and make me see how wicked I am."

"I will as soon as I know what I am to scold about. Unburden yourself, child, and let me see all your iniquity; for, if you begin by being jealous of Mac and Phebe, I'm prepared for any thing," said Dr. Alec, leaning back as if nothing could surprise him now.

"But I am not jealous in that way, sir. I mean I want to be or do something splendid as well as they. I can't write poetry or sing like a bird; but I *should* think I might have my share of glory in some way. I thought perhaps I could paint, and I've tried, but I can only copy: I've no power to invent lovely things, and I'm so discouraged; for that is my one accomplishment. Do you think I have *any* gift that could be cultivated, and do me credit like theirs?" she asked so wistfully that her uncle felt for a moment as if he never could forgive the fairies, who endow babies in their cradles, for being so niggardly to his girl. But one look into the sweet, open face before him, reminded him that the good elves *had* been very generous, and he answered cheerfully, —

"Yes, I do; for you have one of the best and noblest gifts a woman can possess. Music and poetry are fine things; and I don't wonder you want them, or that you envy the pleasant fame they bring. I 've felt just so, and been ready to ask why it did n't please heaven to be more generous to some people; so you need n't be ashamed to tell me all about it."

" I know I ought to be contented, but I 'm not. My life is very comfortable, but so quiet and uneventful I get tired of it, and want to launch out as the others have, and do something, or at least try. I 'm glad you think it is n't very bad of me, and I 'd like to know what my gift is," said Rose, looking less despondent already.

"The art of living for others so patiently and sweetly that we enjoy it as we do the sunshine, and are not half grateful enough for the great blessing."

" It is very kind of you to say so, but I think I 'd like a little fun and fame, nevertheless," and Rose did not look as thankful as she ought.

" Very natural, dear; but the fun and the fame do not last; while the memory of a real helper is kept green long after poetry is forgotten and music silent. Can't you believe that, and be happy?"

" But I do so little, nobody sees or cares, and I don't feel as if I was really of any use," sighed Rose, thinking of the long, dull winter, full of efforts that seemed fruitless.

" Sit here, and let us see if you really do very little, and if no one cares," and, drawing her to his knee, Dr. Alec went on, telling off each item on one of the fingers of the soft hand he held.

" First, an infirm old aunt is kept very happy by the patient, cheerful care of this good-for-nothing niece. Secondly, a crotchety uncle, for whom she reads, runs, writes, and sews so willingly that he cannot get on without her. Thirdly, various relations who are helped in various ways. Fourthly, one dear friend never forgotten, and a certain cousin cheered by the praise which is more to him than the loudest blast Fame could blow. Fifthly, several young girls find her an example of many good works and ways. Sixthly, a motherless baby is cared for as tenderly as if she was a little sister. Seventhly, half a dozen poor ladies made comfortable; and, lastly, some struggling boys and girls with artistic longings are put into a pleasant room furnished with casts, studies, easels, and all manner of helpful things, not to mention free lessons given by this same idle girl, who now sits upon my knee owning to herself that her gift *is* worth having after all."

"Indeed, I am! Uncle, I'd no idea I had done so many things to please you, or that any one guessed how hard I try to fill my place usefully. I've learned to do without gratitude: now I'll learn not to care for praise, but to be contented to do my best, and have only God know."

"He knows, and He rewards in His own good time. I think a quiet life like this often makes itself felt in better ways than one that the world sees and applauds; and some of the noblest are never known till they end, leaving a void in many hearts. Yours may be one of these if you choose to make it so, and no one will be prouder of this success than I, unless it be — Mac."

The clouds were quite gone now, and Rose was looking straight into her uncle's face with a much happier expression, when that last word made it color brightly, and the eyes glance away for a second. Then they came back full of a tender sort of resolution, as she said, —

"That will be the reward I work for," and rose, as if ready to be up and doing with renewed courage.

But her uncle held her long enough to ask quite soberly, though his eyes laughed, —

"Shall I tell him that?"

"No, sir, please don't! When he is tired of other people's praise, he will come home, and then — I 'll see what I can do for him," answered Rose, slipping away to her work with the shy, happy look that sometimes came to give her face the charm it needed.

"He is such a thorough fellow he never is in a hurry to go from one thing to another. An excellent habit, but a trifle trying to impatient people like me," said the doctor, and picking up Dulce, who sat upon the rug with her dolly, he composed his feelings by tossing her till she crowed with delight.

Rose heartily echoed that last remark, but said nothing aloud, only helped her uncle off with dutiful alacrity, and, when he was gone, began to count the days till his return, wishing she had decided to go too.

He wrote often, giving excellent accounts of the "great creatures," as Steve called Phebe and Mac, and seemed to find so much to do in various ways that the second week of absence was nearly over before he set a day for his return, promising to astonish them with the account of his adventures.

Rose felt as if something splendid was going to happen, and set her affairs in order, so that the approaching crisis might find her fully prepared. She had "found out" now, was quite sure, and put away all doubts and fears to be ready to welcome home the cousin whom she was sure uncle would bring as her reward. She was thinking of this one day, as she got out her paper to write a long letter to poor Aunt Clara, who pined for news far away there in Calcutta.

Something in the task reminded her of that other lover whose wooing ended so tragically, and opening the little drawer of keepsakes, she took out the blue bracelet, feeling that she owed Charlie a tender thought in the midst of her new happiness; for of late she *had* forgotten him.

She had worn the trinket hidden under her black sleeve for a long time after his death, with the regretful constancy one sometimes shows in doing some little kindness all too late. But her arm had grown too round to hide the ornament, the forget-me-nots had fallen one by one, the clasp had broken; and that autumn she laid the bracelet away, acknowledging that she had outgrown the souvenir as well as the sentiment that gave it.

She looked at it in silence for a moment, then put it softly back, and, shutting the drawer, took up the little gray book which was her pride, thinking as she contrasted the two men and their influence on her life, — the one sad and disturbing, the other sweet and inspiring, — "Charlie's was passion: Mac's is love."

"Rose! Rose!" called a shrill voice, rudely breaking the pensive reverie, and with a start she shut the desk exclaiming as she ran to the door, —

"They have come! They have come!"

CHAPTER XXI

HOW PHEBE EARNED HER WELCOME

D R. ALEC had not arrived, but bad tidings
had, as Rose guessed the instant her eye
fell upon Aunt Plenty, hobbling downstairs
with her cap awry, her face pale, and a letter flapping
wildly in her hand, as she cried distractedly, —

"Oh, my boy! my boy! sick, and I not there to
nurse him! Malignant fever, so far away. What can
those children do? why did I let Alec go?"

Rose got her into the parlor; and, while the poor
old lady lamented, she read the letter which Phebe
had sent to her that she might "break the news
carefully to Rose."

"DEAR MISS PLENTY, — Please read this to yourself first,
and tell my little mistress as you think best. The dear doctor is very ill; but I am with him, and shall not leave him
day or night till he is safe. So trust me, and do not be
anxious; for every thing shall be done that care and skill
and entire devotion can do. He would not let us tell you
before, fearing you would try to come at the risk of your
health. Indeed it would be useless; for only one nurse is
needed, and I came first, so do not let Rose or anybody else
rob me of my right to the danger and the duty. Mac has
written to his father; for Dr. Alec is now too ill to know
what we do, and we both felt that you ought to be told without further delay. He has a bad malignant fever, caught no

one can tell how, unless among some poor emigrants whom
he met wandering about quite forlorn in a strange city.   He
understood Portuguese, and sent them to a proper place
when they had told their story.   But I fear he has suffered
for his kindness ; for this fever came on rapidly, and before
he knew what it was I was there, and it was too late to send
me away.

"*Now* I can show you how grateful I am, and if need be
give my life so gladly for this friend who has been a father to
me.   Tell Rose his last conscious word and thought were
for her.   'Don't let her come ; keep my darling safe.'   Oh,
do obey him !   Stay safely at home ; and, God helping me,
I 'll bring Uncle Alec back in time.   Mac does all I will let
him.   We have the best physicians, and every thing is going
as well as can be hoped till the fever turns.

"Dear Miss Plenty, pray for him and for me, that I may
do this one happy thing for those who have done so much for

"Your ever dutiful and loving

"PHEBE."

As Rose looked up from the letter, half stunned by
the sudden news and the great danger, she found
that the old lady had already stopped useless bewail-
ing, and was praying heartily, like one who knew
well where help was to be found.   Rose went and
knelt down at her knee, laying her face on the
clasped hands in her lap, and for a few minutes
neither wept nor spoke.   Then a stifled sob broke
from the girl, and Aunt Plenty gathered the young
head in her arms, saying, with the slow tears of age
trickling down her own withered cheeks, —

"Bear up, my lamb, bear up.   The good Lord
won't take him from us I am sure : and that brave
child *will* be allowed to pay her debt to him ; I feel
she will."

"But I want to help. I *must* go, aunty, I must: no matter what the danger is," cried Rose, full of a tender jealousy of Phebe for being first to brave peril for the sake of him who had been a father to them both.

"You can't go, dear, it's no use now; and she is right to say 'Keep away.' I know those fevers, and the ones who nurse often take it, and fare worse for the strain they've been through. Good girl to stand by so bravely, to be so sensible, and not let Mac go too near! She's a grand nurse: Alec couldn't have a better, and she'll never leave him till he's safe," said Miss Plenty, excitedly.

"Ah, you begin to know her now, and value her as you ought. *I* think few would have done as she has; and if she does get ill and die it will be our fault partly; because she'd go through fire and water to make us do her justice, and receive her as we ought," cried Rose, proud of an example which she longed to follow.

"If she brings my boy home, I'll never say another word. She may marry every nephew I've got, if she likes, and I'll give her my blessing," exclaimed Aunt Plenty, feeling that no price would be too much to pay for such a deed.

Rose was going to clap her hands, but wrung them instead; remembering with a sudden pang that the battle was not over yet, and it was much too soon to award the honors.

Before she could speak Uncle Mac and Aunt Jane hurried in; for Mac's letter had come with the other, and dismay fell upon the family at the thought of danger to the well-beloved Uncle Alec. His brother

decided to go at once, and Aunt Jane insisted on
accompanying him: though all agreed that nothing
could be done but wait, and leave Phebe at her post
as long as she held out; since it was too late to save
her from danger now, and Mac reported her quite
equal to the task.

Great was the hurry and confusion till the relief
party was off. Aunt Plenty was heart-broken that
she could not go with them, but felt that she was too
infirm to be useful; and, like a sensible old soul,
tried to content herself with preparing all sorts of
comforts for the invalid. Rose was less patient, and
at first had wild ideas of setting off alone, and forcing
her way to the spot where all her thoughts now
centred. But before she could carry out any rash
project, Aunt Myra's palpitations set in so alarmingly
that they did good service for once, and kept Rose
busy taking her last directions, and trying to soothe
her dying-bed; for each attack was declared fatal,
till the patient demanded toast and tea, when hope
was again allowable and the rally began.

The news flew fast, as such tidings always do: and
Aunt Plenty was constantly employed in answering
inquiries; for her knocker kept up a steady tattoo
for several days. All sorts of people came; gentle-
folk and paupers, children with anxious little faces,
old people full of sympathy, pretty girls sobbing as
they went away, and young men who relieved their
feelings by swearing at all emigrants in general and
Portuguese in particular. It was touching and comforting to see how many loved the good man who
was known only by his benefactions, and now lay
suffering far away, quite unconscious how many un-

suspected charities were brought to light by this grateful solicitude, as hidden flowers spring up when warm rains fall.

If Rose had ever felt that the gift of living for others was a poor one, she saw now how beautiful and blest it was, — how rich the returns, how wide the influence, how much more precious the tender tie which knit so many hearts together, than any breath of fame, or brilliant talent, that dazzled, but did not win and warm.   In after years she found how true her uncle's words had been ; and, listening to eulogies of great men, felt less moved and inspired by praises of their splendid gifts than by the sight of some good man's patient labor for the poorest of his kind.   Her heroes ceased to be the world's favorites ; and became such as Garrison fighting for his chosen people ; Howe restoring lost senses to the deaf, the dumb, and blind ; Sumner unbribable, when other men were bought and sold : and many a large-hearted woman working as quietly as Abby Gibbons, who for thirty years has made Christmas merry for two hundred little paupers in a city almshouse, beside saving Magdalens and teaching convicts.

The lesson came to Rose when she was ready for it, and showed her what a noble profession philanthropy is, made her glad of her choice, and helped fit her for a long life full of the loving labor, and sweet satisfaction unostentatious charity brings to those who ask no reward, and are content if " only God knows."

Several anxious weeks went by with wearing fluctuations of hope and fear ; for Life and Death fought

over the prize each wanted, and more than once
Death seemed to have won. But Phebe stood at her
post, defying both danger and death with the courage
and devotion women often show. All her soul and
strength were in her work; and, when it seemed
most hopeless, she cried out with the passionate
energy which seems to send such appeals straight
up to Heaven, —

"Grant me this one boon, dear Lord, and I will
never ask another for myself!"

Such prayers avail much, and such entire devotion
often seems to work miracles when other aids are
vain. Phebe's cry was answered; her self-forgetful
task accomplished, and her long vigil rewarded with
a happy dawn. Dr. Alec always said that she kept
him alive by the force of her will; and that, during
the hours when he seemed to lie unconscious, he felt
a strong, warm hand holding his, as if keeping him
from the swift current trying to sweep him away.
The happiest hour of all her life was that in which he
knew her, looked up with the shadow of a smile in
his hollow eyes, and tried to say in his old cheery
way, —

"Tell Rose I've turned the corner, thanks to you,
my child."

She answered very quietly, smoothed the pillow,
and saw him drop asleep again, before she stole away
into the other room, meaning to write the good news;
but could only throw herself down, and find relief for
a full heart in the first tears she had shed for weeks.
Mac found her there, and took such care of her that
she was ready to go back to her place, — now indeed
a post of honor, — while he ran off to send home a

telegram which made many hearts sing for joy, and caused Jamie, in his first burst of delight, to propose to ring all the city bells and order out the cannon.

"Saved: thanks to God and Phebe."

That was all; but every one was satisfied, and every one fell a-crying, as if hope needed much salt water to strengthen it. That was soon over, however, and then people went about smiling and saying to one another, with hand-shakes or embraces, "He is better: no doubt of it now!" A general desire to rush away and assure themselves of the truth pervaded the family for some days; and nothing but awful threats from Mac, stern mandates from the doctor, and entreaties from Phebe not to undo her work, kept Miss Plenty, Rose, and Aunt Jessie at home.

As the only way in which they could ease their minds and bear the delay, they set about spring cleaning, with an energy which scared the spiders, and drove char-women distracted. If the old house had been infected with small-pox, it could not have been more vigorously scrubbed, aired, and refreshed. Early as it was, every carpet was routed up, curtains pulled down, cushions banged, and glory-holes turned out, till not a speck of dust, a last year's fly, or stray straw could be found. Then they all sat down and rested in such an immaculate mansion that one hardly dared to move for fear of destroying the shining order everywhere visible.

It was late in April before this was accomplished, and the necessary quarantine of the absentees well over. The first mild days seemed to come early, so that Dr. Alec might return with safety from the journey which had so nearly been his last. It was perfectly impossible to keep any member of the family away on that great occasion. They came from all quarters in spite of express directions to the contrary; for the invalid was still very feeble, and no excitement must be allowed. As if the wind had carried the glad news, Uncle Jem came into port the night before; Will and Geordie got a leave on their own responsibility; Steve would have defied the entire Faculty, had it been necessary; and Uncle Mac and Archie said simultaneously, " Business be hanged to-day."

Of course, the aunts arrived all in their best; all cautioning everybody else to keep quiet, and all gabbling excitedly at the least provocation. Jamie suffered most during that day, so divided was he between the desire to behave well and the frantic impulse to shout at the top of his voice, turn somersaults, and race all over the house. Occasional bolts into the barn, where he let off steam by roaring and dancing jigs, to the great dismay of the fat old horses and two sedate cows, helped him to get through that trying period.

But the heart that was fullest beat and fluttered in Rose's bosom, as she went about putting spring flowers everywhere; very silent, but so radiant with happiness that the aunts watched her, saying softly to one another, " Could an angel look sweeter? "

If angels ever wore pale-green gowns and snow-drops in their hair, had countenances full of serenest joy, and large eyes shining with an inward light that made them very lovely, then Rose did look like one. But she felt like a woman: and well she might; for was not life very rich that day, when uncle, friend, and lover were coming back to her together? Could she ask any thing more, except the power to be to all of them the creature they believed her, and to return the love they gave her with one as faithful, pure, and deep?

Among the portraits in the hall hung one of Dr. Alec, taken soon after his return by Charlie, in one of his brief fits of inspiration. Only a crayon, but wonderfully life-like and carefully finished, as few of the others were. This had been handsomely framed, and now held the place of honor, garlanded with green wreaths, while the great Indian jar below blazed with a pyramid of hot-house flowers sent by Kitty. Rose was giving these a last touch, with Dulce close by, cooing over a handful of sweet " daffydowndillies," when the sound of wheels sent her flying to the door. She meant to have spoken the first welcome and had the first embrace; but when she saw the altered face in the carriage, the feeble figure being borne up the steps by all the boys, she stood motionless till Phebe caught her in her arms, whispering with a laugh and a cry struggling in her voice, —

"I did it for you, my darling, all for you!"

"O Phebe, never say again you owe me any thing! I never can repay you for this," was all Rose had time to answer, as they stood one instant cheek to cheek, heart to heart, both too full of happiness for many words.

Aunt Plenty had heard the wheels also, and, as everybody rose *en masse*, had said as impressively as extreme agitation would allow, while she put her glasses on upside-down, and seized a lace tidy instead of her handkerchief, —

"Stop! all stay here, and let *me* receive Alec.

Remember his weak state, and be calm, quite calm, as I am."

"Yes, aunt, certainly," was the general murmur of assent: but it was as impossible to obey as it would have been to keep feathers still in a gale; and one irresistible impulse carried the whole roomful into the hall, to behold Aunt Plenty beautifully illustrate her own theory of composure by waving the tidy wildly, rushing into Dr. Alec's arms, and laughing and crying with an hysterical abandonment which even Aunt Myra could not have surpassed.

The tearful jubilee was soon over, however; and no one seemed the worse for it: for the instant his arms were at liberty Uncle Alec forgot himself, and began to make other people happy, by saying seriously, though his thin face beamed paternally, as he drew Phebe forward, —

"Aunt Plenty, but for this good daughter I never should have come back to be so welcomed. Love her for my sake."

Then the old lady came out splendidly, and showed her mettle; for, turning to Phebe, she bowed her gray head as if saluting an equal; and, offering her hand, answered with repentance, admiration, and tenderness trembling in her voice, —

"I'm proud to do it for her own sake. I ask pardon for my silly prejudices, and I'll prove that I'm sincere by — where's that boy?"

There were six boys present: but the right one was in exactly the right place at the right moment; and, seizing Archie's hand, Aunt Plenty put Phebe's into it, trying to say something appropriately solemn, but could not: so hugged them both, and sobbed out, —

"If I had a dozen nephews, I'd give them *all* to you, my dear, and dance at the wedding, though I had rheumatism in every limb."

That was better than any oration; for it set them all to laughing, and Dr. Alec was floated to the sofa on a gentle wave of merriment. Once there, every one but Rose and Aunt Plenty was ordered off by Mac, who was in command now, and seemed to have sunk the poet in the physician.

"The house must be perfectly quiet, and he must go to sleep as soon as possible after the journey; so all say 'Good-by' now, and call again to-morrow," he said, watching his uncle anxiously, as he leaned in the sofa corner, with four women taking off his wraps, three boys contending for his overshoes, two brothers shaking hands at short intervals, and Aunt Myra holding a bottle of strong salts under his devoted nose every time there was an opening anywhere.

With difficulty the house was partially cleared: and then, while Aunt Plenty mounted guard over her boy, Rose stole away to see if Mac had gone with the rest; for as yet they had hardly spoken in the joyful flurry, though eyes and hands had met.

CHAPTER XXII

SHORT AND SWEET

IN the hall she found Steve and Kitty; for he had hidden his little sweetheart behind the big couch, feeling that she had a right there, having supported his spirits during the late anxiety with great constancy and courage. They seemed so cosey, billing and cooing in the shadow of the gay vase, that Rose would have slipped silently away if they had not seen and called to her.

"He's not gone: I guess you'll find him in the parlor," said Steve, divining with a lover's instinct the meaning of the quick look she had cast at the hat-rack, as she shut the study-door behind her.

"Mercy, no! Archie and Phebe are there, so he'd have the sense to pop into the sanctum and wait; unless you'd like me to go and bring him out?" added Kitty, smoothing Rose's ruffled hair, and settling the flowers on the bosom where Uncle Alec's head had laid until he fell asleep.

"No, thank you, I'll go to him when I've seen my Phebe. She won't mind me," answered Rose, moving on to the parlor.

"Look here," called Steve, "do advise them to hurry up and all be married at once. We were just ready when uncle fell ill, and now we can *not* wait a day later than the first of May."

" Rather short notice," laughed Rose, looking back with the door-knob in her hand.

" We 'll give up all our splendor, and do it as simply as you like, if *you* will only come too. Think how lovely! three weddings at once! Do fly round and settle things: there 's a dear," implored Kitty, whose imagination was fired with this romantic idea.

" How can I, when I have no bridegroom yet?" began Rose, with conscious color in her tell-tale face.

" Sly creature! you know you 've only got to say a word and have a famous one. Una and her lion will be nothing to it," cried Steve, bent on hastening his brother's affair, which was much too dilatory and peculiar for his taste.

" He has been in no haste to come home, and I am in no haste to leave it. Don't wait for me, ' Mr. and Mrs. Harry Walmers, Jr.; ' I shall be a year at least making up my mind: so you may lead off as splendidly as you like, and I 'll profit by your experience; " and Rose vanished into the parlor, leaving Steve to groan over the perversity of superior women, and Kitty to comfort him by promising to marry him on May-day " all alone."

A very different couple occupied the drawing-room, but a happier one; for they had known the pain of separation, and were now enjoying the bliss of a re-union which was to last unbroken for their lives. Phebe sat in an easy-chair, resting from her labors, pale and thin and worn, but lovelier in Archie's eyes than ever before. It was very evident that he was adoring his divinity; for, after placing a footstool at her feet, he had forgotten to get up, and knelt there, with his elbow on the arm of her chair, looking like a thirsty man drinking long draughts of the purest water.

"Shall I disturb you if I pass through?" asked Rose, loth to spoil the pretty tableau.

"Not if you stop a minute on the way and congratulate me, cousin; for she says 'Yes' at last!" cried Archie, springing up to go and bring her to the arms Phebe opened as she appeared.

"I knew she would reward your patience, and put away her pride when both had been duly tried," said Rose, laying the tired head on her bosom, with such tender admiration in her eyes that Phebe had to shake some bright drops from her own before she could reply in a tone of grateful humility, that showed how much her heart was touched,—

"How can I help it, when they all are so kind to me?   Any pride would melt away under such praise and thanks and loving wishes as I 've had to-day; for every member of the family has taken pains to welcome me, to express far too much gratitude, and to beg me to be one of you.   I needed very little urging; but, when Archie's father and mother came and called me 'daughter,' I would have promised any thing to show my love for them."

"And him," added Rose; but Archie seemed quite satisfied, and kissed the hand he held as if it had been that of a beloved princess, while he said with all the pride Phebe seemed to have lost,—

"Think what she gives up for me: fame and fortune and the admiration of many a better man.   You don't know what a splendid prospect she has of becoming one of the sweet singers who are loved and honored everywhere; and all this she puts away for my sake, content to sing for me alone, with no reward but love."

"I am so glad to make a little sacrifice for a great happiness: I never shall regret it or think my music lost, if it makes home cheerful for my mate. Birds sing sweetest in their own nests, you know," and Phebe bent toward him with a look and gesture which plainly showed how willingly she offered up all ambitious hopes upon the altar of a woman's happy love.

Both seemed to forget that they were not alone, and in a moment they were; for a sudden impulse carried Rose to the door of her sanctum, as if the south wind which seemed to have set in was wafting this little ship also toward the Islands of the Blest, where the others were safely anchored now.

The room was a blaze of sunshine and a bower of spring freshness and fragrance: for here Rose had let her fancy have free play; and each garland, fern, and flower had its meaning. Mac seemed to have been reading this sweet language of symbols, to have guessed why Charlie's little picture was framed in white roses, why pansies hung about his own, why Psyche was half hidden among feathery sprays of maiden's-hair, and a purple passion-flower lay at Cupid's feet. The last fancy evidently pleased him; for he was smiling over it, and humming to himself, as if to beguile his patient waiting, the burden of the air Rose so often sung to him, —

> "Bonny lassie, will ye gang, will ye gang
> To the birks of Aberfeldie?"

"Yes, Mac, anywhere!"

He had not heard her enter, and wheeling round

looked at her with a radiant face, as he said, drawing
a long breath, —

"At last! you were so busy over the dear man, I
got no word. But I can wait: I'm used to it."

Rose stood quite still, surveying him with a new
sort of reverence in her eyes, as she answered with a
sweet solemnity, that made him laugh and redden
with the sensitive joy of one to whom praise from
her lips was very precious.

"You forget that you are not the Mac who went
away. I should have run to meet my cousin, but I
did not dare to be familiar with the poet whom all
begin to honor."

"You like the mixture then? You know I said I'd
try to give you love and poetry together."

"Like it! I'm so glad, so proud, I have n't any
words strong and beautiful enough to half express
my wonder and my admiration. How *could* you do
it, Mac?" and a whole face full of smiles broke loose,
as Rose clapped her hands, looking as if she could
dance with sheer delight at his success.

"It did itself, up there among the hills, and here
with you, or out alone upon the sea. I could write a
heavenly poem this very minute, and put you in as
Spring; you look like her in that green gown with
snowdrops in your bonny hair. Rose, am I getting
on a little? Does a hint of fame help me nearer to the
prize I'm working for? Is your heart more willing
to be won?"

He did not stir a step, but looked at her with such
intense longing that his glance seemed to draw her
nearer like an irresistible appeal; for she went and
stood before him, holding out both hands, as if she

offered all her little store, as she said with simplest
sincerity, —

"It is not worth so much beautiful endeavor; but,
if you still want so poor a thing, it is yours."

He caught the hands in his, and seemed about to
take the rest of her, but hesitated for an instant, unable to believe that so much happiness was true.

"Are you sure, Rose, — very sure? Don't let a
momentary admiration blind you: I'm not a poet
yet; and the best are but mortal men, you know."

"It is not admiration, Mac."

"Nor gratitude for the small share I've taken in
saving uncle? I had my debt to pay, as well as
Phebe, and was as glad to risk my life."

"No: it is not gratitude."

"Nor pity for my patience? I've only done a
little yet, and am as far as ever from being like your
hero. I can work and wait still longer, if you are not
sure; for I must have all or nothing."

"O Mac! why will you be so doubtful? You said
you'd make me love you, and you've done it. Will
you believe me now?" And, with a sort of despera-
tion, she threw herself into his arms, clinging there in
eloquent silence, while he held her close; feeling, with
a thrill of tender triumph, that this was no longer little
Rose, but a loving woman, ready to live and die for
him.

"Now I'm satisfied!" he said presently, when she
lifted up her face, full of maidenly shame at the sudden passion which had carried her out of herself for a
moment. "No: don't slip away so soon; let me
keep you for one blessed minute, and feel that I have
really found my Psyche."

" And I my Cupid," answered Rose, laughing, in spite of her emotion, at the idea of Mac in that sentimental character.

He laughed too, as only a happy lover could; then said, with sudden seriousness, —

" Sweet Soul! lift up your lamp, and look well before it is too late; for I'm no god, only a very faulty man."

" Dear Love! I will. But I have no fear, except that you will fly too high for me to follow, because I have no wings."

" You shall live the poetry, and I will write it; so my little gift will celebrate your greater one."

" No: you shall have all the fame, and I'll be content to be known only as the poet's wife."

" And I'll be proud to own that my best inspiration comes from the beneficent life of a sweet and noble woman."

" O Mac! we'll work together, and try to make the world better by the music and the love we leave behind us when we go."

" Please God, we will! " he answered fervently; and, looking at her as she stood there in the spring sunshine, glowing with the tender happiness, high hopes, and earnest purposes that make life beautiful and sacred, he felt that now the last leaf had folded back, the golden heart lay open to the light, and his Rose had bloomed.

END.